The shining splendor ___ ___ ___
cover of this book refle ___ ___ ___
story inside. Look for th ___ ___ ___
buy a historical romance ___ *guarantees*
the very best in quality and reading entertainment.

BOLD POSSESSION

Laurie gazed at her reflection, and had the thought that the red gown suited her in spite of Carlota's dismayed objection to it.

"But it is so immodest!" Carlota had gasped.

"Not in Paris," Laurie had retorted with a defiant glitter in her eyes.

She wandered from the arched bridge to the carved fountain in a shadowy corner of the alcove. A few stars were reflected in the pool, and she could see her own reflection until a fish shattered it. She laughed softly.

Suddenly her laugh became a gasp when a hand grasped one arm and swung her around. There was no time to scream before a man had her in his arms, holding her much too tightly, his hands roaming much too boldly, shocking her sophisticated European awareness into oblivion.

As she tried to pull away, the man held her more tightly, his hand dangling in the knot of lace at the back of her neck. Laurie had been kissed before, but never like this, never so thoroughly or so savagely, with the man intent on complete possession.

She felt her senses whirl. "Dear heavens," she thought, "What is he doing? What am *I* doing . . . ?"

THE BEST IN HISTORICAL ROMANCES

TIME-KEPT PROMISES (2422, $3.95)
by Constance O'Day Flannery
Sean O'Mara froze when he saw his wife Christina standing before him. She had vanished and the news had been written about in all of the papers—he had even been charged with her murder! But now he had living proof of his innocence, and Sean was not about to let her get away. No matter that the woman was claiming to be someone named Kristine; she still caused his blood to boil.

PASSION'S PRISONER (2573, $3.95)
by Casey Stewart
When Cassandra Lansing put on men's clothing and entered the Rawlings saloon she didn't expect to lose anything—in fact she was sure that she would win back her prized horse Rapscallion that her grandfather lost in a card game. She almost got a smug satisfaction at the thought of fooling the gamblers into believing that she was a man. But once she caught a glimpse of the virile Josh Rawlings, Cassandra wanted to be the woman in his embrace!

ANGEL HEART (2426, $3.95)
by Victoria Thompson
Ever since Angelica's father died, Harlan Snyder had been angling to get his hands on her ranch, the Diamond R. And now, just when she had an important government contract to fulfill, she couldn't find a single cowhand to hire—all because of Snyder's threats. It was only a matter of time before the legendary gunfighter Kid Collins turned up on her doorstep, badly wounded. Angelica assessed his firmly muscled physique and stared into his startling blue eyes. Beneath all that blood and dirt he was the handsomest man she had ever seen, and the one person who could help beat Snyder at his own game.

Renegade Embrace

Virginia Brown

ZEBRA BOOKS
KENSINGTON PUBLISHING CORP.

Dedicated to Wayne and Kay Moose. Thanks, "Mom and Dad," for always being there for me, and for enduring my adolescence so bravely. See? We do grow up!

ZEBRA BOOKS

are published by

Kensington Publishing Corp.
475 Park Avenue South
New York, NY 10016

First printing: November, 1990

Printed in the United States of America

Prologue

I

New Orleans, Louisiana, 1835

Laurette Allen had just turned sixteen that spring of 1835 when she discovered that her life was about to completely change. That morning her father, Phillip Allen, had told her that he intended to remarry after almost sixteen years of being a widower.

Shocked, Laurette could only stare at him for a long moment of silence. "M-m-marry Carlota?" she echoed, hating herself for stuttering. Her fingers tightened into the satin skirts of her fashionable gown, and her wide hoops swayed as she took several steps forward. "But I never thought you would—that you were serious, Papa!"

Phillip Allen smiled slightly, his thin lips curving in amusement. "A man needs a wife, Laurie," he said as gently as possible. "I've been alone a long time now since your mother died."

"But Carlota? She's so . . . so different, and she disapproves of me so—you know she does, Papa!"

Laurie's cry was forlorn and childish, and she could not help the quick start of tears in her large amber eyes. Her lower lip quivered slightly, and Phillip drew

5

her into his embrace, one hand stroking her blond hair.

His poor, beautiful child. She really didn't understand about a man's needs, but one day she would. Phillip spared a brief prayer that his headstrong daughter would find a man who could handle her as well as love her, then tilted up her face, his finger beneath her chin. He almost changed his mind about chiding her when he saw the huge golden eyes swimming with tears, the slight quivering of her full lower lip, and the delicate arching of her winged brows. He steeled himself.

"You've not done a lot to encourage Carlota to approve of you, you know," he said softly. "Some of your escapades have shocked her sensibilities. She was brought up in a strict household, Laurie, and I think some of her discipline would benefit you a great deal. . . ."

"Oh no!" Laurie twisted out of his embrace, and her drenched gold eyes swiftly altered to a biting clarity. "I am not about to become a Spanish simpleton with a prayerbook in one hand and a sanctimonious cloak in the other! Why, I've seen Carlota's family, and they're all just like her, swathed in gray or black from ankles to chin like crows, with those long veils over their heads and faces—they don't know anything about fashion or beautiful things, and. . . ."

"Laurette!" Her father' s voice was sharp. "You have just insulted your future stepmother. Please be so good as to mind your tongue and your manners in my presence. I cannot tolerate such behavior from my daughter."

Much more meekly than she felt, Laurie lowered her rebellious face and muttered, "Yes, Papa."

She kept her eyes on the carpet while her father told her about the wedding plans and his expectations for her behavior.

"And you must no longer ride your horse astride or continue with your fencing lessons," Phillip Allen ended his conversation, bracing himself for the storm to come. He still wasn't prepared for the sharp glitter in Laurie's eyes as her tawny head jerked up. Phillip recoiled slightly when her large, dark-fringed eyes narrowed as she stared at him, and he was reminded more than ever of his late wife. Françoise had had eyes like that, cat's eyes, startling and beautiful and dangerous. . . .

"What? Am I to cease everything I enjoy because it annoys Carlota's *sensibilities?* I refuse!" Laurie grated.

"Laurette," he began warningly, but she rolled over him like a storm cloud.

"Cease riding and my fencing lessons? But you've never minded them before, and you know how I enjoy them, Papa!" Her tone altered from angry to slightly wheedling. "I've done as you asked, and I haven't let Gilbert — Monsieur Rosière — talk me into disguising myself as a man again and joining in another contest. You were right about that, and I. . . ."

"Laurette, you will stop them," Phillip Allen repeated firmly. "If anyone in New Orleans were to discover that you were doing something so common, your reputation would be ruined. I allowed it only because you pleaded so, and I've never been able to withstand your sulks. All that will change now."

Everything will change, Laurie thought with a pang, *everything!*

She was right. Everything did change. Carlota Sanchez y Alvarado swiftly and irrevocably changed the entire household in the space of only a few weeks. Laurie's former freedom was sharply curtailed, all in the name of propriety, and as time for the wedding drew near and the spacious house on Rue Royale became crowded with guests and Carlota's family, the tension grew.

7

"But I don't see why he wants to marry that cold fish!" Laurie raged as she crossed her bedroom to gaze out on the wet New Orleans streets. "She is so . . . so haughty!"

"Ah, *ma petite*," crooned Isabeau Lautrec, "you would not approve of anyone who wanted to marry your *papa*. You have had him to yourself for too long now."

Whirling, Laurie glared at her old nurse. Her small chin tilted stubbornly. "That's not true!"

Isabeau just smiled, her creamy brown face as smooth and placid as always. Laurie's rages and occasional tantrum had no more affect on her now than they had had when the girl was a small child. Granted, Laurette had matured a great deal and no longer threw herself to the floor with her tantrum, but she had not yet learned to keep her anger to herself, either. Isabeau was still trying to convince her tawny-haired charge that one's anger was much more effective if expressed in scathing words rather than with a broken mirror or vase.

"Well," Laurie amended after a moment of Isabeau's silence, "perhaps it is true a small bit."

"*Oui*, perhaps," Isabeau agreed. She continued checking the clothes hanging in the huge armoire against one wall, sliding Laurie an occasional glance. The girl paced the floor, pausing to gaze moodily out the rain-spangled window, then paced back to the fireplace. The fire crackled, and rain hissed softly against the glass windowpanes as Laurie fought her own private misery.

Finally, sinking into a deep-cushioned settee, Laurie looked up at Isabeau's understanding face. "I will try to be nice to her for Papa's sake," she whispered through a throat aching with unshed tears. "But I don't have to like her."

"*Non, ma petite*," Isabeau agreed, "you don't have to

8

like her."

"And as long as we stay here, I suppose everything will be the same," Laurie said reflectively. She shrugged her shoulders. "After all, it's not as if I have to put up with all her relatives for very long."

"That's true," Isabeau said with another sidelong glance at Laurie. "They are here only for the wedding."

Nodding, Laurie propped her small chin in the cup of her palm and sighed. "They jabber in Spanish all the time, so fast that I can barely understand a word they say. And they stare down their long, pointed noses at me as if I had two heads, and tell me that my gowns are too daring and only loose females wear paint."

Isabeau hid a smile. "It is known that well-bred Spanish girls do not use artifices to enhance their beauty, but this — this is New Orleans, and here are many Creoles who believe in fashion."

Laurie laughed. "Like you, Isabeau!"

Smoothing her day dress of fashionable mint-colored brocade, Isabeau gave a self-satisfied "Tch, tch! It is true that I know fashion, while those ladies — ah, they are still wearing muslin, and *no* hoops!"

Laurie laughed again, her eyes sharpening with slight malice. "Those old crows must not get the latest fashions out in California."

"No," Isabeau agreed, and rearranged the full sleeves of her dress. "They must not. But California is a primitive place, and so far from civilization."

"I find it hard to believe that they would travel all this way just for a wedding," Laurie muttered, and Isabeau reminded her that Carlota's relatives had been returning from a visit to Spain.

"And you must recall, that although Señorita Alvarado is from California, they are very well connected. It's just that her father came to New Orleans

9

and she came with him for a time. She had never left her rustic home before, you'll recall." Isabeau smiled at Laurie's scowling face, and smothered a laugh at her delicate shudder.

Laurie murmured, "No wonder Carlota stayed here in New Orleans! If only she would not marry my father, I would not care. But. . . ."

She let her voice drift into silence and rose from the settee to go to the window again. The house was on the corner of Rue Dumaine and Rue Royale, and delicate wrought-iron balustrades enclosed a courtyard that helped muffle the sounds of the busy city. In early spring, the courtyard was filled with fragrant blossoms and new green foliage. Laurie pushed open the window and inhaled the sweet fragrance of spring. A gust of damp air swirled into the room, and Isabeau hurriedly crossed to shut the window. The mulatto maid's face was indignant.

"Do you invite the sickness?" she demanded. "Do you want the shakes, the chills and fever that come with the air?"

Restlessly pacing from the closed window back to the fireplace, Laurie fought against the prick of rebellion that urged her, and lost. She turned to face her nurse with a defiant stare that immediately put Isabeau on her guard. "I shall go to Exchange Alley. That will cure my boredom."

"You know your papa has forbidden it."

"No, he just forbade fencing lessons, not visits to Monsieur Rosière."

Isabeau shrugged, but muttered underneath her breath, "It is an embarrassment that you visit those *maîtres d'armes*, such low-class ruffians! How your papa allows it, I do not know!"

"I heard that," Laurie observed. "Now, come unlace my gown so that I may change."

Still muttering under her breath, the maid did as

her mistress bade her, albeit disapprovingly. As she laced the fresh gown around Laurie's slim waist, Isabeau had the thought that her young mistress was too tempting to allow so much freedom, especially with a hot-blooded Creole. Laurette's maturing beauty had already caught many a young man's eye, and there would be trouble if she was not curbed soon. For what young man blessed with even the most limited sight could long resist the vision of Laurie, with her cloud of golden hair, high cheekbones, pouting mouth, and seductive topaz eyes? Not many at all, Isabeau had found, to her extreme pride. Mixed with that pride, however, was the fear that Laurie's promising beauty would attract the wrong kind of suitor, and her headstrong charge was not prone to advice most of the time. No, she rushed headlong into life, not pausing to think about possible consequences along the way.

Oui, perhaps it was good that the stern Californio would be her step-mama, for Isabeau had seen the effect Laurette had on the gentlemen of New Orleans. That a young woman of breeding should visit the free-spirited men like Gilbert Rosière, even though he was French and had come from a good family, was courting disaster. It was simply not done, and it did not matter if she was chaperoned or not. The friendship would ruin her if it was discovered. What was Phillip Allen thinking of, that he would allow his only child to run about New Orleans so freely?

"Papa is distracted lately," Laurie said slyly, somehow sensing Isabeau's thoughts, and the maid's head jerked up indignantly.

"He should not be that distracted!" was the swift retort.

"But he is, and after the wedding, when Carlota takes up residence here, I shall never get out again, so I intend to take full advantage of it now," Laurie said. Her steady gaze dared Isabeau to object or refuse her, and the maid did not.

"I still think it is a dreadful thing to run about New Orleans like a stevedore's child," Isabeau muttered as she withdrew Laurie's heavy rain cloak from the armoire. "What if someone should see you? What if your *Tante* Annette should see you?"

That gave Laurie a moment's pause, for she loved her mother's sister dearly. But then she gave a characteristic shrug. "She will think I am on my way to the Market, and that is all," Laurie said impatiently. "Now, do hurry, or we shall miss Monsieur Rosière."

With that in mind, Isabeau dawdled as long as she dared, until Laurie threatened to go alone with only old Jaspar as chaperon.

"And him as old as dirt and just as wise!" Isabeau snapped as she grabbed up her own cloak and swirled it around her shoulders. "He is a coachman, not a chaperon!"

Laurie just smiled, and was still smiling when the closed landau rolled to a stop in Exchange Alley. Rain pattered softly on the top of the carriage as old Jaspar climbed slowly down and went to the front door to announce his mistress's arrival. He was back in a moment with a sheet of paper, his leathery face crinkling into a frown as he handed it up to Laurie without a word.

"What is this?" she began, then understood that he had found it nailed to the door. After swiftly scanning the hastily printed words on the paper, she gave a short, determined nod of her head. "Very good. Proceed to the Oaks, Jaspar."

"The Oaks?" Isabeau echoed in a horrified tone. "*Sacré bleu*, you have gone mad!"

Laurie gave Isabeau a hard look. "I most certainly have not. At once, Jaspar," she repeated, and the grizzled old coachman shook his head as he climbed back up to the driver's box.

Laurie could feel Isabeau's disapproving frown even in the dimly lit interior of the landau. She did her best to ignore her. After all, it was only to watch, wasn't it? And didn't everyone in New Orleans know that only the most exciting duels were fought beneath the Oaks? Gilbert Rosière was about to fight a duel, and she intended to be there, to see his skill with an epée demonstrated in a real duel, not just a match.

But once there, Laurie wondered with a sudden lump in her throat if she should have listened to the things she had not allowed Isabeau to say. It was much more bloody than she had ever thought. And it seemed as if Gilbert Rosière, for some astonishing reason, was not faring that well at all.

His opponent seemed relaxed, even amused as he feinted, lunged, parried, and thrust, barring Gilbert's most expert moves with a slim-bladed rapier. Rosière was bleeding from a long scratch on one arm, and his face was grim as they circled on the wet ground beneath the spreading arms of the huge live oaks. A light rain made the ground slippery and treacherous, yet Rosière's opponent had the surefootedness of a large cat as he moved.

Laurie sat forward, her gloved hand clenching the edge of the carriage window, her lips slightly parted as she watched the two men with awe and excitement. Gilbert Rosière was small and slightly built, with a compact frame that hid his sinewy strength.

His opponent was tall and muscular and looked much too large to be as graceful as he was. He moved lightly on the balls of his stockinged feet; his boots lay discarded on the wet grass a few yards away. The rain had plastered his dark hair to his skull, giving him a saturnine appearance that made Laurie shudder and Isabeau cross herself. His bored voice carried through the rain to the carriage.

"Are you tiring, Monsieur Rosière? We can stop anytime you please. . . ."

Rosière's lips tightened into a grim line, and his dark eyes flashed at his opponent. "Do you mock me?" he shouted, and gave a graceful lunge with his rapier. It almost caught the other man, but he moved swiftly out of the way and returned the lunge with a counterthrust that brought blood from a slice across the Frenchman's upper arm. Rosière recoiled in shock, looking from the bloodied arm to his antagonist, who smiled.

"Second blood," was the soft remark. "Do we continue?"

Rosière stiffened. "Of course, Monsieur. I would not dream of stopping now."

Rosière's seconds rushed to his side and anxiously checked his wound, while the tall American waited with a casually indifferent pose. He was lean, and the rain had drenched his loose white shirt so that it clung to his broad shoulders as if a second skin, outlining the smooth flex of his muscles. Laurie stared at him in fascination.

When Rosière stepped forward again and said *"En garde,"* Laurie dragged her attention from his opponent. The fencing master seemed tired, and his eyes were bright with pain.

Excitement drummed in Laurie's ears, and her breath was short and fast as she watched the two men move warily through the rain. The grass under the oaks had been churned by their feet, and it had grown slippery. Once the tall man almost slipped, but he quickly caught himself and returned Rosière's expert rapier thrust, deftly fending off a counterattack. They lunged and parried, and it was apparent that the men were almost equally matched in spite of the difference in their sizes.

Leaning forward, her gaze fastened on the duelists,

14

Laurie did not hear Isabeau's swift order to Jaspar until the carriage lurched forward.

"Wait!" she cried, but Isabeau would not listen.

"It would be a great scandal if you were to be seen!" Isabeau hissed angrily. "I will not allow it!"

"I must know who wins!" Laurie cried, but the carriage rolled on, leaving the Oaks behind.

II

Cade Caldwell was still wet from his duel in the rain. Cursing the weather and his luck, he slammed into the house on Rue Royale and found Cecelia waiting on him, another stroke of the bad luck he'd been suffering lately. Damn it! Hadn't she caused enough trouble already? If he'd known who she was when she began pursuing him, nothing would have come of it. But he hadn't, and now there'd been trouble because of it. He flicked her an impatient glance, noting that she wore nothing other than a thin silk peignoir that did nothing to hide her considerable charms.

"What are you doing here?" he asked in a blunt, harsh tone. He tossed his soaked hat on a table and stalked to the fire burning in the grate. His clothes were plastered to his body, outlining hard ridges of muscle and the fact that Cecelia's scanty attire and firelit curves had begun to interest him.

She noticed his reaction and smiled. "Waiting on you, *mon chèr*," she purred. She walked toward him, and in the dim light afforded by the fire and a candelabra on the table, she could see that Cade's desire was increasing. Her smile grew even wider.

Cade did not move when she reached him and exclaimed softly over the blood on his shirt. Nor did he react when she ran her fingertips lightly over his body

15

to assess the damage. It was only when she began to remove his wet shirt that he grabbed her hand, his fingers tightening around her small wrist.

"Don't."

"But I. . . ."

"But don't. It's only a scratch, nothing serious, and I don't want you fussing over me. Especially if I take into consideration that the duel would not have been necessary had you not decided to spread around your charms."

The brunette beauty blinked, and her full mouth farmed a ripe pout. "But I only flirted a small bit, *chèr*—just to make you jealous—and that is all!"

Cade turned away in irritation. "Your flirting could have cost a man his life, CeCe. Did you stop to think of that?"

She shrugged. "Well, what of it if he is foolish enough to challenge you?"

Turning back, Cade glared at her in the dim light, his eyes raking her perfect features with condemnation. "You don't really care, do you, CeCe?"

She shrugged again. *"Non, chèr,* I do not. It was his choice, you understand."

Unbuckling his sword belt, Cade tossed it to the table beside his hat, then turned in the same smooth motion and jerked Cecelia close. He held her against his hard, wet frame, and she could feel the imprint of him against her stomach. The silk wrapper parted from around her throat and floated to the floor, and she smiled as she curled her arms around his neck.

"Don't you want to know if he's still alive?" Cade asked against her parted lips, and felt her shrug.

"You are alive, and that is all that matters right now, *chèr.*"

Cade lifted her into his arms, and as he strode toward the bedroom he muttered, "You are an amoral cat, CeCe, unlike most women, who possess at least a

16

small degree of conscience."

Wriggling in his arms as he placed her on the bed and bent over her, Cecelia let her small, hot tongue flick over his bare skin before she whispered against him, "I am not at all like most women, who are dull and boring and would not think to do this for you . . . or this. . . ."

Cade pushed her back onto the bed and stripped off his clothes, ignoring her appreciative gaze. Then he was over her, penetrating her without preliminaries, hearing her cries of satisfaction in his ears as he took her.

When it was over, and they lay panting and listening to the beat of rain against the windows, Cade surprised the brunette by pulling her into his embrace and holding her gently. It was all the more surprising to her because of his earlier anger and disgust, and Cecelia snuggled closer to him.

"You like me more than a little," she murmured, and felt the rumble of laughter in his chest.

"I like doing this with you," he said, running a finger over her full breast, then over the curved arch of her ribs to her flat stomach. His hand wandered to the thrust of her hip, then smoothed over her buttocks as he pulled her hard against him. When his palm smacked against her bare buttock she cried out with shock, and he laughed again. "But that's all," he said before smothering her indignant protest with his mouth.

"This is not all you like about me," Cecelia said after several minutes. Her slim arms curved around his neck, and she looked into his handsome face. Her heart gave a funny lurch as she saw the amusement in his dark eyes, and suddenly she knew that he was telling her the truth. She sat up and glared at him. Shaking her long dark hair from her eyes she said, "You fought a duel for me! You must like me more

17

than this, more than the time we share in your bed! I would be a good wife to you, and—"

Cade's burst of sardonic laughter stopped her words, and she stared at him as he uncoiled his lean frame and rose from the bed to look down at her.

"CeCe, *amour*, while I freely admit that I enjoy your charms in the bedroom, I fought the duel only because I was challenged to it. It was a point of honor, not love, that took me to the Oaks. Whatever you may think, I will never marry you."

Stunned, Cecelia de Marchand felt a burning anger. Rising to her knees on the bed, she burst out, "Don't you know who I am?"

Cade's amusement was obvious. "Of course I know who you are. You're the governor's spoiled niece."

Vibrating with rage and rejection, Cecelia clenched her small hands into impotent fists. "You are a nobody, a man with mixed heritage, yet you dare to reject me? To refuse me as a wife?"

"I'm not a marrying man, CeCe. I told you that a long time ago," Cade said impatiently. He stepped into a dry pair of trousers and pulled them up, buttoning them around his lean waist.

"But I never thought you meant . . . meant me," the girl said in such a bewildered voice that Cade felt a pang of pity for her in spite of the fact that she had relentlessly pursued him.

"Look," he said, "I'm sorry you got the wrong idea, but that's the way it is. It has nothing to do with you, but I am just not ready for marriage."

Cecelia's aristocratic nose tilted upward, and her brows drew down over her dark Creole eyes. "That is your misfortune," she said softly, and Cade looked at her through narrowed eyes.

"What do you mean by that?" he demanded, but Cecelia did not reply. He did not discover the answer to his query until the following morning, when a

18

squad of soldiers appeared at the door of his house and arrested him.

"And the charges?" Cade asked as he buttoned his trousers and stepped into his boots.

"Unlawful dueling," the sergeant replied without a flicker.

"Unlawful dueling?" Cade laughed shortly. "How interesting, sergeant. I had no idea the law was being enforced now."

Cade had plenty of time to think about it in the following days as he languished in a damp cell. River breezes did not enhance his small quarters, nor did the occasional meal of weevil-infested rice cereal with chunks of fish floating on the surface.

By the time an official solution presented itself he had long since come to the correct conclusion for his imprisonment.

A stone-faced Creole officer sat behind a desk and did not look up when Cade was escorted into his office. The prisoner's chains rattled slightly as he swayed, and finally the officer looked up with an expression of distaste.

"You smell unpleasant, Monsieur Caldwell," the officer remarked, and put a scented linen handkerchief to his nose. It was an affected gesture, and Cade disliked him on sight.

"How unfortunate for you, but I've grown accustomed to it," Cade said with a lift of one dark brow. His manacled hands clenched into fists behind his back, and he was well aware of his unkempt appearance and the lice in his hair and the fact that his stomach was growling and the Creole had a plate of untouched food on a tray beside his desk. The tempting aroma wafted to his nostrils, and he did his best to school his features into indifference.

The linen square fluttered as the Creole said from behind it, "I'm afraid I have not grown accustomed to the odor. Be so good as to stand back a bit, if you please."

"Look, I didn't ask to come here, so if you object to my presence . . ."

The guard behind Cade slammed his rifle stock across Cade's back and his legs buckled, sending him to his knees. The Creole officer stood and walked a few paces away, looking down at Cade thoughtfully.

"I shall make this very brief, Monsieur Caldwell. You have been arrested for dueling, which is against the law. There are many witnesses who can testify against you, so it is apparent what the outcome of a trial will be. You can spare the state the expense if you will only be sensible."

"I'll think about it," Cade said when it seemed that an answer was expected of him. "What are the conditions of my, uh . . . cooperation?"

Seating himself on the corner of his desk, the officer reached out and plucked a hot roll from the tray. Butter dripped between his fingers as he bit into it, and he seemed to take pleasure from the fact that Cade's stomach was audibly growling. Cade looked away, and a muscle in his jaw twitched with anger.

"It's very simple," the officer said when he had finished the roll and wiped his hands on the linen handkerchief. "You will agree to wed the young lady you have compromised. For some reason, she desires it greatly, and her uncle is very indulgent."

"So I've heard," Cade muttered. "And the alternative to a wedding?"

"A well-attended hanging," was the prompt reply.

"Ah, my choice of deaths. How pleasant."

The officer laughed. "You are very amusing, monsieur! I have heard that the lady is well favored, so perhaps you should think of that, heh? After all, one death is permanent, while the other—well, there are consolations to marriage at times, and you are still young. What—twenty-four years of age? Think about it." He made a gesture to the guard, and Cade was jerked to his feet. "I will send for you tomorrow, and hear your answer."

But it was two days before Cade was summoned again, and he was weak with hunger and from being chained.

"Phew!" the Creole said with a shake of his head and a grimace. "You smell much worse, and I did not think that possible, monsieur!"

Cade said nothing, just stared at the officer with flat, dark eyes. For some reason his direct, piercing gaze made the smaller man shift uneasily, and he retreated behind his desk to look at Cade.

"Your reply, monsieur?"

"Yes."

It was all Cade said, but it was enough, and the Creole hurriedly had him removed from his office and taken away, giving the order that he was to be released at once.

III

"They say he is a devil with a sword," Isabeau remarked as she brushed Laurette's heavy hair into curls on each side of her face.

"He who?" Laurie asked idly, frowning at herself in the mirror over her dresser. She looked pale, too pale, and her eyes had circles under them. It was difficult to pay attention to anything Isabeau was saying when she had so much on her mind lately, but the woman's next words jerked up Laurie's head.

"Cecelia de Marchand's fiancé. He is the one who defeated your precious Monsieur Rosière a fortnight ago." Isabeau smiled at her in the mirror, a slightly malicious smile that made Laurie's eyes narrow.

21

"They say that he fought and won six duels in as many days, and that he compromised the governor's niece and refused to marry her until he was imprisoned for it."

"*They say, they say*—who are they?" Laurie demanded crossly. "And besides, who cares about Cecelia de Marchand? I think she is terribly vain and haughty, and I never have been very fond of her, even though we attended the same classes at the convent last year. Though two years older than I, she was always disrupting the nuns with her silly, constant chatter about men, and I grew tired of her."

"Nonetheless," Isabeau continued imperturbably, "she is to be married, while you are not. And she is only a little older than you are. . . ."

"And marrying a man who went to prison rather than face marriage to her!" Laurie ended with a snap. "If you ask me, he is smart even though he weakened in the end."

"Well, he is not a Creole," Isabeau said, as if that explained his weakening. "His father was American, while his mother was Spanish, a *gauchupine*."

Rising from the dresser chair, Laurie turned away, her face set and pale with misery. "Enough of this. I am much more concerned with Papa's wedding than Cecelia de Marchand's forced vows." She paced the floor, then went to stare out at the dark street. "It will all change somehow, I know it will," she murmured. "I have this feeling that my life is about to change quite drastically."

Isabeau said nothing, though her heart ached for her young mistress. It was quite true that Laurie's life was about to change, for she had overheard Phillip Allen agree with Carlota that his daughter should be sent abroad for a continental education. They would not tell her until after the wedding, and her *pauvre petite* would be given no opportunity to refuse. Laurie

22

would be sent away from New Orleans for four long years, and there would be nothing she could do.

Stepping up behind Laurie, Isabeau said softly, "Just remember, *ma petite,* that you will face whatever the future may bring. You are strong, much stronger than your *maman* ever was."

Laurie turned to look at Isabeau. "Am I? Am I much like my mother, Isabeau? I mean, I know I have her eyes, and her color of hair, but am I *like* her in any other ways?"

After a moment of silence, Isabeau said, "Françoise was delicate and fragile and lovely, just like you are, but she did not have the inner strength, the fire that you have. A strong wind defeated her, where you may bend with it, but you do not break, as did poor Françoise."

"You make it sound as if my mother died of a broken heart," Laurie said in a puzzled tone, and Isabeau nodded.

"That is true," she said, and silence fell again before Isabeau spoke slowly. "There was another child, a boy, and when he died, my *pauvre* Françoise wanted to die also. But then she was *enciente* with you, and so she held on until you were born. Not long after, she died, and the physician said she died of a broken heart, not the milk sickness."

For a long moment Laurie said nothing, then she released her breath in a soft sigh. "Oh," she said. "I see. I had always thought . . . I mean. . . ."

Isabeau hastened to say, "She loved you very much, *ma petite,* truly she did! She could not have stayed alive so long if she did not, but the loss of a child was too much for her, and not even your birth or your papa could keep her alive."

Laurie had the rebellious thought that if her mother had truly wanted to live she would have. Her chin tilted up and her mouth hardened, and she knew

23

that she would never give up so easily.

Seeing her face, Isabeau knew that Laurie would never lie down to die as her mother had, and she gave an inward sigh of relief. She had done the right thing in telling her. Perhaps she would not always be with Laurette, and her old bones had lately been telling her so. But if the girl had a strong will to live, she would survive whatever life dealt her. Isabeau smiled. It would be all right; even if Phillip Allen sent her away, Laurette would be all right.

Chapter One

California, 1840

Standing on solid ground for the first time in so many weeks it seemed like she'd always been aboard a rolling ship, Laurette Allen glanced at the California coastline with a frown. Grudgingly, she admitted to herself that it was beautiful, with blinding white sand along the beaches, and water as blue as the bright sky overhead. Fields of brilliant blossoms dotted rolling hillsides with splashes of color — red, orange, creamy white, and yellow, and the stucco houses with red tiled roofs looked quaint and picturesque.

Yet somehow, actually arriving was even worse than her overactive imagination had visualized. It was hot. And as glad as she was to disembark from the dreadful steamer that had rolled ceaselessly over the swells of the Atlantic and Pacific, she was not glad to be standing on the docks of a sleepy village that looked as ancient as the caves she'd seen in northern Italy.

After leaving Europe, where cities stood in soaring splendor and civilization was crowded, arriving in a primitive coastal town was anathema. Though she was eager to see her father, for after all, it had been almost five long years, Laurie could not help but be dismayed by California.

Why had Phillip Allen accepted the position as diplomatic ambassador between Spanish California, which was a province of Mexico, and the United States? Just because he had Spanish connections through his wife did not mean he should have left gracious New Orleans. A pang hit her at the thought that she no longer had a home in that lovely old city. Of course, her *Tante* Annette was still there, and it was still home, would always be home, yet now here she was in Higuera, California, a tiny coastal town perched amid green hills and overlooking the Pacific Ocean.

There was only a small fort, or *presidio,* in the center of the town, a walled fortress guarded by what looked to be a minimum of soldiers. Fig trees — hence the village's name, she presumed — shaded the *mercado,* or marketplace, in the center of town. There was an air of somnolence, lent credence by the dozing figures in wide-brimmed sombreros and dusty serapes under the trees.

"Señorita," a voice prompted at her elbow, and Laurie turned. "Do you wish to have your trunks put in the wagon?" a young boy asked, pointing to the high mound of baggage stacked on the wharf.

"Yes, I suppose so," Laurie said with a trace of impatience. She looked around again, and saw only strangers and dock workers, busy sailors scurrying over the long wooden docks that jutted into the crisp blue waters of the bay. Gaily dressed men and women swept past her, some throwing her curious glances, but most intent on going out to the ships and steamers to examine the goods aboard.

She had seen the cargo aboard the steamer, the casks of wine and brandy, teas, coffee, sugars, spices, raisins, molasses, hardware, crockery, clothing, boots and shoes, and huge bolts of material. The hold had been crammed with all styles of furniture as well, making Laurie wonder if these Californios produced anything at home.

As she waited on the dock a feeling of uneasiness crept over her, but Laurie determinedly ignored it with a toss of her head. After all, she was twenty-one years of age now, mature enough to travel over half a continent alone, so she would not allow a small thing like having to wait alarm her.

Yet in the back of her mind was the uneasy feeling that she had been forgotten. Hadn't her father received her letter? She had written it months before, giving the approximate time of arrival. A servant sent down to the docks would have been able to discern when the steamer would arrive, because it had already stopped at every tiny port on the California coastline. She would have probably made better time if she'd disembarked in San Diego and taken a carriage the rest of the way.

But she hadn't, and now here she was, waiting, feeling like a small, lost child again as she stood on the dock and looked for a familiar face. Why was no one there to meet her? Was she to find her own lodgings, or had they even gotten her letter? If only Isabeau was still with her, then she would not feel quite so alone.

But Isabeau would never be with her. Her old nurse had taken a chill in the spring before Laurie had been sent to her mother's family in France; and had died in only a few hours. It had been sudden, with little suffering, but had left Laurette more alone than she'd ever felt before. In the past five years she had learned to deal with her new independence, and though she still missed Isabeau's loving, scolding guidance, she rarely felt at a loss.

Now was one of those times. Standing on the wharves and waiting for her absent father, she felt a slight qualm, as if she was truly alone. She turned abruptly.

"Take my baggage to the nearest inn," Laurie told the

waiting boy in a decisive tone that helped banish the qualm of uncertainty. She would send word to her father's house and he could look for her there. *"Pronto!"* she added when the boy just stared at her, and he jumped into action.

But before Laurie had hired a carriage to take her to an inn, her father's carriage arrived with two servants.

"We are from Señor Allen. Are you Señorita Allen?" a voice inquired, and Laurie nodded.

"Yes. It's about time you arrived. Has there been trouble?" she asked as she was handed into the carriage. A surge of relief made her unconsciously haughty, but her smile was tremulous as she looked down at the older man.

"Si, but it has been settled," was the reply from the old man. He smiled, his gnarled hands twisting his hat as he bobbed his head at her.

Laurie smiled back, some of her tension easing. It was never well bred to be impolite, especially to servants, she had been taught, and as she settled back into the cushions of the open carriage she said, "Thank you. Will it take very long to get to my father's house?"

"No, señorita, it will not take long at all," the old man said with another smile. "Unless we run into *soldados* again," he began when the other servant quickly interrupted with a nervous laugh.

"What Tómas means, Señorita Allen, is that unless we must wait for soldiers to clear the road of a fallen tree, we shall be there shortly," the younger man said, nudging Tómas. "I shall finish loading the trunks, Tómas, while you take the señorita home."

Laurie surveyed her new surroundings as the open carriage rolled down quiet streets. Adobe buildings lined dirt and cobblestone lanes and paths, and alleys jutted erratically at every conceivable angle. Thatched roofs adorned some of the buildings, while others had the distinctive red tile that she'd noticed from the steamer. The entire town seemed to cling precariously to the sides of the slopes, rushing seaward, until the buildings looked as if they only waited to slide into the ocean. Though the breeze was brisk and salty, the air was already hot in early June. Laurie waved a painted fan to stir the air and wished she had worn something a bit cooler.

She saw brightly dressed women with lacy shawls over their heads and shoulders and short sleeves that left their arms bare. Amazed, Laurie stared at them; wondering why she had assumed that all Californian women wore only drab gowns with no color. These women wore dresses of silk, crepe, and bright calico. None of them appeared to be wearing corsets, but wore skirts above the ankles and loose blouses circled with a sash. Their shoes were fashioned of kid or satin, and the women all wore necklaces and earrings, sometimes several at once. Bright scarves were worn around necks or draped over shoulders like capes. All the women were dark like Carlota, with long black hair worn loose or in braids. Laurie stared at them with interest, feeling rather out of place with her gold hair and pale complexion.

And the women were staring at her, too, chattering among themselves, obviously wondering about the identity of the newcomer in their midst. Feeling ill at ease, Laurie tried not to notice their stares, or the stares of the men she saw, all of them on horseback.

Nervously smoothing the wrinkles in the shimmering blue skirts of her gown, she lifted her chin in an unconsciously haughty gesture, avoiding their admiring gazes. Why did she feel like a duck in the henhouse, as her cousin would say? She felt very out of place, very different, and even the few comments she overheard did nothing to make her feel more at ease.

Clad in broad-brimmed hats of dark material with gilt hatbands, the men made admiring comments as

Laurie's open carriage rolled slowly through the narrow streets. She slid them surreptitious glances, noting their short jackets, white shirts open at the neck, and straightlegged trousers of velvet or broadcloth. And to her astonishment, in spite of the warm weather, every man wore a long broadcloth cloak of black or dark blue. Some were festooned in a great deal of gilt trim. Even the horses wore trappings of velvet and gilt, with silver bridles and huge saddles.

The men on foot wore loose-fitting garments — white trousers and long shirts, and some of them wore a sort of blanket with a hole in the middle for their head. Those men were barefoot, or sandaled, and obviously from the lower class, Laurie decided. They looked down at their feet and scurried between the long rows of adobe buildings with an indolent haste, carrying baskets of produce or fowl over their shoulders. The women of the class seemed similiarly burdened, with children slung in brightly woven blankets across their backs. Small children ran about the streets either half-clad or clad like their elders.

She had donned her best dress that morning, hoping to impress her father and Carlota by sweeping down the wharf from the ship in a sophisticated arrival. Her exit had been remarked only by sailors and stevedores, however, so she hoped that she would not wilt completely before arriving at her father's home. It would be embarrassing to be all damp and smelling of the ship in spite of the expensive French cologne she wore.

Laurie realized that she was nervous about meeting her father again, and why not? After he had so summarily sent her away immediately following his marriage to Carlota, she had vowed never to see him again. She had been hurt by his detachment and grief stricken over Isabeau, and it had seemed as if her world was ending. But time had slowly eased the pain, and she'd even lingered in Europe for a year after her schooling had ended, visiting with relatives and touring the Continent. When his letter had come pleading with her to return to the United States, she had done so reluctantly. Now she found herself eager to see him again.

Had he changed much? Would he recognize her? After all, he had last seen a red-eyed, rebellious daughter who barely filled out the bodice of her dresses. Now she had matured, and she was no longer that awkward child who had left New Orleans vowing eternal hatred.

Indeed, Laurie had been quite the rage in London, Paris, Barcelona, and Rome, where she had moved in the circles frequented by her French cousins. It had been a gay whirl of laughter and dancing, and she had loved it. Now she was back, only not in her beloved New Orleans but in California, where life moved at a snail's pace and nothing ever happened.

As the carriage rolled to a halt in front of a sprawling adobe structure, Laurie peered out the windows and was pleasantly surprised. A red tile roof and a profusion of greenery lent the house a comfortable atmosphere and made her think of Spain, and so when she was helped down from the carriage and Phillip Allen strode down the walk to greet her, she was smiling.

"Papa!" she cried in a natural way, and the slightly uneasy expression he wore vanished.

"My lovely Laurette!" He opened his arms and she rushed into them as if she had only been gone a week instead of five years. "Oh, my child, my lovely child!" Phillip said over and over, then held her at arm's length to look at her. "Though I suppose I should not be referring to you as a child now. You are definitely quite a young lady, and the most beautiful I have seen!" He said it with such conviction that she laughed.

"And you have grown to be quite a flatterer, I see," she teased, though she was delighted at his words. When she glimpsed Carlota standing in the arched doorway watching them, Laurie decided she could be gracious, so she smiled and said, "I have brought gifts for you, and some pretty things that I hope will please Carlota."

Putting an arm around Laurie's shoulders, Phillip walked her up the tiled pathway to the house. "I am sure she will be delighted with your gifts, Laurie," he said, unconsciously reverting to his old name for her.

Carlota's greeting was reserved, and not as spontaneous as her husband's, but pleasant. And she exclaimed with pleasure over the painted fans Laurie had brought her, and the lace mantilla from Spain.

"Thank you," Carlota said with a smile that made her sallow features light up most attractively. For the first time, Laurie could see what had attracted her father to the Spanish woman. Carlota truly adored Phillip Allen and looked to his every need and whim with genuine attention. The wine had to be exactly the right temperature to suit him, and his chair must be just so and his dressing gown pressed with just the right pleats — Laurette found herself thinking that her own mother must never have devoted herself to him so completely. It would stand to reason, as Françoise had not wanted to even live for her husband.

Forcing such thoughts from her mind, Laurie tried to follow the thread of their conversation as best she could, until finally Carlota noticed her weariness and suggested she get some rest.

"We have been selfish," Carlota said softly, "and not thought of your long journey. I shall have Serita show you to your room."

Gratefully, Laurie followed the young girl down a hallway to her room. "Here we are, señorita!" Serita said with a cheerful smile. She was slender and dark complected, with the lustrous black hair that seemed common in California. She wore a bright yellow skirt, a scoop-necked loose blouse, and a bright orange scarf tied around her slender waist, and Laurie thought she

32

looked very pretty and comfortable. No tight shoes nipped her feet, but a pair of loose leather sandals slapped against the stone floors.

It was obvious Serita was measuring her, too, for her dark eyes flicked over Laurie's fashionable gown and she gave a small sigh of envy. "You are so lovely, with such fine, pale skin—and such lovely gowns, señorita. It must be wonderful to have such things."

Laurie smiled back at her as she unpinned the wide-brimmed bonnet atop her head and noticed that Serita had already hung up all the clothes from her trunks. They stood open and empty, her clothing neatly stored in a huge armoire against one wall. She tossed the bonnet to the bed and sat down in a chair nearby.

"Serita, I have some things that are too small for me now," she said in a burst of generosity. In France it was common for cast-off clothes to be given to the maids in her aunt's house, so she thought nothing of offering her clothes so casually. "Would you care to have them? I think there is a gown that would just fit you if you would like. . . ."

"Oh no!" Serita quickly shook her head. "I could not. It would be . . . dangerous."

"Dangerous?" Laurie laughed. "Come now; it's just a gown, and I assure you that no one will think you stole it."

"That's not it, señorita. If a *soldado* saw it, he might think I had money to pay for such a gown, then he would think my taxes should be raised, and . . . oh, I dare not!"

Puzzled, Laurie would have said more, but the girl quickly ran from the room. Perhaps it wasn't the same here, she mused as she gave a shrug. Alone, Laurie wandered about the large chamber, looking from the turned-down bed to the ornately carved dark Spanish furniture. Some of it appeared to be very old, and she assumed it had been in Carlota's family for years, as

33

was the ranchero. It was a lovely old house, with large, airy rooms and tile floors that kept it cool.

Serita returned to help Laurie get ready for bed, and she seemed so subdued Laurie did not attempt to ask her any questions, just thanked her for her attentiveness. After placing a small carafe of water on the bedside table, Serita left again, and Laurie realized how tired she was after her long journey. A small courtyard filled with greenery and sweet-smelling flowers was just outside her bedchamber. As she lay on the soft mattress that was a welcome relief after the weeks spent on a ship's hard cot, the moonlight streaming through the open doors seemed to smile a welcome to California.

Perhaps it won't be so bad, Laurie thought drowsily just before she drifted to sleep.

She slept soundly, but was awakened in the night by voices. The moonlight had faded, and only pale patches lit the floor of her room. Sitting up, Laurie pushed at tumbled waves of hair in her eyes and strained to hear the voices.

It was a man and a woman, and they were speaking in guarded tones, the man's insistent, the woman's fearful.

"You must do so!" the man was saying, and Laurie heard the woman moan with apprehension.

"But it is so dangerous, and if the alcalde should find out, we would be executed, Juan!"

The man she had called Juan must have grabbed her, for the woman — who sounded like Serita — gave a soft cry. "Oh! I shall do it, but it is so dangerous in these times. To hide monies from the tax collectors invites instant death, even if we starve slowly by paying. . . ."

The voices faded, and Laurie realized that they must have been passing by her open doors and windows. She frowned. What had they meant? The alcalde must be the official responsible for collecting the taxes, and a

34

small amount of resentment was normal, but those two had sounded almost desperate.

Lying back down, Laurie made a mental note to ask her father about it the following day. The thread of true fear in Serita's voice haunted her.

But Phillip Allen did not have an easy answer for her question. He frowned, looking down at his hands. "I do not know who you heard talking," he said, for Laurie had not mentioned a name or that she thought it was Serita, "but I am afraid that they are correct to fear the alcalde. He has imposed rather . . . brutal . . . taxes upon the peons in Higuera."

"The alcalde is the tax collector, then?"

Phillip shook his head. "No, not really. Usually, you see, there is a governor-general who is appointed by the central government in Mexico, but Higuera is too small. You may have noticed the size of the *presidio* — the fort?"

"Yes, and I saw very few soldiers lounging about in the sun."

A wry smile curved his mouth as Phillip nodded. "Yes, it's almost unmanned most of the time. The cannons are old and rusty, and the soldiers undisciplined; usually just peasants from the countryside who hope to better themselves. Higuera, instead of having a general, has a military commandant in charge of the fort, and one alcalde. The alcalde is usually elected by the citizens, but Don Luis was appointed by Mexico after his predecessor's untimely death."

"And now he is heavily taxing the peons."

"Yes, and the hacendados, too, the wealthy land-owners like Carlota's family. But they can afford it. The peons cannot so easily afford it."

"But some of these people must work for you, Papa. Would the taxes be unbearable for them? I mean, could you not cushion the severity of their life?"

"As ambassador, I am required to abide by a few

35

rules myself, Laurie. Foreigners and Protestants are allowed no rights under the law. And I must truthfully report the wages I pay the peons and servants who work for me. The soldiers collect the taxes, and while I do what I can to provide food and lodging for those people, I'm afraid that it is not very much help to their families."

As Carlota joined the breakfast table the conversation changed by unspoken agreement, and Laurie greeted her stepmother with a smile.

"Good morning, Carlota. Did you sleep well?"

"Very well, thank you," Carlota said, blushing slightly and looking shyly at her husband.

Laurie sat in awkward silence; suddenly realizing that her father was a handsome, virile man who loved his wife, and what that meant. A faint flush stained her cheeks, for she had learned a great deal in the past five years, and though she was still a virgin herself, she had listened to the young married girls talk among themselves quite frankly. It had been another part of her education.

"That is a very lovely gown you are wearing," Carlota said after a moment, and Laurie smiled.

"Thank you."

"Don't you think it is a little—immodest?" Phillip asked with a faint lift of his brows.

"Immodest?" Laurie looked down at her gown, at the low scooped neck that bared just the smallest hint of her breasts. It was the latest fashion, and she had made a concession in not wearing one of her other, more daring gowns. In France, such gowns were common, but she had realized from observing Carlota's attire that the fashion had not yet reached the Californios living here. Carlota always wore a scarf around her neck, pinned with an ornate brooch, but modestly covering her.

"Well," Phillip said quickly, voicing her thoughts,

36

"perhaps it's just that the latest fashions have not yet reached California," and Laurie nodded silently.

She had already noticed the modest gowns with pinned scarves, and the large black lace mantillas worn in public by most of the women from the upper classes, covering them from the tops of their heads to their waists in some cases. They adorned themselves with jewelry and glitter, but did not believe in showing too much flesh.

Phillip Allen cleared his throat and pointed to a bowl of fruit, "Some of your favorites are there, and I know how you love fresh melons."

"Yes, I do." Laurie sipped hastily at her chocolate, a thicker version of the hot brew than she was accustomed to drinking. "This is very good," she said when it seemed as if the conversation lagged. "It's richer than what the French prefer."

"But not as good as *café brulot,* eh, Laurie?" her father teased, and she laughed.

"You remembered!"

"How could I forget the scene you made when I refused to allow you to drink it? You were only six, but oh, what a determined child you were!"

Laurie smiled at him over the rim of her cup. "I still am, Papa."

Phillip nodded, and his gaze met hers. "I rather thought so. You always were strong-willed."

"Do you still like to ride?" Carlota asked after a moment. "Everyone rides here, from the smallest child to the oldest."

Laurie nodded. "Yes, I love to ride."

"I will have Paco escort you, if you like. We have some excellent horses, and you may choose your favorite." Carlota slid a shy glance toward her husband. "If we can manage to drag your papa away from his work, perhaps he will ride with us."

"You know I've been very busy lately, but I will try,"

37

Phillip promised with a smile.

After breakfast, Carlota accompanied Laurie outside, where horses roamed freely in the pastures, trailing long ropes the *vaqueros* used to catch them. Laurie stared up the hillside, wide-eyed at the fine-blooded horses peacefully grazing.

"Why, they're beautiful, Carlota!"

"Yes, my father was quite a horseman, and had an eye for bloodlines. These come from his stock."

"Where are the stables?" Laurie asked, and Carlota laughed.

Sweeping her arms out in an expansive gesture, she said, "The hills are their mangers, the mountains their fences. We do not stable them here, as you did in New Orleans. Here, if a man wants to ride, he goes out and catches his mount. When the horse is weary, he gets another one. It is simple, *sí?*"

"I suppose, but don't they run off? Or get stolen?"

"Sometimes. But usually they are returned. We brand them with our mark, so that they can be easily recognized."

"Brand them?"

Carlota nodded, and explained to Laurie how marks were burned into the skin, or the ears notched. They walked as they talked, under huge shady trees and the long-trunked, top-heavy trees called palms. The mountains edged the horizon, and the gentle hillsides were green and fertile, spreading as far as the eye could see. Laurie took a deep breath, detecting the salty tang of the ocean on the currents.

A warm sun beat down, and Laurie was grateful for her thin cotton gown with short, puffed sleeves and a low bodice. It seemed to be drawing Carlota's attention, however, and after a moment the older woman said in a hesitant voice, "Girls here don't usually wear such . . . daring . . . gowns until after they are married, you know."

Laurie laughed gaily. "Really? What's the point after they're married? I mean, I thought a pretty gown was meant to attract a suitor, didn't you?"

"This is not New Orleans," Carlota said after a moment. "It is not the same here. This is a small village, and here the girls must wear proper gowns." She cleared her throat when Laurie did not reply, then said more strongly, "I promised your papa I would say something to you about it. He wants people here—my family and some of the older families—to accept you without reservation."

"And they won't if my gowns are too risqué?" Laurie's voice was brittle, and Carlota gave an unhappy sigh.

"No, they won't. It could endanger your papa's position here, you understand."

Some of the brightness faded from the day, but Laurie could see how unhappy the conversation was making Carlota, and bit back a sharp retort.

"I see," she said. "Perhaps I should wear a modesty bit and a shawl, then."

"Perhaps," Carlota said, and Laurie had the dismaying thought that the auspicious beginning of her stay in California was quickly fading.

When Laurie appeared at lunch in the same gown, she wore a thin scarf tucked into the bodice and pinned, and a light shawl or mantilla was draped over her head and shoulders. Phillip seemed pleased with her concessions, and Carlota smiled gratefully, but to Laurie it was a sharp reminder that California was not New Orleans or Europe.

Here she was called Doña Laurie by the servants, a term of respect accorded her. And she could not leave the hacienda without a dueña right behind her as chaperon, another irritating reminder that she was far from home.

Another reminder came the next day.

Carlota Alvarado y Allen's hacienda lay just on the eastern edge of Higuera, on a slope overlooking the town. To reach the market near the harbor, they had to ride through the town. On this day, soldiers had cordoned off the square, and were publicly flogging a man.

Laurie paled, and turned to her father. "What are they doing, Papa? Why?"

Phillip's face was grim, his mouth a taut line. "Taxes. He must have tried to withhold more than he was supposed to withhold. The new alcalde has invested a great deal of time and energy in collecting the correct amount of taxes, it seems, and raises them every time the wind shifts direction from east to west . . . but I speak out of turn. It's not my place to interfere with the existing government, but to maintain diplomatic relations with the Californian people here."

"How can you remain neutral when that poor man is being beaten?" Laurie demanded. "Doesn't it sicken you?"

"More than you know," Phillip replied tersely, and signaled to the driver to turn around.

It was when the carriage was maneuvering in the tight space bounded by the crowd of silent peons ordered to watch the punishment that Laurie recognized Serita. She was at the edge of the crowd, her face pale and eyes wide as she held up her hands in a pleading gesture. The soldiers paid her no attention, but continued to flog the now-unconscious man tied to a post.

That evening, Laurie confronted the red-eyed maid. "It was you I heard under my window the other night," she said, then put out a hand when Serita gave a frightened gasp. "I don't intend to say anything. But—why, Serita? If you needed more money, why didn't you come to my father or even to me?"

Looking down at her sandaled feet, the girl muttered, "It would not have mattered. If we gave them more, then the next time they would expect the same amount, or even more. And my family, they cannot continue paying such outrageous sums."

"I'll speak to my father, and we. . . ."

"Oh no!" Serita begged. *"Por favor,* Doña Laurie! Do not do so! If Don Luis should discover that one of the peons has complained to the American ambassador, it would be very bad. And at least Juan was only beaten and not killed."

"Don Luis is the alcalde?"

Serita nodded. "Si. And he has spies everywhere. It is not easy now since he came to Higuera, but we must live. Surely you understand."

Staring into the girl's frightened brown eyes, Laurie nodded slowly. "Yes, I suppose I do. If there is anything I can do to help, please let me know."

Serita laughed bitterly. "Unless you can steal back our pesos, there is nothing! We will starve one day, and the alcalde will have no one else to steal from." Then, as if frightened by what she'd said, the girl clapped a hand over her mouth and fled, leaving Laurie to ponder her words.

Chapter Two

It was hot when she awoke the next day, and Laurie lay in her bed staring at the ceiling. She realized it must be late, for the sun stitched a wide golden swathe across the floor, and she sat up, stretching.

Her sleeveless nightdress was damp, and she stood up, crossing the room to gaze out on her courtyard. No hint of a breeze stirred the jasmine or curling tendrils of vine that wound around a lattice screen. Only the sun was evident, and it poured onto the courtyard with a glaring intensity.

Laurie shut her screens and dressed, and when she joined Carlota on the patio outside the main dining room, she discovered they had company. An older, silver-haired gentleman sat at the table, accompanied by a tall, bulky servant who hovered in the background. The gentleman was evidently an aristocrat, a *gauchupine* from an old family. Laurie had met many like him in Spain.

He stood immediately when Carlota introduced her stepdaughter, and made her a formal bow. His trousers and short jacket were immaculate, and his frilled shirt cuffs and ruffled front were heavily starched and perfectly pressed.

"Señorita Allen, it is a pleasure to meet you," he said, and Laurie replied in flawless Castilian Spanish.

"I am honored to meet you, Señor Alvarez. My father has mentioned you with great respect."

Don Benito Alvarez smiled broadly. "Ah, it is so good to hear such a lovely young lady speak so eloquently! I am honored."

Carlota smiled with pleasure and pride, obviously congratulating herself on her good sense in insisting that her stepdaughter travel the Continent. It had given Laurie a great deal of polish to match her considerable beauty. It had been well worth the pain it had caused at the time, she decided as she offered Don Alvarez more wine.

"Gracias, Doña Carlota. Tell me, how did you find Spain?" the don asked Laurie, and she began to tell him of the places she had visited. He smiled and nodded with pleasure, tapping a silver-handled riding crop against one leg as he gazed at her. "Ah, to go again! But I am too old, and since my grandson has only recently returned, I must forget Spain."

Carlota signaled for the don's glass to be refilled as she sympathized, "But surely your grandson could tend to your estates while you're gone, Don Benito?"

Shrugging, the old man gave a shake of his silver head. "I do not think he cares for the *estancia* as I do, Doña Carlota. Ah, but after he finally returned, I had hopes—well, they will all come to naught."

Assuming that his grandson must be fairly young, Laurie soothed, "But when he matures, Don Benito, perhaps he will realize how important his heritage is."

Scowling, the don gave a rude snort, then apologized. "I am sorry, señorita, but of course you cannot know. My grandson is not a youth, but well beyond the age of accountability. He simply does not care." Shrugging, the old man said, "But I air my family problems." Turning to Carlota he asked, "You will attend the fiesta?"

"Of course. We would never miss one of your grand

fiestas, Don Benito!" She smiled when he rose and announced his departure, and extended her hand. After a flourishing kiss on her wrist, the don took his leave, once more saying how delighted he was to meet Laurie. "And be certain you attend the fiesta also," he added.

"A fiesta?" Laurie asked when the don had gone, and Carlota nodded.

"It will be a grand party. There will be music and dancing and tables upon tables of food. Everyone in Higuera will be there, even, perhaps, the alcalde, though Don Benito does not care for him. It is not wise to be his enemy, and Don Benito is very wise."

"It is a shame about his grandson," Laurie said. "Does he not care that he causes his grandfather sorrow?"

"Don Benito's grandson has always been a wild one. I can recall many of his escapades as a boy, especially after his parents died. His father was an American, and died in the war against England when Nicólas was only four or five. Then his mother slowly wasted away. He ran wild for the longest time, until finally his grandfather tried to discipline the boy." Carlota shook her head. "It was no use. Nicólas refused to obey. He was sent abroad for a time for an education, then a tour, and when he returned, he came back to Higuera for a while before leaving again."

"Where did he go?" Laurie asked, interested in spite herself.

"Ah, that is what upset Don Benito so," Carlota said with a sad shake of her head. Her large dark eyes were sympathetic, and her voice lowered so that Laurie did not know what atrocity to expect from Don Benito's errant grandson. When Carlota whispered, "Nicólas fought for the Texas Republic against Mexico," Laurie just stared at her.

"Excuse me?" she asked when it seemed as if Carlota expected some reaction from her.

"The don's grandson fought against Mexico," Carlota repeated, and at last Laurie understood.

"Oh, I see. He took up arms against his grandfather's country. Of course. That would upset the don very much. But isn't his grandson American as well as Spanish?"

Carlota nodded. "Yes, but Don Benito is not, and his grandson's mother was not. She was pure Castilian like her father, and so of course, he was very distressed when Nicólas fought against Mexico."

"But this is California," Laurie pointed out. "I know it is a province of Mexico, but it seems so removed, independent. And didn't Mexico fight for independence from Spain not so very long ago?"

Carlota stared at her, and her large eyes blinked rapidly for a moment. Her thin face puckered in a frown, and she said, "California is very Spanish, as is Mexico. There are the Indians, of course, and there are the pure Spaniards. Intermarriages have brought many changes, some of them good, some of them not. Many of the older *criollas* like Don Benito refuse to relinquish old ways and customs. For his grandson to fight against what the don regards as his homeland was a very bitter blow, indeed."

"Has he disowned him, then?"

"Oh no. There is no other heir to his lands. Don Benito cannot disown him, though he has frequently threatened to leave the Alvarez estates to strangers."

"When is the fiesta?" Laurie asked, idly fanning herself with a palm leaf. "I'm curious to see what this wild renegade is like . . ."

"Oh no!" Carlota said in genuine alarm. "You must stay away from him, Laurette! For all his wild ways, he is very handsome, and many a young girl has been deceived by his charm."

Laughing, Laurie said, "Don't worry about me, Carlota! I have been courted by dukes and flattered by

45

princes, and I will hardly lose my head over an untamed Californio!"

Don Benito's ranchero was several miles away from Higuera, and guests from all over the countryside traveled far to attend. It was a grand affair, with musicians and fountains of wine, and entire steers roasting on spits. Long tables groaning with food were set up on patios and beneath canopies, and the air throbbed with gaiety and guitars.

A bullfight was staged, but it was unlike any bullfight Laurie had ever seen. It was more an exhibition of equestrian skills than anything else, with the rider's object to tire the bull into immobility, rather than to kill it. Laurie enjoyed it much more than she had the brutal bullfights of Spain, and clapped and waved with the other ladies when the rider proved his skill by waving a red cloak at the bull, then dancing out of reach of the wicked horns. No horses were gored, though there were some close calls, and all the riders were celebrated.

The Indian musicians played guitars, horns, and violins, the lively melodies of the *jarabe, jota,* and even the more quiet waltzes from Europe. Gilt-encrusted swains presented themselves to Doña Carlota with effusive compliments on her stepdaughter, all asking for the honor of a dance. Phillip, though skeptical, watched as Laurie was swept into the intricate steps of the dances, and had to admit that his daughter had become quite popular.

The afternoon wore on, and with the music and loud laughter still ringing in her ears, Laurie began to look around for Carlota. Her partner of the moment, a tall, dark young man with a mustache and sweeping whiskers, had gone to fetch her a glass of chilled wine, as she plead weariness and overheating. Laurie glanced around, but knew no one, and wished she could place names with new faces.

"Shall I escort you to your *mama*, Señorita?" a handsome young caballero asked, but she shook her head.

She was so hot, and flushed from the dancing and too much wine, and she wanted to find a quiet corner to retreat to, so she murmured something vague, then moved quickly and politely away. Pushing through the dancers, Laurie found her way outside, to cool breezes, tiled walkways, and fresh air.

Wandering down the walkways and away from the clamor of music and voices, Laurie began to feel better. The grounds were neat and well-tended, with scattered stone fountains and groves of foliage offering seclusion.

Don Benito's sprawling hacienda made her stepmother's seem like a cottage, and she had never dreamed a man could own so much. It was larger than any Louisiana plantation she had ever visited, and Phillip had told her the ranchero encompassed over eighty square miles. It was one of the original Spanish land grants, sweeping from the ocean to the mountains, almost from horizon to horizon. It occurred to her to wonder how Don Benito kept the alcalde from taxing him too heavily, then realized that he must have friends in high places.

If that were so, she wondered, why did Don Benito and other hacendados like himself not stop the predatory actions of the alcalde? Didn't they care that the peons were being brutalized? Didn't they feel a sense of responsibility to them?

A slight frown knit her brow as she strode over a stone bridge to a small courtyard tucked behind a natural screen of palms. Softly gleaming lanterns lit the soft haze of dusk with a warm glow, and she could hear the faint strains of guitar music in the distance.

Pausing to stare down into the pool beneath the bridge, Laurie could hear the musical trickle of a fountain nearby. She gazed at her reflection, and had the thought that the red gown suit her in spite of Carlota's dismayed objection to it.

"But it is so — immodest!" Carlota had said in a gasp.

"Not in Paris," Laurie had said with a defiant glitter in her eyes. Stubbornly, she had decided not to go to the fiesta garbed like a dowdy crow, though she had conceded and tucked a modesty-bit into the plunging neckline. And she had worn a mantilla to cover her bright, burnished hair, though not for the reason Carlota might have wished, and not of a somber color. The rich hue set off her fair coloring, and the lacy wisp was flattering and coquettish, easily used to tease a man when she peeked at him from beneath the sheer red fabric.

She wandered from the arched bridge to the carved fountain in a shadowy corner of the alcove. Leaning on the stone lip of the fountain, Laurie watched the fish dart about beneath the shallow surface of the pool. A few stars were reflected in the pool, and she could see the reflection of her face and mantilla until a fish shattered it. She laughed softly.

Her laugh swiftly altered to a gasp when a hand grasped one arm and swung her around. There was no time to scream before a man had her in his arms, holding her much too tightly, his hands roaming much too boldly over Laurie's shocked curves. Any protest she might have made was strangled by his mouth slanting harshly over her lips, burning into her, shocking her sophisticated European awareness into oblivion. One hand cradled the back of her head, his arm pressing her into his hard male frame; the other hand was tugging at the low bodice of her gown, loosening a small rosette on the sleeve-strap and detaching the modesty-bit.

When she would have pulled away, the man held her more tightly, his hand tangling in the knot of lace on

48

the back of her neck. Laurie had been kissed many times before, but never like this, never so thoroughly or so savagely, with the man intent on complete possession.

Laurie felt her senses whirl. As he pressed forward her head fell back, and to her shock she felt him touch her tongue with his. It sent a thrill of revulsion and excitement through her, warring emotions that left her confused and shaking. A faint protest died in her throat, emerging as only a soft moan, and she thought *Dear heavens, what is he doing? What am I doing?*

When he finally lifted his head and stared down into her face, Laurie saw his eyes register surprise, then amusement. They were dark eyes, hot and liquid, with black shadows dancing in them, set in a face that was darkly handsome.

"You're not Rosa," he said softly.

As wit slowly gained ground on shock, Laurie managed to push the intruder away, bringing one hand up to slap him. Her wrist was caught in a viselike grip.

"No, I am not Rosa!" Laurie hissed furiously. She was trembling from head to toe, her poise and self-confidence as invisible as the wind.

A smile crooked the hard slant of his mouth, and his eyes danced with devilry. "That could be to your advantage, chica," he murmured, and before she realized his intentions he had pulled her into his embrace again, molding her body to his hard frame and kissing her until she couldn't draw a breath.

This time Laurie felt her knees grow weak, felt her head spin and her lungs cease to work properly. And in the pit of her stomach, there began to burn a slow fire, hot and searing, coiling swiftly upward and threatening to consume her with its intensity.

"Monsieur," she protested weakly when he released her lips, unconsciously reverting to French, "please stop!"

49

He replied in perfect French that he saw no reason to do so when they were both enjoying it, and Laurie's fingers dug into his arms. She could hardly stand, and her senses were reeling with the shock of his touch and her reactions to him.

As his hand caressed the ripe curve of her breast, shoving aside the thin material of her chemise, Laurie felt it as if in a daze. She was still held tightly against him, and she slowly became aware that there was very little barrier between their bare chests. His shirt was open almost to the waist, baring his lightly-furred chest, and her bodice was pushed close to her waist. Her hands were trapped between them and almost useless as she tried to push him away.

It felt as if she was moving underwater, her movements sluggish and weighted, and she began to wonder if she was having a nightmare. The situation had taken on a dreamlike state, with the soft splashing of the fountain and the pale glow of lanterns around them, shadows shifting and music in the distance. And always, the hot, high insistence of his mouth and hands, making her feel things she had never felt before.

What was it her cousin Pierre had once told her? Laurie struggled to recall, because it seemed important now for some reason, something about one day finding herself in a situation she could not handle with her quick wit and her sharp tongue. Oh yes, it was how to force a man's unwelcome attentions away from her, something about using her knee and bringing it up sharply.

But when she would have done that, she realized that her wide hoop skirts and multitudinous petticoats would only render her action ridiculous. So with a feeling of hopeless surrender — a feeling completely alien to her — she allowed the tall man with the dark hair and eyes to continue kissing her, his mouth searing from her lips to her throat, making her moan, making her head fall back. It was only when his mouth moved to the aching fullness of her breast that a semblance of her sanity returned, and Laurie felt a sharp jolt of reality that brought her back from her dazed acceptance.

With a suddenness that caught him off guard, she let her body go limp in his arms, so that he was unbalanced. He loosened his grip on her for an instant, and that was all Laurie needed.

With the rage and swiftness of a cat, she brought up her arm and slashed her palm across his cheek, hearing with a great deal of satisfaction the loud crack of her hand against his face. For a split-second he stood there, his eyes boring furiously into her face, then as she lifted her other arm to repeat the action, he seized her wrist in a bone-crushing grip and bent her arm up and behind her, slamming her hard against his body again.

"I don't know what kind of damned game you think you're playing," he ground out between clenched teeth, "but enough is enough!"

"You are so right!" Laurie flashed back. "Enough is more than enough, and you, sir, have crossed that line!"

There was a flicker of doubt on his face for a moment, then he released her with a shove so that she stumbled back and came up short against the edge of the fountain. Laurie stared at him as she fumbled with the bodice of her gown. The strap was ripped, and the rosette gone, and she had no idea where her modesty-bit had fallen or what had happened to her mantilla. But all that seemed insignificant in the face of this tall, dark man's assessing fury.

"You are not with Rosa?" he demanded, and Laurie's chin tilted upward.

She was startled by the quick start of tears in her eyes, and realized that her reactions might overpower her if she did not regain control. Laurie inhaled deeply and let it out slowly, deliberately smoothing her gown

51

as she cudgeled her trembling reactions into control again.

"I should think it obvious, sir, that I have never met you before, nor do I know any Rosa. However, if she knows you as well as you seem to think, I offer her my deepest sympathies!"

His handsome face creased in a brief grin, and he stood back a step to rake her with an assessing glance. As he studied her disheveled face and the blond curls tumbling down around her shoulders, he laughed softly.

"It seems that I have made a mistake, señorita. I offer my apologies."

Stiffening, Laurie snapped, "They are not accepted, sir!"

He shrugged indifferently. "As you wish."

"And what am I supposed to do now?" Laurie demanded with a snap. "My gown is ruined, I see my mantilla in the fountain, and I don't see the modesty-bit that you so rudely tore away!" Her angry gaze swiftly traveled his tall frame from his dark hair, over his broad shoulders and starched white shirt to his snug-fitting trousers and knee-length boots. He was dressed as a gentleman, but his manners were those of a boor and ruffian, and she lost no time in telling him so, an acid edge to her tone as she struggled with her torn strap.

"I am devastated to hear it," he mocked, crossing his arms over his bare chest and leaning back against the curved edge of the fountain. "But it was you who invited my unwelcome, boorish attentions with your, ah—seductive—gown and that lovely expanse of bare flesh. What else was I to think? I was to meet Rosa and her friend here, and there you are, clad in a seductive red gown with a mantilla hiding your hair and your breasts begging me to touch them."

Furious, her cheeks flaming, Laurie unwillingly realized that Carlota had been right. The gown had been an invitation to this man, and she should not have worn it. He had assumed that she was Rosa, who must be very familiar with him — though why she would be was a mystery.

Lifting her chin, Laurie managed to say coolly, "If it would not embarrass my host, I would complain about you, sir! However, I do not wish to distress Don Benito with any disparaging truths about one of his guests, so if you will just go away, I will be silent."

For some reason, the man seemed to find her remark very amusing. He laughed, pushing away from the edge of the fountain to approach her again. Instinctively, Laurie took a quick step back, her breath catching in her throat and her gold eyes wide with apprehension.

Noting her expression, he laughed again, softly, his white teeth flashing in his dark face, making Laurie think of a handsome Mephistopheles — saturnine, brooding, too wickedly handsome to be real. She felt behind her and her hands closed around the limb of a tree. She held on to it for security as he drew closer.

"I shall complain to Don Benito about you if you come any closer!" she said with only the barest trace of panic in her voice. Her legs trembled, and she was glad she could hold to the tree limb for support as he reached out to lift her chin in his warm palm.

His voice was soft, almost lazy, as he drawled, "And do you think Don Benito will have me removed, chica?"

A harsh voice interrupted from the shadows, "No, he will have you whipped if you do not release her at once!"

The man's hand dropped away and he turned with indolent grace, giving a slight, mocking bow as Don Benito stepped out of the shadows and into the light cast by the lanterns.

"Holá. Abuelo," he said, and Don Benito cracked his gold-headed cane against the courtyard tiles.

Grandfather? Laurie thought dazedly, then realized with a rush of understanding the man's amusement. He was Don Benito's scapegrace grandson, Nicólas Alvarez. No wonder he had found her threats to report him amusing!

Don Benito was stiff with anger, his autocratic features drawn into stern lines as he viewed his grandson with cold eyes.

"You shame me, Nicólas! Do you play the rutting bull with every decent female, regardless of her tender years or breeding?"

Again, Nicólas slightly inclined his head in his grandfather's direction, but some of the mockery had faded from his gesture. "It is a case of mistaken identity, Grandfather."

"Ah, I see! And when you discovered your mistake you immediately apologized and offered to make amends!" The old man's voice whipped across his grandson with contempt, and Laurie thought she saw Nicólas flinch slightly. "Do not shame me further with your weak excuses," Don Benito continued in the same scathing tone. "I will see you in my office in the morning. Do not fail to be there. The consequences could be extremely unpleasant!"

The don put out his hand, and said to Laurie, "I will escort you to the main house by the back way, señorita, where you may find a woman who will help you mend your torn gown. And on the way, I shall tender my most abject apologies for having inadvertently subjected you to my grandson's unwelcome attentions."

Laurie silently put her hand in the crook of the don's arm and went with him, her wide hoop skirts swishing over the tiles and her head held high. She did not dare glance at Nicólas Alvarez again, did not dare look at his dark, burning eyes for fear she would see mockery

54

in them, a veiled contempt for her reactions to his caresses. He knew that she had responded, however briefly, to his hot kisses and the touch of his hands on her.

After repairing her gown and returning to the vast ballroom where the musicians were still playing, Laurie found Carlota and went to stand beside her.

Carlota turned with a welcoming smile. "You were gone so long, I began to think you had become lost."

"No, I had to cool off from so much dancing, and then I discovered that one of the straps on my gown was loose, and Don Benito was kind enough to find a woman to sew it down for me," Laurie said in a breathless kind of reply that she hoped sounded convincing. After all, it was the truth, even if a bit rearranged.

To her relief, Carlota accepted her excuse without a murmur, simply flashed her a distracted smile and pointed out the dancers, naming several of those she thought her stepdaughter should know.

"There is Linda Concepción Gonzales y Navarro, who is the alcalde's niece, and very nice in spite of some of the feelings about her uncle. And over there is Teresá Morales y Evans, who is married to a very nice American. Her husband was once a sailor, but met Teresá and decided to stay here and raise cattle and children. And over there. . . ."

Laurie's attention drifted, but she made polite murmurs at all the right intervals as Carlota pointed out several suitable young men. She had already met most of them in the dancing earlier, and had decided that they were gauche and boring, though perfectly nice. Only one man had remotely interested her, an American who had been her partner for two of the dances. Of course, the other man who had made quite an impression on her was the don's grandson, but she had no intention of ever meeting him again! Now she understood why Carlota had been so horrified at the thought of Laurie meeting him. She'd been right. He was unsuitable, a veritable devil, though admittedly a handsome one. And when she saw him again—as she inevitably would—she would put her nose in the air and snub him coldly.

But when Nicólas Alvarez presented himself in front of Laurie and announced to Carlota that his grandfather had sent him to ask her stepdaughter for a dance, Carlota seemed at a loss and Laurie found that she could not snub him without appearing ungracious and attracting unwanted attention. Gold eyes flashed dangerously, but she gave a stiff nod of her head and put her hand in his outstretched palm, trying to ignore his smug grin.

"Did Don Benito truly insist that we dance?" she asked in a low tone when he had pulled her into the swirl of dancers, and he laughed.

"He did suggest something of the sort, along with a few other choice words for my earlier behavior." He put an arm around her waist and held her much too closely for the steps of the waltz, and Laurie pushed at him indignantly. Her reaction only made him laugh softly again, and she hated him at that moment.

"You are no gentleman, sir!" she snapped.

"Ah, and what foolish person ever said I was?"

She glanced up at his face, and saw that he was gazing down at her with laughter, but no mockery. "I am certain that no one who knows you would ever make that mistake," she observed tartly, and he grinned.

"You're very astute for a young lady who is dressed so daringly," he said, and Laurie wished she could stomp his foot and storm from the dance floor.

"I realize that my choice of gowns is daring for this country, but in France. . . ."

"Ah, in France the young ladies rouge their cheeks and lips and even their breasts, and put perfume in places proper young Spanish girls don't know exist," he

56

said in a soft tone that was suggestive and matter-of-fact at the same time.

Drawing in a deep breath of shock and embarrassment, Laurie spat, "Let me go!"

She tried to pull away, no longer caring about attracting attention, but he held her waist tightly. "I won't talk about that, if you object," he said. "But my grandfather is watching, and if I offend you he is liable to have me shot at dawn."

"He is far too late for that!" Laurie snapped back at him. "It should have been done years ago!"

"Nonetheless, I promise not to offend you again if you will finish this dance." His lean body moved in a whirl as graceful as a caress, and Laurie hesitated. She could feel Carlota's worried gaze in her direction, and would have hated to admit to her that she had been wrong in her choice of gowns for the evening. If it got out that she had been so familiarly handled because of her gown, Carlota would never allow her to leave the house attired in anything less than a mantilla to her ankles and necklines to her eyebrows and she knew it.

So Laurie gave a tight nod of her head, and muttered less than graciously, "Just this one dance."

"You honor me," was the prompt, practiced reply, and Laurie flashed him a narrowed glare that he interpreted correctly. "You dislike me, señorita," he observed with the familiar thread of mockery in his voice.

Far too aware of the hard press of his lean body against her and the way he was holding her a bit too closely, Laurie found it difficult to reply. She could not help but recall the touch of his lips against hers, his mouth grazing her bare breast and the familiar way in which he had touched her, and a hot, high flush stained her cheeks.

"Ah," he whispered, "I see that you have not forgotten our first meeting. Neither have I."

Laurie pressed her lips tightly together, refusing to

rise to his bait and praying for the quick end of the dance. When it finally arrived she almost ran back to her stepmother, barely acknowledging the mocking bow he gave her and his polite greeting to Carlota. She was too flustered and upset, and wished she could go home.

"It has been a long time, Señor Caldwell," she heard Carlota say to him, and Laurie's head jerked around. Her stepmother was smiling politely but with obvious strain, and Laurie wondered why she had called him by that name. Wasn't his name Alvarez?

"Yes," Carlota explained to Laurie when he had taken his leave and disappeared into the crowd again, "but that was his mother's name. You are familiar with Spanish custom, Laurie, so you know that both the parents' names are used. As Nicólas — or Cade, as he prefers to be called — is Don Benito's heir, the don insists upon calling him by the family name." She shrugged. "It simplifies matters here in California."

Laurie was frowning. For some reason, the name teased her memory, and when she looked up at her stepmother she saw that she understood.

"In New Orleans," Carlota said, and it all returned to Laurie in a rush. Of course! He was the man who had dueled with Gilbert Rosière and won, and he was the man who had wed the governor's niece and abandoned her at the altar! He truly was a conscienceless scoundrel, and she wondered about his wife. That had been what — five years before? A man like Cade Caldwell probably had several children by now, and Cecelia had more than likely grown fat from it.

That notion pleased her for some reason, and Laurie recalled how she had always disliked Cecelia de Marchand. What irritated her was the fact that for the rest of the evening, her gaze seemed to search for and find Cade Caldwell wherever he happened to be in the crowded room.

And it irritated her that he didn't seem to recall her existence. No, he danced and laughed and played the part of an attentive suitor to every attractive female in the vast ballroom, but he did not even glance at Laurie again. And she found herself wondering why she even thought about him, why his indifference irritated her so.

The fiesta was to go on all night and into the next day, but when Phillip said he and Carlota needed to leave, Laurie quickly said she would go with them, of course. It was not too far from the Alvarado hacienda to the sprawling Alvarez estates, and the ride was quiet in the moonlight. Carlota glanced at her curiously once or twice, but kept her face averted, staring out the window of the closed carriage at the dark countryside.

Later that night when she lay in her own bed and stared at the moonlight-checkered ceiling, she decided Cade intrigued her because he was unavailable. After all, he was married, wasn't he? Even if his wife was so far away? Unless Cecelia had died, or the marriage been dissolved, she added in the next instant. Cade Caldwell certain did not behave like a married man, but then, there were many of her past acquaintance who had conveniently forgotten such a fact. She had thought it amusing then, but now it angered her that this man would stoop to such deception. And it angered her that he was obviously a man who cared little what people thought of him, except, perhaps, for his grandfather.

Well, none of that really mattered. She would not see him again, not unless they attended the same social events, and anyway, his crude arrogance was so abrasive she would only get angry at him.

Laurie kicked at the covers over her, thinking that he was too much like some of the men she had known in Spain. No, he was not the kind of man she would care for, but one of those coldly calculating men who took

59

what they wanted without thought. But just before she fell asleep, she knew he had awakened some latent spark of sensuality inside her that was vaguely frightening.

Chapter Three

Nicólas Cade Alvarez y Caldwell's interview with his grandfather did not begin or end pleasantly. The old don was furious. His steps were quick and angry as he paced the floor in front of his desk and the indolent long form of his grandson that was draped over a chair.

"You insulted the daughter of a friend!" the old man said in a harsh tone. "And you had the temerity to invite one of your *putas* to a fiesta honoring decent guests!"

"Two *putas*," Cade put in lazily. "Rosa brought a friend."

The don's gnarled hands tightened around the riding crop he carried, and his jaw clenched as he glared at Cade. "You are insolent, sir!"

Unfolding his body from the chair, Cade stood up and met his grandfather's irate gaze with a resigned smile. "Nothing has changed, has it Grandfather?"

Don Benito had to look up at his grandson, and he held himself proudly erect, refusing to let his anger fade. "No, it has not! You leave your home and stay away for years, then when you return, you insult the house of your ancestors with loose behavior and women! And I have word of some of your less savory occupations while you've been absent, and it sickens me, Nicólas."

61

Cade leaned back against his grandfather's heavy desk and folded his arms across his chest. It had always been this way, ever since he was a small rebellious boy squirming under the harsh hand of Don Benito's rigid discipline. There were the confrontations, the accusations, the many lashings as a boy. Only now he was a man, and his grandfather could not accept it. He must still have control over him.

"And to think," Don Benito snarled when it appeared that his grandson's attention was wandering, "that you dare to dally with the niece of the alcalde!"

Shrugging, Cade said, "How can I refuse when she summons me to her side? It would be rude."

The short whip snapped against the desk top, and Don Benito shook his head. "It is better to be rude than in bed with the devil! And do you think the alcalde does not know about his niece? Do you think him a foolish man who would sit back and idly watch Señorita Navarro bed you?"

Another lazy shrug as Cade asked softly, "And who has said that I've bedded her? I have not. I ride with Linda only because she insists. She's bored, more bored than I am here, and she longs to leave."

Drawing in a sharp breath, the old don spat, "I wish she would! And take her uncle with her!"

Cade smiled. "That would suit too many people, I'm afraid."

Rounding on his grandson, Don Benito said softly but furiously, "It is too bad you do not care enough to use your sword for a just cause!"

Knowing he could assuage his grandfather's anger with the truth, yet reluctant to tell him too much, Cade said, "I suppose you are referring to my service in the Texan Army."

"Exactly!" The riding crop slashed down on the desk top with a loud crack, but Cade did not flinch. "You dared turn your back on your own people to fight with

62

a band of farmers and frontiersmen!"

Cade met his grandfather's gaze calmly. "They were brave, honorable men fighting for a cause they believed in. I am proud to have served with them, and there are times when I think I should have been with them in San Antonio at the Alamo when Santa Anna and his cowardly troop took two weeks to kill a mere handful of true fighting men! They were given no quarter that day, nor at Goliad, and when we found Santa Anna in San Jacinto, we gave him more mercy than he deserved."

"Bah," The riding crop swished through the empty air. "I am ashamed of your part in that disgraceful spectacle. It is an embarrassment to the Alvarez name and to Higuera."

"And the alcalde is not an embarrassment to the Mexican government?" Cade retorted. "He is a butcher, a madman who would be deposed if there were any worthy men in Higuera!"

Stiffening at the implied insult, Don Benito said, "I am surprised you think yourself capable of recognizing a worthy man, my grandson!"

Cade straightened slowly, and his jaw was tight with anger as he glared at his grandfather. He was well aware of the silent, stalwart figure standing guard in a corner, and he knew that Don Benito's constant companion would not hesitate to shoot him if he became too belligerent and had the temerity to threaten his grandfather, but there were moments when Don Benito went too far.

"Look at you—you come to my hacienda draped in braces of pistols like a bandit," the don was saying, jabbing his whip toward the holsters Cade wore. "Whatever happened to the swords gentlemen wear? Ah, of course, you are no longer a gentleman! I had forgotten for a moment, that you chose to be a disgraced American rather than a man of breeding."

"Do you sneer at all Americans, Grandfather?" Cade couldn't help asking. "If so, why be distressed at my insulting one of them?"

"You know I do not object to Americans, or I would never have allowed my precious Maria to marry your father," the don replied stiffly. "I object to dishonor, no matter the nationality of the man who wears it!"

Cade was silent, smarting from his grandfather's rebuke but not wanting him to know it. He wished he hadn't returned to California. He'd known how it would be, which is why he had delayed his return as long as possible. But now he was here, enduring this uncomfortable interview that had only one, foreseeable end. It was always the same, and he braced himself for it.

Turning back to his grandson, Don Benito took two steps closer. His body was rigid with anger, but to Cade's surprise he did not strike him with the riding crop he held.

"Tell me about your marriage!" the old don snapped, and Cade's mouth thinned.

"There's nothing to tell," he said shortly.

"Nothing to tell? You wed a girl from a good family over five years ago, and there's nothing to tell?" The don lashed out, slashing his whip across Cade's chest and leaving a long, red weal beneath the thin material of his shirt. "I demand to hear it!" The whip sliced down again, but Cade did not flinch from it. His pride would not allow him to try to avoid the blows that crisscrossed his chest with vivid red marks.

Shrugging, fighting the anger his grandfather's blows always provoked, Cade sliced a glance toward Pancho in the corner, who had immediately tensed when the old don erupted into anger. The burly guard held a rifle loosely in his hands as if he expected Cade to attack the old man, and he wanted to laugh with derision. Instead he said coldly, "I wed her because I was

64

forced to it, and that's all."

"She was bearing your child?"

"Not that I know of." Cade shrugged again. "I haven't seen her since the wedding. I immediately joined the Texas Regulars and left New Orleans."

"You are less than a man!" the don spat with disgust, and Cade's face paled with suppressed fury. Taut white lines bracketed his mouth, and his eyes blazed with anger as he glared at his grandfather. The don laughed. "Ah, I see that my words upset you! At least you still have the decency to care what an old man says."

"I care what you think of me," Cade said so tightly that the don gave him a long, thoughtful stare.

"Perhaps you do," he said finally, shaking his head, his shoulders slumping.

Cade saw age in his grandfather, and realized that he was not the strong man he'd always been. He still held himself tall and erect, proudly, with the blood of his old Castilian ancestors flowing hot and vigorous through his veins, but he was getting older. Knowing this, it was easier for him to accept his grandfather's insults and blows.

When Don Benito crossed to the desk and poured two glasses of *aguardiente,* the strong brandy he preferred, Cade knew the interview was close to an end. Returning to Cade's side, he thrust one of the glasses into his hand.

"You will make your amends to the pretty blond señorita and her family," he said without preamble.

"I think she would prefer that I throw myself in the ocean," Cade said dryly.

"Then she shows remarkably good sense for a young woman," the don replied.

"And after I've abased myself?" Cade prompted when his grandfather lapsed into silence. "Am I allowed to return home and into your good graces?" His voice was only slightly mocking.

Don Benito regarded him silently, his eyes quickly raking his grandson's tall, lean frame. He was too cocky, this grandson of his, and always had been. As a youth it had been to cover up his immaturity, but now — now he was a man full-grown, and a man to be reckoned with if his information was correct. But he was still too reckless, too heedless of his family's good reputation, and Don Benito had only a little time left to instill in Cade a respect for the things that time had won for the Alvarez family.

"We will discuss your wife at a later date," the old don said, ignoring Cade's narrowed gaze and the slight thinning of his lips. "I shall study the situation and decide what is to be done. Now, you shall do your best to correct the insult that you visited upon my friend Señor Allen and his family. Doña Carlota is from a fine old family, and there would be bad blood if it were known that you had behaved so badly."

"And you think the girl hasn't told them everything by now?" Cade mocked.

Don Benito shook his head. "No, somehow I do not think she would say anything. She struck me as a sensible young woman."

Cade didn't say what he was thinking, that the girl had eyes like a cat's and morals to match. She had certainly returned his kisses with enthusiasm, though she'd offered the usual token protest. He'd liked the feel of her in his arms, her soft curves and the wealth of silky blond hair that framed a face of exceptional beauty. Señorita Laurette Allen was a definite addition to Higuera, and he meant to stay as far away from her as possible. Though she was lovely and soft, and probably willing, she was trouble. He could sense those kind of things, especially after his troubles with Cecelia de Marchand. He'd learned a valuable lesson from that affair — to trust his first instincts.

Sipping at the potent brandy, Cade listened politely

to his grandfather's plans for the ranchero, grateful the difficult interview was over at last. It had gone badly from the first, and though he wasn't at all pleased with the edict, he'd get it over with quickly enough and be done with it.

There were more important things to think about since he had returned. Higuera was in a state of unrest, and had been for years, since Don Luis Jorge Baptiste y Navarro had become the alcalde, or mayor. Cade had received a letter from his grandfather while still in New Orleans, and after leaving the Texas Army, had gone to Mexico to get Don Luis removed from office.

A wry smile slanted his lips as Cade recalled his grim reception in Mexico City after an officer had remembered him from his service with the Texans. He might still be languishing in one of their prisons if not for the help of a very lovely señorita he'd met at a fiesta. She had bought his way out when she'd learned of his predicament, and he had taken her with him to Spain for a time.

But even the sunny clime of Spain and the attentions of the lovely woman had not lessened his desire to return to Higuera and his grandfather, and so here he was. Carmelita would miss him for a time, but he had left her in the very capable hands of a good friend who had been quite smitten with her. No doubt, if he ever saw her again she would have married Don Francisco and have ten fat babies at her feet.

After murmuring a polite reply to his grandfather's query as to a particular horse, Cade thought that it had been a long time since the people of Higuera had been able to think of little more than survival. He'd seen the way the peasant women scurried around with their eyes down, the short hems of their skirts tattered and their feet bare. It was ridiculous for the peons to be so wretched in a land that was so fertile and productive.

He could recall when they had been a much more happy people, dozing in the mercado during a noonday siesta, fat and content with their vineyards and gardens. Now they all looked sullen and miserable, and it made him angry.

It wasn't so on Don Benito's land, where the people were well fed and treated with kindness and respect. Here things were different. Yet just a few miles away, in the village and on other, smaller *estancias,* they eked out an existence that was barely tolerable. No one smiled anymore.

That's why he had come back, and he intended to end Don Luis's tyranny as soon as possible.

But first he had a domestic matter to attend to, the matter of making peace with Doña Carlota's willful, cat-eyed stepdaughter. Cade almost laughed when he recalled the girl's anger at his kisses. He'd been just as surprised, but pleasantly so, and he knew she wouldn't want to hear that. It should be interesting to see how she would react when she saw him again, he mused, stretching his long legs in front of him as he recalled her flushed, furious face. Yes, it should be very interesting indeed.

Chapter Four

Laurie was not surprised to be informed the following day that she had a visitor. Several of the young men who had danced with her at the Alvarez fiesta had vowed to pay court to her as soon as possible. What did surprise her was the fact that her visitor was Cade Caldwell.

She paused in the doorway, her gold eyes widening with shock, then narrowing with anger.

"To what do I owe this pleasure?" she asked, making her voice as cutting as possible.

"My grandfather," was the immediate, flat response, and Cade looked at her with such blatant effrontery that she had to smile.

"I see. I should have known it wouldn't be your idea."

"Yes, I should think you would," he agreed, sauntering toward her with such confident arrogance that Laurie immediately bridled again.

"And I suppose this is to atone for your disreputable behavior earlier?" she snapped out, crossing the room and avoiding him by a wide arc. Cade laughed softly, his dark eyes glinting with amusement as Laurie paused beside a table to fiddle with an arrangement of fresh flowers.

"Of course it is. My grandfather is afraid I have somehow managed to offend you, and that it will affect his relationship with your father and your mother's family."

"My stepmother," Laurie corrected idly, and flashed him an irritated glance when he laughed again. Of course, he would know that. "Very well," she said again, not caring how rude she sounded, "you have done your duty. I would appreciate your disappearing as quickly as you arrived."

"Without offering your guest refreshment?" Cade managed to sound hurt. "I'm afraid if word got out that you were such a rude hostess, your popularity would suffer much more than mine. . . ."

A flush stained her cheeks, and Laurie wished he would go to the devil even as she tugged at a bell rope to summon a servant. When Serita arrived, Laurie asked her brusquely to serve refreshments on the patio, well aware of Cade's mocking smile and eye on her.

They sat stiffly on the patio as refreshments were served, Laurie strained and uncomfortable, and Cade seeming relaxed and amused by her discomfiture. She longed to ask him what he had done with his wife, but dared not get into such a personal conversation, so she contented herself with getting his visit over with as quickly as possible.

"Your hair is quite lovely in the sunlight," Cade said in a soft voice, startling Laurie into looking up at him.

"Oh . . . thank you," she said, then felt that he was laughing at her. "And you look even more like the devil in daylight," she blurted before thinking, then flushed at his loud burst of laughter.

"Another gracious compliment!" His mouth twisted with amusement. "I find myself quite bedazzled by your diplomacy and tact, Señorita."

Her cup clattered in its saucer as Laurie placed her tea on the table and said irritably, "Oh, stop playing

70

the part of a gentleman! I have not forgotten the other night, and you can tell your grandfather that I have no intention of repeating that disgraceful episode to anyone, so he need not worry about the Alvarez reputation. I am certain you can find other ways to destroy it without my help."

All amusement died from his expression as Cade bent forward, his dark eyes riveting on Laurie's face and his tone quiet and faintly menacing. "I would not be so haughty if I were you, my lovely little hypocrite. I seem to recall your returning my kisses. Perhaps you should worry more about your own reputation than about mine."

What Laurie would have answered remained unspoken, because Carlota chose that moment to appear on the patio, her gaze flicking from one to the other as she approached the table.

"The maid told me that you had come for a visit, Señor Caldwell," Carlota said in a faintly breathless voice, "and I came as quickly as I could."

Rising politely, Cade bent over Carlota's hand. "It is good to see you again, Doña Carlota, but I fear I must be leaving now. My *abielo* has many errands for me to do, and I can't stay." His eyes flicked only briefly to Laurie, who sat with a stiff, averted face. "Señorita, again, it was pleasant seeing you. *Adios.*"

"Adios," Carlota and Laurie chorused, each grateful for his departure for entirely different reasons.

Carlota gazed at her stepdaughter anxiously, noting the girl's high color and the grim set of her mouth. She might have questioned her about Cade Caldwell if not for the arrival of another caller almost on the heels of his departure. This time it was one of the young men she had met at the fiesta, a handsome young man who was obviously quite smitten with Laurie, and who had brought her a large bouquet of sweet-smelling flowers.

"Thank you!" Laurie exclaimed brightly as she took

71

the flowers and buried her nose in them, striving to control the remnants of anger Cade had left behind. The fragrance of the flowers was cloyingly sweet, and she almost choked, but managed to keep her smile as she gave them to Serita to put into a vase. "Do come onto the patio with me, señor," Laurie told the bemused young man, who followed her as gladly as a puppy.

Garbed in the tight-fitting dark trousers and short jacket that was common, the young man — Felipe Herrera — was almost embarrassingly effusive in his compliments to Laurie, praising her golden eyes, golden hair, flawless complexion and rosy lips. Almost apprehensively, she waited to hear him burst into spasms of verse as one young Frenchman had done in Paris. Fortunately, the enthusiastic young suitor did not quote poetry to her, but contented himself with detailed descriptions of romantic sunsets he would show her if only she would agree to ride with him.

Demurely lowering her eyes and feeling like a fraud, Laurie said that she would go only if her stepmother approved and if she was properly chaperoned. How her friends in Paris would laugh if they heard her! Michelle Devereau had once remarked laconically that Laurette was the only person she knew who could walk out alone with the most depraved duke in all of Europe and return untouched by scandal. It had been, of course, a great exaggeration, but nonetheless Laurie had enjoyed unprecedented freedom at times. Now she felt stifled, but when faced with overeager suitors such as Señor Herrera, she was remotely grateful for the social edicts.

In the three days following the Alvarez fiesta, Laurie had a host of gentleman callers. Cade Caldwell did not return, but she did not expect him. And, she told herself, she did not ever want to see him again. He was insulting, and there was something so . . . aware in his

72

gaze when he looked at her, as if he knew her very soul. It made her uncomfortable, and she would never forgive him for his implication that she had invited his coarse kisses and caress that night.

Sometimes she thought about it, when forced by courtesy to endure the visits of Carlóta's family, the dour, stern-faced women who had looked down their noses at her so long ago in New Orleans. Even when she sat demurely stitching an intricate piece of needlework that she would immediately cast aside on their departure, Laurie could feel the weight of their disapproval. She fretted under it, and Carlota sensed her restlessness and tried to make amends by allowing Laurie more freedom.

She rode out with Don Felipe Herrera, and Juan Bautista and Captain José Garcia from the alcalde's honor guard, and an American gentleman from Los Angeles named Paul Anderson. Laurie liked him the best.

Paul Anderson was tall and fair and handsome, and his smile was always kind and admiring. There was no mockery in his eyes, nor in his words, and he did not dote on her so that she was uncomfortable. Instead, Paul Anderson treated her as if she was special, bringing her small gifts and making all her other suitors quite jealous.

"You seem to like Señor Anderson very much," Carlota observed one evening when Laurie returned weary and contented from a long ride in the rolling hills.

"Yes, I think I do," Laurie said as she sank down onto a chair close to Carlota. "Is Papa here tonight?"

Carlota shook her head. "No, there is a small bit of unrest in the village, so he is there to see if he can be of assistance."

"Unrest?" Laurie echoed, already thinking of the new gown she would wear to impress Paul the next day.

He was taking her—and her ever-present chaperon—to a picnic in the hills. Carlota's reply jerked Laurie's attention from the planned picnic to the present.

"Yes, the alcalde has executed a peon for not paying his taxes, and the entire village is in an uproar."

Laurie just stared at her stepmother's troubled face. "A man has been . . . been killed for not paying his taxes?"

Carlota nodded unhappily, and Laurie noticed at last the strain in her thin features as she concentrated on her needlework. "Even the church is becoming involved, I understand, and I am very worried about the situation here," she said in a soft voice. "It was not this way before Don Luis came into power, before he was alcalde. Several of the hacendados have applied to Mexico for the alcalde's replacement, and when he heard of it, I hear that Don Luis had their names placed on a list." She lowered her voice and leaned forward to whisper, "It is said to be a list for execution!"

"But not even the alcalde can do that!" Laurie protested, then lowered her voice at Carlota's frantic motion. "Do you suspect spies?" she whispered with a frown.

"Not among my old, trusted servants, but there are some new ones Don Luis insisted I hire, 'as a favor to the peons,' he said, but I think as spies."

It was a grave situation, Laurie thought, and could not rid herself of the memory of the man being publicly flogged for not paying enough taxes. He had been Serita's *novio,* she had later found out, and had almost died from the whipping.

With a pang of self-recrimination, Laurie realized that lately she had been so caught up in her enjoyment of her suitors as well as her own discontent that she had paid little attention to the events around her. Her one meeting with the alcalde had been brief and uneventful, and she could recall having the thought that he had

74

not appeared to be the monster everyone said he was. Now she felt foolish. She had allowed her own selfish desires to override any concern for injustice, and she had always been the first among her friends to advocate justice for all. They had laughingly teased her about being a radical American while in Europe, but now she knew that she truly felt strongly about it.

Still frowning, and tapping her riding crop against the toe of her boot, Laurie considered the situation. If the alcalde could summarily execute a man for not paying his taxes, what more could he do if he desired? No wonder her father and the wealthy hacendados were concerned!

"Can't anyone stop him?" she wondered, and didn't realize she'd spoken aloud until Carlota answered her.

"Not unless they wish to risk their families' welfare, or their own necks. It is too bad there are not masked men who would defend the poor peons."

Laurie laughed softly. "Masked men? But what good would that do, Carlota?"

A slightly embarrassed smile slanted Carlota's thin lips. "Oh, I suppose it's nonsense, but I had the silly idea that faceless men could return to the peons their hard-earned pesos, thus thwarting the alcalde but risking no one."

"They would simply have to pay the taxes again," Laurie pointed out, and Carlota nodded.

"Yes, but it would be with the same money!"

Laurie looked at her in surprise. "Do you know," she said slowly, "that is not a bad idea, Carlota! If there was just a way to get it back to the peons without being found out—Is there someone who would dare to do such a thing, do you think?"

Giving a little laugh, Carlota said, "Oh, it is not a practical idea, and I am certain there is no one in Higuera who would ever dare to do such a thing. Why, there are so many *soldados,* and the alcalde can be so brutal, that it would be quite useless."

"I wonder," Laurie said, "I wonder."

To her surprise, Cade Caldwell voiced almost the same words the next time she saw him, a chance meeting while out riding with Paul Anderson. Cade's sardonic glance flicked from Laurie to the handsome blond man at her side, and his dark eyes glittered with amusement.

"*Buenos dias,*" Cade greeted them with an incline of his dark head as he kept a steady hand on his horse's rein. The huge black that looked as if it came from the same bloodline as Laurie's danced nervously, snorting and tossing its head.

"That is a fine, spirited animal you're riding," Paul Anderson observed with a lift of his brow.

"*Gracias.* The Alvarez family has always prided themselves on good horses." His gaze raked their mounts, and Laurie stiffened.

"Are you insinuating, sir, that these are not fine animals?"

"Nothing of the kind, señorita! You misunderstood!"

Still not appeased, Laurie's hands tightened around her horse's reins and her gaze narrowed. "I don't think so."

Cade laughed. "Whatever you say, señorita. I would not dream of disagreeing with you."

To fill the awkward void that fell, Paul Anderson said quickly, "I understand that Don Luis has arranged for a count of all the horses in Higuera. It is to simplify the payment of taxes, I hear."

Irritated, Laurie snapped, "The alcalde just wishes to ensure that he is being paid all the monies he is due!"

Cade's brow rose, and he drawled, "Do I understand that you do not agree with our illustrious alcalde, señorita? That could be misconstrued as treason, you know."

"If you had the wit of a chicken, you would not agree

76

with him, either!" Laurie flashed recklessly, then bit her lip as the thought came to her that he could be loyal to Don Luis.

To her relief, Cade laughed. "I don't, but I am not foolish enough to voice my opinion to strangers."

"We're not exactly strangers," she pointed out, then flushed when he laughed again, his eyes dancing with wicked amusement.

"So, you have not forgotten our first meeting? I'm glad to know that," he said softly, and Paul Anderson gave Laurie a curious glance.

Laurie stiffened, and dared not look at Paul. She glared at Cade. "We were talking about the alcalde."

"Ah yes, the alcalde. Tell me, Miss Allen, what do you think should be done about the grave situation? Should the alcalde be allowed to tax us so heavily? Should he be given such free rein with the very lives of the peons?"

Feeling as if he was making fun of her, Laurie gave a toss of her head. "I have not seen evidence of any man in Higuera brave enough to stand up to the alcalde," she said scornfully. "Most are frightened of him — or play at bravery by accosting innocent women."

Her direct gaze and curled upper lip made Cade grin in spite of the prick of anger that prompted him to say, "I take it that you are challenging me?"

"Or any man who has courage instead of fear in his veins."

"That is easy enough for a woman to say when she sits behind a high wall and a man's protection."

"And do you think I could not do what the men in this village are scared to do?" Laurie flashed angrily. "Why, I could show the alcalde that there are people who will not stand for oppression, people who are brave enough to say, 'enough!' And I should think that if a woman would do so, a man would be shamed not to. . . ."

77

"You talk big, Miss Allen, but I don't notice you riding into the mercado with a drawn sword and loud talk." Cade's gaze flicked from Laurie to the uncomfortable Paul Anderson. "You seem more disposed to genteel rides in the countryside than danger."

"Now see here, sir," Anderson began stiffly, "you are talking to a proper young woman, not a man."

Laughing with sardonic amusement, Cade let his dark gaze flick insultingly over Laurie's tight-fitting riding habit and the cocked plumes in her fashionable hat. "I'm not too sure about the 'proper,' but she is a young woman with more notion than nerve," he drawled. "Don Luis is a brutal man, and has enough soldiers to make a precipitate action useless. The *hacendados* are doing what they can by filing a formal protest to Mexico. The alcalde should be removed by law, and if that does not work, then other measures will be considered, I assure you."

"And I think you're afraid, Mister Caldwell," Laurie said softly. She was angry, and embarrassed at the sly reminder of her first meeting with Cade. Sitting rigidly atop her huge black horse, she glared at Cade's mocking face and wished she had an epée in her hands at that very moment. Then she would show him what a little courage and a lot of skill could do for the peons!

Bowing slightly from the waist, Cade reined his mount away from them. "Perhaps you're right, Miss Allen. A female with a sharp tongue is deadlier than an adder. *Adios*."

As he rode away, Laurie turned to see Paul Anderson looking at her with a faintly curious smile. "Mr. Caldwell seems to bring out the worst in you, Miss Allen."

Flushing, she said more sharply than she intended, "He is an arrogant coward, and I would appreciate it if you would not mention him to me again!"

For Laurie, the day was ruined, and she asked that

78

Paul escort her home again, where she pled a headache and retired to her room. Damn that insufferable Cade Caldwell, she fumed as she threw herself across her bed to think. What she wouldn't give to show him up!

Chapter Five

Sullen peons gathered in the mercado, the center of the village, to hear the soldiers' latest proclamation and to pay their taxes. Uniformed soldiers milled around with their weapons ready. Some were mounted, but most of the soldiers clustered in menacing groups as the peons lined up to be counted.

Clad in loose pants, shirts, and serapes, the peons stood silently, approaching one by one the table where the collector sat. A ledger lay opened in front of the soldier who was the collector, and he painstakingly made a mark beside each name as the peon paid. A figure was written beside each name denoting the amount of the tax, and on occasion a man would protest.

"But that is too much, señor!" one mustachioed man said in a pleading voice. "If I pay all of that, my family will go hungry. . . ."

"Basta ya!" the soldier snapped, and held out his hand for the coins. "You will pay it all or your family will surely starve without a man to feed them."

His inference was not lost on the protester, and he paid his tax silently, counting out the last of his coins and placing them on the table with trembling fingers. It was hot, and the sun beat down on the quiet scene with blistering intensity as the collector tossed the pesos carelessly into a leatherbound casket.

"Next," he said without looking up, and the line moved slowly again. Dust hung in a fine haze around the mercado as the muted clink of coins increased the pile in the casket, and the soldiers began to yawn with the heat and inactivity. Swords hung at their sides, unneeded with the quiet procession of peons moving like obedient sheep toward the collection table. Flat-crowned dark hats shaded their faces in the sun, and the red-and-blue cross-striped uniforms grew thick with dust.

As the line slowly shortened, a drumming of hooves could be heard. Only a few of the soldiers bothered to look up. It was the sudden buzz of frightened voices that gathered the interest of the soldiers at last, and by then it was too late.

A black-masked rider, clad in billowing black cape and astride a snorting black stallion, leaped the mount over a low stone wall and into the middle of the mercado, scattering soldiers and peons. The rider's sword flashed briefly as one soldier more alert than the rest offered a token resistance. The sharp clang of swords was over in an instant as the soldier's weapon went sailing through the air to the ground. Then the rider spurred his mount forward and past the collection table, scooping up the casket in a shower of spilling coins and galloping back the way he had come.

It was over so quickly that everyone just looked at one another in surprise, not quite certain what had happened. Only the angry hum of soldiers made it evident to the peons that it had not been an official act. The peons gazed at the soldiers expectantly, and the tax collector still sat in stunned silence, his face pale. Dust slowly settled around him in choking clouds.

"What was that?" a soldier finally thought to ask,

but no one knew.

"He stole the tax money," the collector finally said. "What will I tell the alcalde?"

"Who was it?" someone asked again, and the soldiers all looked at one another, knowing the alcalde would ask the same question.

Don Luis Jorge Baptiste y Navarro did indeed ask the same question, and he did not ask it idly. Nor did he ask it kindly. He was furious, and shouted that heads would roll if he did not have the perpetrator of the crime in his hands within the day.

"But Your Excellency," the commandant protested with panic in his voice, "it was done so quickly no one was able to do anything except Lieutenant Lopez, who had his sword stricken from him!"

Fixing the commandant with a baleful eye, the alcalde snapped out the observation that if his soldiers were such inefficient swordsmen, perhaps he should replace their leaders with capable men.

"And I do not think you will like the lower ranks, *Comandante*," Don Luis added coldly. He paced the floor of his ornate office, his expensive leather boots tapping out a grim tattoo on the stone tiles as he crossed from bare floor to the thick Turkish rugs scattered about. He paused at a table, where he poured a healthy draught of brandy, then downed it in a single gulp, heedless of the fine liquor's potency. "How much did we lose?" he rapped out, and the officer looked at the floor.

"Three thousand pesos," he muttered, adding, "Which is not much, Your Excellency! On a good day, we collect much more in taxes than that!"

Lacing and unlacing his fingers, the commandant waited, watching the alcalde prowl his office, his hands behind his back, his sagging jowls quivering with rage. He was a tall man, with a swordsman's lean frame, but his face showed evidence of self-indulgence. Comandante Trujillo had the thought that the alcalde's physical condition had deteriorated in the past few months due to his high style of living. But that was not for Trujillo to remark upon and he did not, wisely keeping his own counsel and hoping he could leave the alcalde with his head intact.

When Don Luis whipped around and growled a command for the commandant to leave and bring back the bandit, he did not offer a single word as he bowed and backed from the room. Trujillo was grateful to have escaped without serious damage.

Furious, Don Luis snatched up his sword and hacked at the furnishings of the room, slicing candles and drapes. He seethed with rage, and after a moment, stalked to the bell rope and yanked it, demanding more brandy.

His taxes, his precious taxes, gone into the hands of a bandit! "Damn him, I shall see him staked to the village walls," Don Luis growled, and the servant shuddered as he backed from the room.

The alcalde was a man possessed, the servant told the others, and they all crossed themselves and prayed for mercy.

When the pitiful remains of the tax money was sent by guard to Los Angeles to the north, to a private account in the alcalde's name, the soldiers were surprised at a wooded bend in the road. The masked man, with flashing sword and deadly accuracy, once more stole the tax money, leaving a man wounded and bleeding in the road. The frightened soldiers told the commandant that the swordsman was a devil, garbed all in black, with fire shooting from his horse's nostrils and sparks flying from the hooves, his blade magic as it whirled about.

Even discounting the soldiers' efforts to cover their own ineptitude, the commandant was nonplussed to see how easy it was for a single man to steal the alcalde's money. And he had the unpleasant task of informing His Excellency of the latest theft.

There was a moment of dark silence before Don Luis said in a quiet voice that he expected his monies or the heads of the men who allowed it to be taken, and he expected it within two days.

"Sí, Your Excellency," Comandante Trujillo said, backing out as quickly as possible and considering himself lucky to have escaped so lightly.

But the commandant was not fortunate enough to be able to appease the alcalde. For the following two days, it seemed as if the masked rider knew every plan beforehand, knew where the soldiers would be, and how many there would be. And the bandit the peons had begun to refer to as *El Vengador*—the Avenger—did not always strike in the same way.

Sometimes it was like a whirlwind, appearing out of nowhere and striking as swiftly as a rattlesnake, then retreating with caskets of money. And sometimes it was as silent as a thief in the night—stepping up behind a guard or soldier and wielding an expert sword. The swiftness of the blade would quickly detach soldier from money, then the masked man would be gone, disappearing over a wall with an agile leap, or astride his great black stallion. It was as if the soldiers were trying to fight a phantom, a myth, a mirage, for El Vengador would be there one moment, then simply vanish into thin air. Often only the echo of hoofbeats could be heard.

Posters advertising a reward were tacked up on the village walls, and mysteriously torn down or shredded with what appeared to be the tip of a sword. No one saw them defaced or destroyed, they were just hacked to pieces without anyone seeing, most of the time shortly after being put up. Some of them would be simply slashed with the letter V as a sign that El Vengador had been there and gone without being

84

seen.

Only once did a band of soldiers managed to corner the masked figure after a theft, but he so expertly hacked his way through the men that it was humiliating for the entire troop.

Don Luis was furious. The peons were faintly skeptical. The commandant was chagrined. The church was shocked.

For in the poor boxes, there appeared a multitude of pesos marked for the peons' use. Poor Padre Juan was at first unbelieving, then grateful for the gifts, and decided that it was something the alcalde did not need to know. It was distributed back among the peons with a sparing hand, and it was a godsend. It was there when needed, and when the taxes were to be paid, the money mysteriously appeared for every needy family.

"It's an outrage!" Don Luis snarled.

"Isn't it wonderful?" Carlota marveled, and Laurie agreed with her.

"Yes, it is. I wonder who the bandit is?"

Shaking her head, Carlota said, "I cannot imagine, but whoever he is, he is a brave and foolish man!"

Phillip Allen was not as impressed with El Vengador, and said so.

"Why not, Papa?" Laurie asked. "At least he is doing something, while everyone else sits around and waits for a miracle."

"Because this El Vengador has only enraged Don Luis, not rid us of him. No," Phillip said as he shook his head, "it is a dangerous matter to provoke a snake, and that is what the man is doing. Though I must admit, at least he is trying to help."

"It seems to me," Laurie observed tartly, "that if the wealthy hacendados cared about their peons they would have petitioned the governor-general or Mexico to rid Higuera of Don Luis by now!"

"Oh, they have, Laurie. But it takes time."

"I don't mean send them a formal letter of polite protest, Papa. I know they've done that. I mean *go* to the government seat—Los Angeles—and talk to the governor-general, or even go to Mexico City and speak with an official there. Surely if they talked to the President, he could. . . ."

Phillip's words were rueful. "I'm afraid President Bustamante has too many troubles of his own with Santa Anna trying to regain the presidency. He would not be too concerned with our small problems here in Higuera, especially as it concerns the peons instead of the landowners such as Don Benito."

"But even Don Benito has filed a protest," Carlota said softly, and her gaze was troubled as she looked at her husband. "He remarked upon it to me."

"That is probably the best course," Phillip said, but Laurie disagreed.

"I don't think so! I think this El Vengador is doing the right thing!"

Slanting her a sly smile, Carlota said, "Do you say that to the handsome Captain Garcia you are seeing now?"

A slight flush stained her cheeks as Laurie looked at her stepmother. "I enjoy his company, and he is very handsome and charming, but we rarely discuss politics or El Vengador.

Phillip seemed surprised, and stared at his daughter in the light of the ornate silver candelabra on a side table. "I thought you preferred the company of Paul Anderson, Laurie."

"You know young girls," Carlota said as she threaded a needle and continued with her tapestry. "And Laurie is in great demand. With so many young men to choose from, why should she tie herself to only one?"

Phillip's fair head gleamed in the candlelight as he

leaned forward to light his cigar from a burning taper, and he wore a slight frown. "I don't think it's good for you to be too—flighty—right now, Laurie. After all, proper young ladies in California are usually married by the age of sixteen, and you are twenty-one. People might consider it loose of you to be still unmarried and going from man to man."

Drawing herself up, Laurie looked at her father with blazing eyes. "I resent that Papa! And I don't think they expect me to act as they do at all!"

Eager to avoid a quarrel, Carlota interrupted, "I know that none of my acquaintances think harshly of Laurie for being courted by so many young men. Indeed, they all assume that she will soon wed, and have even tried to decide who we will choose." She looked anxiously from Laurie's angry face to her husband's taut features. "Everyone knows that she has been abroad and away from her papa for so long, and only just arrived," she said softly to him, and Phillip relaxed slightly.

"Well," he said after a moment, "I am certain that is true. I just don't want to insult anyone. . . ."

"You certainly don't mind insulting your daughter!" Laurie broke in, unable to hide the hurt in her voice. She had tried so hard to please her papa, and made concessions that she had not wanted to make, and for him to care more for others' opinions than for her feelings was devastating.

It was quiet in the sitting room for a long moment, then Laurie rose from her chair and bade her father and Carlota a stiff goodnight. "You hurt her feelings," Carlota reproved softly when Laurie had gone, and Phillip looked miserable.

"I'm not much of a diplomat, am I?" he asked ruefully.

Carlota tucked her hand into the crook of his arm and put her needlework aside. Rubbing her cheek against the rough material of his shoulder, she said, "It's hard to be a diplomat when it comes to someone you love. Go to her in the morning."

A faint smile tilted his mouth as Phillip covered his wife's hand with his own. "You're right, Carlota. I will talk to her in the morning."

During that night, El Vengador staged another daring raid, this time on the alcalde's own personal coach. The driver was so frightened by the sudden appearance of the black-masked figure and huge horse that he began to babble hysterically and was of no use whatsoever.

When El Vengador yanked open the carriage door, he caught the alcalde by surprise. Don Luis was startled and furious, and his hand immediately fell to the hilt of his sword.

The throaty laugh further infuriated him.

"You are at a decided disadvantage, Your Excellency," came the taunt, and a gloved hand reached out to pluck the sword from its scabbard while the deadly point of an epée pressed lightly against the alcalde's chest. "Now — your purse, if you please," came the velvet command delivered in Castilian Spanish.

Don Luis reached slowly for the heavy purse at his side, always aware of the pressure of the sword against his chest, his flat black eyes narrowed on the hooded figure.

"You will die for this!" Don Luis snarled as he removed his purse and handed it carefully to El Vengador. "I will see your back flayed and your body flung to the four corners of the earth!"

"Such pretty sentiments from one such as you are music to my ears," came the mocking reply. The swordpoint pressed slightly harder, just piercing the alcalde's shirtfront. "I think you should look to your health, Don Luis. The climate here is growing very bad for you. Even the wine could be tainted, or the meat spoiled. Perhaps a change would do you good, eh?"

Don Luis could not speak, afraid to move for the sharp point in his chest, afraid that the slightest movement would end his life. He looked at the masked man with hatred and the beginning of fear in his eyes, and El Vengador saw it. A low laugh whispered in the air, and then the swordpoint withdrew, quickly slashing a V in the upholstery of the carriage before the masked avenger slammed shut the alcalde's carriage door.

The rumble of hoofs echoed in the night, and Don Luis finally gave the order for his driver to go on. His voice was not as harsh as earlier, but more subdued and slightly shaken. But after all, he had barely escaped with his life, he would tell his commandant, and that demon meant to kill him.

"Your Excellency?" Comandante Trujillo asked. "Did he make an attempt on your life?"

"Of course, he did! I would have fought him, but he took my sword and flung it in the bushes, then tried to run me through!"

"What kept him from it?" the commandant asked, his face respectful but his gaze frankly skeptical.

The alcalde whirled on Trujillo, his face red with fury and his eyes wild. "It certainly wasn't my brave *soldados* who kept him from killing me! There were none to be seen! I travel in my coach on a public road, yet I am not safe! Are there no men who can guard their leader? Are all the *soldados* in Higuera cowards?"

Quailing slightly, Trujillo said, "I am sorry, Your Excellency. The men who were to ride with your coach were delayed."

"Delayed? Delayed?" The alcalde ran his hands through his hair so that it stood on end. "What can be so much more important?"

Trujillo coughed, then mumbled, "A tree, Your Excellency."

"What?"

"A tree." Trujillo flushed. "A huge tree suddenly fell into the road. It barred the path. By the time the *soldados* could remove it, El Vengador was gone."

"And so was my money!" came the snarling reply. "Now my life is in danger, and all my food must be tasted before I eat—or drink! Find a peon to do it for me." He leaned forward, and spittle flew from his mouth as he said, "I want my money back, Comandante Trujillo, and I want this menace caught or I shall begin arresting every single man in Higuera, do you understand me? I shall have them all questioned, by whatever means pleases me."

Paling, Trujillo understood what Don Luis meant, and he gave a mute nod of his head. When he was dismissed he fled in relief, and realized that he was sweating profusely. The situation was grim, for none of the soldiers were able to apprehend the bandit. He struck too randomly, and was gone too quickly. How did he do it? How did he know where all the soldiers would be? Trujillo decided to begin there. He would set a trap for this bandit, a trap that would certainly catch him.

Chapter Six

It was hot, and Laurie fanned herself slowly with the palm-leaf fan Carlota had given her. The early morning sun shimmered across the patio, and she was grateful for the shading vines and latticework that kept it from burning her skin.

"Am I disturbing you?" Phillip Allen asked as he came to sit down beside her.

Laurie shook her head. She was sleepy, and her face had a flushed look that made her father glance at her sharply.

"Are you all right?" he asked, and she nodded.

"Just tired. I didn't sleep well," she added, and he reached out to pat her hand.

"I'm sorry about last night, Laurie."

She managed a smile. "I know. I probably shouldn't have reacted as I did."

There was a short silence in which Phillip was served a glass of chilled fruit juice and thinly sliced toast, and when the servant had gone, he said, "I forget that you're a young woman now, not a rebellious girl."

Laughing, she teased, "Even young women have rebellious moments, Papa!"

He agreed with a smile. "I'm very proud of you, you know," he said.

She looked at him. "Are you?"

"Yes. You've grown into a beautiful, poised young lady, and I find it hard to realize that you're my daughter at times. It seems inconceivable that I could produce such a wonderful person."

Laurie smiled, her gold eyes tilting up at the corners and reminding Phillip more than ever of her mother's eyes, cat's eyes, soft and knowing.

"It seems inconceivable to me that we should ever doubt one another," Laurie said. She lifted her fruit juice. "A truce?"

Phillip matched her gesture. "A truce," he agreed with light solemnity, and their glasses clinked together.

When Carlota joined them, Phillip asked Laurie, "Are you riding out this morning with Captain Garcia?"

Shrugging, Laurie said she hadn't decided yet. "Why?"

"I understand there was some trouble last night, and I just want you to be careful, that's all."

Laurie sipped at her juice. "Trouble?" she inquired over the rim of her glass. "What kind of trouble?"

"Don Luis was attacked. . . ."

"*Madre de Dios!*" Carlota gasped crossing herself. "He is dead?"

A wry smile twisted Phillip's lips for a moment. "I'm afraid not. For which we should all be grateful, I suppose. It would go very badly, and there might be suspicions thrown toward the United States if he were to be murdered."

"The United States?" Laurie echoed. "But why? I mean, there are so many Californios who hate him!"

Clearing his throat, Phillip said, "There have been recent clashes between Don Luis and myself as regards some of the finances, but I won't bore you with details. Suffice it to say that he threatened to banish my diplomatic post at one point." He shrugged. "Some might take it that he had tried to do so and I have retaliated."

Laurie laughed in disbelief. "Papa! *You* as El Vengador? Not even your most ardent enemies would be so foolish!"

Phillip asked stiffly, "Is it so ludicrous that I would be dismayed by brutality?"

"Oh, I didn't mean that. I only meant that I cannot see you galloping about the countryside at night with a drawn saber in your hand!"

He relaxed slightly, some of the offense fading from his drawn features. "Well, there are times I have felt like it, but it is true that I have never been much of a swordsman." His smile was brief. "You were always the agile one, Laurie."

"Yes," she said. "I know."

When it was quiet for too long Carlota said into the heavy silence, "Captain Garcia seems quite smitten with you, Laurie. He has appeared on our doorstep every day, it seems."

Laurie's long-lashed amber eyes flickered briefly, and a soft smile touched her lips. "He is very persistent, and very charming. I don't mind spending the time with him at all."

"That's a strange way of admitting interest in a man," Carlota remarked with a puzzled glance at her stepdaughter. "Do you not like him?"

Laurie seemed surprised by the question, but she could not look directly at Carlota as she murmured, "Of course I like him. Why else would I ride out with him?"

Why else, indeed, she thought irritably, wishing she had not promised José she would ride with him that day. It was hot, and she was still tired. And she was weary of being questioned so much.

When she looked up she met her father's narrowed

gaze, and Laurie flushed. It was almost as if he could read her mind, knew what she was thinking and how bored she'd become with the sedentary life in Higuera. El Vengador was the only exciting thing to happen in the sleepy village.

But she wondered if the excitement was worth the danger when she recalled how José Garcia had detailed the punishment that would be meted out to the criminal when he was caught. They had been out riding together again, with the ever-present dueña trailing behind, and Garcia had reminded her of a smug cat with the feathers still between his teeth as he'd recounted the plans.

"Don Luis has vowed to slowly strip his skin from his back, and to hang him up in the mercado for everyone to see! Now that I am in charge of the *presidio*—while Comandante Trujillo is concentrating on other matters—I shall do what I can to see that he is captured." Lightly stroking his mustache with a finger, José had slid Laurie a glance to see if she was impressed with his new status.

But Laurie pretended to be thinking of something else, and had only smiled politely and murmured something vague, leaving Garcia disappointed.

And now she was to ride with him again today, and endure more of his inane talk of how El Vengador would be killed, or at best, tortured and imprisoned. Determined not to let him get the best of her, Laurie decided to play the part of a coquette. It would be fun, and would surely take the captain's mind off the infamous bandit.

Faint smudges of circles beneath her eyes that could not be hidden with powder belied her exuberance when she greeted Captain Garcia, but Laurie was well aware of how lovely she looked in her soft mint green riding outfit and plumed hat. Her golden hair had been carefully coiled into fat ringlets above each ear, bobbing with every graceful motion of her head, and her amber eyes sparkled as she smiled at the bemused young officer.

"*Buenas tardes, Capitán!*" she greeted Garcia. She made her smile as alluring as possible, and was rewarded with the glitter of appreciation in his dark eyes. He tried to hide the desire in his gaze, but it was too obvious, and she was almost tempted to plead a headache and go back into the house.

But as Garcia was useful, and it was good to find out what was planned, she did not, and managed a smile and sweet words. She even allowed the young captain's hands to linger a shade too long around her waist as he lifted her to her mount's back.

"Another superb animal, Doña Laurie?" he asked softly, his lips close to her ear and his breath whisking across her bare neck. "I thought you preferred the same horse all the time."

Laurie could not suppress a shudder. "That is true," she said quickly. "Though I find it disconcerting to ride different horses all the time, this one is fresh, while the other has pulled a muscle in his foreleg, I believe."

"How unfortunate, but then, you have many horses to choose from," the officer said, his mouth quirking in a smile as he gazed at the rolling pastures. "Doña Allen's family is famous in this area for their fine horses."

"So I understand." Laurie's smile was bright, and she glanced at her dueña, who rode a fat, stolid mare that had the same resigned expression as its rider. "I believe that our chaperon is growing weary of our daily rides," she said softly to Garcia, and he laughed.

"Perhaps it is her efforts to keep up with us that has tired her," he suggested, vaulting lightly onto his mount and smoothing his mustache with one finger.

He was proud of his mustaches, and waxed them

daily. They were a sign of virility, and José Garcia had been told that he was especially virile. When he was with the golden Laurie, he felt more virile than ever; just watching her made the blood rush hot and swift through his veins, and he knew if he could ever get her truly alone, she would swoon beneath his caresses. He would make her his, only his, and to be aligned with the Alvarado family even through a second-hand marriage, would not be bad at all. Carlota's family had lived in California for generations, and was well respected, while he—his was just a poor family eking out a living on only a few acres of land with scraggly vineyards.

No, he could do much worse than to wed the fair Laurie, the young captain thought smugly, and besides, she was the most sensual woman he had ever seen. There was something about her, the sultry flash of her golden eyes, or the way she tossed her head, or her fine, straight nose and the full ripe pout of her lips.

Ah, her lips! Capitán Garcia found it hard to resist kissing that mouth, the rich promise of passion that lurked there, and once when she had put out her tongue to wet her lips he had almost lost control. But he would wait. Hadn't he waited patiently until she had finally noticed him? He'd thought for a while that she was more interested in that American, but then she had smiled prettily at him, fluttering her long lashes to hide her eyes and telling him softly that he was very handsome in his uniform.

It had been worth the wait, for now he rode out with her every afternoon.

Sometimes they rode leisurely over the green hills of the Alvarado ranchero, and sometimes they rode through the small village of Higuera. Laurie made him feel much more important than he'd ever thought himself to be, with her constant questions and admiring observations, and Captain Garcia was eager to tell her anything she wanted to know.

Today, with the long-suffering dueña riding at a slow pace behind them, Garcia was certain he would be allowed to kiss Laurie at last, and perhaps—if he was very careful—to touch her breast. It would be done so subtly that she would not know his intentions at first, until then, when his hand was there, feeling her ripe body through the thin material of her riding outfit, she would be flustered and he would soothe her with kisses and promises. Ah yes, the capitán could already feel her velvety skin beneath his fingers, and he was almost impatient for them to be in the green hills above Higuera.

But he felt a pang of disappointment when Laurie asked softly, "Oh, I had thought we might ride into the village today! Do you mind *mi Capitán?*"

Swallowing his disappointment, Garcia said graciously, "No, of course not! It would be an honor to ride anywhere with you, lovely lady."

Dust rose behind their horses as they rode slowly down the main street of the village. A brisk salt breeze was blowing in from the ocean, and it lifted Laurie's tawny curls from her neck. She smiled against the wind, and thought that it was the one good thing about California. A breeze always blew near the ocean.

In the distance she could hear the mission bells ring, and Laurie wondered why they were ringing at this time of day.

"A public proclamation from the alcalde," Garcia replied when she asked him.

"A proclamation? Of what sort?"

Shrugging, the handsome young officer said casually, "A warning to El Vengador, or to anyone who accepts his help."

"Warning?" Laurie felt a cold lump in her throat.

97

"What kind of warning?"

"Don Luis has declared that any peon found with stolen monies will have his right hand removed at the wrist. And when El Vengador is captured, he will be publicly flogged before being hung." His voice lowered and he leaned from his mount to say softly, "I predict that El Vengador will be captured within twenty-four hours!"

A chill ran down her spine, but she forced a smile. "Do you know his identity?"

Instead of replying directly, Garcia asked, "Do you know Don Benito Alvarez?" When Laurie nodded he said, "His grandson is very high on the list of suspects, I am told."

"His grandson?"

"Si. Perhaps you have not met him, but he was born here in Higuera." The captain's voice grew scornful. "He is said to be a disgrace to his mother's house, and has been a bane to his *abielo* since he was a child."

"I met him. At Don Benito's fiesta," Laurie clarified when Garcia gave her a quick glance. "And I've seen him a few times since, but only in passing." She smiled at the captain and briefly lowered her lashes before lifting them, a trick she had learned watching the Parisian courtesans who plied their trades in the best opera houses and even in the palaces of France. There were few wealthy Frenchmen who did not escort beautiful young ladies of pleasure upon their arms. "I found Señor Caldwell to be quite — well, decadent," she said with a mock shudder, and the captain agreed.

"Es cierto!" Leaning closer to her, stretching the distance between their mounts with his body, the captain said in a confidential tone, "The alcalde had a most disagreeable interview with him, it is said!"

"And the outcome?" Laurie couldn't help asking.

Again the captain shrugged, sitting back in his saddle and thinking how appealing the young American señorita was when she bit her lower lip with her small, white teeth. If it was not for that sour-faced dueña riding too close behind them, he would take Laurie's face between his palms and kiss her so thoroughly she would swoon.

"Señor Caldwell has not been arrested—yet."

The veiled remark had the effect of quieting Laurie, and some of the animation faded from her face as she stared thoughtfully ahead.

As far as Capitán Garcia was concerned, the rest of the ride into the village did not even draw near his earlier expectations. Even when he boasted that the soldados had a clever trap ready for El Vengador, and that it was one so tightly drawn he would not escape, she did not respond as he'd wished. Instead of exclaiming over his cleverness or admiring their courage, Laurie seemed to be frightened, and the captain cursed his unfortunate choice of conversation. He should not have talked to a delicately reared young girl about such horrible things, for she had grown very quiet and barely smiled when he said witty things to her.

And when they had the misfortune to meet Cade Caldwell in the mercado, he noticed that Doña Laurie became very quiet and reserved then, too. Of course, it could have been because he was trying to draw her out, and had taken her hand and pressed it to his lips when Caldwell paused to look up at them with a faint smirk, his voice light and mocking as he greeted them. It might have embarrassed the pretty señorita to be seen in such an obvious position, the capitán thought, because she was so well bred and shy.

But that wasn't it at all. What made Laurie Allen so quiet was the fact that if she opened her mouth, she might burst into some very explicit abuse directed toward Cade Caldwell. Captain Garcia must not speak fluent French, for if he had, he would most certainly have been incensed by Cade's remarks.

And Cade knew it. He stood looking at them, his dark eyes mocking her, watching a slow flush suffuse her face in bright color.

As much as Laurie would have liked to reply in scathing French that he was the son of a pig with vain pretensions to masculinity, she did not. Instead, she lowered her lashes and murmured a soft, "You speak out of turn, monsieur."

Only the tightening of her gloved hands on her horse's bridle indicated her anger, and she dared not lift her lashes for fear that her eyes would give her away. Phillip had always said Laurie's eyes were the window to her moods, and he was right. At that moment, Cade Caldwell would have seen murderous violence in Laurie's wide, golden gaze if she had looked at him.

A slight grin crooked his mouth as he recognized her restraint, and Cade's eyes flicked to Captain Garcia. His grin widened.

"Capitán," he said with exaggerated courtesy, "I see that you have the rabble well under control today." He indicated the quiet mercado with a sweep of his arm. "No insurrection, no violence—how boring for the troops."

"Not really, señor," Captain Garcia said coldly. He did not like Caldwell, did not like any of the wealthy hacendados, but this one—a man who denied his heritage and did not appreciate his wealth—irritated him more than the others.

"Ah, I'm certain the alcalde's guard finds other, more entertaining amusements than flaying a few peons' backs until they are raw," Cade said then, and enjoyed the brief flare of fury in the captain's eyes.

"If I were not in the presence of a lady, señor, I would see that you retracted that remark," Garcia ground out. His hand toyed with the hilt of his sword as if he longed to pull it, and Cade laughed aloud.

"Ah, you forget—I've seen you wield a sword, Capitán! It is a most amusing—and sad—sight."

Garcia's mouth thinned, and he gave a slight start from his saddle that made Laurie instinctively reach out. "No! Oh, please, no quarreling, señores! It makes me quite ill to see violence!"

She was trembling so that Garcia was immediately penitent, his anger forgotten as he assumed that the poor, delicate creature was almost faint from the idea of it.

"Of course. I shall escort you home at once, Doña Laurie," he said, with a glance toward Cade that told him how lucky he was not to have had to fight.

Still trembling, but with anger instead of revulsion, Laurie allowed the captain to turn her horse around and lead her from the mercado. She did not give Cade Caldwell the satisfaction of a single glance back, but somehow had the uncomfortable feeling that he had seen through her and known what she was thinking. It was very disquieting, almost as disquieting as the things Capitán Garcia had been telling her.

Though Laurie's afternoon had been spoiled, the young officer was elated when he left the Allen hacienda. A smug, pleased smile curved his lips beneath the mustache, and he had the thought that at least the day had not ended as badly as he'd thought it would.

Laurie Allen had not offered a protest when Garcia had taken her in his arms before leaving, but had tilted back her head and allowed him to kiss her not once, but twice. She had felt so good in his arms, her mouth soft and pliant and her curves pressed against him until he had wanted to do much more than kiss

101

her. Only Laurie's firm hand and soft eyes had stopped him from doing more, and Garcia had contented himself with the kisses . . . for now. Later, there would be more — much more. She felt something for him, he knew it.

But Laurie had felt only a strong desire to run to the washstand and wipe away the scratchy feel of his mouth against hers, the taste of him on her lips. It wasn't that she disliked him, especially, it was just that he had not sparked a similar admiration in her. She had enjoyed Paul Anderson's kisses, and the kisses of the men she'd known in Europe, but not Captain Garcia's. Nor, she recalled, had she enjoyed the kisses of Cade Caldwell.

His kisses had been more like an invasion than anything else, and she wondered why she had responded to them. No one had ever kissed her like that before, and Cade Caldwell was a man she despised, yet she could not deny that his touch had aroused something in her she'd never felt before. She couldn't say she'd actually enjoyed his caresses, because they were vaguely frightening, but she could say his touch had certainly been unforgettable. Sometimes, at night when she could not sleep, she would think of that evening by the fountain when Cade had mistaken her for another woman. And then she would wonder if he'd found the other woman, Rosa, and if he'd kissed her just as deeply and arousingly.

Those nights when she thought of him were the most difficult, for she would feel those unfamiliar yearnings in her body and remember some of the things the giggling girls at her convent school had said. The school hadn't been too bad, really, though at the time she had missed Isabeau dreadfully and still been furious with her father. The long nights sitting up with the girls in their narrow cots and talking of things the gentle nuns would have been shocked to hear remained with her still, and Laurie could recall as if only the day before some of their conversations.

They'd been innocent enough, a few of the more daring girls had actually tried some of the things they discussed and come back to tell the others about it. The conversation had centered around men and sex and how terrible or wonderful it all was. Laurie had listened in fascination but always felt a detached revulsion for the entire process as it was described to her.

Let a man do those things to her? Not in a hundred years! No, she would kiss a man, and she had learned from watching others how to coax admiration and even pretty gifts from men with a flash of the eyes, a smile, a soft touch, and just the barest of intimacies, but that was as far as she intended to go with it.

Perhaps that was why Cade Caldwell frightened her so. He hadn't asked to kiss her and hadn't been abashed by her outrage, but only amused. And he had dared imply that she'd enjoyed his touch! What made it much, much worse was the fact that she had, for the briefest of moments, enjoyed it. It still haunted her.

Chapter Seven

Dark shadows enveloped the thick trees just above the sea road leading down into Higuera. It was the first of the month, and the payroll for the troops was due to arrive at any time. In the past month of raids by El Vengador, it would have been normal to assume that he would strike. This night, however, the payroll was scantily guarded. Few men rode beside it, and instead of being brought into the village in the normal manner, it was brought in by mules and carts.

It was so obvious a lure that a child could have seen through it, yet the alcalde hoped it would be too powerful a prize to resist. And he was ready for El Vengador, more ready than most of the soldiers knew. For in some of the carts, hidden beneath innocent-looking burlap, soldiers were crouched, armed and ready to battle El Vengador to the death, if necessary.

But it was all for naught, since El Vengador did not strike the payroll. Instead the masked outlaw rode down from the thick trees long before it arrived, and robbed a coach bearing Don Luis's sultry niece, his portly wife, and two of his sisters. They were wearing a king's ransom in jewels.

"Be certain to inform the alcalde of my appreciation for his providing such rich prizes," El Vengador said in a husky, mocking voice as the sobbing women

104

were stripped of their glittering finery. "It was very thoughtful of him," El Vengador added, blinking at the women from behind the dark mask that covered his head and most of his face. Only his lips were visible below the black cloth. A wide, voluminous cape swung behind the masked figure as it backed away, long sword in one gloved hand and the jewels in the other. "*Adios, señoras!*"

The carriage lanterns were still burning, and as El Vengador passed them a thrust of the sword shattered glass and extinguished the fitful light they cast, plunging the road into darkness and the women into hysteria. As hoof beats sounded on the road, El Vengador vaulted to the back of a huge black stallion the Navarro women would later declare to be from the bowels of Hell, and rode away up the steep slope overlooking the sea road.

By the time the soldiers arrived at the coach, almost overriding it in the dark, El Vengador was gone.

"He vanished in a puff of black smoke!" one of the more hysterical Navarro women screamed. She then fainted into the arms of the commandant, who appeared more than a little disgruntled.

"Here, take her," he growled to one of the soldiers, thrusting the hefty señora into his arms. "I will follow El Vengador!"

But in the dark, and with the added hindrance of the hysterical women who might inform Don Luis of less than cavalier treatment, the commandant could do little more than make a cursory search in the dark, cursing his bad fortune and the certainty of the alcalde's fury.

"There is no way El Vengador could have disappeared, I tell you!" Commandant Trujillo shouted, staring about him wildly. "It is not possible! There were *soldados* behind and a small troop not far in front, so that he would have had to pass one of

105

them. . . ."

"I tell you, he disappeared straight up in a cloud of black smoke," one of the women insisted, pointing to the steep slope rising almost straight up beside them. Commandant Trujillo was frustrated. He barely glanced at the thickly wooded slope, then dismissed the possibility that any rider could get up such an incline.

Above them in a secluded copse of trees stood El Vengador, listening to the faint sounds of the soldiers thrashing about in the bushes below, and the shrill voices of the Navarro women berating them. With one hand pressed over the stallion's nostrils to keep it from snorting, El Vengador watched and waited. It had been a difficult climb up the slope, much more difficult in the dark than the practice climb in the daylight hours. Though moonlight would have helped him see, the darkness had concealed everything.

Now the moonlight was finally appearing in scattered patches of silvery glitter, lighting up the copse of trees and the horse and masked bandit. That was when El Vengador discovered that they were not alone.

"*En garde,*" came a softly menacing voice, and the caped figure swirled around to meet the challenge.

Swiftly El Vengador's sword flashed up in the dim light and was met by the harsh clash of steel. No word was spoken, no sound uttered. Only the ringing clang of sword against sword could be heard in the trees as each swordsman parried deadly thrusts.

In the close network of tree branches and clinging vines it was difficult to fight without tripping, and the long black cape that El Vengador wore further hampered the masked outlaw's efforts. Harsh breaths rasped in the air as they met, closed, and sprang apart again.

For the first time it seemed as if El Vengador had

106

met a worthy opponent. The tall, lean man fought viciously, ruthlessly, giving little ground and slowly beating back El Vengador with each bone-jarring thrust.

It wasn't until El Vengador tripped over a half-hidden root and went to one knee that an advantage was gained, and the opponent drove in a wicked slash with the slicing edge of his blade.

El Vengador could not hold back a cry, and dropped the slender rapier to the ground to grab at the wound. Blood spurted and in the bright glare of the moonlight, Cade Caldwell could see that he had managed to deliver a victorious blow to his opponent. He stepped forward, about to mock the caped figure, when to his surprise El Vengador slumped to the ground in a dead faint.

"What in the hell?" Caldwell muttered. He knelt beside the prone figure and ripped aside the cape and the black blouse, then sat back on his heels in shock. After an instant's hesitation, Cade reached up and tore away the concealing hood and mask.

Golden hair spilled out onto the ground, and Laurie Allen's lovely face looked as pale as death in the moonlight.

"Well, I'll be damned!" Cade said softly.

Chapter Eight

"Leave me alone!" Laurie snapped, sitting up and putting a hand to her arm in an effort to still its steady pounding. Cade Caldwell brushed aside her hand as easily as her words.

"Don't be stupid."

Laurie glared at him in the moonlight. "It's only a scratch!"

Looking up into her blazing eyes, Cade said, "I know that. But if you don't clean it, you'll get blood poisoning from my blade. It's not exactly clean, you know."

"I can well imagine," Laurie said as she tried to get to her feet. When she shoved aside his helping hand, Cade rocked back on his heels to watch her.

"So, *you're* El Vengador," he said in a calm voice, and she slanted him a sharp glance as she swayed to her feet.

"What are you going to do now? Do you intend to tell the alcalde?"

"Do you think I should?" Cade countered. His smile was lazy and amused, and Laurie bridled.

"I would not dream of telling you what you should do!"

"You're the first woman who's been able to resist," Cade said in the mocking voice that she'd grown to hate. He kept a sharp eye on her in spite of his outward indifference, looking for signs of dizziness. She'd not lost much blood, but it was hard to tell how weak she would grow from the little she'd lost.

Uncertain what to do next, Laurie just stood there far a long moment, feeling the slight trickle of blood down her arm and Cade's steady gaze on her. He'd torn her blouse open, and she had to hold the ripped edges together over her breasts, which she did with great difficulty. Her arm ached where his blade had sliced it, but she knew it wasn't a bad injury. It would barely leave a scar, but that didn't matter now. Now she had to think about getting back home before anyone discovered her missing from her room.

Laurie's gaze flicked from Cade's watchful face to her horse, then back.

"You'd never make it," he said, reading her thoughts. "Soldiers are as thick as ants out there tonight."

"What are you doing up here?" she demanded irritably. "Why were you watching me?"

"I wasn't watching you—I was avoiding the coach down there when you just bolted up the hill."

"Why?"

A soft laugh was followed by, "Señora Navarro. I was supposed to ride with her in the coach tonight, but managed to avoid it at the last minute."

Laurie shrugged, though his mention of riding with Señora Navarro gave her an angry twinge. Must he bed every woman in Higuera? Her voice was sharp when she said, "It's just as well, since there was a trap set for El Vengador tonight. I knew about it, and. . . ."

"Ah, the cooperative Captain Garcia, I presume."

Laurie's amber gaze should have withered him, but Cade merely laughed at her glare.

"Yes," she ground out, "Captain Garcia was unwittingly cooperative, but. . . ."

"Unwitting is a good word for Garcia," Cade said, rising to his feet and towering over her. "Where did you learn to fence?" he asked so abruptly she was startled.

"W-w-why?" she stammered, then hated herself for hesitating and lifted her chin to meet his gaze with more control than she felt.

As she tossed back her heavy mane of tawny hair and the moonlight caught in its waves, Cade felt the familiar stirring of desire for her. She knew how tempting she looked in the form-fitting trousers she wore, trousers that outlined the ripe curve of her slender hips and the long legs that ended in tight, knee-high boots. The torn blouse and pale skin beneath was an invitation that he wondered if he should accept. His desire was stronger now than it had been since the night of the fiesta, and he wondered if she could tell how he felt or if it was the question that had startled her.

"Well?" he prompted. "Who taught you to fence?"

"An old friend," Laurie said, stubbornly refusing to reply. Who did he think he was, demanding to know such personal details about her? And what did it matter anyway, unless he meant to turn her over to the alcalde, which she strongly suspected that he did not.

"A talented friend," Cade commented, but Laurie was not listening anymore. She'd stepped close to the edge of the slope to peer into the darkness below.

"I think they've gone," she said after a moment, then turned to look at him. He was right behind her, his dark eyes narrowed on her, his mouth thinned to a mocking line that made her want to slap him.

"You ride down there and you'll find out just how mistaken you are," Cade said softly. He grabbed her arm when she tried to push past him, and whirled her around. "Don't ruin everything by being stupid or

110

in a hurry."

She jerked her arm away, wincing at the pain that action brought. "What do you mean by that?"

"For the first time in a long while, the peons have hope. Don't ruin it by being caught."

"I don't intend to!"

"But you will if you don't listen to reason," Cade said. His dark eyes glittered in the moonlight, and Laurie could see fine lines of tension on each side of his mouth.

As she looked at his mouth she remembered that first night she'd seen him, when he had kissed her so intimately, and made her feel things she'd never felt before. He was looking at her now in almost the same way as he'd looked at her then, with a cool appraisal in his gaze that made her feel like an awkward school-girl. Laurie silently damned him for it. Why should he so easily be able to fluster her? It wasn't fair, not when he remained so cool and composed.

Lifting her chin slightly, she said, "I can take care of myself, thank you, Mister Caldwell!"

"Can you?" Cade's eyes raked her derisively, lingering on the cut still oozing blood, then shifting to her torn blouse. She was still holding the edges together, but he could see the curve of her breast between them, the soft skin that he remembered touching before.

When Laurie didn't answer, but stood there gazing at him with defiant anger, he shrugged and bent to scoop up her sword. "Here," he said, tossing it at her. "You'll need this if you go down there now."

Laurie caught it clumsily, trying to hold her blouse with one hand and flinching from the pain of her cut. The wound began throbbing again, and she felt a surge of weakness that made her almost faint.

"All right, you've made your point," she said after a moment. "I won't go down there right now. But I certainly don't wish to stay here with you!"

"Frightened?" he asked softly, with something like a speculative glitter in his eyes.

"Of you? Never!"

"Never's a long time," Cade said as he strode across the small clearing to the horses. He grabbed both sets of reins in one hand and motioned for Laurie to follow as he began to walk higher up the slope.

"Where are you going?" she demanded, following him even as she asked. "And what are you doing with my horse?"

"There's a spot near here where we can wait for the soldiers to leave. I don't think they'll find us there. It's kind of remote."

"How convenient that you should know all the hiding spots in the area," Laurie remarked with all the sarcasm she could muster. Her arm and head hurt, and she was finally frightened of what she'd been doing. Cade Caldwell knew her identity, and she had no assurance that he would not decide to turn her in whenever he chose.

"Have you ever considered the fact that you might be caught?" Cade asked, glancing at her over one shoulder.

"Yes, but never as much as now." When he laughed Laurie could not help but look behind her, wondering as they pushed through the moonlight and shadows if the soldiers were right behind them. She could still hear them below, hear faint shouts and an occasional thrashing about in the bushes.

"Good. Maybe caution will temper your recklessness," Cade said when they reached the top of the ridge, and when Laurie stared at him blankly he explained, "If you think I will betray you, you might think twice about playing this dangerous game again."

"And you might think twice about being an accomplice with your silence!" Laurie shot back, then gave a silent groan at her foolishness. When would she ever learn to curb her quick tongue and temper? And what if he took her words to heart and told what he knew?

Cade shook his head and began walking at a right angle across the high ridge. "Are you your own worst enemy, El Vengador?" he mocked.

"It seems that way," she admitted, "though I had the thought you might be."

Cade stopped and stared at her, then laughed softly. "I think your injury has confused your brain," he said when she glared at him again. "You've not made much sense since I met you, but you're positively confused now."

"I'm confused?" she hissed. "If I remember correctly, Cade Caldwell, it was *you* who mistook me for one of your girlfriends at your grandfather's fiesta!"

She half-stumbled, and Cade put out a hand to catch her before he said with drawling amusement, "Rosa isn't a girlfriend, chica. She's a very talented *puta*."

Jerking her hand away, Laurie gasped with fury and shock. "You mistook me for a whore?" she finally demanded. "How dare you! Why, I should slice you to ribbons for that! If it wasn't for. . . ."

"Quiet!" Cade grabbed her quickly, glaring at her in the moonlight. "Do you want the soldiers up here? It's your life, Doña Laurie!"

Forgetting her injury, Laurie put both hands on her hips and tossed her hair back from her eyes. She was smarting from humiliation and the knowledge that he had kissed her so familiarly only because he'd thought she was a whore. He hadn't been swept away with her charm and beauty, but had merely been handling a purchase.

"I hate you, Cade Caldwell, and I hope you go back to wherever it is you came from!" she burst out

113

childishly, knowing she was being foolish but not caring. All she wanted was to strike out, to wipe that smug look of complacency from his face.

When she noticed where Cade's gaze had drifted, she glanced down and saw the gaping edges of her torn blouse. Bare skin gleamed beneath and Laurie instinctively reached up to pull the shredded pieces together, but it was too late.

Dropping the horses' reins, Cade took two steps back to her.

"You've been playing a dangerous game," he said into her startled face, his hands biting into her shoulders. "I don't think you know that Don Luis doesn't care if you're a man or a woman right now. He wants the blood of El Vengador, and he's going to do everything he can to get it. You've made a fool of him, and while you may have the gratitude of the peons and even some of the hacendados, you won't have their assistance should you be caught."

"You're just jealous because you weren't brave enough to do something like this," Laurie spat back at him, her words hot and sharp. She didn't want to let him know how weak his proximity made her feel, how just the harsh touch of his hands on her shoulders made her want to lean into him and feel his mouth on hers again. Was she insane to want such a thing? To recall the hot burning of his lips, to wonder if she would feel that way again?

"Jealous?" Cade was repeating, and his dark eyes narrowed with a sort of amused anger. "Jealous of someone idiotic enough to risk their lives for a lost cause? I hardly think so, chica!"

"You're horrible!" Laurie said, feeling foolish even as she said it. It was such an understatement of the way she felt that she wished she dared call him the name she wanted to say.

Cade laughed softly. "Horrible? You know you

want to say worse than that," he mocked. "I can see it in your eyes, as well as something you don't want me to see."

Pushed to her limit, Laurie said with brutal frankness, "I admit that you . . . interested me—but only because I have never met such a savage, unprincipled man before. I've never been afraid to experiment, though I must say you leave me rather disappointed."

His hands curled into her shoulders more painfully and Laurie flinched slightly, her chin lifting as she faced him with a haughty defiance. Cade's eyes were cold and indifferent as he said in a softly menacing tone, "So you were disappointed in my touch, chica? I'll see what I can do about that."

"No! I never meant. . . ."

It was too late. Cade dragged her to his hard frame and held her tightly against him, so tightly she could feel the hard press of his body against her curves. She gasped, and he took advantage of her parted lips to thrust his tongue between, raping her mouth with fiery thrusts that left her vibrating with fear and a strange kind of excitement. What was it about him that made her react so? she wondered in a dazed kind of way, then shivered when his hands moved boldly to her bared breast.

There was no tenderness in this kiss, this savage raping of her mouth and her mind, only a brutal insistence that left her weak and clinging to him. Instead of the fury she should feel, Laurie felt only a strange, fevered pulse of the blood through her veins, a hot gushing that left her totally confused.

Without realizing it at first, her arms rose to wind around his neck, holding him, her mouth opening willingly for a duel of tongues. When Cade's hand moved up the ridge of her spine to her neck to cradle her head, she shivered again, and moaned softly as his mouth trailed a fiery path from her lips to her

115

earlobe.

"Laurie," he muttered huskily in her ear; and somewhere in the dim recesses of her mind she knew she should not be allowing him such liberties with her, but she could not say the words that would stop him. It was too much of an effort to speak, and the slow burning that was deep in the pit of her stomach was suffusing her body with a raging heat.

When she finally would have uttered the words that may have stopped him, Cade covered her mouth with his lips again, stifling them, and she shuddered in his close embrace. And when his dark head lowered and he began to kiss her breasts, lingeringly, teasingly, Laurie cried out incoherently and grasped his head with both her hands.

She felt drained, powerless to stop him, and there was a brief moment when she realized that she didn't want to.

As if realizing her sudden surrender, Cade laughed softly, and her blouse fell away, baring her upper body to the night air and the moonlight.

"You're beautiful, you know," he said in a voice rough with desire and fatalism.

There wasn't an answer for that, and she arched against him wordlessly, wanting an end to the grating tension that was building higher and higher in her, but not knowing how to achieve it. Laurie was conscious of his throbbing hardness against her, his muscled thighs pressing against her legs and stomach, of the absence of a barrier between their bodies.

Dimly, she recalled the whispered conversations at the convent school, and had the vague thought that now she knew what they had been talking about. Now she knew how it felt to want to yield to a man, to want an ending to the raging need inside. She tried to remember what they'd said would ease the longing, but the answer wouldn't come to her; she could think of little but Cade's strong arms and hot body, his hotter kisses and the insistence as he laid her down on a bed of pine needles.

The sky reeled above her, and the raw ground beneath her gave little cushion, but Laurie didn't care. At the moment all she could think about was Cade and the deep fires inside her.

But then there was a shout nearby, and the muffled sound of men thrashing through underbrush, and she heard Cade curse softly as he lifted his head. Not understanding at first, Laurie moaned a protest, wanting an ending to the need, but when he spoke sharply, she began to emerge from her flushed trance.

"Get up! We've got to get out of here," he was saying, rising in a smooth, swift motion like the uncoiling of a snake. Laurie looked at him uncomprehendingly for a moment as he rebuttoned his pants, then flushed with shame and put her hands over her bared breasts.

"Here," he said, and flung her cape toward her. "Unless you want to reenact the same scene with a half-dozen troops, I suggest you hurry."

His indifference and casual words brought her back as nothing else would have, and Laurie snatched up the cape and stood.

"It's just as well that this happened," Cade said as he caught the horses' trailing reins. "Curious innocents like you are only trouble, Laurie Allen."

"I'm certain you're more accustomed to very *experienced* women, Cade Caldwell!" Laurie shot back at him, her cheeks hot with humiliation. She adjusted her blouse and the cape to hide her body.

"I prefer it that way. Experienced women know what to do and don't bother with silly word games," Cade said in a sharp tone. "Now, come on. I don't want the good *soldados* of Don Luis to think I had anything to do with the so-brave El Vengador."

117

Smarting under his mockery, Laurie followed silently. He was so mocking, his dark eyes alight with amusement, and Laurie thought that she had never hated anyone so much in her entire life.

Hot tears stung Laurie's eyes for some reason, and she wiped them away angrily as she followed Cade Caldwell over the top of the ridge and down the other side.

Chapter Nine

Red and purple streamers barely lightened the morning sky when Cade finally returned Laurie to the Allen hacienda on the edge of town. He paused on the ridge overlooking the still-quiet adobe house and turned to look at her.

She wouldn't look at him, but averted her face. Faint pink stains flushed her cheeks.

"How are you going to get into the house without being seen?" Cade asked, and Laurie gave a sullen shrug.

"Usually it's dark, and I'm not noticeable in my black cape."

Cade's voice was dry as he scanned her tumbled hair, torn blouse, and dragging cape. "Well, you're certainly noticeable now."

"Thanks to your rough handling!" she flashed, and he laughed.

"I didn't know who you were, and I'm not sure it would have made any difference if I had." A faintly mocking smile curled the corners of his mouth. "And you didn't seem to mind it that much, so you shouldn't be complaining now."

Her mouth tightened with anger, but she managed to say through clenched teeth, "It's no wonder you have to hire whores — no decent woman would let you

119

near her!"

"If you're judging decent women by your standards, *chica,*" Cade said softly, "I'm not sure there's a lot of difference between the two."

Stiffening, and wishing she dared lash out at him with her sword, Laurie said hoarsely, "How I hate you!"

"Look, don't blame me because of your unsatisfied curiosity. You know I want you, and if you'd be honest enough to admit it, you want me, too. At least whores are honest about what they want, while 'decent women' are full of nasty little tricks that would ruin a man if he'd let them." Cade's face was dark with anger, and his mouth thinned as he stared at her with cold eyes. "God save us all from 'decent women'!"

"You sound as if you've a grudge against decent women, Señor Caldwell," Laurie said, and remembered Cecelia. "Is it because of your wife?"

Cade's gaze became murderous. Suddenly, frightened of his reaction, Laurie took an instinctive step back. He looked as if he'd like to kill her, and fine white lines framed his mouth as he obviously struggled for control.

"How do you know about that?"

"I . . . I used to live in New Orleans, and Carlota reminded me of her not long ago. I went to school with Cecelia." Why was her voice so fearful and shaky? she wondered, irritated because she'd allowed him to know he frightened her.

"Well, it is a small world, I suppose," Cade said after a moment, and his voice was full of the familiar mockery again. His dark handsome face was carefully blank, and one eyebrow arched high as he stared at her. Laurie wished for a single instant that she could know what he was thinking, then thought it was probably better that she couldn't. He wouldn't be having very charitable thoughts about her right now, but really—she didn't care anyway.

"If you will hand me my horse's reins, I will go now," she said when the silence stretched tautly. "The sky is getting lighter by the moment, and unless I want to explain to my father why I am dressed this way and where I've been, I'd best hurry."

Silently, Cade put the long leather reins of her stallion into Laurie's outstretched palm. His gaze briefly met hers, dark eyes locking with gold, then he was gone, stepping back to his waiting horse and into the saddle. Only the echo of hoofbeats was left to remind Laurie of the unbelievable night, and she mounted her horse and walked it down the slope to the hacienda.

Good fortune was with her. No one saw her ride into the small yard and unsaddle her horse, nor was she seen slipping into her bedchamber via the walled terrace adjoining it.

Weary and strangely disconcerted, Laurie tumbled into her bed and feigned illness when Serita arrived to wake her for the day.

"You are ill, Doña Laurie?" the girl asked with a worried frown. "Perhaps I should go to fetch Doña Carlota, and. . . ."

"No! No, Serita," Laurie said more calmly, "I'll be all right. It's just my time, that's all."

"Ah," Serita said with a wise nod of understanding. "I have something for that illness, Doña Laurie. It cures any ache you may have."

Because she couldn't very well refuse without inviting conjecture and comment, Laurie agreed, and the girl rushed from the room. When she reappeared with a particularly noxious drink, Laurie wished that she had thought of an excuse, but forced herself to drink it. It was bitter, and smelled dreadful, but when she had finished it, Serita smiled.

"You will feel much better soon," the girl promised,

and Laurie managed a nod.

"Gracias, Serita. Now I think I'll sleep for a while."

Tiptoeing around the room, Serita closed the shutters, then left as quietly as possible. Laurie stared at the shadowed ceiling above her bed for a long time before she went to sleep, thinking about Cade Caldwell and El Vengador.

For some reason, she was more worried about Cade than about being exposed as the bandit who had been harassing the alcalde. Cade's touch affected her so quickly, so strongly, that she wondered why. Was the rushing sweep of emotion that she'd felt the same thing as the passion her school friends had discussed so thoroughly? If so, why hadn't she felt a surge of that thing called desire? Desire and the hot burning inside her could not be the same thing, because you were supposed to be in love with a man to feel that. And she certainly didn't love Cade Caldwell! In fact, she hated him. He was arrogant and a savage, little removed from the Indians she'd heard so much about before arriving in California.

But then she recalled the Indians she had seen, the shabby, nearly naked men who were more slaves than the fierce, marauding savages she'd imagined. Though she had also heard of the raids farther north, Higuera had been fortunate not to suffer any raids since her arrival. An uneasy truce seemed to exist, but the cannons were kept ready in the *presidio* just in case.

She shivered, and thought that Cade was the most savage she wanted to encounter.

Laurie's thoughts began to grow hazy, and just before she drifted into a heavy sleep she remembered that Cade had been the man who had bested Gilbert Rosiére in a duel. No wonder he had outdueled her so easily! Well, she would definitely think of a way to pay him back for his humiliation of her, damn him.

If Laurie had known it, she would have been delighted to discover that Cade was damning her, too, and he was not dismissing her as easily as he should have. Instead he could not stop thinking about the feel of her in his arms and the taste of her on his lips. Damn her cat's eyes, he told himself with a harsh shake of his head. No woman had lingered long in his memory since Cecelia, and he was determined that no woman ever would.

Cecelia de Marchand had been education enough. Cade didn't need any other woman to play the same tricks on him. And somehow it didn't really surprise him to find that Laurie had known Cecelia. Women so alike would naturally gravitate toward one another, he decided.

Now that Laurie had decided to take vengeance into her own hands in such a misguided fashion, his plan was thrown to the four winds. How could he pursue the removal of the alcalde now? He shook his head, angrily thinking that Laurie's meddling had caused a great deal of trouble.

He had been carefully courting Doña Linda Navarro, Don Luis's sultry niece, extracting information from her. To that end, he had wanted to keep his position in the village hierarchy above reproach. But now, he'd learned, he was one of the men suspected of being El Vengador. It could ruin everything.

Stretching his long frame out on a settee on the patio, Cade smoked one of the thin cigarillos he favored, squinting against the smoke and staring across his grandfather's land. He crossed his legs at the ankles and relaxed, blowing lazy smoke rings toward the vines woven into a roof overhead.

"Well, my grandson, are you hard at work as usual?" came a sarcastic voice some time later, and Cade stifled a groan.

Levering his lean body up from the settee, he met

Don Benito's clear gaze. "As you can see, I am busy thinking," Cade replied with a self-mocking smile.

Don Benito's riding crop tapped against the top of his calf-length boot as he stared irritably at Cade. "I hear that you and a certain captain of the alcalde's guards had a misunderstanding in the village."

Cade's brow lifted. "That was two days ago. Your sources are getting slower. Usually news travels fast, especially when it's bad," he said. "José Garcia and I have never liked each other. That shouldn't surprise you."

"No, but your bold behavior does. Tempers are too thin at this time. To antagonize the alcalde's captain is only asking for trouble."

"What about antagonizing me? Shouldn't the brave capitán be worried about that?"

Don Benito gave an impatient shake of his head. "It is not the capitán who has been questioned about his activities lately! Don't make any more enemies, Nicólas."

Cade shrugged. "I'm afraid it's too late for that. The fair Linda has already informed me that her uncle suspects me of being El Vengador."

"Madre de Dios!" There was a long moment of silence before Don Benito asked, "And are you?"

A ringing laugh answered his question, and Cade mockingly elaborated, "Do you really think I care enough to put myself in that kind of danger?"

Don Benito stared at him. "I seem to recall a young boy who cared enough about others to champion the causes of the weak and unfortunate, yes. Has life changed you that much, Nicólas?"

"Not life, Grandfather — people. I've discovered that one does not garner gratitude for endangering oneself for someone else's cause. Usually, the reward earned is all the blame and a generous amount of trouble."

"You've grown bitter and cynical."

"Yes," Cade agreed without emotion. "But wiser."

"That remains to be seen," Don Benito said, and Cade did not reply.

The don sat down heavily, his gray brows knitting into a frown as he stared out over the rolling hills of the ranchero.

"All this has been in the Alvarez family for generation upon generation," he said after a moment, softly, as if to himself. "It has been a struggle to keep it at times as the land has changed countries, but now — now I think the time is near when California will be a part of America. The Spanish and Mexican influence will die out, melt into the nationalities of the Americans, and one day no one will know or remember the Alvarez family. We will be as one of the grains of sand upon the shore, as tiny and insignificant as all the other grains of sand."

"It's important to you that we're not?" Cade asked when it looked as if his grandfather was through speaking.

The old don looked at him with surprise. "Of course."

Cade was silent. He didn't care about the future. He didn't care about the Alvarez lands or even the name, except as it pertained to his grandfather. Perhaps one day he would, but now he didn't. Now there were too many other things that were important to him. He'd seen the dawning of a new freedom, had helped to bring it about, and he itched to be back in the Republic of Texas, the Lone Star Republic, as it was called.

The months he'd spent fighting with the Texans for independence had been the best of his life. It wasn't the danger that intrigued him, nor the thought that he might be making history. It was the realization that he had made a difference, and even as he thought that, Cade suddenly understood why Laurie

Allen had been reckless enough to don a disguise and ride out into the night to fight injustice. It was just that kind of crazy recklessness that had formed the Republic of Texas, and he wondered why he'd been so surprised to find it in a woman.

Hadn't he seen women fighting beside their men? Loading and shooting a long Kentucky rifle, burning their hands and still not stopping? He'd thought Laurette Allen different, a haughty, spoiled girl who thought of little but herself—until he'd seen her the night before. An unwilling smile slanted Cade's mouth as he recalled how skillfully she wielded a sword. If she knew that several times he'd begun to wonder as to the victor, she would be too swelled with conceit to stand. God knows, she had to be vain enough already, with most of the available young men in Higuera sniffing at her heels every time she walked out the door.

Cade felt a tightening in his gut, a spasm of irritation that surprised him. Why should it matter to him if she had every man in town at her beck and call? He certainly wasn't among that number, nor did he intend ever to see her again unless circumstances unavoidably threw them together.

A faint smile curled his mouth when Cade recalled her spitting fury the night before. She'd reminded him of a tawny cat, all claws and hisses, and her great golden eyes had shone in the moonlight like cat eyes. Almost absentmindedly, he moved his hand to rub at a long scratch on his arm, a scratch that she'd put there with her sword. She had not noticed, and he'd no intention of telling her. It would only make her think she might be able to best him one day.

With a little shock, Cade realized that the woman had begun to intrigue him, a definite sign of danger.

Standing, he announced abruptly to his grandfather that he was going into the mountains for a few days. Don Benito gazed at him with a resigned smile touching his lips.

"I know that you ride almost every night, sometimes until the morning sun comes up. You cannot sleep, and now—are you running away from or to something, my grandson?" he asked caustically.

A careless shrug briefly lifted Cade's broad shoulders. "Neither, but that doesn't matter. I just feel the need to be alone for a while."

"Bah! This passion for solitude that you have is quite ridiculous! Always you run into the mountains, and when you come back you look like a renegade and smell like a goat!"

Laughing, Cade said, "I'm pleased you noticed."

Don Benito just shook his gray head and mumbled something that Cade wasn't certain he wanted to hear so he didn't ask him to repeat it.

"Will you be back by Friday?" the don asked after a moment, and Cade shrugged again.

"I'll be back whenever the *aguardiente* runs out."

"Drunk, I suppose," Don Benito muttered.

"Maybe," Cade agreed, and nothing else was said. Each knew the other's limits, and each knew that the other would not change.

Chapter Ten

Laurie spent the week following her dangerous escape in deep thought. She was overly gay and unusually quiet by turns, until Carlota thought she must be coming down with a grave illness.

"Nonsense!" Laurie said more sharply than she intended when her stepmother suggested she see the physician. "I'm only a bit tired at times, and bored. I'm not accustomed to such a sedentary life, with no balls or opera or gay soireés to attend. . . ." She paused and threw Carlota a penitent smile. "It's not that I don't like it here, because I do, but I still feel as if I don't fit in."

Carlota plucked at her dark skirt for a moment, then looked up at Laurie. "I've been thinking about giving a belated birthday fiesta for you, but I wasn't certain you would like that, or that your papa would allow it. After all, there's his position to consider, and we have to be careful about appearances. Some might take it amiss if we were to seem too frivolous with money or gaiety." She paused, then said in a rush, "Or we could travel to Los Angeles, where there are many things to see and do and no one to care! I used to go there often with my parents, and there are lots of amusements, and fine shops with goods from France and other wonderful places."

Brightening at the thought of actually shopping again, and visiting a theater and strolling along a crowded boulevard, Laurie was enthusiastic. "Do you think we could, Carlota? Would Papa allow it?"

"He might, if we proceeded very carefully in how we asked him," Carlota replied, her dark eyes twinkling with mischief.

For the first time, Laurie felt a real closeness with her stepmother, and they laughed together. "It would be wonderful!" Laurie exclaimed, and they began to plan their trip.

In spite of Phillip Allen's reluctance, doubt, and worry that the infamous El Vengador might swoop down on their carriage, Carlota and Laurie convinced him to allow them to undertake the journey to Los Angeles. After all, it had been some time since certain goods had been purchased for the household, and Phillip *had* been promising Carlota he would take her to see some of her relatives one day soon. Now that Laurie was there and fretting with boredom, it was a good time to go.

Phillip yielded to their pleas and hired an armed guard of six men to accompany them to Los Angeles. Though it was well known that Don Luis was El Vengador's target, and though since the last narrow escape he had not struck again, Phillip did not intend to take any chances with his wife and daughter's welfare.

Serita packed for Laurie, filling several trunks with her prettiest gowns.

"Do you not think this one would be best for a fiesta, Doña Laurie?" Serita asked, lifting a deep emerald gown with straps for sleeves and a very low-cut bodice. "It needs only a small scarf at the neck to be presentable."

Laurie made a face. "A scarf would ruin the lines

of the dress, Serita, but I suppose I must abide by the proper conventions, however silly they seem."

Surprised, Serita looked up at her. "Don't the señores think women are loose when they wear gowns like this, Doña Laurie?" she blurted out, then flushed, her dark skin growing crimson. "Oh, *por favor*—I did not mean to insult you!"

Recalling that night at Don Benito's fiesta, Laurie knew what Serita meant, and she smiled. "I'm not insulted, Serita. I suppose it's natural for California women to wear scarves, while in New Orleans and France, it's natural for the women to show more of their skin. It's considered very fashionable, you understand."

A furrow knit her brow as Serita slowly re-folded a lacy chemise and put it into the trunk. Then she lifted the corset Laurie had brought, a whalebone reinforced garment that looked to the Indian maid more like an instrument of torture than an article of underclothing.

"This I do not understand," she said frankly, holding it up and making Laurie laugh. "You are already small—*muy pico,* yet you have me pull laces so tight that you can barely breathe. Why?"

"To make me even smaller and more appealing to men," Laurie said wryly. "I begin to see your point, Serita!"

"But how could a man think a woman who cannot breathe is appealing?" Serita shook her dark head, wisps of hair flying about her face, and her expression was amused. "Juan would think me very dull indeed, if I could not speak but in a whisper, and found it hard to walk up the hill with him."

"But if I don't wear the corset, I cannot fit into any of my gowns," Laurie pointed out with a sigh. "So, unless I buy new gowns, I'm afraid that I will continue to wear my corset."

Making a face, Serita put it back into the trunk. "Doña Carlota has bolts and bolts of material in the storehouses, and laces and silks and enough leather for a hundred pairs of new shoes." She slid Laurie a sly glance. "There is just enough time to have Teresa sew you a new gown, one that you can breathe in."

Carlota thought it was an excellent idea, and for the three days before they left for Los Angeles, the hacienda seamstresses worked feverishly, sewing new gowns for Laurie and Carlota.

"This is my favorite!" Serita exclaimed, holding up a deep burgundy gown with flounced sleeves. "And see? The waist is still small, as you are, Doña Laurie."

"I must admit that the California styles are much freer and more comfortable," Laurie said with a pleased smile. "But they also make me feel decadent in a way, as if I am not wearing enough clothes."

Carlota laughed at that, and when Phillip appeared in the doorway and asked why they were so amused, no one would tell him.

"You would be shocked, Papa," Laurie said with a laugh. "We were merely comparing the differences in what's enough and what's too little."

It was true, she reflected later. While the Californios considered corsets and the multitude of petticoats too bulky and awkward, they covered their breasts and shoulders with lacy scarves that allowed only the barest glimpse of bare skin. Wouldn't they have been shocked by the styles of only a few years before? she thought. Then European women had worn clinging muslin with no petticoats at all, and had even wet it so that it clung to their curves with a daring flouting of convention. But that was Europe and this was California, and much more than mere miles separated the two.

Laurie found that she was looking forward to the trip to Los Angeles, to a more lively social atmosphere than the lazy, sun-drenched days in Higuera. And she was certainly glad that she would not have to see Cade Caldwell again for a while, she thought later when she and Carlota rode down into the village.

Carlota had insisted, saying that there was to be a contest of horsemanship skills that day, and her cousin Alfredo was one of the contestants.

"You will enjoy watching it, Laurie," Carlota promised, as they rode toward the seashore.

A crowd was already gathering, and Carlota introduced Laurie to people whose names she would never remember, but she made polite replies and smiled so much her jaws began to ache from the strain. A carnival atmosphere pervaded the village, an atmosphere even the uniformed soldiers did not affect. Indeed, some of the soldiers were among the men who were to test their skills.

Laurie didn't realize she'd been watching for him until she saw Cade. Then her heart lurched crazily and her breath came more quickly as she tried to pretend she hadn't seen him.

Mounted on a huge gray Arab stallion draped in bright blankets, he rode directly toward them, sweeping his broad-brimmed hat from his head as he greeted Carlota.

"Doña Carlota, it is good to see you again. You have come for the spectacle, I suppose?"

Carlota nervously smoothed her many-tiered, flounced skirts with one hand, darting glances between Cade and Laurie from beneath her lowered lashes. "We had thought to watch them for a short time, si, Don Nicólas."

Grinning at her discomfiture, Cade said smoothly, "Good. I will ride with you, so that none of the bolder *caballeros* confront you."

There seemed to be no way to politely refuse, and Carlota nodded unhappily. Laurie, however, fumed silently as Cade deliberately wedged his stallion between her and Carlota.

"I don't believe your mount cares for the proximity of my horse," she said stiffly when her gelding tossed its head and snorted.

"I believe it is your horse that does not care for mine," Cade said in the same formal tone she was using, and her eyes flashed at him.

"Perhaps it's just the rider my horse objects to, then! If you would please make an effort to control your animal, Señor Caldwell, I would appreciate it very much."

"Are you suggesting that I am incapable of doing so?" Cade's grin widened. "In California, we learn to ride our horses as soon as we learn to walk. There are very few Californios who cannot control their mounts."

Laurie's hands clenched around her leather reins, and she said with an effort, "Then do so!"

Still grinning, Cade nudged his stallion just ahead of her, so that she had to slow her horse. She glared at him, but he ignored her.

Indifference, Cade had learned, would pique a woman's interest much more than ardent desire. Hadn't he noticed that with CeCe? And with a dozen other women? Laurie Allen was no different. If he went to her and told her he wanted her, that he wanted to hold her in his arms and feel her soft, velvety skin beneath his hands and lips, then she would snub him quite rudely. But if he pretended that he did not care about her, did not think she was lovely, then her female pride would be pricked and she would do her best to lure him.

It was a game men and women played with one

another, and a quite effective one. Like now—the *vaqueros* who swaggered up and down the sandy beach preparing for a contest of skills wanted to impress the ladies more than each other.

"Are you riding, Don Nicólas?" Carlota leaned forward to ask, and he shook his head.

"No, I'm just a spectator. Your cousin Alfredo is riding today, isn't he?"

"Sí. He has won the last three contests, and Tia Anita is quite proud of him, though she is worried he'll be hurt."

Slightly leery of the nature of the contest, having endured a bull and bear baiting two weeks before, Laurie asked cautiously, "Isn't this a test of equestrian skills between the young men?"

Cade laughed. "Yes, and no blood-letting today." He leaned close, his dark eyes fixed on her face. "I realize you must feel squeamish at the sight of blood, Doña Laurie, but this is California! There are dangerous villains out here in the wilderness, swordsmen who challenge our brave soldiers and champion the plight of the peons. We are a barbaric people, much less civilized than the East."

She flicked him a scathing glance and wished she dared say the things that came to mind. She didn't, but merely smiled sweetly and said that she could not bear the sight of blood.

"Especially your own, I would imagine," Cade said, and she stiffened. "But only a chicken is in danger today," he added, "so there is no need to worry."

Laurie tried to concentrate on the contest, though it was hard with Cade beside her, feeling his amused glances at her, and Carlota's frowning bewilderment. Poor Carlota. She must wonder why Cade and Laurie were always baiting one another!

"Which one is your cousin Alfredo?" Laurie

asked, to get Carlota's mind off her and Cade.

Carlota searched the gaily dressed *vaqueros*, then pointed. "That one. The tall young man standing beside the bay horse. Oh, look! He is the next contestant!"

Laurie watched as Alfredo vaulted atop his horse and wheeled it around to the far end of the beach. The object of the contest was to ride at a full gallop past a rooster partially buried in the sand, then pluck it successfully without breaking stride or killing the fowl. It was difficult—almost impossible—for the rider had to bend low from his mount and scoop up the squawking, pecking bird as it tried to avoid the flying hooves and sand. There were many casualties in games like them.

Looking away, Laurie wondered why she always felt sympathy for the animal instead of admiration for the rider's skills. It had been the same when she had gone to the bullfights in Spain, and she had not watched when the matador had killed the bloodied bull. Killing an animal for food was one thing; for sport was something else. It was the waste of life that bothered her, not the necessary killing.

After all, hadn't she attended a *matanza*, where freshly killed beef roasted on huge spits? From July until October the *vaqueros* rounded up the free-roaming cattle that were to be used for food and hides. Some of the beef was dried; some was used for shoes, lariats, and clothing, and some for candles and soap. It seemed vaguely wasteful to Laurie, when she saw that only a few hundred pounds of the carcass was used. The rest was left lying for the wild animals to clean.

She had learned that cowhides were the most valuable form of currency for the Californios, besides silver. They exported most of it to foreign countries, including the United States. Each hide brought from a dollar to two dollars and a half, causing the American sailors to dub the hides "California banknotes."

Close to the huge warehouses near the wharves, a stench filled the air as the raw hides were brought in and stored, and Laurie usually avoided the area. Even now, though they were two miles away, she could detect a faint nuance of the stench as the wind carried it.

"California perfume," Cade said in her ear, somehow sensing her thoughts, and Laurie looked up at him in surprise. "You wrinkled your nose," he said by way of explanation, and she gave him a reluctant smile.

"I suppose I'm much more transparent than I thought."

"Most of the time, yes. It's your eyes."

"That's what Papa has always said." Laurie tugged at the ends of the lacy shawl draped over her head and shading her face, and wished for an instant that Cade's thoughts were as readable.

When she looked at him again, she felt the oddest leap of her heart, then quickly looked away. A soft flush stained her high cheekbones, and she felt a moment's irritation that he could do that to her.

Cade began talking to Carlota again, his voice polite and distant, and Laurie tried not to recall that dusk on his grandfather's patio. She was too aware of him next to her, sitting so easily on his big Arab, his long frame draped in the ornate Spanish saddle. Today he was dressed just like one of the *vaqueros,* in an open-necked white shirt, long cape carelessly draped over his broad shoulders, and gilt-encrusted *calzones* with the flared hems. The usual red sash was around his lean waist, and his silver-handled sword dangled at one side. He looked

136

wickedly handsome—and very dangerous, she decided.

Laurie was glad when the festivities were over, when each *vaquero* claimed his prize and rode away with the girl of his choice. And she was even more glad when Cade Caldwell rode to only the gate of the Alvarado *estancia*, and left them with polite good-byes.

Every time she saw him, Laurie reflected, he left her thoughts in turmoil. Why did she care what he thought of her? Or if he thought of her?

Well, it didn't matter anyway, because they were leaving for Los Angeles in the morning and she wouldn't have to see him again for a long time.

Los Angeles was just the thing to enliven Laurie. She was delighted with the city, even though it was poor in comparison to Paris or Barcelona. It was new, and pulsed with promise and excitement.

Many of the streets were unpaved, and the buildings were both Spanish-influenced and American. The majority of the business district was near the waterfront, with rough seamen and well-armed men walking the streets. Laurie was grateful for their armed escort, and did not protest when Carlota insisted she go nowhere alone.

Carlota had a large family of relatives in Los Angeles who were exuberantly glad to see her and meet her stepdaughter. Laurie found them to be exceedingly gracious, and she was immediately caught up in a whirlwind of socials that reminded her of her beloved New Orleans. Though the social structure was quite different, and the young girls her age were either married or looked upon as spinsters, she did not find it so restrictive as she had worried it might be.

One of Carlota's young cousins, named Concepción but called Concha, was irrepressible and lively, and liked Laurie at once.

"Your hair is so lovely!" she said admiringly. "Rarely have I seen such a shade of gold. It even matches your eyes, so that you look like a cat," she ended with a little laugh that made Laurie smile. "You will go with us to the Ramirez ball, will you not?" Concha asked in the next breath. "It is always the grandest fiesta of the year, and simply everyone is there!"

"I wouldn't miss it," Laurie replied promptly.

The Ramirez fiesta turned out to be much more exciting than Laurie had ever dreamed.

Garbed in her new finery, and with Carlota, Concha, and Señora Portolá, Concha's mother, Laurie soon found herself riding in an open carriage through the uneven Los Angeles streets on her way to the fiesta. She smoothed the satin skirts of her new gown, a deep burgundy that flattered her creamy skin and light hair and eyes. The bodice was cut daringly low, with severe lines that only emphasized her curves, and the elbow-length sleeves were wide and flounced.

"It makes your waist look so tiny!" the larger Concha had said without a trace of envy in her voice. She knew that she was lovely, too, with her dark hair and eyes and deep complexion. Her rich rose-colored gown enhanced her vivid coloring, and Señora Portolá decided that Laurie and her daughter made a perfect foil for one another.

"See? Light and dark! Do they not look lovely together?"

Apparently, the young men at the fiesta thought so too, for Laurie and Concha were immediately engulfed by a swarm of handsome suitors all vying for their attention. Not all of them were Spanish.

Indeed, Laurie was delighted to find not only Americans there, but Frenchmen.

As a major seaport, Los Angeles enjoyed a variety of cultures, and the Ramirez family was not prejudiced against anyone who would add to their roster of friends and acquaintances. There were even Russians, tall and somber and with a remarkable capacity for liquor.

To her shock, Laurie saw Cade Caldwell among the guests, and when she turned toward Carlota, she saw the same shock mirrored in her stepmother's face.

"Of course, he would be invited," Carlota murmured unhappily, and Laurie wondered why she sounded so dismayed. After all, Carlota had no idea her stepdaughter had spent long hours in the dark with him!

Laurie couldn't know that her stepmother's unease stemmed from the obvious attraction Carlota recognized in the tilted amber eyes that drifted again and again to Cade. Women came naturally to him; they always had. It was a well-known fact in Higuera, but Carlota had not wanted to add to his mystique any more than had already been done. She had recognized the flicker of interest in Laurie's eyes the night of Don Benito's fiesta, when the girl had stared at Cade with a speculative gaze.

And even now, when Laurie saw Cade across the room, her attitude subtly altered. She began to flirt with the young men around her more gaily, until she had quite a crowd of eager suitors vying for the next dance. Always, she seemed to be waiting. An air of expectation shrouded her, and when she caught Cade looking in her direction, Laurie took great pains to pretend she didn't know he was there.

A soft breeze blew across the courtyard and into

the ballroom, but it did not penetrate the crowd of dancers. Hot and flushed from her dancing, Laurie found it necessary to retreat to the walled veranda for some fresh air. Her partner of the moment, a fair, handsome Frenchman who had, once, a long time before, lived in Paris, offered to fetch her a cool glass of fruity wine, and Laurie accepted.

"You are too kind, monsieur," she said in French, and he lifted her hand to his lips, overcome with his good fortune in finding a beautiful girl who had lived in France and who spoke such fluent French.

"And you are too beautiful for words, mademoiselle," he replied huskily, then dared to pull her into his arms to steal a kiss.

Laurie allowed it, giddy with excitement and the brandy she had drunk, putting back her head and closing her eyes. If Carlota or Señor Portolá saw her they would swoon with dismay, but she enjoyed feeling reckless tonight.

The Frenchman, Jacques Poirier, felt reckless, too, and he kissed her deeply, his hands pulling her against him so that her wide hoop skirts belled out in a swish of satin. He could feel the press of her breasts against his chest and wondered if the lovely Laurette would allow him any more liberties. But he would have to proceed carefully, very carefully, for she was obviously gently reared and he could not frighten her. Yet she had lived in Paris, and she spoke of people he knew of only by reputation, though he came from a very good family. Her mother's people were obviously well connected, Jacques thought as he reluctantly relinquished her to fetch more champagne punch.

"I shall return quickly," he said with a smile he hoped was intriguing. "You will wait upon me?"

"I would not dare leave until your return," Laurie said into his smiling face. Her heart was beating only a bit faster, and she hoped she'd hidden her disappointment well. His kiss had not excited her, but had merely been pleasant. And the fact that he was a viscount did not excite her either, though Concha had declared herself to be consumed with jealousy over the fact. Laurie had known many viscounts in France, and she found found most of them to be as boring as any other men who thought only of their own interests and expected everyone else to be as fascinated with their exploits as they were.

When the Vicomte de la Poirier had vanished into the crowded ballroom, Laurie walked restlessly along the low wall edging the veranda. Huge stone pots filled with overflowing ivy and sweet-blooming flowers squatted at intervals, and she paused beside one particularly fragrant profusion to lift a blossom into her hand.

Rubbing her nose over the velvety petals, she inhaled deeply, closing her eyes.

"Stealing hearts instead of jewels?" a familiar, mocking voice asked from just beyond the stone wall, and Laurie's eyes opened with a snap as Cade Caldwell vaulted the wall.

"What are you doing here?" she demanded angrily, and took a step back, accidentally pulling the blossom from the vine. It dropped to the stone tiles of the veranda, and Cade bent to pick it up.

He presented it to Laurie with a flourish. "Believe it or not, I was invited." He smiled, a predatory smile, she thought as he reached out to lift her limp hand in his. He pressed the flower into her palm, and her fingers closed around it.

For some reason Laurie noticed how handsome he was, with his dark hair just brushing the high collar of his shirt and his short jacket snugly fitting his broad shoulders. The bright red sash at his waist added a flair to his dark trousers and emphasized his lean waist. He looked every inch the well-bred gentleman this evening, except for his wicked grin and the lights dancing in his dark eyes.

"What? No rude comments to make?" he asked softly, and Laurie found her anger dissolving.

Perhaps it was easier to tame this savage with honeyed words instead of the truth, she thought as she gazed up at him with honest admiration in her eyes. And there was no point in reminding herself what a rogue he was, because right now her heart was pounding too fast to hear.

Tilting her head to one side, Laurie let her lips curve into a ripe, promising smile, and she let her lashes dip briefly before lifting them again.

"Should I be rude?" she asked. "Is that what you want from me?"

"I've already told you what I want from you, Laurie Allen," Cade replied, and she felt a tiny thrill shoot through her body. He was still smiling lazily, his dark eyes warm and assessing, and she knew what he meant. She had recalled that last conversation over and over, had recalled his harshness as well as his hot kisses and the feel of his hard body pressing against her. Although she had promised herself she would make him pay for his humiliation of her, she was finding it difficult to concentrate on that when he was standing beside her, close enough for her to reach out and touch the dark, crisp hair over his collar.

Then Cade reached out and took her hand and turned it over, opening her fingers to remove the slightly crushed blossom he had placed there. Without speaking, he tucked it into her bodice, nestling it in the creamy swell of her breasts. The brush of his fingers against her breasts made Laurie's breath quicken, and she wondered if he could feel the

142

rapid thud of her heart.

"Walk with me," he said, and Laurie found herself going down a set of wide steps with him into the garden. Tall trees and bushes trimmed into shapes lined narrow paths, forming a large pattern of squares.

"Carlota will faint if she discovers that I have slipped away without a chaperon," Laurie said after a few moments, and Cade laughed softly.

"Do you care?"

"Yes, and no. I'm not accustomed to having someone at my heels all the time, but I would not want to distress or embarrass Carlota."

Cade stopped and turned Laurie to face him. Moonlight filtered through thick leaves overhead to spangle his face with light, and she tried to read his expression but could not. His voice was soft, yet held an edge of something she couldn't identify.

"Why did you come out here with me, Laurie Allen?" he asked. "There's no one nearby, and we're all alone, you know that, don't you?"

She nodded, unable to force words past the sudden lump in her throat. Why had she come? She didn't know, except that she'd realized she'd wanted to be with him for a long time. He was the only man who had ever excited her, who had interested her long enough that now she thought about him even when she didn't want to.

"I've been watching you tonight," he was saying, and his voice was husky. "You've teased every man here."

"Not you," she said, and he laughed again.

"No," he agreed, "not me. I don't play those kind of games, I told you that."

She looked up at him. "I know."

He seemed to be waiting for something, but she didn't know what, and when he took her arm again

143

and pulled her with him deeper into the maze of secluded paths, Laurie did not protest. It wasn't until they reached a small gazebo that she realized where he was taking her. Laurie hung back slightly, her breath coming fast and her heart pounding so furiously she was certain he could hear it.

Thick vines wove a tapestry over the wood and stone structure, and Cade stepped up the two shallow steps and into the shadowed interior. He turned and looked at her, and as if in a dream, Laurie found herself going up the steps with him, walking into the close, fragrant air of the gazebo, where it seemed as if time stood still. Somewhere a nightbird sang a soft, sad song, and she could hear the faint strains of music from the main house that was only a glow in the distance. Looking up at his shadowed face, she offered a smile and a light, teasing remark.

"Did you bring me out here to dance?"

"No, and I didn't bring you out here for casual talk. I've never had much patience for light flirtations in the moonlight, chica, and I still don't. If you want to remain innocent, you'd better pick up your skirts and run back to the house, because if you stay here with me I'm going to do much more than kiss you," he said roughly, and there was a hard edge of harshness in his voice that made her catch her breath.

A feeling of panic swept through Laurie as she gazed at him. She thought that she should run, but couldn't. She seemed to have lost all power of movement and coherent thought. All she could hear was the rapid pulsing of blood in her ears, and the rasp of her breath as she finally released it.

When she didn't move, but remained staring up at him with thick-lashed gold eyes full of moonlight, Cade took her into his arms and carried her to a wide, cushioned ledge. He didn't lay her on it but stood her beside it, holding her against him, his hands moving caressingly over her back, his mouth lightly grazing her parted lips as he loosened her hair.

Laurie stood there stiffly, her body as cold as ice, and she was trembling so violently he murmured soft words in her ear and held her closer. She didn't know what he said, and it didn't matter. She could feel the deep timbre of his voice in every nerve, and the words didn't matter to her then. Nothing mattered but the man.

"Cold?" he asked softly when she shivered, his hands skimming over her bare shoulders with a light, lingering touch. Laurie shook her head.

"No," she whispered, and her voice sounded too loud in the thick silence.

"Look at me," Cade commanded, and she tilted up her head obediently. A faint smile curved his mouth as he saw the sheen of fear in her eyes, like that of a frightened rabbit, and for some reason he felt a surge of protection for her. "I won't hurt you," he murmured.

Slowly Laurie began to relax as he talked to her in a soft, husky voice between warm kisses, and when he finally lifted her and laid her back against the cushion of the bench, she did not offer a protest. He just held her for a few minutes, comfortingly, until he felt her tensed muscles loosen. As he held her next to him and she felt his warm breath slip over her cheek in the dark, she wondered what she was supposed to do. It had never occurred to her that there might be a certain way of doing this, yet she now realized that she had no idea where to begin. Did he? Of course, he must. Hadn't she heard how he'd left a string of broken hearts behind him? Or was that merely one of those tidbits of gossip enhanced with each telling? Laurie didn't know, and she wasn't certain she wanted to know.

Laurie's throat was dry, and she found it hard to say, "Cade, I've never . . ."

"I know," he interrupted her. "Don't do anything. Just be still, and let me do it all."

Cade's hands were warm and his mouth hot, so that when he caressed and kissed her he transferred some of that heat to her stiff, cold body and lips. There was a moment in which she wondered with another trace of panic why she hadn't run, but then he was unbuttoning her pretty gown and sliding it from her shoulders. The chemise and wide hoop petticoats she wore presented him with little mystery, and Laurie had the hazy thought that he was fairly familiar with the workings of a woman's clothing as he untied the laces and freed her from them.

Left in only her pantalettes and stockings, Laurie made the shocked discovery that Cade wanted her completely nude, and it frightened her. What if someone came to the gazebo? What if they were discovered?

But Cade brushed aside her fears with a careless, "No one ever comes way out here unless they're up to something. And we were here first."

It was scant comfort, but then he was pulling away the last of her clothing and she was left shivering in the dark shadows until he covered her body with his. She squeezed her eyes shut, suddenly painfully shy and mortified at what she was doing. She might have changed her mind then, as she felt his bare skin against her naked body, but he didn't give her the chance.

Gathering her slender curves into his arms, Cade kissed her until she couldn't breathe, his mouth hot and searing, his tongue probing between her lips with fierce intensity. Laurie responded; forgetting everything around her, forgetting everything but Cade.

Arching against him when his mouth found and lingered upon the tightened bud of her breast, Laurie tangled her fingers in his hair and gasped aloud. A coiling fire flared deep inside, banishing the coolness she'd felt, filling her body with such a raging need that she moaned. Cade heard her and smiled against her breast. Deliberately, slowly, he kissed and caressed her until Laurie was writhing beneath him, until she was clutching at him and saying his name, her head thrashing back and forth on the cushion.

"Cade," she whispered, "Cade. . . ."

Taking one of her hands, Cade pulled it to him and traced her fingers over his chest, down over the hard band of muscles that ridged his belly. He felt her instinctive recoil and did not press her.

"That's all right, love," he muttered. "We won't push you too far this first time."

Shivering uncontrollably, Laurie wondered how he would end this pulsing need inside her, wondered if there was an ending to it or if it just went on until she exploded from it.

Then Cade lifted slightly to poise over her, one knee thrusting between her trembling thighs, his voice light and coaxing.

"Open for me, love," he was saying, and when she still could not, he reached down a hand to gently part her thighs and lie between them. "It'll be all right, you know that, don't you?" he asked, and Laurie nodded mutely, wondering if he could see her in the shadows.

She stared up at him, at the way the light cast a hazy glow over him, leaving half his face shadowed. Her hand grazed the furred pelt on his chest as she reached up to touch his face, and her caress was hesitant. Cade took her hand in his and held it against his jaw, then to his mouth, his lips moving against her palm.

Feeling him nudge against her, against the soft swell between her thighs, Laurie gasped as she felt his heat. For some reason she had never imagined it like this, never imagined the strength of a man, or the prodding insistence. Why hadn't she listened more closely when her school friends had talked? Then she might know what was about to happen, might know more than just the vaguest imaginings.

At the first sharp stab of him against her, Laurie bit her lower lip between her teeth, her arms going around him in an instinctive reflex. As he began to penetrate, Cade muffled her cries with his mouth, his own breathing harsh and rough. When Laurie twisted and heaved against him, her hands moving to push him away, he caught her wrists in one of his hands and pulled them over her head, gently but firmly, his mouth never leaving hers. He held her that way a long moment, his body resting between her thighs, his lips slowly easing her tension until she relaxed beneath him.

She felt him shift slightly, but before she could brace herself he thrust forward in a swift, hard lunge that took away her breath and made her slender body arch against him. Shocked by the sudden splinter of pain that seared through her, Laurie's eyes widened.

"Don't! Oh Cade, *don't.*"

"It's done, love," he said hoarsely, staying deep within her and not moving. He kissed her again, her mouth and then her closed eyelids as she shut her eyes. "Relax, Laurie, and it won't hurt again."

Disbelieving, she opened her eyes to look at him with a reproachful stare, and Cade couldn't help but laugh softly.

"Didn't you know what it would be like your first time?" he asked her, and she shook her head.

"No," she said in a faintly sullen voice. "I heard so many different stories I didn't know which one to believe."

"Well, now you know," Cade said, and kissed the tip of her straight little nose. "And now it just gets better, I promise."

Still slightly unbelieving, Laurie tensed when he began to move again, but found that he hadn't lied. There was no more pain, only a vague kind of soreness that disappeared when he began to kiss her again, his movements quickening. She felt his hard, driving thrusts with mounting excitement and matched his rhythm, her breath coming quick and fast and her heart beginning to pound harder and harder. But it wasn't until a shuddering release coursed through her body that she knew the ending, knew why she was there. It was a rush of quivering excitement that all seemed to build to a single point before bursting into wave after wave of hot, totally encompassing ecstasy.

And when it faded, it left her weak and drained and limp in his arms. Cade held her loosely, his mouth close to her ear, his body relaxing atop her and his breathing deep and steady. His voice was lazy when he said, "That wasn't so bad, was it?"

Laurie stirred slightly, and managed to roll her head back and forth on the cushion. "Not too bad," she murmured so softly he wasn't certain he heard her.

Still cradling her in his arms, Cade shifted to lie next to her, one leg thrown across her body. They lay that way for a long time, listening to the far-away sounds of the fiesta. Neither of them wanted to return, but both knew that they must. Laurie had been gone so long now that her stepmother was surely searching for her, and what if the viscomte reported her missing?

She turned into his chest to bury her face against him and inhale deeply, feeling his arms tighten briefly around her. He kissed the top of her head, a comforting gesture that made her smile against the dark hairs tickling her nose.

When she tilted back her head to tell him that they needed to return, Cade kissed her again, soft and vaguely arousing, and she forgot what she'd wanted to say. She forgot everything but Cade again, and felt him strengthen against her. This time she was ready for him, and matched his pace with eager arches of her body, her breasts quivering as he kissed first one, then the other. And when he was rocking against her and whispering soft words in her ear, Laurie knew she had never felt this way in her entire life.

So this is what it was all about, she thought when they once more lay spent and drifting in a satisfied haze. Her life would never be the same; never would she wonder or fear it.

But afterward, when he helped her dress in the shadows, his hands swift and certain while hers trembled, Laurie could not bring herself to ask him the question on her mind! did it end here? There had been no promises made, no word of later. But she hadn't asked, and didn't know how she'd feel when she saw him again.

Shyly, she let Cade pin her hair up, his hands as sure and efficient as a ladies' maid's as he slid the Spanish combs through the thick blond tresses. Gazing at her with a critical eye in the faint sheen of moonlight spilling into the gazebo through the latticed roof, Cade saw that her eyes were hazy and replete, her mouth swollen and bruised from his kisses.

"One good look at you in the light, and they'll know what you've been doing," he said grimly. His hand reached out to lightly touch a soft mark on her neck, and he gave a sigh. "You'll have to go home, and that's all there is to it. Do you want me to call you a carriage?"

Stricken, suddenly afraid of public censure, and feeling like a hypocrite, Laurie nodded. "Yes, and please — if you would tell Concha that I became ill and you called it for me, perhaps no one will worry unduly."

"If Carlota discovers it was me who called a carriage for you, she'll know everything," Cade said with a lift of his brow. "She's no idiot, and she's known me since I was a boy."

A little sharply, Laurie said, "I take it this is something you do frequently, then!"

White teeth flashed as Cade laughed. "Not necessarily. My reputation is not wholly deserved, you know."

"I'm not at all certain that is a comforting thing to know," Laurie muttered, feeling suddenly unendurably weary.

"I'll have a friend tell your cousin that you've been taken ill and gone home," Cade said then. "That should still any gossip."

She couldn't help but wonder, now that it was over and she was left with a tangle of lies to weave, if she should have yielded to the spurring desire she felt for him. It wasn't until she looked up at his handsome face again, at the sensual line of his mouth and the dark, glistening eyes, that Laurie knew she would do the same thing over again if given the choice.

"I'll call on you," Cade said when he handed her into a hired carriage and gave the driver Señora

Portolá's address. His hand briefly cradled her chin and he leaned forward to brush her mouth with his lips, then he stepped back and shut the door.

Laurie was to remember later that he had never mentioned love.

Chapter Eleven

"Are you certain you're all right?" Concha asked for what must have been the tenth time in as many minutes. She gazed at Laurie with her dark head tilted to one side, a frown creasing her pretty face.

"I'm fine. I think I just grew overhot from all the dancing, and the wine and brandy made me feel nauseated. That's all," Laurie said with a forced smile.

"Oh." Concha was quiet, then shrugged and said, "I did not know what to think when Consuela came to tell me that she had called you a carriage. I've never liked her very much, you know." She leaned forward, her voice dropping slightly. "She has a *reputation* for being a bit loose!"

Laurie found it hard not to react, but she was silently damning Cade Caldwell for enlisting the aid of a woman he had obviously been intimate with. Her fingers closed convulsively over the coverlet across her lap, and she felt truly ill for a moment.

"And Tia Carlota was almost beside herself with worry," the girl went on without noticing how still and pale Laurie had gotten. "Nothing would do but that we come home immediately and make certain you were all right." Yawning, Concha did not seem to bear any ill will toward Laurie for having shortened her evening. Instead, she seemed to be more than satisfied with the fiesta. "There will be many callers today," she remarked slyly, and Laurie found to her dismay that Concha was right.

Fortunately, she could dismiss the callers who came to see her with a plea of illness, but the one caller she hoped to see did not come. There was no note, nor a gift or message from him. She didn't know quite what she had expected, but Laurie realized that she had expected some sort of acknowledgment from Cade.

"The French viscomte was quite distressed that he could not see you," Concha said late that night when she came to bed. "He was still worried that you had left so early last night."

Laurie gazed sullenly at the huge bouquet of flowers at the side of her bed, one of several that had been brought to her that day. Why this preoccupation with flowers? she wondered irritably, and thought of the single blossom that Cade had tucked into her bodice. She still had it, but did not remember picking it up. It was wilted now, brown around the edges and limp, but she'd carefully pressed it between the pages of a book. It was the only flower that meant anything to her, but the man who had casually given it to her and taken her virginity did not come to visit.

Nor did he come the next day, nor the next, and Laurie began to feel the cold chill of rejection. She forced herself not to think of him, not to leap with anticipation each time a caller was announced, but she couldn't help it at night when she lay alone in her bed and gazed at the ceiling. Hot tears burned her eyes, and she would blink them away and bury her face in her pillow.

It was becoming more and more obvious that she'd meant nothing more than another conquest to him. How foolish and vain she had been to think otherwise!

Laurie was so subdued in the three days following the fiesta that Carlota became convinced she was ill, and announced their immediate departure from Los Angeles.

"We must return home, where she can rest," her worried stepmother said, and no one argued. They had all seen the faint circles beneath Laurie's eyes, the pinched look to her face and the dreamlike state she was in.

But the announcement had the affect of rejuvenating Laurie, and she resisted.

"No, I'm much better," she said firmly, suddenly realizing that she did not want Cade to think his defection had upset her. "In fact, I'm looking forward to the fiesta at the Santana hacienda this evening!"

Carefully, deliberately, Laurie put any thought of Cade Caldwell to the back of her mind. She would not allow herself to think of him, to remember his kisses in the dark or the intimate way in which his hands roamed her body. She would not think of how foolish she'd been, and how she had thought he might want to marry her. He was married to another, she remembered belatedly, and though he could have at least said he loved her and promised to get a divorce, he had not. But she didn't care. Marriage was for other women, anyway. Hadn't she always said that she would never be a man's possession, owned by him as surely as he owned a horse? Of course, she had, and even when her girlfriends had laughed at her saying she would be the first to marry, she had thought not. Well, she had seen them all wed before she'd left Europe, and now she was here in California and unwed and didn't care. It was more fun flirting with a man, seeing him stumble over his words and beg for a kiss, or fetch her a glass of something cool to drink. Yes, that was decidedly preferable to dancing attendance on him, fearing his cross words and trembling at his anger.

So Laurie went to the Santana fiesta and flirted with every man there, and they all threw themselves at her feet and declared her the most beautiful woman there. Even Concha, who had not considered her a serious rival, began to grow a little concerned at her cousin's flirtations.

"Juana Lopez is very angry with you for flirting so with her *novio*," Concha whispered into Laurie's ear at one point. "He has not left your side all evening, and she is glaring so at you!"

Laurie shrugged. "If she can't keep his interest, it's certainly not my fault," was her cold reply, and Concha stared at her for a long moment.

"Something has happened to you," the girl said softly. "I think, perhaps you are still ill and do not know it. You are not the same person you were just a few days ago."

No, I'm certainly not, Laurie thought with a pang, then shrugged it away.

"I don't know what you mean."

"I'm not certain what I mean, either," Concha said with the same worried frown on her face. "I only know that you are different."

By then the young man who had gone to fetch her a glass of chilled punch had returned, and Laurie bent her attention on him, laughing gaily at his witticisms and speculations about the other young men who crowded around her. He was amusing and made her laugh, and it did not matter that he was affianced to another. She had no intentions of allowing matters to progress far anyway, and if she'd cared enough, she would have told Juana Lopez not to worry about it. But she didn't care enough. Every time she allowed herself to think, she thought about things that hurt, so she concentrated only on gaiety and exciting distractions.

And always she was aware of Cade Caldwell, who had come into the vast ballroom and stood there watching her for a long time. Each time she glanced his way he was looking at her with his flat, dark eyes, his eyebrow lifted in that mocking way she hated, and a small smile on his lips—lips that she too vividly recalled kissing her intimately.

He did not approach her, but instead lounged against a wall and made polite replies to the questions from those around him. Several young women cast their eyes in his direction, giggling behind fans or the sweep of a lace mantilla that half covered their faces, but Cade ignored them. He was in no mood for light flirtations; he'd never enjoyed them.

Now, seeing Laurie again, he was filled with a restless hunger that made him wish he'd never met her. He'd tried to ignore her in the past days, knowing that he should never have taken her to the gazebo, should never have yielded to the desire he'd felt for her, but he had. And after that night, he'd known that he could not endanger her reputation any more than he already had. After all, everyone knew that he was married, even if his bride was two thousand miles away and he hadn't seen her since his wedding night. His attention could only hurt Laurie, and Cade had realized that he liked her too much to do that. She was strong-willed and stubborn, and though he hadn't given her any illusions about his intentions, he could not give her any hope that there might be more one day. So he'd decided that the kindest thing was to end it at once. A quick severing of the relationship and it was over with a minimum of pain and suffering.

Yet as he watched Laurie bend low to whisper something in one of her suitors' ears, her pale blond hair shimmering in the candlelight and her curves alluring and provocative, he felt a harsh surge of desire that he couldn't deny, and he damned her for it.

And he damned her even more when they were thrown together in a reel, and the other dancers seemed to fade into oblivion as he looked down at her with his narrowed dark gaze and saw her face flush angrily.

Laurie tried to ignore the rapid thudding of her heart, and the disquieting feeling his touch gave her as he took her hand in the progress of the dance. She looked away, unwilling to meet his dark, amused gaze, unwilling for him to perhaps see the raw pain that she still felt at his rejection.

How dared he act as if nothing had happened? As if they had not performed the most intimate of acts together? And how dared he not throw himself at her feet and demand that she never leave his side. . . .

"Why, Señor Caldwell!" she said with a tiny little pout that she hoped showed him how little she cared for him, "I do believe that I haven't seen you in a while."

Cade's eyes crinkled slightly at the corners, and his mouth twisted. "No, you haven't," he agreed, deftly spinning her around with one hand at her waist and the other holding her hand.

Laurie's long-lashed eyelids lowered briefly before lifting again, and she saw in his face the amusement at her trick. It did not endear him to her, that he knew what she was doing.

"I thought perhaps you'd left Los Angeles," she said when he met her again in the forward movement of the dance.

"Really?" Cade's smile was as noncommittal as his

158

reply, and she stiffened.

"Yes, but perhaps someone told me that. I really don't recall, because I've been so busy lately."

"So I see," he said, and there was a note of suppressed anger in his voice that startled her. Did he care if she was surrounded by adoring men? Perhaps he did; perhaps his apparent indifference was not real, and the thought made her claws sharpen.

A small laugh filled the close space between them as they stepped forward again, hands joined and lifted. "Yes, I don't know when I've met so many fascinating and exciting people! Why, my bedchamber is simply filled to overflowing with bouquets of flowers and gifts!"

Cade's grip on her hands tightened briefly, and his voice was soft. "It's amazing how little it takes to purchase a woman these days," he drawled. "A few flowers, a cheap trinket, and she's yours. . . ."

Laurie gasped with outrage, and her eyes sparkled with fury as she snatched away her hands. "You could never have enough money to buy me!" she spat, blithely ignoring the fact that he had not given her anything but had taken her virginity in a secluded gazebo without even a promise.

"Then it's fortunate you gave yourself so freely," he mocked her, and Laurie might have flung herself at him in a rage if not for the end of the music and the dance. She could feel interested gazes flick in their direction, and knew that Carlota must be half faint with dismay, so she put on a smile and forced a laugh.

Her voice was low and soft so that only he could hear, and she kept the smile on her face so that no one would know what she was saying. "You are a rude, arrogant savage, Cade Caldwell, and I promise you that you'll pay for that remark one day!"

Bowing low over her hand with a courtesy that

matched hers, Cade said against her wrist, "I await your vengeance with a hopeful heart, Señorita!"

His mockery made her snatch her hand away, and she turned on her heel and stalked from the dance floor. Cade watched her go with a smile pressing at the corners of his mouth, but his eyes were cold and filled with anger. She was a hateful little cat, a wanton, and damn him—he had only opened the door for her with his little performance in the gazebo. She'd been ripe to fall, and he had been foolish enough to oblige her, just as he had Cecelia so long ago. It only went to prove, Cade thought cynically, that though a man might think he had learned his lesson, he didn't always do so.

No one noticed that evening how brittle Laurie's laughter had grown, or how forced were her smiles and witty remarks that had those around her laughing. And of course, no one could see the raw pain inside her that she hid so well.

Chapter Twelve

Even after returning to Higuera, Laurie was filled with pain and an anger that threatened to erupt at the least little inconvenience. She was moody, and often found Carlota or her father gazing at her with puzzled expressions. Well, she couldn't tell them what was wrong and so they would just have to wonder about it, Laurie thought with a flash of irritation at having to think about their reactions.

She was too caught up in her own misery to think about them, or about anything but the long, boring days and tedious nights that stretched endlessly before her.

"I want to go back to New Orleans," she told Phillip Allen abruptly one night, startling him into silence. "I'm not happy here."

She stood stiffly, her arms folded across her chest, avoiding his hurt gaze. It didn't matter if he didn't understand. She could no longer remain in the same town with Cade Caldwell, and there was no way she could say that to her father.

"New Orleans?" Phillip finally echoed in a slow voice that betrayed his bewilderment. "But I thought you were happy here, Laurie, and that you and Carlota — well, that you were friends."

"Oh, it has nothing to do with Carlota, or with

161

you, Papa. It has to do with me, and how I feel inside."

Looking at her, Phillip could not deny that his only child was unhappy, so he sighed and said he would think about it.

"But perhaps you could try a little harder to adjust, Laurie?" he ended so hopefully that she nodded.

She'd try, but the restlessness inside her was constant now, and nothing seemed to ease it. How could she be happy here, where every place seemed to hold a memory of Cade? It seemed as if she'd see him everywhere, the memory of him lounging gracefully at her table that day he'd come to call and make amends for his mistaken kiss; the hillside where she and Cade had exchanged barbed comments about courage in front of a bewildered Paul Anderson; and the mercado where she had seen him the day she'd discovered the trap the alcalde had set for El Vengador. And when she closed her eyes at night and tried to sleep, she'd seen his handsome face just above hers, his dark eyes glittering with passion and his mouth awakening her own slumbering desires.

And there was another problem. Now, at night, instead of lying in her solitary bed and wondering what it would be like to make love with a man, she would remember his touch and the feel of him, the searing closeness of his body and the aching need inside her. It was disconcerting; it was maddening; it was heartbreaking.

Finally, more from desperate boredom and to escape her inner turmoil than anything else, Laurie decided that El Vengador should have one last coup before fading into oblivion. It would be so easy now. In the past month of no robberies or sign of the masked rider, Don Luis and his soldiers had grown secure and lax again. It was almost as if it had never happened, as if the masked swordsman had not ever come riding into the mercado and stolen the tax monies.

"We frightened him away that last time," José Garcia boasted to her, his swaggering bravado grating on Laurie's nerves and making her want to tell him the truth. "He saw how fierce we were, how prepared, and decided that nothing was worth his life. It is just as well, for I fear Don Luis would soon have begun executing every peon in sight in retaliation."

Laurie looked at him in the glow of the patio lanterns, where they sat on the cool terrace with a forbidding dueña nearby. Since her prolonged disappearance at the Ramirez fiesta, Carlota had insisted that Laurie be constantly chaperoned.

"Doesn't it strike you a bit harsh that the alcalde should be so drastic?" Laurie asked José and he looked at her in surprise.

"But how else would he ever keep his tax monies safe?"

"By not overtaxing the peons!" Laurie snapped. "Did His Excellency ever stop to think that if he was as generous as his predecessors, he might get even more work out of the campesinos who till his fields and work his vineyards? But instead, he works them into exhaustion, then demands the meager sums they have to live on, and wonders why they are sullen, and grateful for a champion!"

"You sound as if you admire this El Vengador," José said stiffly, and Laurie made an exasperated sound.

"And you sound like a fool," she said, ignoring the social edicts she had been taught since childhood. No matter one's true opinion, it was ill-bred as well as impolite to insult a guest, and she had crossed that line so unmistakably that José was stunned and her dueña was aghast with horror.

Tilting her chin stubbornly, Laurie refused to re-

163

tract her words or try to make amends. She was tired of José Garcia and his constant attempts to brush a hand across her breast and pretend it was innocent. Or his efforts to kiss her when the dueña was not looking, quick, wet kisses that left her cold and wishing he would leave. And when he sat close beside her as he was now, he would try to press his leg against her thigh, though what he thought he might feel through her yards of skirt and hoop petticoats Laurie could not imagine.

"I see that I have offended you in some manner," José was saying so stiltedly that Laurie felt a slight pang of penitence. She slid her dueña a half-guilty glance in spite of the rebellion she felt. Why must she always say what she didn't mean, just to be polite? How much easier it would be to just say *José, you are boring me to tears and I wish you would go away!* In Europe it was easier to say what one felt, though of course, it still had to be couched in polite terms. But there was none of the pretense that she'd found here, none of the insistence upon effusive flattery or false modesty that she found so irritating.

But she wasn't in Europe any longer, and as she knew that Carlota would be exceedingly upset when the dueña reported her rudeness, Laurie stifled a sigh and said in the most apologetic tone she could manage, "I'm sorry if I have given you that impression, Capitán. There are times I speak out of turn, and do not choose my words very carefully."

Thawing slightly, Captain Garcia gave her a cold nod, and took up one of her hands in his. Laurie resisted the urge to yank it away, and wondered irritably why her dueña just sat there like a lump of clay. Couldn't the woman at least remind him of her presence?

"Would you ride with me tomorrow?" Garcia was asking, and because she couldn't think of a good reason to stall him, Laurie heard herself agree.

"But only for a little while," she added. "I haven't been well lately."

Captain Garcia pressed his wet lips against her hand and Laurie shuddered. He obviously mistook her shudder for passion, for he smiled up at her, one finger stroking his mustache as he murmured huskily, "I can hardly wait to be alone with you, too, *mi corazón*."

There was the muffled scraping of boots against the stone floor, followed by a slight cough, and Laurie was saved from answering as she looked up to see who had joined them. Her relieved smile froze in place when she saw Cade Caldwell, his dark eyes alight with mockery and some other, stronger emotion she couldn't recognize.

"Am I interrupting an intimate moment?" Cade asked so smoothly no one would have guessed at the fierce rage inside him. Against his better judgment, he had finally yielded to the desire to see Laurie again, and had found her practically in the captain's lap! And Garcia looked so smug Cade was coldly certain there was much more between them than met the eye.

"Yes, you are," Garcia said as he rose to face Cade, and Laurie's first brief joy at seeing Cade quickly faded in the face of his mockery.

"Ah, a thousand pardons! I would not deny a starving man his satisfaction," Cade said with an enigmatic smile, then bowed briefly before adding, "I only came by to inform Señora Allen that my grandfather wishes to present her with a cask of his finest wine, a gift for her generosity with the loan of her peons to help in its harvest last year."

"So you're now your *abielo*'s messenger boy?" Garcia asked with a smirk, and Cade's amused eyes raked over him with an assessing glance.

"Better a messenger boy for my *abielo* than a murderer for the alcalde," Cade replied, and Garcia tensed.

"One day you will go too far, Señor Caldwell, and I will test you with my sword!"

"I long for that day to come," was Cade's smooth reply. "It would be my pleasure to rid the world of another fool."

"Gentlemen, please!" Laurie interrupted as the two men glared at one another with hostility so thick she could almost feel its weight. Cade's hand brushed the hilt of the sword he wore, and Captain Garcia was toying with the hilt of his as if he meant to draw it at any moment. Laurie shuddered at the idea of the two men dueling on Carlota's patio, and she knew her stepmother would faint with horror. "If you must quarrel," Laurie said with an edge of desperation in her voice, "please leave this house! I will not have it on my doorstep!"

Cade's eyes flicked in her direction. "As I am the intruder, I will leave." He bowed stiffly. "Please give Señora Allen my grandfather's message. Until we meet again, Capitán," he said, then pivoted on his boot heel and stalked from the patio.

Afterward, Laurie could barely recall Garcia's brief farewell or his departure. For some reason her eyes felt hot and heavy and her throat ached as she stared at the door through which Cade had gone.

It was the following day before a servant found the wilted bouquet of flowers that Cade had tossed into the cactus plants outside the house.

Laurie took to her bed in the week after she returned from Los Angeles, and once more Serita brought her that horrid potion to ease her comfort.

"It's wretched," Laurie muttered, making a face at the maid and feeling a vague disappointment that she didn't understand. Perhaps it was because she'd harbored an unconscious hope that she still carried a part of Cade within her, but in the next instant she was glad and relieved that she did not. That would have been the ruin of her, and her family would have been too shamed to remain in Higuera. No, it was much better this way, and she knew it.

When she felt better, Laurie stealthily gathered the black cape, hood, and mask and stole out into the dark to saddle the black stallion she favored. She had told Carlota that she was still unwell, and so she earned a night of privacy from prying eyes. Everyone thought she was asleep under the influence of Serita's potion.

Captain Garcia had divulged more information, telling her about a payroll delivery that was to be that night. This time, Laurie thought grimly, she would steal enough back from the alcalde to last the poor peons for a long time! Don Luis still did not know that the church was pouring his money back into the pockets of those from whom he'd stolen it. He only suspected its return, but did not know how it was being done. According to José Garcia, Don Luis wasn't certain if the hacendados were helping the peons, or if the peons were behind the thefts. And now that El Vengador seemed to have disappeared into the oblivion from which he'd come, the alcalde was harsher than ever.

Laurie saw what Cade had meant when he'd said she was not really helping, for she could not keep up the thefts forever. Somehow, the impractical, romantic side of her had wanted the wicked alcalde to resign his post for fear of El Vengador, but that had not happened. This last theft was a final tweaking of his nose that she hoped would make him wary in the future, but that was all.

Rather ruefully, Laurie realized that she had not become at all like the hero of a novel she'd read in

England, about an English yeoman by the name of Robin Hood. It was far easier to read such wild tales than it was to reenact them, she decided as she walked her horse out of the stableyard that dark, moonless night.

Once more garbed in her disguise, Laurie waited on the road leading into Higuera. She had laid a trap for the wagon by dragging a fallen tree onto the road. When they stopped to remove it, she would surprise them. Surprise was the main key to her success, and without it, she doubted she could have accomplished such daring raids so many times. Surprise and the supersitition of the peons, who had begun to regard El Vengador as a phantom instead of a real figure, were important. Only Don Luis still regarded El Vengador as a very real menace.

Sitting astride her stallion, Laurie loosened her sword wrist by flexing it several times, her blade swishing through the air. Never in her wildest dreams had she imagined that she would one day actually use that sword against men, and she still recalled her first time, when she had knocked a soldier's sword from his hand to send it spinning into the dust. It had given her a sense of power, a sense of omnipotence to defeat a man. All the years of living in a man's world, where women were considered lesser beings and often only as brood mares, had culminated in a fierce surge of joy at that moment, a joy Laurie could not have envisioned.

Her early ideas of philanthropy had somehow melded into an overpowering desire to defeat Don Luis, and she had let her vanity rule instead of her mind. If she had not met Cade Caldwell that night and he had not shown her that she could still be defeated, she might have been caught, for she had become too reckless.

She reminded herself of that as she waited in the

night for the payroll wagon from Mexico. She would be cautious, and not take too many chances.

The stallion's hooves were muffled against a cushion of pine needles, and he blew softly, his nostrils widening and his ears pricking forward as he listened. Laurie drew her mask down and made certain her hair was tucked beneath the concealing hood, and felt a tightening of her stomach. She drew in a deep, steadying breath to calm her nerves, as she always did.

Once the action began, she would think only of reacting instead of possible failure, and that was what kept her from making too many mistakes.

But this night, she must not have succeeded, for she made a fatal mistake. She waited just a shade too long, and the escort with the wagon had almost succeeded in removing the tree when she rode down the slope and crashed from the thick trees, her sword flashing as she quickly disposed of a half-drawn rapier. Wheeling her horse, she deftly caught the man's sword just beneath the hilt with the tip of her blade and sent it flying into the air, then pivoted to parry another thrust. Several more men swarmed toward her, and Laurie realized with a sense of rising panic that these men were no clumsy peons who had been drafted into the alcalde's service. These were true swordsmen, and she was in trouble.

"El Vengador!" someone cried hoarsely, and that seemed to galvanize them all into action.

Turning, slicing, thrusting, parrying, Laurie barely managed to hack a path through the men toward the wagon, where she had just enough time to scoop up a single bag of silver before fleeing. The soldiers were right behind her, and she fled through the night with her cape billowing out, wishing she knew the land as well as Cade Caldwell. He had known every bend and twist in the road, every rocky ridge, but she did not.

The stallion pounded down the road with the soldiers in hot pursuit. Laurie's heartbeat almost matched the frantic pace of the hoofbeats, and she could feel her muscles tense with fear as the distance began to close between her and the Mexican soldiers. Leaning over the horse's neck, feeling the whip of the wind against her mask and the snap of it through her long cape, Laurie searched the road ahead for possible escape. If she could just get out of sight, perhaps she could detour, double back, then flee without being seen. But she was losing the advantage fast, and she knew it.

What if she was forced into a corner and she had to kill a man to survive? she wondered then, and had the sudden thought that she could not do it. Dueling was one thing; killing was quite another. She could expertly cross blades with a man, even draw blood, but to deliberately kill was beyond her ken.

When a sudden clearing opened just off the road ahead of her, Laurie took it without thinking twice, reining the stallion down the road at a breakneck pace. She hoped she did not stumble across a barrier, for the horse was going so fast she would be killed if he went down. As she sped down the road, Laurie realized it was vaguely familiar, then realized that she had ridden onto Don Benito's land.

She felt a surge of triumph, for she knew her way home now, knew how to get back through the hills without going near the road again, and if she could just manage to avoid being seen for only a few hundred yards, she would escape.

When a horseman bolted in front of her, reining his mount to a halt so quickly that the animal half-reared, Laurie thought that all was lost. Then she recognized Cade Caldwell in the dim, moonless night, and half-sobbed, "Oh, help me! Soldiers . . ."

"Perdición!" Cade swore roughly. "I thought as much. It was too tempting for you to listen to anyone, wasn't it?"

"Oh, please! Not now! They're right behind me, and . . ."

"And you want me to help you escape," Cade finished harshly.

"Yes!"

She sawed at her stallion's reins, and saw the flare of his nostrils as he bellowed at Cade's stallion. With a shock, Laurie saw that Cade was also riding a black horse. It was growing more difficult for her to handle her horse, as he was strong and the other stallion was so close. Cade, she noticed distractedly, was not having the same kind of trouble, but was easily controlling his mount.

"They're right behind me," she began again as she fought her headstrong mount, and Cade cut her off.

"Follow me. And don't talk, just concentrate on keeping that crazy horse from throwing you!"

Smarting from his sarcasm and contempt, she bit her tongue and followed him, letting her stallion race neck and neck with his over the hills.

"Take that goddamned cape off!" Cade shouted over the thunder of hoofbeats. "Throw it away!"

Struggling to stay on, she managed to untie her cape and peel off her hood and mask, and tossed them aside as they streaked over the rolling hills of the Alvarez ranchero. She could hear the shouts of their pursuers, and knew that at any moment they could be caught.

When she heard Cade's soft curse, she realized that they were in grave danger, and her head whipped up as she clawed at the loose blond hair in her eyes. Just ahead waited a band of soldiers, blocking the ravine down which they were riding. Cade slowed his mount to a gallop, then a trot, and a walk, and she did the same, her heart pounding and her mouth dry.

Would she be shot, perhaps, like the poor peon who had cheated on his taxes? Or would the alcalde be merciful and only imprison her for her crimes against him? Either option did not appeal to Laurie as she slowed her horse.

"When I give the word," Cade said softly, jerking her head around, "spur your horse through them. Don't stop for anything, and don't look back."

"But I can't leave you to . . ."

"Just do it!" he snapped out.

Laurie's hands tightened on the reins, and she saw the dim glitter of Cade's sword in his hand. Did he mean to fight them all? she wondered incredulously. It was insane! He would be killed before two minutes were up. These soldiers weren't the untrained peons from Higuera, but precision-trained soldiers from Mexico.

"Cade," she said softly, urgently, "these soldiers are from Mexico!"

He understood what she meant, and flicked her a wry glance. "Then we are both in trouble, chica. . . ."

It turned out to be an understatement.

After a brief, fierce battle, Cade was surrounded and dragged from his horse. Laurie couldn't see him for the men pressing close to her, grabbing at her stallion's bridle and trying to avoid the vicious blows she aimed at them with her booted feet.

Madre de Dios!" one of the soldiers muttered when her foot caught him on the cheek, and he snarled as he reached up to yank her down. He held her against him, her arms behind her, her breasts straining at the thin black material of her blouse. "I have caught me a ripe little pigeon this time, Miguel!" he shouted, and pulled Laurie into the fickle light from a torch.

Clouds scudded across the sickle moon overhead, and in the shadows, she could see the sudden interest in the soldiers' eyes as they saw the slender girl with full breasts and a wild tumble of gold hair.

Her heart lurched with fear, but Laurie said calmly, "I am an American, and the daughter of a diplomat. If you so much as harm one hair on my head, there will be severe reprisals."

America and Mexico enjoyed an uneasy truce at the moment in spite of the recent war with Texas, and the men hesitated. Cade, by now only half-conscious from repeated blows, could hear them discuss what to do with her.

Spitting blood from his mouth, he suggested they let them go.

"After all, we were only taking a night ride together, and you must know how that is."

"Then why did you run when we chased?" an officer demanded with a scornful laugh. "You are El Vengador!"

"Do I look like El Vengador? Am I wearing a cape and mask?" Cade countered.

There was a brief hesitation, then the same officer said in a cold voice, "If we look, I imagine we will find it somewhere back there."

Cade shrugged. "Maybe. What is certain is that my *abielo* is Don Benito Alvarez, and he is well known in Mexico City. If you do not believe me, you are free to ask anyone who lives in Higuera."

The soldier stirred uneasily, looking at Cade. Perhaps it was true. After all, though he spoke perfect English, he also spoke Castilian Spanish instead of the rough *mestizo* dialect. And he looked like a *criolla*, one of the aristocratic *gauchupines* who'd descended from Spanish ancestors and were inordinately proud of blood untainted by Indian or Mexican blood.

Cade might have convinced the Mexican soldiers to release them if not for the untimely arrival of Capitán José Garcia.

"Alto!" Garcia snapped as he rode his horse into the group. "Do not release that man! He has long been suspected of being El Vengador." Garcia's gaze shifted to Laurie, who stared up at him with wide gold eyes, her heavy hair spilling over her shoulders. His mouth thinned with anger, and he looked back at Cade. So that was the way it was. No wonder she was cold to him most of the time. She and the sneering grandson of Don Benito were lovers. Why hadn't he seen it before? And he, fool that he was, had patiently waited for her to fall into his arms!

Gesturing, Captain Garcia said, "Take the woman to her home, and I will personally escort this son of a pig to the alcalde."

"No!" Laurie shrieked, twisting away from the soldier who held her. "You don't understand! He is not El Vengador, and if you take him to the alcalde, he will be killed."

"Get her out of here," Garcia said without emotion, and the glance he gave Laurie was cold and final. "You were a fool to choose him over me, Señorita. Within two days, he will be little more than food for the dogs."

With that, Garcia reined his mount around and gestured for the soldiers to bring Cade, while Laurie was dragged protesting and screaming to her horse.

If she'd expected help from her father, she was doomed to disappointment. Phillip Allen, white-faced and furious, said very little when the soldiers politely informed him that his daughter had been in the company of the infamous El Vengador when he had been captured.

"Thank you," Phillip said, while Carlota gasped and looked from Phillip to Laurie's angry face. "I will see that she is more closely watched."

"Papa!" Laurie cried. "Listen to me! They have the wrong man, and they won't believe me when I tell them. . . ."

The officer laughed deprecatingly. "She has tried to tell us that she is El Vengador, Señor, so you can understand why we do not listen to her."

Phillip's gaze flicked to his daughter. "Yes, that is quite ridiculous, isn't it?"

Spreading his hands, the officer shrugged and said, "El Vengador outdueled some of our best swordsmen, so you can see how ridiculous we found it, too."

"But it was me!" Laurie raged, her eyes spitting fire as she glared at them. "Do you care to see another demonstration? Just give me your sword for a moment, and I will prove to you that I am El Vengador!"

"*Niña, niña,*" the soldier soothed in a patronizing tone that made Laurie want to kick him, "if I were to give you my sword, you might cut yourself. It is very sharp, eh?"

"But I tell you—"

"Laurette!" her father snapped out, and she jerked her head to look at him. "That is enough of this nonsense. Go to your room!"

"But . . ."

"Now!" he barked in a tone she had never heard him use, and Laurie stiffened, her chin lifting in defiant pride and her spine straightening. Turning on her heel, she stalked to her room, well aware of the Mexican officer's admiring gaze as she passed him in her snug-fitting trousers and blouse.

It was several minutes before Phillip came to her room, and she was waiting on him with her arms crossed over her chest and her eyes blazing.

"I don't want to hear anymore about your being El

Vengador," Phillip said as soon as he walked in. "It does not matter to me if you are."

"And what does that mean?" she demanded. "Does that mean you will allow an innocent man to be punished for my crimes?"

"I'm sorry about that," Phillip said. "But from what the officer tells me, he made his own choice."

"They know he's not . . ."

"No, they only know that there was one rider, then suddenly there was two. I think I'm intelligent enough to figure out the rest."

"You believe me, then." It was a statement, not a question, and Phillip shrugged.

"As I said, it does not matter to me if you are. No more will be said about it, do you understand?"

Staring at him in utter disbelief, Laurie did not realize her voice was wailing as she asked, "But why?"

"Because relations between the United States and Mexico would be strained if this were to be found out. It is a good thing for us that Cade Caldwell came to your aid. It averted an international incident."

"What? Do you mean, that you will allow him to be led to the slaughter like a lamb?"

"No, no, Laurie," Phillip said with an impatient shake of his head. "His grandfather is very powerful in Mexico! I have a great deal of confidence that Don Benito can arrange for Cade's release."

Uncertain, and wondering if her father could really know that, Laurie hesitated. He pressed his advantage at once. "Now, be a good girl and go to bed. We can talk about this more tomorrow."

"But Cade. . . ."

"Will be just fine for tonight. I will do what I can tomorrow, I promise."

When Phillip left her room, Laurie was stunned to

hear the metallic click of a key in her door. When she tried it, she found it to be locked. Leaning against it, she felt a strange premonition run through her. There was a lot her father wasn't telling her, and when she crossed her room to the patio outside and found a guard, she was certain of it.

Why would he lock her in, and put a guard outside her door? This was totally unexpected, and even considering that he was concerned about his diplomatic status and her actions reflecting on him and creating a serious incident, he did not have to lock her in her room. Why didn't he trust her?

Shivering, Laurie walked to her bed and sat on the edge of the mattress. She had to leave California as soon as possible. She would go mad here if she stayed, and suddenly nothing was the same. Tomorrow, after clearing Cade—though why she was so worried about him she didn't know—she would tell her father to send her back to New Orleans or Europe. That would settle any crisis she may have caused with her actions, perhaps, or at least mollify the alcalde.

She would go back to where she belonged, though at times she wondered if she truly belonged anywhere. She'd tasted freedom too liberally, and could not live in the strait-laced atmosphere of Spanish California, nor could she endure the boredom. Long, lazy days only stretched intolerably for her, and she detested needlework and the other things well-bred young girls were trained to do. She liked floating down the Seine in a boat, with a handsome young swain teasing her and the wind tugging at her hat. And she liked the rich, colorful streets of New Orleans, where even the smells were exciting.

Collapsing onto her bed, Laurie buried her face in her palms and thought that she had never been so unhappy until Cade Caldwll had come into her life.

He had ruined everything, with his wicked good looks and casual taking of her. She had once so naively thought that it would not matter, that the loss of her virginity was only a prelude to better things, but now she knew she'd been wrong. If given to the wrong man — as was so obviously the case — it only made one unhappy and miserable, and left her feeling used and despised.

There had been no whispered words of love, no feverish vows of eternal loyalty — nothing but, "You know that I want you."

Laurie cringed at the memory. She had fallen so easily! No wonder he'd not come back to her. He'd probably laughed at the silly, moonstruck girl who'd gazed at him with wide eyes full of romance and no logic.

Of all men to allow such liberties, she had chosen a man known for his rakish reputation, a man who had been forced to wed a girl in New Orleans, and for all she knew, a man who was still married to her.

And it didn't help to know that there was still that crafty, wheedling memory inside her, an imp that suggested she had enjoyed Cade Caldwell's kisses, missed his hands on her body and the sweet release he had given her.

But at least, the small, insistent voice whispered, he had come to her rescue that night. Didn't that mean something? Didn't that mean that perhaps he cared for her?

It was a long time before Laurie fell asleep.

Chapter Thirteen

Marched across the sun-seared courtyard and dragged up a series of wide-stone steps, Cade found himself shoved roughly into the dim corridors of the alcalde's sprawling quarters. He blinked to adjust his eyes to the rapid change from bright to dark and was thrust blindly down a hallway, his hands heavily manacled behind him.

A cold feeling of fate settled in his gut, and he had the cynically amused thought that he had brought this on himself with his gallant rescue of Laurie Allen. Why had he done it—he, who had prided himself on keeping a coolly detached regard for women? Yet he had gone charging into the midst of a fight that he had no interest in, just to save her lovely skin.

Maybe it was the memory of that lovely skin that had prompted his cavalier behavior, that lovely soft skin like the velvet furring of a rose petal, smelling just as sweet with the expensive perfume she wore; and her hair, the clouds of golden hair like strands of silk, tempting him to tangle his hands in it and kiss her soft, pouting mouth until she was breathless. Maybe it was those things that had made him forget his normal detachment and ride to her rescue.

And now? Now she was safely at her father's hacienda while he had languished in a damp cell in the *presidio* all night, his hands chained to a wall behind him and his ankles tethered by a brief length of heavy chain that allowed him to take only short steps.

The sharp jab of a rifle barrel in his back made Cade half-stumble and curse his guard.

"You are not so brave now that you are in chains, eh, El Vengador?" the guard mocked him, and Cade did not deign to reply. "The alcalde is eager to see you, so you must walk faster." Again the jab of the rifle in his back, and Cade felt a rise of fury that was useless.

When the guard swung open a door and shoved him into a spacious room, Cade could almost smell the triumph in his gesture. "El Vengador, Your Excellency!" he announced, and Cade saw the alcalde rise from behind his desk.

Cade was brought up short by the guard's tug on his chains, and halted in a heavy clink of metal just inside the door. He saw Don Luis rake him with a sardonic glance, and knew how he looked, with his torn, dirty clothing and the bruises and dried blood on his face.

"So," Don Luis said as he came out from behind the desk and gestured to the guard to bring Cade forward, "this is the infamous El Vengador who has so easily terrorized my *soldados* and stolen my money."

"*Your* money, Your Excellency?" Cade mocked. "Somehow, I thought it belonged to the peons from whom you stole. . . ."

The guard's rifle snapped into his back again, and Cade half-turned to stare at him with narrowed eyes.

"No, no, let him continue, Commandant Trujillo," Don Luis said with a slight smile curling his mouth. "I find myself interested in hearing why he is so sympathetic to the peons' plight."

Not bothering to deny that he was El Vengador—after all, no one would believe him—Cade shrugged.

"I'm more interested in why an official of Mexico would take money from his government and keep it for himself instead of—"

"Basta ya!" Don Luis snapped with a harsh glitter in his eyes. He dismissed the guard with a quick flip of one hand, and when the door had shut behind him, he asked, "Why do you think this, Señor Alvarez?"

Cade shrugged again, and his chains clinked. "I hear things."

"And you do not deny that you are El Vengador?"

"I didn't say that." Cade's eyes met the alcalde's, and he could see the quick flare in them.

"Ah yes, I had heard that there was a young woman with you, and she claimed to be the efficient swordsman who has bested my *soldados!*" Don Luis's lips twitched. "Did she think I would be more lenient on her than on you, perhaps? Or did you coax her into an admission to save yourself?"

"Why don't you ask the lady?"

"That has already been done, and she vows that she was forced by you to say those foolish things. Though she was quite tearful and exceedingly repentant, the fair Señorita Allen confessed the truth."

For some reason Cade believed him. Fine white lines pressed against the corners of his mouth as he remembered Laurie's vow to make him pay for insulting her. Would she go this far?

Then he knew she would, because Phillip Allen and his daughter were announced, and Laurie came into the alcalde's room with a wide kind of stare that she could not seem to focus on him. Cade listened to her stumbling replies to the alcalde's gentle, probing questions with growing contempt and fury—both directed at himself.

God, what a fool he was! Had she somehow known where he would be riding that night, or just taken advantage of his presence to focus the blame on him? Damn her gold eyes to hell! She couldn't even look at him! She just stood there holding to her father's arm as if the entire procedure upset her, her gaze constantly shifting.

And there he was, draped in chains and covered with blood and shame, and it was because of her. . . .

But Laurie couldn't really concentrate on what was being asked of her, or the tall, lean man who looked so achingly familiar except for the heavy chains he wore. Her head hurt, and her eyes refused to focus. She didn't know what was the matter with her, but ever since drinking the *cafe brulot* that Serita had brought her, she had been quite out of sorts. Like now, when she gazed around her and realized that she wasn't at home, but was someplace quite different, and then she fuzzily recalled a carriage ride through the streets and her father's comforting arm around her shoulders. His voice had been a constant drone in her ear, telling her this and that, but it was too hard to remember it now.

Was she on the steamer again? The floor kept rocking beneath her, rising in a swell before slowly falling again, like the motion of a ship at sea. Laurie clutched at her father's arm, and a soft whimper erupted from her lips as she realized he was nudging her.

Her gaze searched for and found the man who was asking her questions, and he seemed to be wanting her to agree with him.

"Yes," she whispered in a numb desperation, "yes!" *I will say anything if you will only let me lie down again . . .* Had she said that aloud? She didn't know, but she must have communicated her desires, because Phillip was pulling her with him and murmuring in her ear, telling her she had done just fine and he was sorry it had come to this, and they would be home very shortly and she could go to sleep and wake up feeling herself again.

"So now you see, Don Nicólas," Don Luis said when the door had closed behind Laurie and her father. "I knew you might be hesitant about a confession, so I took the liberty of having the good Señor Allen bring in his daughter so you could hear it for yourself."

182

"How thoughtful," Cade replied with a sardonic lift of his brow. "And now I'm supposed to fling myself at your feet and beg for mercy?"

Don Luis smiled. "Something like that, yes."

"And if I refuse?"

"It really won't make much of a difference, I'm afraid. The outcome will be the same."

"I see." Cade did see. The brief, murderous flicker in his eyes as Don Luis waited for a pleading confession with such certainty did not go unseen, and he had the slight satisfaction of seeing the alcalde shift uneasily.

Spreading his hands out to his sides and softening his voice to one of commiseration, the alcalde shrugged. "It is not a nice thing to discover the perfidy of women, is it, Don Nicólas?"

"I've been well acquainted with it for a long time," Cade replied in a toneless voice. "But there are times it still astonishes me."

"You must sign a confession," Don Luis said after a moment, "and things will go easier for you."

"You really mean, that as the grandson of a powerful hacendado with connections in Mexico City, I must sign a confession before you can have me shot," Cade drawled, and his faintly amused awareness infuriated Don Luis.

Straightening with a jerk, Don Luis snapped, "No! That is not so! As the alcalde I can deal with you as I see fit, but a confession might temper my judgment."

"You are asking the wrong person for a confession," Cade said then. "I am not El Vengador."

"Perhaps after a few days of lingering with my guard your memory will improve, Señor Caldwell," the alcalde said with a small, sinister smile, reverting to Cade's American name to let him know that his Spanish connections would not help him now. "Our accommodations are not, alas, always comfortable, and some of the guards can be quite unpleasant, I've

183

heard. But I'm certain you know that, and that you would not do anything to provoke them."

An ironic smile slanted his mouth as Cade stared at Don Luis. "Of course not, but I have the inescapable feeling that won't matter at all."

"You amaze me with your powers of perception," the alcalde said as he strode to the door and flung it open. "Garcia!"

When Captain Garcia arrived at the door, Cade knew he was in for much more than an unpleasant stay in the Higuera *Presidio*. The malicious glitter in the Mexican capitán's eyes spoke volumes.

"Take our prisoner back to his cell, Capitán Garcia," Don Luis said, "and treat him with great attention. When he wishes to sign a confession, I want to be notified at once."

"Of course, Your Excellency," Garcia said with a slight bow, and gave a jerk of his arm to two soldiers outside the door.

In the long days that followed, Cade discovered just how inventive the captain could be, and Garcia found that the *criolla* he so despised was unshakeably stubborn. He would not budge from his silent contempt, no matter the number of lashes he received, or how long he was left staked out in the blazing sun.

No, the damned, sneering bandit only looked at Garcia with unveiled contempt in his eyes, a contempt that cut as deeply as the lash he used against the prisoner's back. It reminded Garcia of all the slights he had suffered as the son of a poor *campesino,* the times he had watched with a driving hunger as the wealthy hacendados had spent more on one fiesta than twenty *campesinos* could earn in a year. He had vowed then to be among them one day, and when he rose above his station in life, slight enough though it was, he had treated the peons and *campesinos* with the same uncaring contempt. As captain of the alcalde's guards, José Garcia was a man to be feared, a man to command respect, and the fact that this arrogant *criolla* still regarded him with a mocking disdain drove him into a frenzy of retaliation.

"You will give the alcalde his signed confession or I will see every inch of skin stripped from your back!" Garcia snarled once, when Cade was almost unconscious from the captain's efforts to make him speak.

Sweat poured down his body and stung the raw cuts in his back as Cade lifted his head to gaze at Garcia. Though his eyes were glazed with pain, his voice was as contemptuous as always. "One day, *mi capitán,* you shall make the mistake of allowing yourself to be alone with me, and I will pin you to the wall with my blade. . . ."

His hoarse words made a shudder prance down Garcia's spine in spite of the blazing heat, and for a moment he felt the quick bite of fear before he remembered that Cade Caldwell was in heavy chains and could not possibly escape.

"You speak bravely for a dead man," Garcia said, and gave the signal to dismiss the weary man wielding the whip. "I will allow you to rest for now. Don Luis objects to my killing you yet, though if you prolong this too much, I am certain he will change his mind."

Cade didn't care what the captain said at the moment. He was concentrating on keeping his strength and determination, and when it faltered, he would conjure the image of Laurie as he had last seen her, her wild mane of heavy blond hair tumbling over her shoulders as if she had just risen from bed, her alluring curves covered in a demure gown from neck to ankles, and her wide golden gaze distracted and unfocused. Would she be at his execution? Probably, he decided in the next instant. She would want to ensure that her secret died with him.

Oddly enough, instead of being disheartened by her treachery, he found it strengthened him. He entertained visions of having Laurie in his hands, his fingers curled around her slender white throat as he slowly squeezed the life from her. Then her face would meld with that of Cecelia de Marchand's, and it would be as if he was killing them both.

Ah, the lovely CeCe and the beautiful Laurie — how they both must gloat!

Cade's hatred kept him alive during the six days that Captain Garcia tried to force a confession from him, and when the frustrated Mexican had to report to the alcalde that it could not be done without killing him, Don Luis ordered a mock trial, with the *corregidor,* or Spanish magistrate, sitting attendance.

"We must make an example of him!" he snarled, knowing that the peons had begun to regard El Vengador as a hero. "I cannot allow him to be canonized by them! Already they murmur that he is a savior, come to rescue them from the burden of taxes and work, dogs that they are!" The alcalde's voice was sneering, rough with hatred and scorn. "We will see how brave he is when he is faced with a *fusillade!*"

"Si, Your Excellency," Captain Garcia said, but had the private thought that death was infinitely preferable to the days just past. Somehow, he did not think Cade Caldwell would mind dying as much as he had minded the treachery of his woman. And she was his woman. Garcia knew that now, knew it from the swollen look of her eyes when he went to question her again, and the trapped, desperate glances she had given her father and the constant guard around her. Yes, Laurie Allen had been his woman, for a brief time at least. Garcia wondered with a detached curiosity if she would forget Caldwell in time, and then he would take her as he should have done, had he known she would be that easy. It galled him that Cade had known. . . .

"It is too bad I never had the opportunity to test your skill with my blade," the captain told Cade when he went to fetch him for the trial. "Now it is too late."

A faint smile curled Cade's mouth as he moved slowly and stiffly at Garcia's side. "Give me just a moment and a sword, and I will show you death, Capitán."

Garcia snorted. "You will show me your death, you mean! Do not feel hopeful because you are being given the courtesy of a trial. It is necessary, and that is all. It is only a formality before your death in front of a firing squad."

As if he didn't know! Cade managed a careless shrug in spite of the pain of the puckering scars across his back. His obvious indifference further galled the Mexican captain of the guard, and Cade knew it.

It helped him get through the mockery of a trial, the sight of Laurie with José Garcia at her side, attentive and whispering in her ear, her soft, almost inaudible replies to the questions posed her by the corregidor at the head of the council. It helped him erase the memory of his *abielo*'s face as he stood with autocratic stiffness and stated that he was ashamed of his grandson.

"I leave him at the mercy of the court," Don Benito said, and Cade could not help but feel a shock at the words. Always, he had counted on Don Benito's stiff-necked pride and family loyalty. In spite of their words at times, and his grandfather's disdain and contempt for his actions, he had always known Don Benito would never countenance an insult to the Alvarez family, would never allow his grandson to be judged without a fair trial by a higher court. Yet now he heard him relinquish him to the mercy of Don Luis, and Cade could hardly believe it.

It hit him with all the force of a hammer, and the shock showed in his face.

Don Benito could not look at his grandson, could not see the expression of disbelief in his eyes. If he did, he might weaken, and that would be the ruin of it all. There was not enough time to contact his connections in Mexico, and he had to rely on cunning and treachery to free Cade from the alcalde's grasp.

Following correct procedure, the alcalde had commissioned the minutes to be taken and would send them to the governor-general at the government seat. Small municipal matters were generally decided upon by the alcalde, but as this involved the theft of the payroll from Mexico City, not even the commandant had juridiction. And anyway, it was well known that the commandant was afraid of Don Luis, and would do whatever he was told.

Don Benito had already sent men to Mexico City in an effort to secure a referral to the Mexican courts, but that would take too long. So he had used his position and influence to bend the ear of the corregidor—who usually sat in the pocket of Don Luis—and hinted that grave results would attend the execution of Nicólas Alvarez if any corregidor were so foolish as to command it. Imprisonment now, that would be acceptable to the don, and he would not argue the verdict. But there had been no way to let his grandson know this, and an angry part of Don Benito thought that it was just as well. Let the foolish rogue suffer for a time! Perhaps that would temper his judgment the next time he was tempted to behave unwisely.

As for Laurie Allen, any fool could see that she was under sedation, and saying whatever she'd been told to say. It bothered him that her father would stoop to such a trick, but in a way Don Benito could understand. The sacrifice of his daughter's reputation as El Vengador's mistress was worth it if it avoided an international incident, as would surely happen should she be arrested for the crime. As a man who firmly believed in his duty, Phillip Allen would not hesitate to make that decision, and Don Benito could not blame him. Perhaps he would do the same.

But now his main concern was his foolish grandson. It had already been arranged, that when he was being

188

transported to a prison in Mexico, there would be a slight delay, until Don Nicólas Alvarez could be pardoned or acquitted by the Mexican government. It had been difficult to arrange, and even now Don Benito wasn't certain how successful he would be. After all, if the delay dragged out too long, his grandson would still need to spend a certain amount of time in prison before he could be released. There would be an unavoidable exile from California until the proper paperwork was executed, but when it was all over, Nicólas would be free. What point was there in having influence with men in high places if they could not be of use when needed? They were needed now, and Don Benito had no doubts that they would acquiesce to the requests of so old and valued a friend from the wealthy Alvarez family. Until then, he had to keep his grandson alive by whatever means possible.

Don Luis, however, was furious with the corregidor's judgment, and lost no time in telling him so.

"I wanted him used as an example!" the alcalde raged, his sword slashing about him so viciously that the corregidor trembled with fear. Candles toppled, guttered, and died as he sliced them in two, and the heavy draperies over the windows fluttered in mere ribbons of material.

"But Your Excellency," the corregidor squeaked, "if I were to sentence the son of a prominent hacendado to death without the benefit of a confession, it could endanger your position! Only think, what if Don Benito were to protest the decision to Mexico City? An investigation could turn up very unpleasant things. . . ."

He let his voice drift into silence, knowing Don Luis would understand what he meant.

Frustration filled the alcalde's voice as he said, "But I wanted the peons to see what happens to champions who flaunt my authority."

"They will know," the corregidor soothed him. "We will make an example of him, parade him through the streets in heavy chains so that they will see how death would be an easy end instead of the long languishing he will suffer."

Though he would have much preferred the satisfaction of seeing Cade Caldwell shot by a firing squad, Don Luis had to admit that the corregidor was right. A quick end to him would only martyr him to the credulous peons. No, a slow, living death would show the peons that El Vengador could not save himself, could not be the champion they had espoused so eagerly. At last a smile curled the alcalde's lips, and the corregidor breathed a sigh of relief.

Chapter Fourteen

The fog shrouding Laurie lifted slowly. For a week she had been feeling like she was in a strange sort of waking dream, only vaguely aware of what was happening around her. Images floated in and out of her consciousness like drifts of cloud. One particular image haunted her, the image of Cade, his dark eyes burning into her like firebrands, his mouth twisting with anger. Somehow, she knew he was angry with her but wasn't certain why. If only her head didn't ache so, and if she wasn't so sleepy all the time, and confused. Maybe then she would remember something that was prodding insistently at the back of her mind, a nagging feeling that she was supposed to do or say something important.

"Laurie," a voice said close behind her, and she looked up with a frown to see Carlota gazing at her. "Laurie, I brought you your supper. It's your favorite, the *arroz con pollo* that you like so well." Carlota hesitated, then said quickly, "And I brought your medicine, so that you can sleep."

From somewhere deep inside, Laurie gathered the conviction to say firmly, "No! I don't want anymore. I am sleeping too much, and I don't think. . . ." Her voice faded as her thoughts drifted, and she tried to remember what it was that made her not want the bitter-tasting medicine. For the first night after . . . after the

191

soldiers had brought her home, it had been a blessed relief, but now she dimly realized that it was keeping her from remembering things she had to remember.

"But you must drink it," Carlota was saying, and Laurie looked up at her with the clearest gaze she'd had in the past week.

"I will not drink it, and don't think you can put it in my food," she said strongly. She rose from the chair and strode to the doors of her courtyard. A desultory breeze filtered lazily in, and in the bright glitter of moonlight that shone on the stone tiles, she could see the guard. He was there, as always, and now she remembered why she was being kept a virtual prisoner. It came back slowly, in bits and pieces, like shards of a broken mirror, giving her a distorted reflection of what had happened.

Whirling so quickly that a sharp pain splintered through her head, Laurie looked at Carlota's face and saw that she knew.

"What did they do to him?" she demanded.

"To — him?"

"You know who I mean! Cade Caldwell — Nicólas Alvarez! What did they *do* to him?"

Carlota stared down at her laced hands, and she took a deep breath. "He was found guilty of being the infamous El Vengador and has been sent to a prison in Mexico."

Laurie's face whitened, and she had to grab the back of a tall chair for support. "And you let them?" she asked in such a distraught voice that quick tears stung Carlota's eyes.

"You know the situation, *niña* — what was I to do? And your papa, he was so worried that something would happen to you. . . ."

"You mean he was worried that his position would be jeopardized!" Laurie's voice whipped cruelly, and when she saw Carlota's faint wince she knew she'd come close to the truth. "So, in spite of knowing the truth, he allowed an innocent man to be condemned for another's crime! Am I to thank him for this?"

"No," Phillip Allen said from the doorway, and his tone was heavy. "But you must understand why I chose to do as I did, Laurie."

"I'll never understand!" She was close to angry tears, and held them back with an effort. The drugs in her system were still making her weak and vulnerable, and she fought against them. "Do you think I'm a coward who would quail at punishment for what I did? Do you think I would hide behind another?"

"That's not it at all." Phillip walked closer to her, his eyes beseeching her to understand. "I was entrusted with a job, and I took an oath to do my duty. It's part of my duty to avoid international incidents at all costs."

"Even the cost of your daughter?" Laurie shot back, and saw that her inference had struck its target.

"Even at the cost of my daughter," Phillip agreed in a quiet tone. "I had hoped for only the loss of your reputation when you were discovered with Caldwell, but it seems that you are determined to lose everything."

"It's a lot easier to face the condemnation in the faces of those around me than it will be to face myself in the mirror," Laurie replied. Her pale face with the dark circles under the eyes held more clarity than it had in some time, and Phillip knew that he had lost her.

"I'm sorry," he said, but it wasn't enough.

"I'm leaving California, Papa. I am going back to New Orleans, maybe to Paris, but I will not stay here another week."

Phillip nodded. He had expected as much. "I'll make the arrangements. . . ."

"I'll make my own, thank you." Laurie clung to the back of the tall chair with the desperation of a drowning victim, hoping he would leave before her strength gave out and she collapsed in a heap of hysteria on the floor. "Now, if you will be so good as to leave me to the privacy of my own thoughts, I would appreciate it."

When Phillip and Carlota had gone, shutting the door quietly behind them, Laurie made her way to her bed and sank to its welcoming surface. She shut her eyes tightly against the recurring vision of Cade's dark, condemning eyes. What must he think of her? Surely he realized that she had not known what she was saying, had not been aware of her surroundings. And Don Benito—what must he think?

A feeling of helpless panic strengthened, until Laurie thought she would go mad from it. Her hands knotted and unknotted in her lap, until they were red and chapped from the constant friction. What could she do? What could she say to Cade—if there was ever the opportunity? Was there *anyone* who could help him?

She rose from the bed and began pacing the floor, still twisting her hands together. When the answer came to her, it was so simple as to make her laugh aloud, and she had the brief thought that anyone seeing her would surely think she had gone mad. But the solution was so simple that she wondered why it had not occurred to her immediately—Don Benito would know how to help his grandson, even if he had to be persuaded to do it. She vaguely recalled his stiff posture in the courtroom, his unyielding anger with Cade. Was there a possibility he was not as angry as he'd seemed?

Early the next morning, Laurie had a mount saddled for a visit to the don. No one tried to stop her, and sometime during the night, her guard had gone. The reason for her imprisonment was over, for Cade had been taken away and now her reputation was in shreds. There was no longer even a reason for a dueña, as Laurie coldly pointed out to her stepmother, for no brazen mistress ever bothered with one. And she was the most famous mistress in the district since Cade's arrest and trial. Hadn't she been found in the arms of El Vengador? And hadn't she protested his arrest with the ridiculous claim of being the infamous bandit? Only a well-used woman would allow herself to be so degraded, so it was naturally assumed that El Vengador had enjoyed her favors.

Even José Garcia's slight restraint had vanished, and when he had come to visit Laurie his manner had been bold, and confident.

"Since your—*amante* has gone, Doña Laurie, I am sure that you will be lonely," Garcia had said so smugly she had cut him sharply.

"Do not think yourself worthy of replacing him!" Laurie lashed out, and Garcia's swarthy face had darkened with fury.

The visit had ended abruptly when Laurie had stormed from the room, but Garcia had promised in a voice that still haunted her that he would return for what was his.

What gives him a right? she'd wondered, then knew with a sick feeling that her liaison with Cade had made her a public whore. In this straitlaced social structure, her behavior had condemned her.

Fortunately, Don Benito did not condemn her, though he did say dryly, "I'm amazed that you had the courage to come here, Señorita Allen."

Laurie nodded stiffly, and her words were cool and to the point. "I want to right the wrong that has been done him."

Don Benito felt a growing respect for her. There were no words of remorse or denial, no whining about the misdeeds that had been visited upon her, but simply a short statement of fact. He looked at her for a long moment, then gestured to his servant.

"We will have wine on the patio, Pancho. Please see that Juana brings it."

Seated across from the don, Laurie waited for him to speak. Her nerves were taut, her hands clenched tightly together. There were still faint circles like bruises beneath her eyes, but Don Benito had the swift thought that he had never seen a more lovely woman. Her eyes were glowing like new-minted gold, and her soft mouth was thinned into a line of determination that impressed him. He smiled at her.

"It is not as bad as you may fear. I have influential friends, and when my stubborn grandson reaches Mexico City, he will be miraculously free."

There was a lot he didn't say, and Laurie sensed it. She was quiet for a moment, then asked, "And after his freedom, I assume that he will not be able to return home for a time?"

Don Benito nodded, and his wise old eyes smiled approval at her. She was no *idiota,* this one!

"That is true."

"Do you know where he will go?"

Tilting his head to one side, Don Benito asked in faint surprise, "Do you intend to find him, Señorita? I do not think that wise at this time. Nicólas is not — well, he is not aware of the duress under which you acted during his trial. I'm afraid he would not be glad to see you."

Laurie's chin lifted slightly. "I will convince him of my loyalty."

Tapping one toe against the stone tiles of the patio, Don Benito regarded her with an assessing gaze, then gave a brief nod of his head. "My grandson is very fortunate to have your loyalty, Doña Laurie. When you see him, give him my compliments."

For the first time, a genuine smile curved Laurie's mouth, reaching her eyes and making them glow. "I will do so, Don Benito. . . ."

Chapter Fifteen

But when Laurie reached Tijuana, where Cade was supposed to be delayed, she found to her dismay that nothing had gone as planned. Instead of a prolonged delay and eventual release, as Don Benito had carefully planned, it seemed that somehow, someone had engineered his escape.

Bruised soldiers, some with near-fatal wounds, had come back to the army post to tell how they had been set upon by heavily armed brigands. Several men had been killed, and in the chaos, the prisoner from Higuera had escaped.

Stunned, Laurie sat thinking of how much she had risked to go to him, and how that he would probably never know it now. The captain, a well-bred officer of Spanish descent and a gentleman, kindly offered to escort her to a room at an inn until she could return to Higuera.

"I know you are distressed at not being able to visit him in prison, Señora Alvarez," he said, for that was the name she'd given him. "But he will be caught soon. I fear that it will go badly with him, and he will not be allowed visitors for some time, but perhaps you can return in a few months."

Stifling the sharp words of frustration that dogged her tongue, Laurie merely nodded. "Gracias, Capitán.

I am certain that the family will be contacting you very soon."

"Ah, and you — his lovely wife — will be most sad until you see him again, is that not so?"

Laurie nodded stiffly. It had been Don Benito's idea that she masquerade as his wife, for her own protection and perhaps as a deterrent to Cade's anger when she finally saw him again.

Wearily, she wondered what she should do now. There had been a distasteful scene with her father when she'd left Higuera, and she had told him she would not be returning. Perhaps that was best. San Diego was a major seaport and the capital of Upper and Lower California, and it was only a few miles away. She would go there and wait until she could gain passage on a ship or steamer bound for New Orleans. It would be good to go home again, to see familiar faces and familiar places, and to laugh and not worry about whether anyone would disapprove. In New Orleans, no one would know that she had been named a wanton woman, a bandit's *puta*. And she still had an aunt there, Tante Annette, who had always loved her like she was her own. Yes, she would go home, go back to a civilized world instead of this raw, primitive land where people were so fickle.

Laurie waited in the capital city of San Diego for a ship bound for Panama, where she would be able to secure passage to New Orleans. It was there she met Paul Anderson again, the young American merchant who had been her escort for such a short time.

Half-embarrassed, she'd not been able to look directly at him when he approached her in the *sala* of the *posada* where she was lodging.

"What must you think of me now?" she murmured ruefully, and Anderson shrugged.

"That you are a very impetuous young woman," he said in a soft voice that made her look up at him.

Laurie stared into his bright blue eyes, and had the

thought that even Paul Anderson did not look at her with the same condemnation she'd seen in her own father's eyes. A soft ocean breeze blew in through the open windows of the inn, lifting wisps of hair at her temples, and she brushed them away as she said, "You are fond of understatement, I see."

He laughed. "Perhaps. Or perhaps I understand the emotion that might compel a young woman to behave as you did."

Staring at him warily, Laurie asked, "What do you mean?"

"Simply that you were either motivated by love, or by compassion. May I sit down?" He indicated the chair opposite her and Laurie nodded.

"So which reason do you think motivated me, Mister Anderson?"

"Can we go back to Paul again? It's easier, and more familiar."

Laurie's eyes darkened, and her voice was stiff. "If you think I am immoral now because of what happened in Higuera, I. . . ."

"No, that is not it at all," he hastened to say. "I only meant to put you at your ease."

Drumming her fingers against the cloth-covered table, Laurie finally nodded. "All right. I suppose I am very sensitive to every nuance now. There were some . . . comments made that have put me on my guard."

Looking earnestly into her eyes, Paul Anderson took her hand and said softly, "I am not here to judge you. I merely thought we might pass the time together while we wait for passage."

Some of her wariness eased, and she asked, "Where are you going, Paul?"

"San Francisco. My company is selling back California hides in the guise of shoes." He grinned. "Those cowhides have been twice around the Cape, and now they'll be sold back to the Californios for five times what they were sold for originally."

"Isn't it a lot of trouble for you to come this far for an American company?"

"Boston is a long way, but I'm making a lot of money." Paul hesitated, then said, "And I would never have met you if I had not come to California."

"That's hardly in your favor."

Paul smiled, and Laurie noticed for the first time that he had a nice smile. He was really a good-looking man, his fair skin lightly bronzed from the sun, his tall frame clad in expertly cut clothes. But he wasn't Cade; he did not have the power to make her heart race and her breath shorten, and she felt nothing when he let his fingers brush across her hand almost as if by accident. No, it would never do to renew their earlier friendship, for nothing could come of it now.

Regretfully, Laurie soon excused herself from Paul, pleading a headache, saying that perhaps she would walk out with him the next day.

"I don't know, really. So much has happened, and I'm so tired. I just want to go home." She managed a smile. "Do you understand?"

"Of course, I do. And I want you to rest, so if you do not feel like walking out tomorrow with me, I'll wait until you do." He paused, and took a deep breath, his words half-breathless as he added quickly, "I'll wait for you forever, if I have to, Miss Allen!"

Dismayed, she murmured something, she wasn't certain what later, and almost ran from him, fleeing to her small room and slamming the door. She leaned against it, staring up at the rough ceiling, wondering if she would ever get over Cade Caldwell.

In the following days she rebuffed every overture Paul Anderson made, until finally he reluctantly left San Diego to continue north along the coastline.

"But I'll never forget you, Miss Allen," he said so sincerely that Laurie let him kiss her good-bye.

She felt nothing but a vague impatience when he took her into his arms on the shaded patio outside the

200

posada, his lips gently pressing, against hers. As if sensing it, Paul smiled faintly, then kissed her on the forehead and left. And, inexplicably, Laurie cried when his ship sailed.

Though she remained secluded in her room at the *posada* most of the time, she found the waiting bearable. For some reason there was an element of sadness in leaving California, perhaps because that was where she had fallen in love with Cade Caldwell.

Yes, she admitted it to herself now, she was in love with him. Perhaps she'd been in love with him since that first night he had mistaken her for a *puta* and kissed her so thoroughly. There was something about him that intrigued her, though she would never have admitted it to him. Maybe it was easier to think about it now that she knew she would never see him again. After all, he had escaped, and would surely never return to Higuera. But at least he was alive. Laurie comforted herself with that thought, clung to it in the long hours between dusk and dawn when she longed to see him again, hear his soft, mocking laugh and feel the sweet press of his lips against hers.

Those were the hardest hours, and she wondered at times if he ever thought about her, if he knew that she had not deliberately betrayed him.

Laurie would not have been very gratified to know that though Cade did think of her—and often—it was not with a gentle longing. No, when he thought of her he damned her gold eyes to hell, and then wished he could be the one to personally escort her there.

"Why do you think of her at all, *querido?*" Linda Navarro pouted when Cade would stare into the empty air with a hot, narrowed gaze. "You know she is not worth it."

Slanting the alcalde's niece a smiling glance, Cade shrugged. "Perhaps I'm just wishing I had her slender white neck between my hands."

Linda scooted closer and looked up at him with

201

greedy eyes. "But you have me here, and much more than just my neck," she reminded.

As her dark eyes and sultry face moved in closer for a kiss, Cade obliged, thinking that of all the people to have engineered his escape, he would never have considered the alcalde's niece to be the one. But she had done it, and managed it so skillfully that no one suspected. Even now, when soldiers were beating the bushes near Tijuana looking for him, he was in San Diego, ensconced in a comfortable cottage with Linda that was perched on a hillock of white sand near the ocean. When the furor died down, he would secure passage on a ship and leave California. Linda begged to go with him, begged him to take her to Spain, but he knew he would not.

No, Cade had made up his mind to return to Texas, and to take part in the building of a new land. He'd explained that to Linda in the beginning, refusing to allow her any futile hopes, but still she held to a slender thread of hope that he would change his mind.

"You're a fool!" she'd raged once. "You think only of the woman who betrayed you!"

"Perhaps, but not in the way you mean," Cade had agreed, and his eyes were so dangerous that Linda had not dared say it again. He didn't want to admit that he could not make up his mind whether he hated Laurie or just wanted to forget her. There was a fine distinction there, and it was elusive. Cecelia, he had wanted to forget existed, had wanted to rub her memory from his mind as if a wet sponge on slate. But for some reason Laurie remained firmly imbedded in his memory.

Rising abruptly from his chair, Cade paced restlessly. He didn't want to think about her, didn't want to remember anything about her. But there were times, such as when a faint scent would invoke the memory of her perfume, or when he would glimpse a woman with clouds of silken blond hair, and he would suddenly think of Laurie. It would hit him with the swiftness and force of a hammer, and there would be a sick feeling in the pit of his stomach. Would he ever be able to erase her memory from his mind? Would he ever see her again, and if he did, would he kill her before or after he'd made love to her. . . .

Then one lazy afternoon when Linda was napping and he was bored and restless again, Cade ignored the danger of being recognized and strolled down to the *cantinas* on the waterfront. There he saw Laurie walking on the beach near the harbor, and all his indecision was gone in an instant. He knew as soon as he saw her what he would do.

It was late, and Laurie lay in the wide bed of her room that rose above the harbor, looking out the window at the moonlight on the water. Tiny glints of light danced in the slow slapping of waves against stone quays and wooden pilings lining the waterfront. Though it was a peaceful scene, and should have been soothing, she was restless. And she was hot, even though there was a cool breeze blowing in her open window, lifting the sheer fabric of the curtains in a soft billowing motion that reminded her of her walk earlier in the day.

A faint smile curved her mouth as she recalled how easily she had succumbed to the beauty of the lacy waves curling onto wet sand, the wind in her hair and the sun on her face. She had been so bored, so restless, and a walk along the seafront had eased her mood. The bright, burning blue of the ocean had assaulted senses she'd begun to think numb, and she hadn't even noticed when a capricious gust of wind had lifted the long mantilla she'd worn to hide her hair. In San Diego, blonde women were a rarity, and she had already had too many encounters to risk inviting more. That was why she'd worn the mantilla, but when the wind had tugged it from her head and sent it drifting on an air current,

203

she had tilted back her head and smiled blindly into the sun. For one short moment she was a child again, enjoying with the free pleasure of a child the whisk of wind and burn of sun, the sharp, salty tang of the ocean and the feel of the hot white sands beneath her feet. Even through the thin slippers she wore, she could feel the shifting heat of sand as pure white as virgin snow. Her skirts flapped around her legs, the wind outlining her form with pristine precision until she finally realized that she was being observed.

Snatching up her mantilla, Laurie had once more covered her head, ignoring the tall, shadowy form leaning on a stone seawall above and behind her. She had not wanted to talk to anyone, not wanted to allow any intrusion into her self-imposed exile, and so she had returned to the spartan, stark interior of her room to wait.

Now she lay tossing and turning, wondering when a ship would be able to take her away. The days had stretched from two into five, and the steamer she was to take still sat outside the harbor awaiting a berth. "Paperwork" the shipping agent had told her when she'd impatiently inquired about the delay, and she had seen the large number of vessels waiting to come in. She was growing eager to leave San Diego, leave California and her memories behind. It was a long time before she fell asleep that night.

Slept only to be awakened by a hand over her mouth and a harsh, angry voice in her ear.

Laurie's heart pounded furiously, and she could not breathe for the warm fingers pressing down over her nose and mouth so tightly, but what made her entire body freeze was the savage bite to the familiar voice.

"Enjoying your freedom, Señorita?"

Cade. How had he found her? What was he doing here? And would he listen to anything she had to say? Laurie tried to see him in the dim light, but the moon was behind him and his dark face was shadowed. There was only the hard inflection of his voice and the faint glitter of his eyes shining that warned her not to speak too quickly.

The mattress dipped with his weight as Cade bent a knee to the surface, his grip still tight, one hand curved behind her neck and the other still splayed over her face. She could almost feel his gaze raking her, and a high, hot flush compounded her misery as she realized how very little she wore in the sticky night air of San Diego.

Though he'd seen her without her clothes before, it was very different this time. This time he wasn't holding her softly and calling her *amor, amante, querida.* No, this time he was gazing at her with murderous eyes. She could feel it, and she shrank from him.

"Scared?" he mocked her. "You should be. It would be so easy for me to crush the life from you, you know, to put my hands around your small little neck just so. . . ." His hands shifted to curve around her throat, and Laurie could not utter a sound. "See? Maybe I will rid the world of you, so that you don't play any more of those little games you seem to favor. Did you think it amusing to see me accused of the crimes you'd committed, *pequeña?*"

His caressing voice did not fool her for a moment, nor did his use of an endearment. Cade was coldly, deadly furious, and to be fair, she couldn't blame him. But if he would only allow her to explain, to tell him that she hadn't betrayed him. . . .

"Cade," she tried to whisper through stiff lips, but her voice was constricted by his hands around her throat. A swift feeling of panic enveloped her, and Laurie opened her eyes wide as she arched against him. Did he really mean to kill her?

Cade was debating the question. He'd thought about it a lot while in the stinking prison cell, and again when Garcia was mocking him while trying to force a confession. Just the thought of having her here like this had been comforting, and now here she was. A tight smile curled Cade's mouth as he gazed down at her moonlit face, at the wide golden eyes and the look of terror in them, and the tumbled mane of hair that looked more silver than gold in the dim light. Oh yes, he'd dreamed of this moment, and hadn't been able to believe his good fortune in finding her in San Diego.

His hard gaze shifted from her frightened face to the barely visible curves beneath her thin nightdress. That had haunted him, too, the memory of her soft body beneath his, closing around him with the hot velvet press of passion. He had thought of it a lot, even when with Linda, and somehow she'd known it.

"You still want her!" the alcalde's niece had spat at him and he hadn't been able to deny it, nor had he bothered to. Why should he? It was normal enough to want a desirable woman, and Laurette Allen was certainly desirable.

Laurie, with her ripe beauty and golden hair; Laurie, with a rich promise in sultry, exotically-slanted eyes, and fulfillment in her sensual curves. Yes, he still wanted her and she knew it.

She felt his desire in the subtle altering of his hands on her, in the quick flare she could see in his dark eyes and the hardness of him against her. And she knew before he did that he would take her.

Laurie didn't struggle, didn't protest. She didn't care why he wanted her, only that he did. It was enough for now, enough after those weeks of longing for him, of wondering why he didn't come, and then his arrest and the realization that he might never hold her again. Later she'd worry about his motives; now she only wanted him as close to her as a man could get to a woman.

Without soft words or tender caresses, Cade shoved the hem of her nightdress up, uncovering himself and pressing against her without preliminaries. But instead of being too brutal or harsh, he was urgent, and his urgency transferred to Laurie. She arched to meet him when he thrust forward, a glad union of body and pent-up longings.

It was vastly different from the first time. Then there had been a slow build-up of desire in her, until he had given her release. There was no slow progress this time, but a rapid acceleration that ended in a searing explosion. Laurie cried out against him, and he muffled her cries with his mouth, a half-angry press of his lips against hers.

He spoke to her in French and Spanish, his breath tickling her ear as he muttered words that should have been curses but sounded more like endearments. Clinging to him, her fingers digging into the back of his shirt as she held tightly, Laurie tried to recall why she'd been afraid of him but couldn't. That didn't come until later, after he'd taken her again, when she'd surged to meet him with tight, eager thrusts of her body. Then, as they lay wearily in a tangle of damp sheets and arms and legs, she heard him say, "I should have killed you before this."

Pressing her face to his bare shoulder where the shirt had fallen away, Laurie closed her eyes. "Why didn't you?"

She felt him shrug. "I don't know. Maybe I wanted you one more time, first."

Inhaling deeply, Laurie managed to say in a calm voice, "Well, now it's over. What are you doing to do?"

"Maybe you don't know how fine a line you're walking, Laurie," he said tightly. His hands closed around her shoulders and pushed her away, and when she opened her eyes to look up at him, she saw the anger and bitterness in his face. His high, sharp cheekbones and the weight he'd lost in the past weeks made him look harsher, predatory, and she wondered if she was being foolish when she refused to yield to the silent voice that urged caution.

"As long as it's the same fine line you're on, I don't

care," she said so recklessly that she saw his surprise. "I don't care about anything right now, Cade."

"When did you ever care about anything but yourself?"

"You misunderstood. . . ."

"Oh no. I understand you much better now than I once did, though I have to admit that at least then you bothered to keep up appearances." His hands moved to bite into her shoulders again, his thumb dragging across the faint pink scar on her upper arm where his blade had scratched her. "I made the mistake of thinking you were intriguing because you were daring enough to put on a man's clothes and wield a rapier like a man," he said. "I thought maybe you cared about injustice, but now I know that you were only amusing yourself, and the peons didn't really matter."

"That's not true! I did—do—care about the peons, and what the alcalde is doing to them!" Laurie tried not to flinch from his harsh grip, and kept her gaze fastened on his shadowed face.

"I wish I could believe you."

"Believe me. I'm telling you the truth."

"The same truth you told the alcalde?" Cade mocked. "The same truth you told the corregidor at my trial? Oh, I would be a fool indeed if I believed you, Laurie Allen!"

His anger slapped her across the face, hurting her much more than the cruel fingers digging into her tender flesh. All the careful words she had rehearsed on her way to Tijuana fled her now, so that she could only look at him with a helpless kind of pleading that did nothing to alleviate his anger.

Slowly she lifted one hand to trace a soft pattern over his face, from his narrowed, hard eyes over the sharp jut of his cheekbones, to the tensed muscle in his jaw, her fingers light and caressing. He didn't move, didn't jerk away, but he didn't respond.

"Cade, I tried to find you," she began, and he gave a

quick shake of his head.

"Don't."

"It's true!"

"It doesn't matter," he said, and she saw in his face that it didn't. She could not soothe his anger or erase his bitterness with the truth, not now. Maybe later, when it wasn't still such a raw memory. Now, she used the only weapon she had that would have any affect on him — her body. She did it without a shred of remorse, simply rationalizing that he had to give her enough time to prove herself to him.

Tangling her fingers in his dark hair, she pulled his face to hers, ignoring the gleam of mockery in his eyes or his reluctant yielding. He didn't intend to make it easy for her, but she filed away the important fact that he didn't push her away, either.

Lightly at first, like the elusive touch of the wind, she kissed him, brushing her mouth over the straight line of his lips in a fleeting caress. When her kisses grew more bold, straying from the harsh thrust of his jaw over his neck and down to his chest, she could feel his muscles tense against her touch. She smiled into the mat of dark hair curling over his chest, and he felt that, too.

The pads of her fingers wandered up and along the strong sweep of bone, sinew, and muscle until they grazed the cleft in his chin, then her mouth followed in deliberate, provocative kisses designed to make his breath quicken.

"Do you really think this is going to work?" she heard Cade ask a few moments later as she lavished steamy kisses over him, and she didn't bother to reply. It was enough of an answer when he coiled an arm around her and jerked her up to meet his hard mouth.

Neither could deny the explosive passion that existed between them, the searing fire that consumed and scorched them, leaving their better intentions in ashes. And after, when Cade reflected with a touch of self-mockery and bitter self-recriminations that she had somehow won after all, he had to admit the victory was shared. Both of them had gained from the encounter, whether they wanted to admit to the other's victory or not.

"So — Señora Alvarez," Cade rasped as the sun slowly rose to pinken the room on the upper floor of the seaside *posada,* "when did you become my wife?"

The growing light gilded Laurie's face and revealed the faint tinge of embarrassment in her cheeks, but her voice was steady. "When I arrived in Tijuana."

"I always thought you were a bold piece of goods." Cade curled his hand around her shoulder, pressing her deeper into the feather mattress. His mouth traveled from her throat to her breast, so that his words were muffled by warm flesh when he asked, "Am I now a bigamist? Do I still have my first wife, or have you managed to rid me of her?"

Laurie stirred beneath his mouth and hands, recognizing the coiled tension in him that had nothing to do with passion. "It was only to facilitate your release, and to keep unpleasant inquiries at bay," she said as his hand traveled leisurely from her breast to the flat plane of her stomach.

"Is that so?" His mouth was warm, his voice filled with carefully sensual humor that made Laurie tremble. "And I flattered myself by thinking you longed to be my bride," he whispered against the undercurve of her breast.

"Cade, I . . . I wish you would listen. . . ."

"Oh, I've listened to quite enough already, heard every word you said before the corregidor." Cade pushed away with an abrupt motion, sitting up to stare down at her with unfathomable dark eyes. "None of the usual female wiles will work on me, Laurie. I've heard them all before. And you really aren't that believable."

A surge of anger flooded her, and she sat up, too, her face twisting with frustration. "You think you know everything there is to know, don't you! If you weren't so stubborn, and would just think for a moment. . . ."

One hand closed around her jaw, squeezing the words into silence. "I've thought a lot, Laurie. I've thought about it so much my muscles are tired from the effort not to strangle the life from you." She swallowed hard as she saw the restraint in his eyes, aware from the suppressed tightness in his voice and the crush of his hand around her jaw that he was very near to doing just that. Then his fingers relaxed and she felt the blood rush back into her starved veins in a painful surge, and Laurie leaned away from him.

"I'm sorry, Cade."

The three simple words, said in a soft, sorrowful tone, reached him as nothing else she could have said would do. The bleak light in his eyes faded, and some of the tension in his taut body and face eased.

"That's easy enough to say," he said after a moment, and she nodded.

"Yes. But I mean it."

Rising from the bed, Cade turned his back to her and strode unselfconsciously to the window, where the sheer curtains billowed outward. He stood outlined against the growing light, his naked body a splendid reminder of the passion they had just shared. Laurie winced at the vivid tracks across his back, the marks of the whip he had endured, and rose to go to his side. She said nothing, but curled her hand around his upper arm and stood at his side, as bare as he was, and as unselfconscious. She rested her head against his shoulder, staring with him out to where the sea breakers rolled unceasingly shoreward.

When Cade finally turned to her, there was no emotion, no inflection to his flat voice. His eyes were as cold and empty as when he'd first come into her room, his face carefully expressionless.

"I'm taking you with me," he said, and Laurie didn't know whether to be glad or not.

Chapter Sixteen

Laurie stood on the sun-drenched pier with Cade, her eyes gilded with fret as she watched him. They were to board the ship bumping against the wooden quay, but there was a delay. Cargo and passengers had to be completely disgorged before they would take on new ones, and the delay, the waiting on the open dock until boarding, was dangerous. What if soldiers should happen by? What if they should see Cade standing there and recognize him? After all, Nicólas Alvarez was still an escaped prisoner.

Cade was taut, his posture stiff and wary as he stood beside Laurie, waiting. She could feel the cold nudge of a pistol strapped to his lean thigh beneath the long coat he wore, and wondered when he had begun wearing a gun instead of the more aristocratic sword. Laurie struggled for a serene posture, beginning to be nervous as the waiting dragged on. Once she smiled at him, but he only stared at her with narrowed eyes and she gave a half-shrug.

Biting her lower lip, Laurie tried not to let her unease show too obviously. She was still sore from the night before, her lips still bruised from his fierce kisses and her body still aching. She'd almost lost track of time and place since Cade had come into her room, lost herself in his moods. He had not asked nor offered any information, but had tersely told her to dress, gather any baggage she wanted, and to come with him.

His hand on her arm was an almost constant reminder of his presence and his restrained anger. It lay just below the surface, a volatile emotion waiting to explode, and for some reason Laurie did not want to provoke him. Though she told herself she wasn't afraid of him, she was. She was frightened of his anger, and frightened that he might be right when he blamed her for his imprisonment. Common sense told her differently, but it was hard to listen to common sense when Cade was standing over her, his eyes hard and cold and his condemnation evident.

She tried not to think about that as they stood on the pier waiting to board the ship that rose and dipped with the incoming waves. Gulls screeched on air currents, drifting overhead, then dropping like stones to scoop food from the water before rising again in graceful, soaring flight. Laurie envied them their freedom. For a brief instant she thought about her father and Carlota, then dismissed them from her mind. She needed to concentrate on the immediate problems, on the fine lines of tension in Cade's face, the hard, implacable gaze he turned on her again and again. Was this the face of a man in love? A man who couldn't go into exile without her? Somehow, she didn't think so.

Clearing her throat, Laurie looked back at the ship that was to carry them to Panama, where they would cross the small finger of land to the Gulf of Mexico and board another vessel. The arrangements had been made, Cade had told her earlier, his voice brisk, emotionless, and she had not commented. He'd seemed to be waiting for an argument, and she didn't want to provoke one, not now, not when there was still so much unresolved between them.

Finally the wooden gangplank was lowered again,

and a whistle shrilled. Cade turned to beckon for a boy to carry Laurie's luggage aboard, and had just put his hand on her arm to pull her up the narrow bridge between pier and ship when a loud cry floated toward them.

"Nicólas!"

Startled, Laurie turned to see who had called, hearing Cade's swift, harsh curse in her ear, feeling the ruthless grip of his hand on her arm.

"Don't make a scene," he snarled in her ear, "or I'll see that you regret it! I don't need any more attention on us than there already will be. . . ."

His words were smothered by the arrival of a woman shrouded in yards of material from her head to her toes, and Laurie was astonished to see Señorita Linda Navarro storm to a halt by them.

"What is this?" she demanded of Cade, her voice hissing from beneath the sheer material of her veil. Curious stares were being leveled in their direction, and Cade spoke quickly.

"Don't draw any attention, Linda."

Gesturing dramatically toward Laurie, Linda snapped, "So this is the way you repay me? By leaving with her? This *puta* who betrayed you, who caused you torture and suffering and banishment from your home?" Tears thickened her voice, and Laurie stared at her, too paralyzed with shock to offer a protest. "I cannot believe you would do this, Nicólas," Linda ended with a broken sob.

Cade held tightly to Laurie when she would have snatched her arm from his grip, and he gave her a harsh tug as she tried to pull away.

"You know why, Linda," he said, ignoring Laurie's angry gasp. "Soldiers were killed in my escape. I need a hostage, and it's obvious I can't take you. I need her for now, at least until I get away from California."

"And then?" Linda asked. "What will you do with

her?"

Laurie stared at the fluttering veil with detached fascination, hearing them discuss her as if she was only a vase, or a chair. How foolish she had been! She had thought he might love her, but he was only using her. Numbly, she looked up at Cade in shocked silence.

When Cade saw her blank, stunned expression, he gave a shrug. "It was Linda who helped me, as I'm certain you've guessed by now."

Laurie's words were faltering and hesitant. "Then that is who . . . where you've been staying since your escape?"

Cade gave a short nod. "She's been more loyal than any other woman I've ever known," he drawled, and Laurie could not help but feel a pang of guilt.

Linda gave a loud sniff of contempt, and drew her long skirts back as if Laurie might contaminate them.

"This *puta* is not worth your time, Nicólas! Do not bother taking her with you. Surely there is another you can take—I would be a much better hostage, as my uncle is the alcalde, and . . ."

"And every soldier in California, Mexico, and even the United States would be out looking for me then," Cade finished for her. "No, Linda, *querida*, you cannot go. I owe you my life, and for that I thank you, but it's best that I not risk you."

Sobbing, Linda shook her head, and Cade, still holding Laurie's arm in spite of her struggles, gently lifted the veil she wore and kissed her full on the mouth. He ignored Laurie's indignant gasp as he kissed Linda and whispered something in her ear, then stepped back and watched her half-run back down the pier toward the row of buildings.

As he turned back toward Laurie, he was met with the crashing blow of her open hand across his cheek. A loud shout of laughter greeted that action, and Cade was only vaguely aware of the watching sailors who were quite entertained by the show on the dock.

"You bastard!" Laurie raged, lifting her hand to strike him again. Cade caught it with his free hand, still not releasing her other wrist, his fingers digging cruelly into her tender flesh. She didn't care, didn't care that there were people watching, didn't care what anyone else thought. All that mattered right now was Cade's humiliation of her, and the even more humiliating realization that she had whispered words of love to him the night before. How he must have laughed at her! How he must have enjoyed her capitulation!

"Laurie," Cade began in a warning tone, but she was past listening.

"You damned bastard!" she spat again, this time resorting to kicking him in the shins. Another wave of loud laughter floated down from the ship's rail, where all the seamen had gathered to watch.

"You're causing a scene," Cade grated from between clenched teeth. "Do you want the soldiers down on me?"

"Yes! God, yes! I hope they all come to get you, and put you in front of a firing squad!" Provoked to near-mindless fury, Laurie didn't care at the moment. Her pain and anger overcame every rational thought.

Jerking her close, Cade's snarl barely penetrated her anger. "You crazy bitch, if I have to knock you out I will, so don't tempt me!"

But Laurie was past listening, past hearing anything he had to say. Fueled by injured pride and deep humiliation, she was in a frenzy of rage.

"I'll scream until every soldier in San Diego comes!" she said in a panting voice that was breathless from his tight grip and crushing arms.

Speaking over her head, Cade told a wide-eyed

youth nearby to carry their baggage aboard, that his wife was not well and he had to calm her.

"Wife?" Laurie repeated in a faint shriek mixed with bitter laughter. "So now you choose to claim me as a wife? You already have a wife, Cade Caldwell, and it's not me, so you can just . . ."

"Laurie," he said in a quiet voice so filled with menace that it finally penetrated her haze of anger, "if you do not quiet down *now*, I will silence you in the only way left."

"Oh, you would!" she said, but her voice had grown more quiet, and she began to sob, hiccoughing helplessly and hating herself for it. "I suppose you would . . ." She coughed and strangled before finishing, "knock me out!"

"Exactly."

He held her tightly, one arm behind her to press her against him, the other holding both her wrists with one strong hand. She tried to jerk away, her lips pressed tightly together as she fought her silent battle, knowing somehow that she was only making herself look ridiculous, but unable to go without offering some kind of a struggle.

Cade half-dragged, half-carried her up the wooden walk to the ship under the amused, raucous stares of the sailors who enjoyed the spectacle and offered words of advice on how to tame a shrewish wife.

"Got ter beat 'er once a day, mate," one man called as Cade yanked Laurie aboard.

"Naw, a woman like that needs more'n a beatin'," another crew member drawled, and they all laughed. "Ya got ter have th' right rod ter beat her with," he added, and Laurie could feel her cheeks flame with embarrassment at the crude innuendo and the guffaws it produced.

Surging against him, Laurie felt her heel connect with Cade's shin, heard his soft curse, and had only an instant's satisfaction before he'd wheeled her

217

around and slapped her deliberately, lightly, across one cheek, the sharp sting of his blow shocking her into silence.

"I've told you," Cade said into the sudden quiet, making his voice placating as if soothing a child, "there is nothing to be afraid of on a ship. You won't drown."

Before she could contradict him, he was asking for and receiving the directions to their cabin, propelling Laurie ahead of him with such a painful grip on her upper arm that she clawed at his hand.

"Let go of me!" she raged as he pushed her ahead of him down a steep, shadowed stairwell that led below deck.

Whirling her around again, Cade pushed her up and hard against the side of the narrow passageway, and she could see the murderous glints in his dark eyes.

"You and I are going to be alone in a small cabin for several days," he bit out slowly, fiercely, "and if I were you, I would be trying to appease me, not provoke me to murder."

Laurie could not move. He had her pinned against the wall with his hard body, one hand on each side of her head and his face only inches from hers. She could feel the anger in him, feel it vibrating through his taut muscles, and finally sensed how close she was to pushing him into violence. But she offered one, final shot.

"I'll scream for help. . . ."

"And do you think one of those men up there would come to your aid after the shrewish performance you just gave?"

"I'll run the first chance I get," she began, and he pressed his body even closer, grinding her into the rough wooden sides of the passageway.

"Now, get this straight! You're my hostage, my ticket to freedom, and I'll do what I have to do to keep you. Do you understand what I'm saying, or do I have to give you all the nasty details?"

She swallowed hard, and saw the muscle leaping in his clenched jaw. Without realizing it, Laurie made the same sound in the back of her throat as a wounded animal makes, and stared at Cade with wide eyes.

"No," she whispered around the lump in her throat, "I can imagine what you mean."

His grip loosened slightly, but he didn't lift his body from hers. "Good," he said in a tight, grim voice. "Now see if you can keep quiet until we're in our cabin. I'm tired of listening to you whine. . . ."

Laurie pressed her lips together to keep her teeth from chattering, and wondered why she was shivering when it was warm and balmy.

"Since you seem to have the idea you want to escape," Cade said once they were in their cabin and the door was closed behind them, "I think it's necessary to ensure that you don't do anything foolish."

Numbly, Laurie just watched as he uncoiled a length of thin rope and walked toward her. She didn't protest, only stared sullenly when he tied her wrists together, then looped a longer line from them to the bunk built into the wall.

"That ought to hold you until I get back," he said, and was surprised by the quick flash of hate and defiance in Laurie's upturned gaze.

"You can't hold me forever," was all she said, and he did not bother to reply.

Laurie stared at the closed door for a long time after he had gone, feeling a numb weariness seep into her bones to leave her exhausted. The shock of the past twenty-four hours had left her dazed, left her feeling emotionally drained, and she had not yet wept. Somehow, the tears would not come. She still wasn't certain what had happened.

She'd thought — hoped — that he wanted her with

him for love, not vengeance or his own safety. The knowledge that she had so easily played into his hands galled her, and she reflected with a bitter twist of her mouth that he should be very satisfied with himself right now. Not only had he played upon her gullibility, but he had humiliated her in front of the alcalde's wife and the entire crew of the ship taking them—taking them where? She still didn't know their ultimate destination.

Her shoulders slumped, and Laurie tested the strength of the thin ropes holding her. It was an exercise in futility, as she had known it would be, but she'd had to try.

She looked around the cabin, and saw nothing that might help her. It was small and sparsely furnished, and her fine leather trunks stood neatly in one corner. A table and two chairs hugged the corner across from her. A washstand was attached to one wall, with a cupboard built beneath it and a chamberpot glistening on a shelf. Several hooks for clothing jutted from the wall, and the bunk she perched on so stiffly was narrow, just barely wide enough for two people, but quite comfortable for one. She had no illusions about the sleeping arrangements: they would be at Cade's discretion.

Shifting, Laurie tried to make herself comfortable until his return, but her thoughts were dismal and gloomy as the long hours limped slowly past.

She must have dozed, for she was jerked awake by Cade's return and the slamming of the door. He stood there, a tray in one hand, his eyes raking her cramped form where she crouched on the end of the bed.

"Why didn't you lie down?"

Laurie shrugged, and indicated the extent of the rope. "Your prisoner is tied too tightly."

He slid the tray onto the small table in the corner and approached the bunk where Laurie huddled with a wary gaze.

"If my prisoner didn't threaten to escape," he said in a faintly mocking tone, "she wouldn't be tied so tightly."

"As long as we're speaking in the third person," Laurie snapped, "I'd like to mention that my jailor has the wit of a seagull! Where does he think I'd go while in the middle of the ocean?"

Cade gazed at her with amusement in the dark depths of his eyes.

"The ship is following the coastline, not that far from shore, and I never underestimate the power of a woman when it comes to sailors."

"I assume you mean that I might use my charms on one of those devastating creatures I saw hanging over the rail earlier?" Laurie eyed him coldly. "Do you really think I would stoop that low?"

"You continually surprise me," Cade replied as he tugged at the tight bonds on her wrists. "Why invite trouble? After all, I never thought you'd seduce Garcia."

Not deigning to reply to that remark, Laurie contented herself with rubbing at her chafed wrists to restore the circulation. She didn't look at Cade but was well aware of him looming over her, his thumbs tucked into the waistband of his pants as he stood only a foot or two away.

"I brought you something to eat," he said after a moment, and Laurie shrugged.

"Am I supposed to be grateful?"

"No, you're supposed to eat." His tone was sharp and irritated, and she experienced a moment's triumph at eliciting a reaction from him.

"I'm not hungry," she began, but Cade shook his head.

"No, we're not going to play that game, Laurie. You will eat if I have to shove it down your throat."

Her eyes flashed, but when he took a step closer,

221

she rose from the bunk and went hastily to the table. There was no denying that he was stronger, and she certainly didn't want another humiliating show-down between them. The memory of her ignominious boarding still rankled, and her cheeks flamed when she recalled the raucous laughter at her expense. No, any confrontation would have to be verbal, or she was lost.

Sulkily, she slumped into one of the chairs and looked down at the unappealing mass of food congealing on a tin plate. "What is it?" she muttered, not really expecting an answer and not receiving one. Even after spooning several bites into her mouth and almost gagging, she still didn't recognize the fare, and thought it best not to push the issue. There were times when a little knowledge could be a dangerous thing.

"I can't say much for the accommodations," Laurie observed when she had forced enough food down her throat to appease Cade. She was eyeing the chamber pot and trying to think of a way to communicate her needs without too much embarrassment when he bluntly told her that he'd turn his back until she was through.

A resentful flare leaped in her eyes, and with fiery cheeks and more than a little humiliation, Laurie pulled out the enamel chamberpot.

"I draw the line at emptying it," Cade said when she was through, and pointed to the door. "Set it outside for the steward."

"No wonder this ship smells like . . . smells bad," Laurie muttered when she had shut the door. She couldn't look at Cade, but could feel his eyes on her.

"Good God! You're embarrassed about natural functions, yet you didn't quail at seducing Captain Garcia," he said in a brutal tone that made her gasp with anger. "Of course, I suppose with Garcia, it's very close to the same thing. Maybe you were embarrassed."

"You're a beast! A degenerate bastard, and . . ."

That was as far as she got before Cade had yanked her up to within an inch of his face, his gaze boring into her with a cold fury.

"You're on thin ice, sweetheart! In case you don't understand the analogy, it means that you're in danger of drowning."

"I know what it means," she managed to say without her voice shaking. His fingers bit into her upper arms, and she tried to keep from flinching. "But you're wrong about the other. I was never intimate with Captain Garcia."

Cade released her abruptly, and stalked to where the thin ropes lay on the bed. "You're a facile liar, Laurie, but I know the truth."

"No, you. . . ."

"Forget it!" He held up the ropes. "Come here."

Like a sleepwalker, Laurie obeyed, taking the few steps separating them as if in a trance. She held out her wrists when he told her to, watching apathetically as he retied them, more loosely this time, and not so painfully.

Flinging back the quilt from the bunk, Cade indicated that she should lie down, which she did slowly. She could feel his gaze on her as she turned her back to him, could hear him pull out one of the chairs and sit down. There was the faint clink of a bottle and glass, then the slick splash of liquid, and she could detect the subtle scent of brandy. Laurie stared at the wall, her posture stiff and uncomfortable as she waited.

When he came to bed after dousing the lantern, only a faint sheen filled the cabin. Moonlight filtered in through a high, round porthole up above the table, shining across the cabin to the bunk. Laurie shifted, her nerves stretched to a fine tautness by Cade's silence. He lay beside her, one arm reaching out to hook around her body and drag her into the angle of his, and she began to struggle. Her arms and legs felt oddly heavy, and her skirts hindered her struggle. Casually, almost lazily, Cade put one long leg over her body to hold her down, until finally she exhausted herself. Panting with her efforts, she ceased fighting and lay still. She heard Cade's mocking laugh, and felt his warm breath whisper across her neck.

"There's not much room for any other position, love," he said, then added with a wicked chuckle, "Unless you'd rather I get on top?"

When she didn't answer, but buried her face into the thin pillow provided, Cade gave another mocking laugh.

"I didn't think so, love."

He uses the word love so casually, she thought with a pang. *Why did I ever think it held meaning for him?*

Feeling helpless, she sagged into his embrace, knowing he could do anything he wanted and she was powerless to stop him. There was no one who would stop him, believing that she was his wife, a lie she had begun in order to rescue him. A bitter tide of self-mockery rose in a choking wave, and Laurie trembled with the force of it. How utterly foolish she had been! And now he would take what he wanted whether she wanted him to or not. She was achingly aware of her own helplessness at his hands, of her vulnerability, and it terrified her. Tense and stiff, she waited for the inevitable.

But to her surprise, she soon heard the steady cadence of his breathing and knew he was asleep. That irritated her almost as much as the idea of rape. How dare he sleep so soundly when she could not? When she was tied up as snugly as a recalcitrant donkey? And why did she feel a vague sense of disappointment?

She was still pondering those abstract questions

MORE PASSION AND ADVENTURE AWAIT... YOUR TRIP TO A BIG ADVENTUROUS WORLD BEGINS WHEN YOU ACCEPT YOUR FIRST 4 NOVELS ABSOLUTELY *FREE*
(AN $18.00 VALUE)

Accept your Free gift and start to experience more of the passion and adventure you like in a historical romance novel. Each Zebra novel is filled with proud men, spirited women and tempestuous love that you'll remember long after you turn the last page.

Zebra Historical Romances are the finest novels of their kind. They are written by authors who really know how to weave tales of romance and adventure in the historical settings you love. You'll feel like you've actually gone back in time with the thrilling stories that each Zebra novel offers.

GET YOUR FREE GIFT WITH THE START OF YOUR HOME SUBSCRIPTION

Our readers tell us that these books sell out very fast in book stores and often they miss the newest titles. So Zebra has made arrangements for you to receive the four newest novels published each month.

You'll be guaranteed that you'll never miss a title, and home delivery is so convenient. And to show you just how easy it is to get Zebra Historical Romances, we'll send you your first 4 books absolutely FREE! Our gift to you just for trying our home subscription service.

BIG SAVINGS AND FREE HOME DELIVERY

Each month, you'll receive the four newest titles as soon as they are published. You'll probably receive them even before the bookstores do. What's more, you may preview these exciting novels free for 10 days. If you like them as much as we think you will, just pay the low preferred subscriber's price of just $3.75 each. *You'll save $3.00 each month off the publisher's price.* AND, your savings are even greater because there are never any shipping, handling or other hidden charges—FREE Home Delivery. Of course you can return any shipment within 10 days for full credit, no questions asked. There is no minimum number of books you must buy.

4 FREE BOOKS

GET
FOUR
FREE
BOOKS

(AN $18.00 VALUE)

ZEBRA HOME SUBSCRIPTION
SERVICE, INC.
P.O. Box 5214
120 BRIGHTON ROAD
CLIFTON, NEW JERSEY 07015-5214

when she finally drifted to sleep.

The next few days passed in a blur of sameness, in a routine that she quickly grew accustomed to and hated. Cade allowed her no freedom, and the only time he took her above deck — grudgingly yielding to her teary pleas that she was going mad locked in the small cabin — there was a dangerous confrontation.

Wind whipped at her cheeks with a raw bite as she stood on the deck breathing deeply of salt air and limited freedom. Laurie felt it mold her long skirts to her body, felt it claw at her hair, loosening it from the ribbon she wore and sending it in cascading whirls about her head, making her think of a child's pinwheel. But she didn't care. The sun glittered on white-capped waves, and clouds scudded overhead, running on the wind, making playful shadows on the water. In the distance she could see a dark blur that Cade told her was the coast of Baja California, the distended peninsula that separated Mexico from the Pacific Ocean. Soon they would reach Panama, the tiny country that separated North and South America. It was a short land journey across Panama to the Gulf of Mexico, and there they would board another ship.

But that was still several days away, and this was here and now, and she had only the present to worry about. There was nothing she could do about the future, or the past. And it was too much for her weary brain to absorb, so she let her mind drift as lazily as the distant blur of land, put her elbows on the ship's rail and concentrating on nothing.

Watching her, Cade felt a sharp tug of desire. It made his eyes narrow, and he let his gaze roam from her wind-whipped golden hair over the alluring curves outlined by the stiff breeze against her gown. Her high, firm breasts caressed by wind and sun seemed to beg for the touch of his hand, and her long legs and rounded thighs molded by the thin material of her skirts whispered of sensuous mysteries to the man who took her. He leaned one arm against the top of the rail nearby, watching and waiting.

Cade wasn't the only man there watching her. Besides several crewmen who paused in their labors to stare at her with piqued interest, another passenger stood on the foredeck and gazed long and hard at Laurie. She wasn't the only woman on board, but she was certainly the most lovely. And she didn't even seem aware of the stares, which made it even more intriguing.

Christopher Martin took two steps forward, his eyes fastened intently on Laurie, his steps hesitant. What if she spurned him? The tall young man with blond hair and anxious eyes never saw the dark brooding man behind Laurie, didn't know that she was not alone. All his attention was focused on the girl, the beautiful girl with the dreamy smile and pink cheeks, the exotically slanted eyes as golden as the sun.

And when he finally nerved himself enough to approach, and she turned with a surprised smile, Christopher Martin was lost.

"Excuse me," he said in a slight stammer, "but I thought you might like some company."

Aware of Cade's dark gaze fastened on her, Laurie felt a reckless defiance surge through her. Her long lashes lay like silken wings on her cheek for a moment before she lifted them with devastating effect, her smile potent and seeming to caress him.

"Pleasant company is always welcome," she said, and the wind carried her words along the deck to where Cade leaned on the rail. He didn't move, didn't react, but watched her.

Laurie had learned to flirt while still in short skirts, and she'd learned the invaluable tricks that

226

made a man sigh with pleasure and not realize she'd given him nothing in return for his admiration. She also knew that Cade Caldwell would immediately recognize what she was doing, and that it would irritate him.

Martin's response was enthusiastic, his smile stretching his mouth wide as he silently congratulated himself on his good fortune. The girl was lovely, with a ripe mouth moist from the quick slide of her tongue over her lips, her eyes dancing with light golden flecks. And her sweet body seemed to ache for a man to hold it, to explore the luscious curves and hollows with reverent adoration.

"I'm Christopher Martin," he said after a moment of silent appreciation, and she smiled, a dimple flashing enchantingly in one cheek.

"My name is Laurie Allen," she replied with a tilt of her head, and wisps of golden hair fluttered like angel wings around her face.

"Where are you going?" Martin asked when he realized that he could not stand there just staring at her, and Laurie gave a light little laugh.

"Panama."

"And from there?" he pursued, drowning in the wide sheen of her eyes, in the delicate bone structure of her face and the sweet smile she was turning on him.

Laurie's lashes flickered briefly, then she gave a quick shrug before saying, "New Orleans. That is my home."

And, oh God, how I wish I was there! she added in a silent sigh.

"New Orleans? But what a coincidence! That is where I am going!"

"Are you really? But how wonderful!" Laurie clapped her hands together with genuine delight. "I miss it so, miss the tempting fragrance of warm croissants and steaming coffee in the Market, and the iron balconies and even the rain. . . ." As she spoke, she could feel an overwhelming wave of homesickness, and it was conveyed in her expressive eyes.

"I would like to see it with you," Martin said in a soft voice, and she was slightly startled.

Looking up at his open, earnest face, seeing his admiration and desire to please her, she had the beginning of an idea.

Even as the idea occurred to her, Laurie could feel Cade's sudden movement behind her, the pushing of his lean frame away from the rail, and his slow, measured tread as he approached them.

"Hello, love," he said in a deceptively casual tone, and slid one arm around Laurie's waist, his hand gripping her tightly at her involuntary recoil. Cade's gaze encompassed Martin, who stared with some confusion from Laurie to Cade, and then back. Martin's cheeks colored when Cade continued in the same drawling voice, "Want to introduce me to your new friend?"

"This is Christopher Martin," Laurie said unwillingly, her tone sharp. Her mind raced. If Martin was going to New Orleans, then why couldn't she somehow manage to go with him? There had to be a way, and she could tell him that she was a hostage— no, she couldn't dare that. Cade would have no scruples at killing him, and even her, if she tried to do that. No, she would say she was leaving a cruel husband, that was it! Appeal to his protective instincts, then beg him to take her to her aunt.

"Cade Caldwell," Cade was saying, putting out his hand to grasp the embarrassed Martin's.

"Yes," the man said as he flicked a puzzled glance toward Laurie, "I was just telling your . . . wife . . . that I am on the way to New Orleans, also. I've business there."

Laurie thought quickly, sensing Cade's coiled ten-

228

sion. Giving Martin a glance that was half-pleading, half-promising, she said, "I was telling Mr. Martin how much I miss New Orleans. . . ."

"But we're not going there," Cade cut in with a lift of his dark brows, his smile cold and not quite reaching his eyes. There was an air of menace about him that transferred to Martin, and the young man shifted uneasily.

This wasn't at all what he'd expected when he had approached a girl he thought to be alone. And there was something wrong here, he could see it in the quick start of tears in her eyes at Caldwell's words, the slight quiver of her lower lip.

"Oh, I understood Miss Allen to say you were going to New Orleans," Martin began, and Cade cut him off once more.

"She misunderstood." Cade's hand rose to caress the nape of Laurie's neck, his long fingers massaging the skin below her ear in a circular motion that should have been soothing but wasn't. She shivered beneath his touch and Martin noticed that, too.

He was confused. The girl's name was Laurie Allen, the man's Cade Caldwell, yet no one had contradicted his usage of the term *wife*. That led him to believe the girl was just traveling with Caldwell, and not married to him, yet she was obviously intimidated by him. Could she be in trouble?

It wasn't until Martin had left them after another few minutes of stiff conversation, his glance dark and uncertain, that Cade turned Laurie to face him.

"That was a stupid thing to do," he said shortly, and she snatched her arm away from his grip.

"Do you expect me to just follow you meekly?"

"If you want to keep foolish admirers like Martin alive — yes."

"What — do you think I'd risk anyone else's life?" she demanded angrily, ignoring the fact that she had just done so.

Cade brought the tip of one finger along the line of her jaw, and when she tried to jerk away his hand closed around her chin, holding her still, gazing into her sun-drenched face with a mocking smile pressing his lips into a slight curve.

"I think you'd do whatever you had to do to suit your own ends," he said, his fingers tightening when she tried to twist away. "Just remember, Laurie—I'm a wanted man, an outlaw, a renegade, and I won't hesitate to do whatever is necessary to stay free."

Laurie briefly wondered if she should tell him that Don Benito had gained his pardon, then remembered that Cade's escape had certainly negated any pardon he may have received.

His finger dragged over her slightly parted lips, gathering moisture as he slid it along the smooth curves, an action that should have been seductive but was vaguely frightening instead, perhaps because his eyes were cold and hard.

"And whether you realize it or not, because you're with me, you're a renegade too," he said then, making her head jerk up and her breath catch in her throat.

"But I'm not!" she cried, her gaze squinting against the high glare of the sun overhead. "It was Linda who helped you escape, not me!"

"And do you think anyone would believe the niece of the alcalde—a man who tried to have me executed—would be foolish enough to rescue me?" Cade's laugh was filled with scorn. "No, my little renegade, you are in this as deeply as I am."

Furious, and filled with the sudden terrifying realization that he was right, Laurie tried to twist away from him, her hands balling into fists as she beat at his broad chest.

"No! No, I won't be!"

"Laurie! Stop it before I slap your hysterical face!" Cade barked, his hands shifting to grip her upper arms in a grasp of iron. He pushed her hard against the ship's rail, and she could feel the sea-spray wetting her long hair hanging over the side.

Half-panting, still struggling, Laurie pushed at him until he laughed at her, his amusement whipping her into an even greater frenzy of denial.

"I hate you!" she screamed, and the wind carried the words along the decks of the ship.

On the upper deck, the captain of the ship saw the commotion, and saw the stares of his crew and the agitation of Christopher Martin, and knew there was about to be some trouble. He started down to the lower deck, but Martin was ahead of him, long legs eating up the distance between the foredeck and Laurie Allen.

"Let go of her!" Martin shouted as he made the mistake of grabbing Cade to spin him around. When Cade turned, he swore softly as Martin saw the pistol he wore beneath his coat.

"Stay out of this," he advised coldly as Martin took a quick step back, and his eyes reinforced the warning.

"Here now, here now!" the captain puffed as he finally reached them. "There's no reason for a gun!"

"There's no reason for him to interfere," Cade pointed out, but he let his coat fall back over the pistol in his belt. He could feel Laurie's quick movement behind him, and slung out one arm to hold her.

"But he's abusing her, and she's not even his wife!" Martin protested, caught up in a fervent desire to protect the fragile creature who had snared his interest and desire. And who knew how grateful she might be later?

"She's with me," Cade said in a flat, hard tone, and even the captain could not refute that.

Looking from Cade to Martin, the captain, a large man with a bulbous nose and thick gray brows, said heavily, "He is right, Mr. Martin, and you can't go around causing trouble between the passengers."

"Do you allow this sort of thing aboard your ship?" Martin countered, his eyes fastening on Laurie's face. She was staring down at her feet, half-hidden by Caldwell, obviously frightened to death. Her fear lent Martin courage and he said more strongly, "Even if she is with him, I do not approve of men beating up on helpless women!"

Heaving a great sigh, the captain looked at Laurie and said kindly, "If you are in danger, now is the time to say so. If not, I would appreciate your putting an end to this situation before it gets out of hand."

This was her chance, but Laurie realized with a bitter wave of defeat that to speak against Cade was to endanger herself. He would have no scruples about doing what he threatened, and she could not risk the gallant but foolish Christopher Martin for her own selfishness.

Not looking up, Laurie said to the heaving, sea-washed deck beneath her feet, "I am not in any danger," and that satisfied the captain, who led a disappointed and gravely puzzled Martin back to the foredeck, where he gave him a stern lecture on interfering in other people's business.

The wind scoured the decks and blew her hair around her face as Laurie avoided Cade's dark gaze, and when he took her arm and led her back below deck, she went meekly.

"Sometimes you amaze me," Cade said as he shut the cabin door and began to shrug out of his long coat. Laurie heard the metallic clink of his gunbelt being unbuckled as she moved to stare out the small porthole. She could see nothing but sea and sky.

"Why?" she asked. "Because I did not want to cause any more trouble for that young man? That shouldn't amaze you."

"No, that was simply self-preservation on your part. I think you know I'd come after you first."

He crossed the cabin to stand behind her, his hands moving to circle her slender waist, his long hard frame pressing against her. Laurie could feel the tension in him, could feel the harsh touch of this hands on her, and she shivered.

"I was talking about your foolish plan to seduce Martin into taking you to New Orleans." Before she could offer a lame protest, he continued, "I said you would choose a sailor, but I was wrong."

His hands moved swiftly up the curve of her spine to her shoulders, tunneling into her tangled hair, the pads of his fingers moving in slow, somehow menacing, circles.

"You aren't very discriminating, are you, love?" he asked in a soft voice. "First Garcia, now that cow-eyed boy who couldn't be more than twenty."

Jerking away from him, Laurie kept her voice as hard as possible. "No, you were my first indiscrimination, Cade," she said. Her eyes lifted to meet his, defiant, blazing with hot gold sparks. "But you won't be my last."

Cade's jaw tightened, and Laurie knew from the quick flare in his eyes what he would do before he even moved. An icy chill invaded her, seizing her lungs with cold fingers to squeeze the breath from her.

Her eyes were bright, glittery orbs of gold like pieces of coin, her expression trapped as he moved swiftly to capture her face between his palms.

"No — don't touch me," she whispered through painfully dry lips, her heart beating a fierce tattoo in her chest.

"Why not? You gave yourself quite freely before, why not now? And since you plan on having more lovers, what difference could one more man make to you, love?" he was asking in a savage tone that fell on her ears like blows.

Swinging her by one arm toward the narrow bunk on the wall, Cade saw that she was staring at him like an animal at bay, trapped, mesmerized by danger, terrified. For an instant he hesitated, his gaze raking over the uncombed, tangled wealth of hair that tumbled over her shoulders in a tawny spill that reached almost to her waist. She looked as wild and feral as a golden gypsy, with her slanted amber eyes and high cheekbones, the full lips and sultry body, and it was the thought of that body, her ripe curves and the careless way she had taken Garcia so easily into her bed, her deliberate flirtation with Martin, that strengthened Cade's purpose.

"Take off your clothes," he said, jerking a thumb toward the bunk. He was already unbuttoning his shirt, shrugging out of it, his hands moving to the waistband of his trousers while she still stood as unmoving as a statue. "Didn't you hear me?" he asked as he kicked off his boots, and Laurie jerked from her trance.

"I won't do it!" Her gaze fell on his pistol still in the holster and lying on the table, and she lunged for it, snatching it up and swirling toward him in a swift motion. "I'll see you dead before I let you humiliate me again!"

But when she lifted the heavy pistol with trembling hands she could not figure out how to fire it, and Cade reached out in an easy motion and plucked it from her fingers, one arm swinging around to send her flying. She fell half across the bunk, hitting her head against the wall behind it, momentarily dazing her. Cade tossed the pistol back to the table with a careless contempt.

"You ought to know by now that there's no point in your trying to fight me, Laurie," he said as he bent over her, his hands swift and sure as he undressed her, ignoring her frantic struggles.

A single lantern swayed overhead, casting a fitful light over the pair on the bunk, light and shadow adding a surrealistic aura to Laurie's despair. Cade's face was in the shadows, and she half-sobbed as she grabbed frantically for the blanket to hide herself from his gaze. He laughed huskily.

"Do you think that will dissuade me, love?" One hand stroked back a honeyed curl from her forehead. "You underestimate your charms."

Strangled gasps of fury escaped her as she tried to avoid his touch, the lingering exploration of his hands on her curves, sliding up over her bare thighs to the flat plane of her stomach, slipping over her shrinking flesh to the gentle roundness of a breast and cupping it in his palm.

"You've got a body made for love, Laurie," he said in a thoughtful tone. "Maybe I shouldn't be selfish. Maybe I shouldn't resent sharing you." His head lowered and his mouth captured a nipple, teasing it with his tongue as she writhed helplessly beneath him. "Tell you what," he said a moment later, lifting his head to stare into her glazed eyes, "After we're through, I'll take you above deck and let you share your lovely body with all those sailors who were admiring you. Would that make you happy?"

"You bastard! I hate you! Oh, I wish to God I'd never seen you, never thought you were anything but an animal!"

She struggled more fiercely, but he threw a long leg over her to pin her down to the mattress, one hand moving to coil around her wrists and pull her arms over her head. He held her motionless beneath him, the weight of his body and his harsh grip rendering her helpless as he took his time in exploring her body, exacting a response in spite of her sobbing vows of hatred.

"Do you hate me, sweet Laurie?" he murmured

against the heavy underside of one breast, his lips searing a trail that made her shudder. "Your body doesn't."

And because he was right, and because she couldn't fight him anymore, Laurie yielded, cursing him and herself as she gave herself up to him. A harsh rape would have been kinder somehow, because then there would have been no decision on her part, but this—this was much crueler in a subtle way, because she could not deny the hunger inside her for his touch, for the caresses and sweet fires he sparked.

Even as she arched upward, she moaned, "No, Cade, no, please don't!" but he ignored her, whispering soft words in her ears, love words in Spanish, English, and French, his voice thick and urgent, his body hot and hard against her.

Cade's mouth and hands aroused her to a fever-pitch of aching desire, until she could think of nothing but release from the driving urgency filling her. Whimpering, twisting, and turning beneath his surging body, Laurie heard herself whisper back to him, betraying words of passion that would haunt her later, but that didn't matter now. What mattered now was Cade, the pounding ache that seemed to fill her entire body, until at last she crested that peak where infinity passed in but a moment of sighing release, then slid slowly back to awareness.

The sound of the sea filled her ears, the slap of the waves against the ship, the rush of the wind drowning out everything but her own erratic heart-beat.

And then, lying in his arms, feeling his heartbeat match hers, she felt the shame of her body's betrayal. A soft sob caught in her throat, and Cade's head lifted as he gazed down at her face with narrowed eyes.

"Oh, for Chrissake!" he muttered in obvious disgust. All gentleness faded as he sat up, looking at her through half-slitted eyes, uncomfortable with the wrenching sobs that racked her slender body. "Disappointed?"

Turning her face from the tear-soaked pillow, Laurie glared at him. "No, because I don't expect much from you!"

Stiffening, Cade looked as if he wanted to throttle her, and Laurie smeared the tears from her face as she sat up to face him.

"Please, Cade," she said, catching his arm as he swung his legs over the side of the bed to stand, "please let me go. You're free now, and I can't be of any use to you. I want to go home, and I promise I won't betray you."

"Too bad I can't believe you," Cade said after a moment of thick silence. "I can't risk it, Laurie. Not now. But I will let you go later, when I've got things straightened out."

It was as much of a concession as he would make, and she had to content herself with it, with that and the uneasy truce between them. She'd discovered in herself a surprising capacity for passion, for the swift arousal of her sensuality under Cade's expert hands, and it dismayed as well as astounded her.

Slowly lifting her chin to face him, Laurie said in a voice tinged with bewilderment, "But that may take a long time."

A faint smile curled the ends of his mouth, and he reached out to drag her against him, his palms sliding over her bare skin to cup her buttocks, holding her hard against his thighs.

"We can keep busy until then," he said softly, but she pushed hard at him with the heels of her hands.

"Don't mistake me for one of your *putas!*" she spat fiercely, still stinging from the humiliation of her body's betrayal.

Cade's hand coiled around her wrist and he forced

her back against the tangled sheets of the bunk, his eyes cold and angry. "Don't worry—even the worst whore knows more than you do," he snarled into her hissing fury.

Kissing her into silence, he took her again, this time without bothering to arouse her, his body slamming into her until she cried out against him.

Chapter Seventeen

Sea waves rolled high, and the steamer poised on the crest for barely a heartbeat before slipping down the side of the wave and plunging into the trough of foaming water. Laurie's stomach lurched with the movement, and she closed her eyes. When she opened them again, the steamer had settled into another wave, and she gripped the edge of the bunk with tight fingers.

She was alone in the tiny cabin, a room smaller than on the last ship, something she never would have believed until she'd seen it with her own eyes. They were on the last leg of their sea journey, Cade had told her in his brusque, pitiless manner, and she would have to bear it. Of course, if she hadn't been so reckless on the last ship, he pointed out, she could have come above deck with the other passengers, but Laurie had thought it was just as well that she stayed below. She had seen the other passengers crowded onto the steamer, obvious refugees. Most of them were shabbily dressed, or peasant women with shapeless bodies and blank faces, women that haunted her nightmares. How had life done such a thing to them?

Following on the heels of that thought had come the fear that she would end the same way. Perhaps she could be beaten down as they had, yielding to the inevitable, letting life's disasters crush her. And then she had known that she would not, that she would fight to survive.

The past week had been filled with tension, and she had avoided any confrontation with Cade by retreating into herself. His jibes and caustic comments couldn't touch her if she didn't hear them, didn't respond in any way.

Since boarding the steamer bound for the United States, she had held tightly to her restraint, praying for an end to the turmoil inside her.

Cade seemed almost as preoccupied, and Laurie assumed he was contemplating his next move. While traveling across the Isthmus of Panama, they had chanced upon an officer from the Mexican Army, and Cade had found it easy enough to draw him out, to learn how things stood between Mexico and the new republic of Texas. She knew how he felt about Texas, remembered his conversations about it so long ago. Now that seemed like another time, another life. Had they ever just made simple conversation instead of having of every word be a tense confrontation? She couldn't imagine that happening now.

Neither could Cade, and he avoided being alone with Laurie. Since the night he had taken her so roughly, he had not been able to look at her without seeing an unspoken accusation in her wide, golden gaze, an accusation that he deserved. She had withdrawn from him after that, retreating into a shell so he couldn't hurt her.

Her icy unapproachability and unbreakable poise irritated him, but he understood it. He couldn't reach her anymore, couldn't make her feel the pain he felt, couldn't make her react to him even when he took her. Maybe he could wrest a response from her unwilling body, but that was all. The essence of Laurie still eluded him. She had retreated into a private part of herself that he couldn't touch no matter how hard he tried, and it frustrated him. Knowing it was his fault only whipped him with a greater determination to see her open and vulnerable again.

But Laurie was far stronger than he imagined. Scooting up beneath the light quilt over the bunk, she kicked off her shoes and curled her stockinged toes under its warmth. She propped her elbows on her bent knees and read a volume of poetry cradled in the crook of her arms. She had to do something to keep from going mad, and English poets seemed as good a way as any, she reflected as she idly flipped the pages.

The steamer rocked up and down, rolling from wave to wave with such deep plunges that Laurie soon abandoned her efforts at reading. She rolled onto her stomach and cupped her chin in her palms, frowning at the wood-paneled walls.

At times like this, when she couldn't keep her mind occupied with other things, she began to think of escape again, a constant preoccupation with her. Escape. Freedom. Distance from Cade, miles separating them, years separating them. She longed for it, wanted it so badly the wanting was almost a tangible thing.

She didn't even know herself anymore, that stranger she had glimpsed in a mirror the day before, the golden-eyed girl with hollows in her cheeks and an unsmiling face. It was as if she was seeing herself for the first time. Had she changed that much? she wondered, then knew that she had.

Her pride had been dragged through the dust, trampled beneath Cade's feet, then hung out for everyone to see, and she could not forget that. It burned in her, the memory as sharp and searing as the smoldering coals in the brass brazier of the tiny cabin.

Laurie closed her eyes against the memory, willing it away. When she opened them again, Cade Caldwell was standing in the open doorway.

"Hello, love," he said, his voice caressing the word *love* with a teasing mockery that made her tawny eyes flash hotly. He laughed, knowing how she hated it when he called her that.

"Back so soon?" she shot at him, sitting up, hooking her arms around her legs as if in self-defense. "I was hoping you'd fallen overboard."

"And leave you alone to the attentions of other men?" He moved across the cabin to the bunk where she sat staring up at him warily. "Not hardly. Not yet, anyway."

"Too bad," she muttered, recoiling from the touch of his hand when he reached out to lift a thick golden ringlet of her hair in his palm. He held it, gazing down at her with a thoughtful frown, then let his fingers graze ever so lightly across the arc of her jaw.

"We'll be in port tomorrow," he said then, flatly, as if it wasn't important, and Laurie's eye flew up to meet his dark, searching gaze.

Even while her amber eyes darted hate at him, her mind was leaping excitedly from possibility to possibility—was it possible she would be freed? Had he done with her?

But almost as if he could see beneath the riot of gold hair to the feverishly working brain beneath, Cade's mouth curled in a derisive smile.

"Don't get excited—I'm not through with you yet. We won't be in New Orleans, but you knew that. We dock in a busy little place called Galveston, Texas."

Laurie's heart sank, and even while her eyes shot daggers at him, her mouth spouted questions she couldn't hold back.

"But you'll let me go then, Cade? What will you do in Galveston? How far is that from New Orleans?"

None of Laurie's questions, or the quick spurt of anger she tried to hold back, provoked Cade into telling her any more, and she had to be satisfied with knowing their destination. It was small comfort, but something to hold onto in the long night.

Cade watched her, pouring himself a glass of whiskey from a leather flask, his eyes raking Laurie's flushed face and high cheekbones, skimming over the interesting hollows and planes of her face, then over her thick, fragrant wealth of tawny hair to the curves pressing against the thin material of her gown. Why her? he wondered with a detached curiosity, tossing down his drink. Why this slender girl with the big gold eyes like a cat's? Why did she have the ability to get to him when none other ever had before? Not even CeCe had mattered to him like this girl did, and it was unsettling.

The knowledge rankled, and goaded him into cruelty.

Cade's eyes narrowed at her. "You look like a cat, *amante*, just waiting for something. Me, perhaps? Are you anxious to get me into bed?"

Laurie's straight brows dipped over her eyes, and the gold orbs darkened to a smoky bronze. "No! Don't you ever get tired of baiting me?"

"Ah, is that what I'm doing, *amante?*"

"*Amante!* I'm not your lover, I'm your prisoner, and you know it! Don't try to dignify your actions with honeyed words that mean nothing."

Before she could rise from the bunk, Cade reached down and tucked his long fingers under her chin, tilting back her head to gaze down at her with slitted eyes as dark as pitch.

"You're the one who uses honeyed words, Laurie-love. Of course, you saved the sweetest for Capitan Garcia, but the few you used on Martin almost caused a fight, didn't they? Is that your pattern, love? Cause dissension between your admirers and watch them kill each other off?" His fingers tightened cruelly, but she refused to give him the pleasure of seeing her flinch. "You remind me of a spider, the black widow, that mates with her victims then kills them. Is that what you're doing, love?"

"Get away from me!" she snapped in spite of the fear that curled in her chest. Her hands trembled slightly, and she hid them in the folds of her skirt. "You're drunk!"

"No, not yet. Not on whiskey. Drunk with desire, maybe, or vengeance, but not whiskey."

Schooling her features into composure, Laurie managed to say in a flat voice, "I hate you, Cade Caldwell."

"You're becoming repetitive, love." He laughed softly, and his fingers increased the pressure on her chin. "You tempt me to find out just how much you hate me, *querida*," he husked in the next instant.

Instead of releasing her, Cade's hands moved to lift her up and hard against him, then shifted to mold her body tightly to his. He watched for her reaction, but she was careful to let nothing show in her face, including the fact that she was alarmingly aware of his arousal.

This had become a familiar scene, a familiar game of cat and mouse that he played with her, taunting her into a reaction, then attacking with swift efficiency, the outcome always the same. Laurie's fingers curled into tight balls as she wedged her hands between them, a silent protest, an indication of her aversion.

"What? No struggle?" he mocked when she remained silent and stiff. "Why is it I'm not surprised," he murmured then, his mouth moving to brush against the top of her head. When she kept her face carefully averted, he put a finger beneath her chin and tilted back her head again, then let his mouth graze her closed lips. "Open for me, love," he said softly, his hard arms belying his tone and words.

She wasn't fooled. She knew how quickly he could change from loving to harsh, leaving her feeling as if she had just been slammed into a stone wall.

But Cade was an expert at coaxing a response from her, and his mouth and hands worked magic, his fingers massaging her body with supple strokes, his tongue teasing its way between her half-parted lips. Laurie leaned back, but his arms held her so tightly she couldn't lean far enough away. Outrage filled her at his disregard for her feelings, but she knew he would only laugh if she protested.

A feeling of dizzy helplessness made her cling to him with desperate fingers, and Laurie wished for what must have been the hundredth time that things were different. She knew Cade's body almost as well as she knew her own by now, yet she didn't know him at all. He was not the man she had once thought him, but the reckless, arrogant grandson of a wealthy *hacendado* who cared only for his own pleasure. There was a streak of cruelty in him, yet there were moments when he could be gentle. And she could still recall that first, wild night together, in the arbor where she had given herself to him so willingly, swept away by passion, moonlight, and the handsome man who gazed at her with glints of admiration in his eyes.

Laurie wanted to fight him, to struggle against the man who held her now, for it wasn't the same man who'd held her then. That Cade had been at least gentle and loving, while this Cade was made of stone, immovable, hard, unfeeling.

But maybe there was another way to reach him, and Laurie made her voice husky, lifting her arms to coil them around his neck, pressing her body close against his, rubbing her hips suggestively against his hard, male frame.

"Do you remember our first night together?" She paused when his hand moved to impatiently push aside the bodice of her gown, steeling her resolve, then continued softly, "I can't forget it, can't forget how you made me feel that night, Cade. It was wonderful."

As his fingers untied the laces to her chemise, Laurie swallowed hard, trying to repress a shiver. Why didn't he say something? Why didn't he respond instead of acting as if he didn't hear her?

But then she wished she'd left well enough alone, because when she pasted a bright smile of seduction on her face and curled her hands into the unbuttoned flap of his half-open shirt, he caught her hands in his and twisted her wrists cruelly.

"Don't! I respect your hate more than I do this awkward attempt at seduction, Laurie!"

He shoved her away from him, his face dark and angry, and she put her hands to her hot cheeks, staring back at him, just as angry.

"You just can't make up your mind what you want, can you!" she flared. "You say you want me only as a hostage, yet every night you try to force me to participate in a degrading, humiliating act! Why do you bother? Why don't you just admit to yourself that you're seeking vengeance by raping me?"

"Rape?" In spite of the anger in his gaze, he flashed her a tight smile. "Not rape, Laurie. Persuasive coaxing, maybe, but not rape. You participate too quickly and easily to call it that." His voice lowered to a soft, menacing curl of words. "And even if it was, don't you think you deserve some sort of reward for betrayal?"

"*Betrayal!* You still won't listen to the truth, will you?" She laughed bitterly. "Don't dignify your behavior by mouthing platitudes of how wronged you've been! I've been wronged, too."

White lines of fury bracketed Cade's thinned lips, and his dark eyes were blazing with hot fires.

"*You* weren't arrested for something you didn't do, for trying to help someone too stubborn to admit she

246

was playing a game too dangerous to win, were you?" He looked down at her with contempt. "Did you know that I almost had all the evidence I needed to evict the alcalde from his position? It took me months to get it, Laurie, months of careful spying and risking not only my life, but the lives of the peons who were helping me. And you ruined it with your foolish masquerade."

Her throat closed, and she choked out, "Why didn't you tell me?"

"And risk everything? One wrong word, one little slip, and it would have meant the lives of men with families, men who were risking a great deal instead of recklessly dashing around the country like a bored child at play."

One hand shot out to curl around her wrist and drag her back up from the bunk where she'd fallen when he shoved her away, and his voice was tight. "I warned you what might happen, but you wouldn't listen, and when I saw that you were in danger of being caught, I didn't think about myself, but about you. Now I wish I had let them take you." His voice became mocking. "What a fool I was! I didn't know you had Capitan Garcia beneath your skirts. No, I thought I was being gallant in rescuing you from the alcalde's soldiers, and my reward was torture and imprisonment. You've seen the scars on my back from the whip, Laurie. How do you think they got there? Because of you, and you dare to whine about my treatment of you?" He gave her another rough shove that sent her plummeting back to the bunk. "You deserve whatever you get," he ended in a flat tone as she sobbed into her cupped hands.

It was my fault, Laurie thought as she tried to stop her racking sobs. *If I had just listened to him when he told me not to keep on, but I didn't! I wanted to show them one more time that El Vengador was invincible, and now it's ruined both our lives. . . .*

247

But she couldn't say that to Cade. Not now. He was in no mood to listen to her, and she didn't know if she could talk without sobbing anyway. She didn't look up when she heard him slam out the door and lock it behind him, but remained in a miserable heap on the bunk.

Nothing was said when Cade returned hours later, and she lay with her face to the wall, stiff and cold and full of apprehension. To her relief, he did nothing, said nothing, but undressed and lay down next to her without touching her. She could smell the rich, potent fumes of the whiskey he'd been drinking, and spared a prayer of gratitude that he fell asleep almost immediately. Another confrontation like the last, and she would be nothing but a whimpering mass of guilt and hysteria.

That was one of the reasons why, the next day when they disembarked in the hot, humid air of Galveston, Laurie did not offer any protest when Cade put her into a carriage without a word of explanation. The silence that lay between them was thick and heavy, rife with accusation, and she did not want to endure any more cutting words.

She was too aware of him next to her, of his lean thigh pressing against hers, his arm nudging her ribs as he leaned forward to give the driver directions, and she tried to concentrate on the passing streets instead of Cade. She could feel his tension, the occasional cold glance, and she kept her face turned away.

"Stop here," Cade told the driver, and Laurie glanced out the carriage window at the one-story stucco building he indicated. "Deliver the bags to the front desk." There was a rattle of coins, then Cade was pulling Laurie from the carriage and setting her feet on the paved walkway.

She looked dubiously at the hotel, where a painted sign read simply HOTEL, then back at Cade.

248

"Don't worry," he said curtly when he saw her doubtful gaze, "it'll do fine for the short time we're going to be here."

"I suppose it would be too much to expect you to tell me just where we're going?" Laurie couldn't help snapping.

Cade's gaze was faintly amused. "Right."

Laurie subsided into a smoldering silence again, still wary of invoking his anger, though she would have liked to throw a tantrum that would rival any of those she had thrown as an adolescent.

And Cade must have seen the rebellion in her eyes, in the quick, slanted glance she gave him, for he grinned in that irritating way he had and asked softly, "Still want to shoot me?"

"Yes!" she hissed, heedless of the boy waiting patiently to carry in her baggage, heedless of the carriage driver and any curious eyes. Her body vibrated with tension, and she longed to do more than silently curse him.

"You may get your chance one day," Cade said, and took her arm and pulled her with him up the short walkway and into the hotel. Faded carpets were scattered across scuffed floors, and drab velvet draperies hung dispiritedly over tall windows that looked out over the street and the curve of water beyond.

In a room visible off the main lobby, she could see layers of cigar smoke and hear the unmistakable clink of coins and raucous laughter that indicated a gaming hall and dance hall. Shrill curls of forced gaiety and an occasional shriek convinced her that Cade had brought her to a less than reputable hotel. She half-turned, her tawny eyes flashing with anger.

"Is this the best Galveston has to offer?" Laurie could not keep from asking, and he shot her a quelling glance as he pulled her across the lobby with him.

A clerk as faded and drab as the hotel looked at

them without curiosity, pushing a yellowed ledger across the desk. "Sign here," he drawled, not bothering to look at the names as he reached for a room key. "First room on the right at the end of the hallway. No smoking in the room, no muddy boots on the bed, no firing of weapons inside. Enjoy your stay."

With those laconic rules still ringing in her ears, Laurie followed Cade down a shadowy hallway and waited while he unlocked the door and swung it open. She wasn't surprised to find the same type of accommodations in the room, a bed that sagged, a tilted washstand with a cracked pitcher and bowl, and a dresser mirror so smoky she could barely see her reflection.

Cade did not seem even to see those things. He shut the door and strode to the window looking out over the gray-blue waters of the Gulf, his arms folded over his chest.

"Better get some rest," he said after a moment. "We leave early in the morning."

"Leave?" she echoed, sweeping dust off the coverlet before she sank to the sparse comfort of the bed. "Leave for where?"

Cade turned. "Don't ask so many damned questions."

"Why not?" she flared, forgetting her resolve to remain distant and quiet. "Why shouldn't I know where you're taking me?"

A faint smile flickered on his mouth. "I liked it better when you were pretending to be remote, Laurie. Do you suppose you could sulk again?"

Pushing at the humidity-dampened strands of hair in her eyes, Laurie said impatiently, "I thought you were going to set me free once you were safe. Well, you're in Texas and you're safe, so why not let me go?"

He stared at her, his eyes narrowed against the bright shaft of sunlight slanting through the dusty

250

window. "I'll let you go when I'm ready. Not until then. Don't nag me, or I might be tempted to gag that pretty, vicious little mouth of yours."

Gasping with outrage, and not sure he wouldn't do what he threatened, Laurie contented herself with a stiff, contemptuous silence. She remained silent when Cade ordered food and a bath from the pretty little maid who came to their door, remained silent when the food arrived just before a high-backed copper tub and several buckets of steaming water.

"Do you want to eat or bathe first?" Cade asked, and she considered briefly.

It had been weeks since she'd had a real bath, in a tub with soap and hot water and the slick, delicious feeling of being really clean, but the food smelled tempting, too.

"A bath," she decided, and stood expectantly, waiting for him to be courteous enough to leave.

She should have known better.

"Fine," he said, and tossed her a cake of scented soap and a thick towel. "I'll eat while you bathe. Hurry it up. I like my bath reasonably warm."

Laurie stood there, and her shock must have shown on her face, because he added impatiently, "The water won't stay hot for long. If you're not going to use it, tell me so I can."

Her gaze flicked from the tub to the small screen in one corner, a low screen that wasn't nearly large enough to provide any privacy.

"Would you please leave?" she asked with as much dignity as she could muster, and knew from his raised brow and mocking smile that it had been a futile question.

"No, but I'll help you undress if you don't hurry."

And in the end, he did undress her, ignoring her sputtering fury and shrieks of humiliation, plopping her in the tub and scrubbing her tender skin so roughly she was certain she looked like a boiled chicken when he was through. Cade even washed her hair, pushing her below the surface of the water and laughing when she choked, wiping soap from her eyes along with wet ringlets as she glared at him and used all the curse words she'd ever heard.

"You're going to have to do better than that if you want to impress me," he said, and finally tiring of her curses, pushed her below the water one last time. He hauled her up and stood her on the floor, wrapping a thick towel around her shaking body. "Now my dinner is cold, and so is the water, so I'm not going to be in the best of moods. Think you can dry yourself off?"

"You bastard!"

"Is that the only name you know, Laurie? It's getting tiresome. Maybe I'll take the time to teach you some real curses one day, but right now I just want to get to my food and bath."

If she hadn't been wrapped so tightly in the towel, and if he hadn't sensed her reaction and kept his grip on her so that she could barely wiggle much less lift an arm, Laurie would have done her best to scratch out his eyes. But Cade held her wet, squirming body up against his hard chest until she stopped wiggling and stood there, panting from her exertions, her rage spent. His arm was across her body just under her breasts, squeezing until she was breathless every time she moved, his voice a warm whisper across the back of her damp neck.

"You feel almost as good wet as you do dry," he was saying in a thoughtful tone, and one hand slipped under the towel to caress her moist skin.

"Stop it," she muttered through clenched teeth, willing her muscles not to react to his touch. "Aren't you tired of mistreating me yet?"

"Is that what you call this . . . and this?" His hand moved under the towel to cup her breast, his fingers

252

teasing the taut peak until her head fell back against his shoulder and her eyes closed. He could feel the rapid rhythm of her lungs and heart beneath his palm as he slid it from her breast to the small round of her belly and lower, and when Laurie moaned softly he smiled.

Despair filled her as his hands roamed wherever he chose, and she knew that her struggles would be ignored, so to keep every last shred of dignity she possessed, she ground her teeth together and thought of something else, anything else to distract her from what he was doing. She visualized the ocean on the California coast, the powdery white sands and the blue, blue sky and lacy waves washing ashore. She tried to recall the seawinds in her hair and the salty tang they brought with them, the bright nodding blossoms of huge poppies that grew wild everywhere, the startling shades of yellow, orange, and rich cream exploding across hillsides so green as to hurt the eyes.

As Cade unwound the towel from around her and let it fall to the floor, Laurie shuddered, then gave a sigh of relief when there was a knock at the door. When he released her and went to answer it, she scooped up the towel and a dressing gown from her trunk and dived behind the low screen beside the copper tub. Hastily she pulled on the light gown and immediately felt better, more in control as she heard the mutter of voices, then Cade shut the door again.

"Sorry I can't stick around to finish what I started, but if you're good I may later," he said, grinning at her furious gasp. He was reaching for the pistol he'd placed on the table, slinging the leather holster around his waist and buckling it on as he met her snapping gaze. "Don't even think about escape, love. You wouldn't like the consequences, I promise."

She didn't say anything as he stepped out the door and closed it softly behind him, just stared as she

253

heard the key click in the lock. She wasn't surprised, but had held out the faint hope that this one time he might forget. So much for that, she thought as she sank to the edge of the bed and stared at the puddles of water on the floor next to the tub. Her gaze moved to the tray of food, and shrugging, she rose and crossed to the small table.

Upon lifting the lid to the covered bowl, she found a large heap of boiled shrimp, oysters, and freshwater clams. A tangy sauce had been spooned into another bowl, and there was a platter of fresh, crusty bread as well as shredded cabbage and carrots mixed together with another sauce and liberal amounts of black pepper. A bottle of white wine sat in a small bucket of ice, and after a moment's indecision, Laurie poured some in a glass.

Her first swallow was too much, and she half-choked, then sipped at it more slowly, feeling the warmth of the pale wine slide down her throat. Sipping the wine reminded her of France and the many dinners she had eaten there, the wines and excellent cuisine, the brisk table conversation. A half-smile curled her lips as she recalled her *cousine* Mignon. She wondered what Mignon was doing now, and if she was happy. Much sought-after, a petite brunette with doe eyes and a quick, smiling mouth, Mignon had exchanged many confidences with Laurie in the nights spent whispering in a large double bed. They had dreamed about the man they would fall in love with one day, and never in her most imaginative dreams of love had Laurie ever thought it would be a man like Cade Caldwell. What would Mignon say?

Turning to pace restlessly around the room, the bottle of wine in one hand and her half-filled glass in the other, Laurie reflected that she was lost. She didn't know if she still loved Cade, or indeed, if she ever really had, but only justified her actions with grandiose notions of love. Perhaps that was what she had done, otherwise, how could she hate him so much now?

On the heels of that thought was the wry thought that he'd been right when he'd said her body didn't hate him. In spite of all her best resolutions, she could not help an uninhibited response to his kisses and caresses, and she had no idea why. Were the body and mind that far apart? She had always thought the brain controlled the body, but there were times when she had no control at all over her reaction to Cade. Laurie shrugged and poured herself another glass of wine.

The hem of her dressing gown dragged across the carpets as she moved to the window. She pushed aside the dusty fold of drapery and tried the window, but as she had expected, it was nailed shut. Sighing, she stared out over the unkempt garden to the white line of beach across the street. Freedom was so near, just within reach, but so far. Dared she cause a disturbance that would bring the desk clerk to open the door? Or had Cade taken care of that somehow?

After several yanks of the bellpull to summon a maid, and no answer, Laurie beat on the door. No one came, and she hadn't really thought they would. Even in her room, she could hear the noise from the gaming hall, the loud music and laughter that would drown out any noise she could make. Stepping back to the window, she retrieved the bottle of wine, ignoring her glass.

Leaning against the wooden frame, Laurie watched the sun sink on the horizon, a blazing ball of fire that cast long streamers of light over the silky waves rolling endlessly to the beach.

When night fell in a soft dark blanket, shrouding sea and sky, she began to feel sleepy, and discovered to her surprise that the bottle of wine was empty. The floor dipped and slanted as she turned from the window toward the bed, and she stumbled.

A soft giggle escaped her. She was reminded of her Uncle Jean-Claude in New Orleans, and how he had walked just this way one Christmas. *Tante* Annette had pretended to be angry with him, but had smiled when he didn't see. Papa had laughed, too, but then, he had been just as awkward and clumsy as Uncle Jean-Claude and laughed at everything.

She had never drunk too much wine before, except that night she had been feeling so reckless, the night she had gone with Cade to the leafy arbor and lain on the padded bench and fallen in love with him. Her smile faded, turning to tears as she fell across the bed. Things had gone so wrong, so wrong, and she still didn't quite understand how it had happened. But it made her head ache to think about that now, to think about anything. And she was so sleepy, when she had thought she would never be able to sleep in this wretched room that had grown so hot and stuffy. The only air was from a transom high overhead, and it was opened barely a crack, so that the fresh air teased instead of refreshed.

Laurie rolled to her stomach, and the wine bottle slipped from her hand to the floor, rolling across the shabby carpet to stop against the small screen in the corner. Her hands clutched the bedspread as she held on to keep the bed from spinning so crazily, and she had the vague thought that she wasn't as happy as she should have been after a full bottle of wine. Instead, she was much sadder, and couldn't stop the flood of tears that welled in her eyes and scalded her cheeks.

Curling up in a fetal position, Laurie tucked her hands under her chin and gave a long sigh as she fell into a deep, dreamless sleep.

That was how Cade found her, curled into a ball, tear tracks still on her face and the dressing gown draped loosely over her. He stood in the room lit only by a flood of moonlight through the closed window, staring down at her with a bemused expression, half-regretful, half-amused. So she'd gotten drunk, had she? Well, she wasn't the only one.

He'd spent the evening hours with an acquaintance, an old comrade from the war for Texas's independence, and they had drunk whiskey and made plans in one of the busy saloons just off the main street. There was a lot to think about even without Laurie, and he had found himself thinking about her anyway, his mind drifting from their conversation to the sweet, sulky girl waiting for him in a dingy hotel. Finally Cade had stood up and said he was leaving, even though Jim Tyler had tried to get him to stay.

"C'mon, Caldwell! You ain' gotta go back yet," the man had slurred, his eyes as bleary as Cade's. "We still got a few things to 'member."

"Tomorrow, Tyler," Cade had said, tossing enough money to the table to pay for both their bottles.

"We leave early," Tyler reminded, and Cade gave a short nod.

"I know."

Early would be before the first light, and a smile touched the corners of Cade's mouth when he envisioned Laurie's condition at that time of the day. Especially after drinking too much. He could see the faint glassy sheen of the empty wine bottle on the floor. The copper tub still stood amidst almost dry puddles, and the towel he'd used to dry Laurie lay in a heap beside it. The memory of her soft skin beneath his hands and his lips made his body leap with anticipation, but he stifled his reaction. It was late, and there would be plenty of time later, although when Laurie found out where he was taking her she would be so furious she would probably fight him tooth and claw every time he got near her.

But that was all right, too, because Cade was growing tired of having to fight her. Maybe it'd be best if he did let her go, he thought as he lay down beside her, but in the next instant she curled her sleeping body into the hard angle of his as if seeking his comfort, and he knew he was not yet ready to do that. He wasn't ready to relinquish the feel of her next to him, willing or unwilling.

Cade put one arm over her and molded his fully clad frame next to her, then fell asleep.

Laurie was the first to waken, her eyes opening as she felt a movement behind her, her brain struggling to make sense of her surroundings. She had been dreaming she was in New Orleans again, and lying in the bed she'd had since childhood, with Isabeau coming soon to wake her up for the day. Dear Isabeau, with her broad, creamy face and wide smile, the kind, old eyes glowing with unadulterated love . . . there was an aching void where the love once was and Laurie tried to remember why. She missed her so, missed that accepting love that required nothing from her but a return of it.

But as she struggled from the clinging fog of sleep to reality, she realized that she wasn't in New Orleans in her own bed, and that Isabeau would never come to wake her for the day again. Instead, she slept beside Cade Caldwell, and he had one long leg thrown carelessly across her.

Her head throbbed terribly, her stomach felt queasy, and there was a cottony feel to her mouth and throat—but worst was the discovery that she couldn't move without waking Cade. His breathing was deep and easy, and she lay without moving for several moments, the pale light in the room gradually growing brighter. It was near dawn, and the quiet world appeared to be waiting for the sun.

She slid Cade a glance from beneath slitted lashes, and found him gazing at her. Drawing in a sharp breath, Laurie tensed. She knew that light in his eyes,

258

that hot, intense glitter that usually accompanied desire.

"No," she muttered through dry, stiff lips, pushing at him as his arm tightened around her. "No!"

"Always no, sweet love—don't you ever say yes?" Cade murmured, but it was merely a rhetorical question, because he didn't pause to wait for a reply. His hands skimmed over her body and beneath the dressing gown she wore, grazing her soft thighs, kneading the tight flesh of her belly, exploring the contours of her rib cage, then moving to cup her breasts in his palms. A familiar pattern, and Laurie knew it was useless but protested anyway.

"Not today, Cade! Please! I'm . . . I'm sick," she added with sudden inspiration, and felt him draw back slightly to frown at her.

"Sick?"

She nodded, her lashes lowering so he wouldn't see the lie in her eyes, her lower lip quivering just the slightest bit.

"Yes. You know. . . ."

She let her voice trail into silence, hoping he would fill in what she didn't say, hoping he wouldn't want any more details. And really, it was almost that time, and she wasn't lying by but a few days.

To her relief he rolled away from her without saying anything else, and she kept her gaze downcast as if embarrassed. What was happening to her? Just a few short months ago she would have been horrified at the very idea of a man knowing about such things, but now she had boldly suggested it herself! She'd changed so much, and now she buried her face in her hands as she realized how low she'd sunk.

Cade's dry voice came softly through the shadows. "I'd hang my head, too, if I couldn't think of a better lie than that."

Laurie's cheeks flamed hotly, and she felt the prickly

259

sting of tears in her eyed. How mortifying! He knew she had stooped to lying about . . . that.

Few words were exchanged as Cade washed and changed into clean clothes, and Laurie did her best not to get in his way. It was only after she'd dressed and packed her trunk again that he told her, "We're on our way to Austin, so pack light."

She stared at him. "What?"

"Austin—the new capital of Texas. It used to be called Waterloo, until last year. Now it's Austin, after Stephen Austin."

Laurie's brain was numb with shock. Where was Austin? How far away from New Orleans? And how much longer would he force her to stay with him?

Reading the questions in her eyes, Cade almost smiled. "I'll let you go soon, love. Try not to wear out your welcome until then."

Dismay clouded her eyes with tears, and Laurie looked at her trunks stacked on the floor. "What am I allowed to take?"

"Just a few changes of clothes and any necessities. We'll be traveling through rough country and can't risk too much weight."

Her face paled even more. When her lashes lifted to reveal amber eyes wide with fright, her voice was surprisingly steady. "And how far did you say Austin is?"

"It's roughly four hundred miles through Indian country. That's a warning," he added when she just looked at him. "Since the white men have been taking over everything, some of the Indians aren't so friendly anymore. Some never were." He shrugged. "That's a risk we'll just have to take."

"How generous of you to risk me, too!" The fright in her eyes took on the color of anger, and Laurie glared at him in the early morning light filtering in through the dirty, unwashed windowpanes.

"We're already late, baby, so hurry up," Cade said

without the slightest trace of remorse. "And if I have to carry you out of here kicking and screaming, I will, so don't be tempted to cause one of your famous little scenes. My temper isn't as even as it usually is, and I might just break your straight little nose before I can stop myself."

Because she wasn't sure he wouldn't do as he'd threatened, Laurie did no more than grumble to herself as she stuffed the few things she could carry into a leather bag and followed Cade. What would happen to her now?

Chapter Eighteen

Laurie quickly grew to hate Texas, with its vast sweep of hot land unbroken by green trees or lovely landscape. A constant burn of sun and dust reddened her skin and gnawed at her clothes, until she longed for just the touch of water on her parched skin. Would they never reach their destination? Would she never be able to look at something besides the east end of a westbound horse?

Cade kept her with him, her mount close to his, away from the others with them. There were only two more men with them, hard, crusty men that made Laurie nervous when they glanced at her sideways, obviously wondering as to her relationship with Cade. Of course, they must realize where she slept at night—her blanket-wrapped body on the hard ground right beside Cade—but her sharp words and stiff silences were an excellent indication she wasn't with him willingly. Did they know? Did they realize that she was his prisoner and not his mistress?

Chewing her bottom lip, Laurie wondered if one of them might be disposed to helping her get away from Cade, help her get back to New Orleans. It was an idea borne of desperation, borne of fear and hatred for the hot, dusty land that stretched to infinity. How could Cade say he loved Texas? All the Texans she'd met had been rough, crude people filled with self-importance and prone to outrageous claims.

Maybe that was it, she answered herself sourly, maybe that was why Cade liked Texas so well, because he was just like those people. And at night, when she crouched as far away from him as she could get, she couldn't help but hear some of their plans for the republic, plans that included annexation to the United States. She laughed silently. As if the United States would ever truly accept this brawling country of braggarts and rowdies. No, it would be better if it was taken by Mexico again, as the Mexicans were reported to intend. She shuddered at the thought of another war over the republic and put her hands over her ears when the men talked about the battles they had fought to gain Texas her independence.

The Alamo. Buffalo Bayou. Goliad. San Jacinto — I'll go mad if I hear those names again! she thought once when a particularly brutal series of battles was recalled. "And I don't really believe it happened that way, anyway!" she made the mistake of saying aloud, capturing the immediate attention of all three men.

It was Cade who responded first, uncoiling his long body in a smooth motion like a rattlesnake unwinding, his eyes hot and hard in the evening firelight.

"Oh, you don't? Any reason for this educated speculation, Laurie?"

Obstinately clinging to the opposite theory despite the uneasy suspicion that she might be wrong, Laurie tilted back her head to glare up at him from the flat rock near the fire where she sat.

"In the first place, Santa Anna's numbers were so overwhelming, I do not think a decisive battle could have been won at San Jacinto. In the second place,

263

the men at the Alamo were said to have been offered opportunity for surrender and did not. It left the Mexican general with very little choice, the way I see it." Her gaze shifted from Tyler, who had been staring at her courteously, to Cade.

Cade's mouth had thinned to a slash in his sunburned face, and his eyes narrowed. "Where did you get your information?"

She hesitated, then said, "From the newspapers. And my uncle has friends in the American Embassy."

"Where were you in 1836, Laurie?"

She flushed. "France."

"And you're prepared to make a decision when you were not even in the United States?" Cade laughed harshly. "If you want to argue, sweetheart, just tell me, and I'll be glad to oblige you on any other subject." His voice dropped to a menacing whisper. "But don't ever make the mistake of talking about this again, not unless you know a lot more than you do now!"

Retreating into offended silence, Laurie sat apart from them, listening as their voices lowered to rumbles and soft murmurs, feeling miserable and more alone than she'd ever felt in her entire life. The night sky was black and vast, and she could hear the eerie cries of animals Cade had told her were coyotes, their howls penetrating the blackness in mournful wails that made her want to howl with them. Their campfire was the only pinprick of life in this land that ran to infinity, from distant jagged edges of mountain peaks that gnawed harshly at the sky, to the miles and miles of flat, dry sand and scrub. How could Cade say he loved Texas?

It was so raw, so primitive, and it made California seem as civilized as Paris by contrast. A faint smile touched just the corners of her mouth. She'd never thought she would consider California anything but uncivilized, but there were worse places, she supposed. Carlota had tried to tell her that, but in her supreme ignorance and arrogance, she had just laughed at her stepmother.

"Worse than California?" she'd mocked. "I doubt it!"

Was this her punishment for being so arrogant? Was this—her abduction and unwilling introduction to reality—divine retribution? Her convent education returned in a swift rush. She shivered, and wished she'd paid more attention to Father Richard's homilies. She tried to pray and found to her dismay that she couldn't find the words, couldn't think of the right way to begin.

Closing her eyes, Laurie searched her memory and began to repeat the prayers she'd learned in childhood, the old, familiar prayers that were comforting. It worked, and she was so deep in thought she did not hear the approaching bootsteps.

"Ma'am? Am I bothering you?"

Laurie's head jerked up, and her gaze focused on Tyler. "Bothering me? No, no, I was just . . . just thinking."

Holding his hat in his hands, Tyler, a gruff, crusty man almost as tall as Cade but heavier, smiled at her. "In Texas, the mind lends itself to thoughts as grand as the republic. I guess it's because out here there's little else to distract a man—or a woman—from thinking."

Doubtfully, she murmured agreement. "Yes, I suppose so."

He laughed, and it was a genuine laugh with no mockery or hidden meanings. Laurie smiled as he said, "You don't sound as convinced as I'd hoped."

"No, I'm not."

"Well, I know you're not here because you want to be."

265

"Did—did he tell you that?" Her breath caught, and her cheeks flamed with sudden embarrassment that this man knew her predicament.

"Caldwell? Naw, he don't say much about his business, and you are his business, ma'am, pardon my saying it like that." There was a brief pause while he looked at her with troubled eyes, then Tyler added, "But I just want you to know that none of us—me, nor Caldwell, nor Davis—will let anything happen to you, so don't be scared."

Laurie's mind was working swiftly. If Tyler was sympathetic to her, mightn't he help her escape Cade? It was a slim possibility, but it *was a* possibility.

But Cade, as if sensing the direction of her thoughts, appeared right behind Tyler, his lean frame blocking out the light from the fire.

"Flirting with my woman, Tyler?" he asked lightly, but there was a thread of ice in his voice that made Tyler turn quickly and shake his head.

"Naw, you know me better'n that, Cade! I was just trying to tell the little lady that she needn't be scared of anything out here, that we'd take care of her."

Cade's dark gaze shifted to Laurie's flushed, guilty face, and he knew what she'd been thinking, how she had interpreted Tyler's gesture.

"My mistake," Cade said, his eyes remaining on Laurie, and with a mumbled apology, Tyler walked away, leaving them alone.

Cade stepped closer to her and Laurie edged away, her hands scraping roughly on the flat rock as she avoided him.

"I know what's in that fertile little brain of yours, Laurie Allen," Cade said softly, "but you can forget it! I guess I should have made it clear to Tyler and Davis on the head end of this trip just how it stands with us, so there wouldn't be any misguided efforts

266

at pleasing you."

"I . . . I don't know what you mean," Laurie said as she backed away further.

"Oh yes you do. You were going to be 'friends' with Tyler, and then ask him to help you escape, while poor Jim wouldn't even know what hit him. He's not a devious man, Laurie, just a man who takes things at face value. He wouldn't stop to think that you might have ulterior motives."

"You're crazy!" she snapped when she reached the edge of the rock and could go no farther. Her tawny eyes jerked back to Cade, and her chin lifted.

"Maybe. But not crazy enough to let you get away with this. Have you forgotten that you're in this just as deep as I am? After all, love, everyone in California will believe that you helped me escape since you tried to take the blame for my crimes." His voice grew sarcastic, and she noticed the inflection on the word *my* but then he was saying, "No more games, Laurie. Leave Tyler and Davis alone for the rest of the trip, do you understand?" His hand flashed out to grab her by the arm, and he jerked her to him. When she opened her mouth to scream he said in her ear, "Don't bother. They won't interfere."

He was right, because Tyler and Davis did not turn their heads from the fire when Cade pulled her with him out into the flat land beyond the arcing glow of flames, out to where Laurie had been staring only minutes before. He dragged her when she stumbled over a clump of grass, ignoring her angry cries, pausing only for an instant to allow her to half-regain her feet before he pulled her with him again. The dark shapes of cactus and mesquite broke the shadows of night, and once Laurie bumped into the thorny spines of a saguaro. She yelped, and Cade swore softly.

When he stopped, the campfire was just a tiny

flicker of light in the distance, almost a pinprick. Laurie looked up at him with a defiant tilt of her chin.

"What are you going to do?" she demanded in spite of the tingle of fear that made her shiver. He wouldn't kill her— No, he hadn't brought her this far just to leave her on the prairie.

Instead of answering, Cade whirled her to face him. A high moon overhead silvered his face and hers, showing him the sheen of fear in her eyes, the bright glitter that made her eyes shimmer like splinters of gold, and for a brief instant he hesitated. Then the soaring wail of a coyote hung in the air, and he thought of all the predatory beasts he'd known, and how like them Laurie could be. Selfish to a fault, and deadly. Didn't he have the stripes on his back to prove it?

"Ever hear of branding, Laurie?" One hand moved to idly stroke back a strand of hair from her forehead, while his other kept a firm grip on her arm. "Actually, the Spanish brought it to America, but it's caught on pretty good here. See, with all the wide-open spaces out here, cattle roam a vast area. Some of them get lost, or mixed up with another man's herd. . . ."

"Of course, I've heard of it! Do you think I didn't pay any attention at the *matanzas?* Why are you boring me with this story?" Laurie shot up at him, trying to jerk away, suddenly afraid of the light in his eyes and the turn of the conversation.

Cade's grip tightened, and he went on as if she hadn't interrupted.

"So the only way to tell whose is whose, is to brand them. It's done with a hot iron, with the owner's mark burned into the hide. . . ." His finger traced a path across her cheek that made Laurie shudder. "That way, when a cow gets lost, the owner can prove it's his by the mark on it. Do you understand?"

Laurie made her voice steady. "I'm not an idiot! And I don't care a whit about cattle or branding, or if they're lost or found." Her voice trembled slightly and she sucked in a deep breath. "But it's late and you always get me up early, so I'd like to go back to the camp now."

Tension vibrated between them, and she held her breath as she waited to see what Cade would do. She could see the distant flicker of the fire over his shoulder, the tiny figures of Tyler and Davis, and felt slightly comforted. Though they were far away, they were within shouting distance, and she hoped neither man would approve of Cade actually harming her.

But then he was gathering her into his arms in a fierce hold, his mouth searing across her lips in a startling, hot kiss that left her momentarily confused. What did he mean to do? She was crushed against him, his hands moving over her body with a familiar urgency that made her heart leap and her breath shorten, and Laurie struggled more against her own responses than against Cade. This was ridiculous! He had only to kiss her, and her body responded to his touch with a yearning that was as inexplicable as it was overpowering.

A brisk night breeze skimmed her bare skin, and Laurie realized with a shock that Cade had somehow unlaced her gown and was peeling it away from her. The knowledge whipped her back to reality, and she pushed away from him.

"Stop it!"

"Ah no, sweet love. It's gone too far to stop now," he said, curling his fingers into the remaining strap of her gown and pulling it down. "I intend to brand you, to let Tyler and Davis and anyone else know that you're mine. Mine until I don't want you any-

269

more, anyway," he added brutally, and swept her from her feet into his arms.

As she pounded her hands against him, raging that he couldn't just take her like an animal in the dirt and dust of the prairie, Cade stripped away her last garment. Sobbing and shivering, she continued to struggle against him, her cries of rage and hurt whipping on the night wind.

"I hate you, Cade Caldwell!" she screamed, and wondered if Davis and Tyler would come to her rescue.

"They won't lift a finger to help you," Cade said, reading her mind, his mouth slanted into a derisive smile. Laurie saw that he'd undressed, too, and tried to roll away from him. He stopped her, his hands catching her around the ribcage, his palms quickly moving to cup her breasts. "And you don't really want them to, do you?" he said in the next breath.

"Yes! I hate you!" Laurie snatched at her clothes lying in a heap within inches of her, and Cade reached around her to push them away.

His warm breath fanned across her cheek as he leaned over her, her back pressed close against his chest and hard thighs, and she could feel the heat of him nudging her.

"Oh please, Cade, let me go," she whispered in a voice broken with sobs.

"But I can't, Laurie," he said. His voice was harsh and faintly puzzled. "You've gotten to me, somehow, like a sand flea, nestled just under my skin and worrying the hell out of me. I can't let you go, and I don't want you with me, and it's driving me crazy."

Holding her breath, she could tell from the ravaged bite of his voice that he was just as tortured as she was, and for the first time, Laurie realized that though he hadn't meant to let her know so much, he was as trapped as she was.

Somehow, knowing that, made it easier for her to give in to the urgent demands of her body and his, made it easier to soothe the prick of conscience that told her she was being a fool again. She should scream at him, tell him just what she thought of him, but the surging ache in her body made her return his kisses, her greedy hands moving to arouse him as much as she was aroused, and she had the vague thought that she had never dreamed love and hate were so inexplicably entwined.

Pinpricks of light frosted the night sky that dipped to meet the horizon, and she tilted back her head as Cade took her, his body driving into hers with a savage need that threatened to consume them both, and Laurie shuddered with the force of it. Her fingers traced the faint scars on his back as she held him, as he moved inside her, and her hips arched upward.

"We're both branded," she said, her voice sounding faint and faraway, as remote as the stars.

Cade drew back slightly, lifting himself to stare down at her moonlight-drenched face, his in shadow, his voice harsh. "Remember that the next time you try to tempt a man to your bed, Laurie."

Gasping with shock and a swift return of anger, Laurie dug her nails into his back, hearing his grunt of pain with a surge of satisfaction until he grabbed her wrists and pulled her arms over her head.

"You bloodthirsty little bitch," Cade swore softly, his fingers biting into her flesh with a vengeance. Then his mouth came down over her half-parted lips in a savage kiss that drove everything from her mind but the aching need for release.

And after, as she lay sullen and with lips and eyes still swollen with remnants of passion, she heard Cade say as he tossed her clothes to her, "Get dressed. I hear something."

Sulkily, with her hands trembling from reaction,

she sat up and smoothed back a tangle of hair from her eyes. "I don't know how you can hear anything. All I hear is the wind. And coyotes."

"Those aren't coyotes," Cade said, reaching down to jerk her to her feet, his mood as swiftly business-like as it had been passionate just moments before. "And if you don't hurry it up, love, you may find that pretty gold hair of yours has parted company with your head."

Before she could ask him what he meant, he was pushing her ahead of him, then half-dragging her back to the camp. Laurie could see that the fire was out, and wondered why even as she felt a surge of gratitude that it was. She didn't want Tyler and Davis to see her tumbled hair and flushed cheeks, even though she knew they had to be aware of what had happened.

"Caldwell," came a soft voice from the shadows, and Cade shoved Laurie behind a cluster of huge rocks and dropped beside her.

"How many do you think there are?" Davis asked, and there was a taut note to his voice that made Laurie's throat tighten.

"What's going on," she began, but Cade told her to shut up and be still.

"Ten, maybe more from the sound of it," Cade added to Davis, and Laurie could see the shadow that was Tyler shift position.

"I'd say Comanches," Tyler muttered, and Cade nodded.

Comanches. Just the word made Laurie's blood freeze. Had they been out there in the shadows, listening to her and Cade? Cade's next words confirmed her suspicion.

"If I'd been paying attention as I should have," he said in a low voice, "I'd have heard them sneak up. But I was distracted."

272

Tyler's teeth flashed in the moonlight. "Yeah. I kinda guessed as much."

A hot wave washed over Laurie's cheeks and made her eyes water, but she didn't care so much about the embarrassment as the fact that she could be killed or captured by savage Indians.

"What do they want?" she asked in a choked voice.

Cade shrugged. "Our horses. Us dead. Something like that."

"Well, give them the horses!" she almost screamed, curling her hands into tight fists.

Cade looked amused. "Sure. I'll just go out there, hand them our horses, wait for them to say thanks, and march back into camp safe and sound." He shook his head. "It doesn't work like that, Laurie."

Frozen with fear, she sat there for a long moment, staring into the inky blackness where death waited. There was only the sound of the wind, coyotes, and the metallic click of the rifles being loaded.

No one had time to answer her questions or still her fears. They were too busy with their weapons, and Laurie found it difficult to restrain the tremors that racked her body. She was too young to die, and she hadn't done all the things she'd wanted to do yet. This was so very different from her confrontations with the alcalde's soldiers, and even the final flight, before they had caught her.

At least, then, she had controlled the battle, and been the one to initiate it. Now, there were men out there—men she'd never seen and had no feelings for or against—and they wanted to kill her. Nameless faces, savage warriors with hard brown bodies and hate in their eyes for all white men, wanted to kill her and take her hair as a trophy. She shuddered, still exploring the boundaries of unreality. It could not be happening to her. How had she come to this? How had she—Laurette Allen—ended up alone in a

273

strange and frightening land where even the plants were enemies?

"Guess those Comanches still got their backs up," Davis commented in a laconic tone. Laurie jerked to look at him.

"What do you mean?" she whispered as Cade and Tyler concentrated on loading rifles and handguns. She wiped her sweaty palms on her skirts, and licked suddenly dry lips.

Shrugging, Davis said, "Back in March a delegation of Comanche dignitaries went to San Antonio to meet with white leaders. Wanted to discuss the tradin' of white prisoners the Comanche held, in exchange for certain concessions from Texans. Well, when the Texans saw the condition of the white prisoners—only two, a Mexican boy and a young girl who'd been tortured—they did the worst thing they coulda done. They leaped on the Comanches and tried to take the leaders prisoner. 'Course, they fought back, and it ended up with about twelve of the chiefs and a score of warriors bein' killed."

"And now the Comanches are set on revenge," Laurie whispered through stiff, cold lips.

Davis nodded. "Right. Those Comanches, see, have been lords of the desert for more'n a hunnered years. Drove off all the other Indians, includin' the Apaches, and so they thought they'd parley with the white man." He shook his head. "Don't look like talkin' worked."

"No," Laurie said around the icy lump in her throat, "it doesn't."

She might have descended into hysteria then if Cade hadn't shoved a rifle into her unwilling hands with the order to load it.

"I don't know how," she said, staring down at the heavy weapon with an expression of acute distaste. "All I know is a sword. An epée is much more . . .

274

civilized."

"Well, you'll see how civilized a rifle can be when you've got painted warriors howling in your face," Cade shot back coldly, then instructed her on the finer points of firearms. He kept his Paterson revolver—the pistol invented by Samuel Colt and known as the Texas model—for himself.

The night dragged on as they sat sleeplessly waiting for the first light that would bring an attack, and Laurie found herself as tense and wide-eyed as the men. She'd had to load and reload until Cade was certain she knew how to operate one of the rifles, his voice hard and impatient in her ear until she'd longed to tell him to shut up. But fear drove her on, and she tried to concentrate on what he was telling her as the night slowly faded into a faint glow on the eastern ridge of land.

"Now," Cade said softly, and they all readied themselves.

But when Laurie had meticulously poured in the powder and rammed a cartridge into the long barrel of the rifle, she still wasn't prepared for the deafening explosion of it being fired close to her. A squeal of fright accompanied the first shot, and she cowered behind the rock until Cade dragged her up and handed her the hot rifle to load again.

"Keep at it!" he snapped. "And don't use so much powder this time!"

Over the thundering roar of pistols and carbines, she could hear the bone-chilling scream of the Comanches, and her movements became smoother, methodical, so that she didn't have much time to worry about death. Apparently the Indians hadn't expected the Texans to be ready for them, and they finally withdrew.

"They're discussing what to do next," Cade said, and Laurie looked up at his grim, soot-smeared face.

There was a red streak across one cheek—blood?—
and she barely had time to reach up a hand before
he was shaking her away, his gaze intent on the
brightening expanse of land beyond them.

Moments later, another wave of screaming, yelling
warriors flung themselves at the men in the rocks,
and were once again met with a withering fusillade
of gunfire. This time they were mounted on horses
with wild eyes and streaks of warpaint, and one warrior managed to leap his mount over the rocks and
into the small clearing where Laurie sat with a lapful
of rifles she was loading. Her head snapped up, and
her eyes were wide and dilated with fear.

The Comanche paused almost imperceptibly, his
black, obsidian gaze boring into her, before he
wheeled his horse and lashed out at Davis with his
lance. Cade was firing at oncoming warriors, and
Tyler was half-turned, trying to keep more at bay
from another side. It was only Laurie and Davis,
back to back, battling the fierce Comanche.

When Davis fired the last shot from his revolver,
she quickly handed him a loaded carbine, but the
Comanche was quicker. With a swift, brutal blow, he
gashed Davis with the sharp edge of his lance, sending him to the ground. Then he pivoted his mount
to lean down and grab Laurie.

Shrieking, she fought him, using a rifle as a club
before her hand found and identified Cade's sword as
a possible weapon. This she was familiar with, and
she jerked free for a moment, sweeping up the sword
in the same smooth motion, the blade flashing in the
sunlight and startling the Comanche.

"Aiiee!" he shouted, obviously struck by the sight of
a woman wielding a sword. And when Laurie thrust
forward, the tip of the sword slashing toward the
warrior and making his horse rear in fright, he
lashed out with his war club. But her sword was

swifter, and sliced a path through the Comanche's breechclout and flesh in a smooth, sickening thrust of blade against bone.

Withdrawing the blade, Laurie would have struck out at him again, beyond reason, beyond terror, but the warrior managed to wheel his horse, and her blade struck only thin air. Gouts of blood clung to the blade, and adrenalin pumped through her veins in a rushing tide that sent her over the rocks and after him. There was no reason in her reaction, no method, only a savage, fierce desire to kill the man who had terrified her. She lashed out again, the flat of her blade striking the fleeing warrior across his back, and he wheezed. Blood was dripping down his leg and splattering on the ground, and her blade had left a wide red stripe across the bare skin of his back. The horse shrilled, half-rearing as the warrior almost fell from its back, and Laurie finally realized that the man was badly wounded. A surge of triumph shot through her, and she leaped to the crest of a rock and brandished her sword.

"Damn you!" she shouted, balancing on the rock, "Damn you!"

A hand on her arm made her swing around and bring up the sword at the same time, her eyes widening with fear and reaction. Too late she saw Cade, heard his harsh curse, and then the sword was slicing through his flesh. With a shock, she felt it grate against bone.

He stared at her in a kind of stunned surprise, but there was no time for comment as he grabbed her around the waist and slung her to the ground. An arrow whined overhead as he fell beside her, his long body pinning her down.

Laurie could see the incredulity in his gaze, could feel the warm trickle of his blood soaking her gown, and she couldn't move.

Finally, a wry smile twisted his mouth, and he said in a steady voice, "If I didn't know better, I'd think you did that on purpose."

"But I didn't."

Her voice sounded strangely alien to her ears, as if it came through yards of cotton batting, and she felt him move slightly and saw his grimace.

"I know. If I really thought you had, you'd be dead."

She said nothing, watching his dark eyes, seeing the pain in them. There was a faintly baffled expression, too, as if he was wondering just how far she could be pushed, but no anger.

"There's no time for this now," he was saying then, pushing himself up, bringing her with him, running low and crouched back toward the pile of rocks where Tyler lay with the wounded Davis.

It seemed unbelievable to Laurie that only a few short months before she had been safe and sound in France, with only the happy chatter of her cousins in her ears instead of the deafening roar of rifles. Now here she was, an ocean away, with the acrid smell of gunpowder in her nostrils and blistered fingers from fumbling with hot rifles. Frozen with fear, half-crouched, half-lying on the rocky ground with her head hidden behind a large thrust of rock, Laurie tried to obey Cade's terse commands to reload his rifle. She kept her eyes glued to the weapon even when she heard his voice rise in warning.

"Tyler! To the left!"

Was that really Cade? He sounded so different, so harsh and rasping, almost unrecognizable.

A heavy thud nearby jerked her head up, and Laurie's eyes widened at the sight of a Comanche warrior sprawled on the ground almost at her feet. And then, just beyond, she could see Cade grappling with another warrior, straining to keep a knife from plunging into his abdomen.

Fascinated, horrified, Laurie could not tear her gaze from the two men locked in silent, grim combat. Somewhere beyond she could hear Tyler, and even the bloodied Davis, shooting, shouting, but she paid them little heed. All her attention was focused on Cade and the Comanche.

Half-lifting the heavy rifle she held, Laurie let it drop in the next instant as she knew she could not bring herself to fire it. Besides, she could just as well hit Cade instead of the Comanche. She saw the half-naked warrior slash Cade with the knife, saw the bright spring of blood along his arm, saw Cade step sideways to avoid another wicked thrust of the knife. He made no sound or indicated that he'd even felt the cut, but remained taut and wary, circling the warrior, his mouth grim and his eyes narrowed. The Comanche lunged again, and they met, muscles straining as Cade fought to keep the blade from his belly.

"Oh God," someone said, and then she realized she had spoken aloud. Fear clogged her throat, fear that Cade would be killed, and that she would have to see it, have to sit by helplessly and watch.

With her gaze riveted on the men rolling over and over on the hard, dry ground, she was only vaguely aware that the shooting around her had lessened, with only occasional shots being fired.

Tensely, she watched Cade and the Comanche separate, then circle one another, Cade warily watching the knife in the warrior's hand. He spoke to him in a guttural voice, words that Laurie did not understand, but that the Indian apparently did. With a howl of rage, the Comanche flung himself forward, striking out at Cade with the knife. Cade neatly sidestepped the lunge, bringing the side of his hand down on the Comanche's arm as he turned in a

279

smooth motion. The knife clattered to the rocks, and he bent and scooped it up, still turning, slashing upward with the blade just as the Comanche reached for him.

They seemed to hang suspended in mid-air for a long moment, the Comanche staring into Cade's blood and sweat-streaked face with slowly glazing eyes. Then he dropped to the ground without a sound, and Cade stood there with his own blood and the Comanche's on him.

Somehow, Laurie found herself beside Cade, her breath locked in her throat. She put a hand on his bloody arm, and Cade swung his eyes toward her.

"Better take cover," he said softly, and gave her a push toward the rocks.

She went, wondering why she felt suddenly safer. She stayed there until the firing stopped, until the Comanches had taken their dead and ridden away, leaving them alone in the arid, desolate country with buzzards already circling overhead.

She looked up to see Cade beside her, his dark eyes skimming over her. Self-consciously she put up a hand to push the hair from her eyes, leaving streaks of dirt across her face. He held out a hand.

"It's all right, you can come out now," he said in a voice that was harsh and soft at the same time. She just stared at him.

Gently, he reached down to lift her into his arms, holding her, stroking back the hair from her eyes and letting her shiver and tremble until at last she was quiet, all the time whispering soft words to her.

"It's all over, Laurie," he said finally, and she rubbed her cheek across his shirt and sighed.

"I know."

"And we have to get on the move. Davis needs to see a doctor as soon as possible, and we're still a ways from a town."

Tyler shook his head, muttering that Davis "don't look none too good, but I reckon he'll live."

Steeling herself, Laurie said, "Let me look at his wound."

It was a mess, with congealing blood and dirt mixed with mats of his hair, and she took the knife Cade offered her and gingerly cut away portions of his hair.

"Ouch!" Davis protested weakly. "Are you scalpin' me or nursin' me?"

"I'm not sure," Laurie said, trying to still the violent heaving of her stomach. "But if you'll just sit still I'll do what I can until we can get you to the doctor." Finally she glanced up at Cade, who was watching her efforts. "How far is the nearest town?"

"A ways," he said, and she had the resigned thought that everything in Texas was "a ways."

Chapter Nineteen

When Laurie looked at it later, Cade's wound was not as bad as she'd first thought. Still, she felt guilty as she bandaged it, in spite of Cade's assurance that he'd had much worse wounds and managed to survive.

"Anyway, I couldn't let you get the best of me by dying just to please you," he said in a voice that was slightly mocking, and she tied a strip of clean linen with a sharp tug that made him wince.

One of his ribs had deflected the sword's thrust, and he had bled profusely, soaking his shirt and even his pants so that he looked as if he'd been mortally wounded. His dark eyes rested on her flushed face as she finished her inexpert medical care, and a half-smile tugged at the corners of his mouth.

"You know, maybe I didn't give you enough credit for being able to take care of yourself, Laurie," he said after a moment, and she glanced up at him in surprise.

"Maybe I didn't give you enough credit for being able to take care of me," she returned in a matter-of-fact tone as she wiped her hands on a cloth. Her eyes shifted from his steady gaze. "I'm still alive, so I suppose I should be grateful."

"You sound like it," he said dryly.

"Well—what did you expect? You have dragged me from California across Panama and the Gulf of Mexico, and halfway through Texas, and you expect gratitude? Don't bet on it!"

"I've learned not to bet on anything as far as you're concerned." Cade's brow lifted, and his tone was thoughtful as he stared at her. "But you never cease to surprise me."

Sullenly, Laurie swung her eyes back to him, and had the thought that he often surprised her, too. Who would have thought that the man she considered a spoiled aristocrat could be so fierce? That he could wield a sword expertly, shoot a rifle so straight, and even battle a Comanche with a knife? She had never thought him more than a handsome *criolla,* pampered and petted and used to luxury. Now she knew better, and she felt a reluctant admiration for him.

"Truce?" Cade asked softly, and she frowned. "Suppose we call our private battle quits for now. After all, we can always resume it later."

"I don't know," she began, but he was putting out a hand to tilt up her face, and his lips were curving in a smile.

"Truce," he said firmly. "We've got more to think about than our own quarrel. And Laurie, if you'll only be a little more patient, and have a little more confidence in me, everything will be all right. I was going to tell you—before the Comanches came—that by tomorrow night we'll be in San Antonio. Maybe I'll leave you there, or get you some transportation to New Orleans."

She stared at him warily. "Do you mean it?"

Nodding, he said, "Yeah. It's too dangerous out here for you right now."

"What will you do? Just abandon me?"

His hand dropped away from her face, and his

voice was hard again. "Aren't you ever satisfied?"

"I'll be satisfied when I'm back in New Orleans eating gumbo," she shot at him. "How are you going to get me back? Do you intend to leave me with just anyone?"

But even though she stormed at him and even asked sweetly, Cade would not tell her anymore. He helped Davis onto his horse, then helped Tyler saddle their horses, and they were ready to move on again.

As she sat her horse, staring ahead at the endless horizon, Laurie clutched at the promise of freedom like a banner. Free to walk to the Market with her aunt, free to sleep alone in a big bed at night, without wondering if she would be jerked from her slumber with searing kisses—it sounded too good to be true. But even as she thought that, she had a twinge of dismay at the thought of her relatives' reaction to her sojourn in the company of Cade Caldwell. What would they say? She was a ruined woman in Higuera—was she ruined in New Orleans as well? Had her father written to them to tell them of her disgrace? Or did he know about this latest humiliation?

Biting her lower lip between her teeth, Laurie worried over the possibilities. Well, I can always go back to Paris and my cousins, she decided when her head began to ache from the strain. Dust rose in choking clouds around her, and she could see Cade several feet away. He always sat his mount so straight and easily, as if he had been born in the saddle, she thought resentfully.

Well, soon she would be free of him. Free of his tyranny and dominance, free to do what she pleased. But somehow that did not please her as much as it should have.

It was late when they got to San Antonio, and most of the buildings were dark. Laurie had a vague impression of two-story stucco buildings, live oak trees in a plaza, and streets lined with shops and awnings. She was too weary to think about it, too weary to do more than slide from her mount and let someone take it away while Cade tended to the baggage.

Cade rented a room in a hotel, and Laurie went in gratefully. All she could think about was a bath, hot food, and a soft bed, and when he tried to help her up the short flight of stairs to the room, she jerked away, irritable and exhausted.

"Leave me alone! Haven't you done enough?"

"Apparently not," he said, and the familiar mockery was back in his tone. "Look, princess, if you don't mind, I'd prefer you not be such a bitch. I'm tired too, and I damn sure don't want to listen to any of your shrewish remarks."

"Then you'd better stay out of earshot," she said as she turned on the top step to glare at him. She was near tears and she didn't know why, except that it was late, she was exhausted, and Cade had said very casually that he would soon be shed of her.

He hadn't said it to her, but she had heard him say it to Tyler, and though she'd been furious at first, the thought that he didn't want her anymore rankled somehow. As if she had not been through enough with him! And because of him! And now here she was, hundreds of miles away from anything and everything she knew, and she was to be discarded like so much rubbish.

Conveniently forgetting that she had wanted this very thing for the past month, Laurie turned away from Cade with the comment that she was glad he wouldn't have to be bothered with her anymore.

Cade's brows dipped briefly, then he grinned. Fortunately, she didn't see his amusement as she stormed ahead of him. He reached around her to open the door to the room and Laurie stood stiff and still, refusing to look at him as she waited. And when it was open and she'd swept in as regally as royalty, Cade shut it softly behind her.

Swirling around, she gazed at the closed door with wide eyes. Her lower lip trembled, and she wondered with a kind of self-mockery why she was being so foolish and so contradictory. After all, it wasn't as if she was really in love with him, though she had been foolish enough to think so for a long time. And it wasn't as if he would ever marry her, as he was still married to Cecelia de Marchand, and somehow that last thought made her totally miserable.

Even the hot bath, the hot food, and the soft bed did not make her less miserable, and before she fell asleep—alone in the big bed between clean white sheets—Laurie had the vague thought that she would never be the same person again.

The thought lingered the next morning, when she was served breakfast on a tiny balcony just off the room and rimmed by a wrought-iron railing. It looked out over a huge courtyard filled with trees and flowers and sunshine, and it was the first pretty place she had seen since arriving in Texas.

Nibbling at a bowl of iced fruit, Laurie wondered where Cade had spent the night, then forced her mind away from him. He occupied her thoughts too much, and she would have to learn to think of something else. She let her gaze drift over the tiled walkways below, where slow-moving strollers enjoyed the softly-scented air and the breeze from the San Antonio River that edged the courtyard. Sunlight glittered on the slowly winding river. Why did the sun seem so much softer here, instead of harsh and searing, as it had out on the prairie?

Squares of sunlight checkered her balcony, making the china and crystal on the table glitter, almost hurting her eyes, and she looked away again. She was wrapped in a soft robe she'd found at the foot of her bed that morning—a gift from Cade, perhaps? She didn't know, but had not been able to resist the loose, soft material that flowed around her in a graceful swirl. Nor had she been able to resist the sweet, hot chocolate that the maid had brought on the silver tray with the fruit and buttery rolls. But as the time passed and Cade did not come to her room, Laurie found that her earlier acceptance altered to resentment. The hot chocolate grew cold, the fruit warm, and her temper frayed, and still he had not come to explain anything to her.

Rising from the chair overlooking the balcony railing, she paced her room restlessly, scarcely noticing the plush chairs, gilded mirror, and ornate dressing screen. She was too agitated to pay any attention to anything but the direction of her thoughts.

Did he mean to just leave her here like a stray cat? Was that what he intended to do? A rush of panic swept through her as she wondered if he'd already gone. How far was Austin? Was she locked in her room again?

But when she hurriedly dressed and tried the door, she found to her surprise that it wasn't locked and she was free to go out. Cautiously, half-expecting Cade to appear at any moment and shove her back into the room, Laurie went down the short flight of stairs into the spacious main lobby. Baskets of green plants hung from every conceivable spot, and a smiling clerk told her that "Si, Señor Caldwell was still a guest, and no, he was not in at the moment. Would the señorita like to wait at a table in the lobby for him?"

She most certainly would, and Laurie found herself placed by a window looking out over the street. San Antonio was a lot larger than she'd thought, and even had the appearance of civilization, something she hadn't noticed the night before in her exhaustion and the dark. Drumming her fingertips against the linen-draped table, she waited for almost two hours before she saw Cade's tall frame come through the arched doorway. He was with a tall man, the tallest man she'd ever seen, and she hesitated, wondering if she should confront him now.

But Cade had seen her, and he said something to the man and they changed direction to come to her table.

"General, this is Laurette Allen—a friend. Laurie, this is General Houston. You've heard me speak of him."

"Of course." A practiced social smile curved her lips as she greeted the general, and though she would never have admitted it to Cade, she was impressed. Though rough-speaking, he was a very commanding man, with craggy features and a full head of fiery hair. When he smiled, as he did now, his entire visage was transformed into a most likable one.

"You were right, Caldwell," the general was saying in his loud, rough voice, "She's a beauty. Being a newly married man, I can't say she's the loveliest woman I've ever seen, but she's real close to Margaret!"

"Thank you, General," Laurie said as Cade just stood there with an amused smile. "I appreciate your kindness."

"I'm a truthful man, not a kind one, my dear, as my wife may attest."

Turning to Cade, Houston stuck out a huge, rawboned hand and said, "I will count on your cooperation, Caldwell, and count myself fortunate to have a man like you with me."

Laurie wondered what he meant as Cade stepped aside with the general, and when Houston had left, bidding her a smiling farewell, she looked up at

288

Cade with a lifted brow.

But he would answer none of her questions, only say that she didn't need to know too much.

"Is that why you let me think you'd abandoned me here?" she asked tartly. "I woke up and you weren't there!"

"But I left early, and you were still sleeping," Cade said with a quirk of his lips that irritated her even more. "Did you miss me, love?"

"Like a boil!" She sat stiffly, hoping her dislike was evident. "You knew I'd think you'd abandoned me without any money or transportation home."

Turning the chair beside her around so that he was close, Cade shook his head. "No, but if I'd known you were still so bitchy, I might have."

"What did you expect?"

"That a good night's sleep would have improved that prickly temper of yours," he said flatly, and when he slid her a quick glance from beneath lowered brows, she took a deep breath.

"Well, it did, sort of. I was just worried, that's all. I mean . . ." Her voice faltered. "I wasn't sure you'd come back for me."

"I said I'd take care of you, didn't I?"

"You said a lot of things."

Cade raked a hand through his dark hair, then shook his head. "So did you. But I meant what I said. I'll see that you get to New Orleans. After that, you're on your own."

Silence stretched between them, and Laurie found herself looking at him through a veil of eyelashes, trying to see what he was thinking. If only his thoughts would show on his face, then perhaps she would know what to do, what to feel.

"What will you do?" she asked after a moment.

Shrugging, he said, "Since Houston's here in San Antonio, and we don't have to go on to Austin, I guess I'll take care of what I've got to do quicker than I thought."

"Why is General Houston here?"

"He's been touring with his new wife, but she's going back east." A faint smile flickered on his mouth as he looked at Laurie. "She's not as hardy as you are, love. The general is traveling to San Augustine to court, while the lovely Mrs. Houston is going to New Orleans." His eyes flicked over her briefly. "Maybe it'd be a good idea if you two women traveled together."

"I don't know about that," Laurie began stiffly, not knowing how she would explain her relationship with Cade to someone else.

A high flush stained her cheeks, and Cade correctly guessed the reason for it.

"Then again, maybe you're right. The general's wife is said to be pretty religious, and she might not approve of . . ."

"Of a dishonored female?" Laurie couldn't help blurting out. "And whose fault is that, Cade Caldwell?"

"Are we back to that again?" He sat back in his chair, and his eyes darkened. "I seem to remember a night in an arbor when you weren't so unwilling."

"You took advantage of me!"

"Oh, for Chrissake, Laurie! You knew what you were doing, and you were the one who came after me in San Diego, remember?"

"I came to help you!" she spat, near tears but too furious to let him know it. "I wish now that they'd shot you."

"Well, it's too late for that, and too late for anything else. And I damn sure don't feel like sitting here in the lobby arguing with you. I've got to meet Houston and Tyler. I just came back to tell you that I've arranged for you to Galveston, and from there to

New Orleans or wherever you want." His tone was impatient, and he stood up, looking down at her pale face and the sheen of tears in her gold eyes. "Damn it, Laurie, do we have to part angry? thought that maybe on your last night here we could at least be friends."

A huge lump in her throat kept her from answering for a moment, but finally she was able to nod her head and manage a smile.

"Yes, I suppose we could. After all, I doubt if we'll ever see each other again."

Cade gave a short nod, and his face was impassive as he agreed. "That's possible."

That night was to remain in Laurie's memory for a long time. Spanish music that made her think of California filled the air, and lanterns that hung from trees and walls lent the air a softness. A fountain splashed in one corner of the courtyard, and Cade had claimed a table near it. Palm fronds waved gently in the breeze, and the San Antonio River glittered with the reflection of the lanterns and stars.

"It's beautiful here," Laurie murmured, and Cade smiled.

"So you've found something in Texas that you like?"

She turned her head to look at him, and saw from the quick flare in his eyes that he'd been staring at her. She knew she looked better than she had in some time, knew that the gown she wore flattered her, and the maid Cade had sent to her room had wound bright flowers in her blond hair and tucked in a gilded comb or two. She wore a light shawl around her shoulders, and the gown she'd hurriedly packed the morning they'd left Galveston was one of her ballgowns, an impractical fact she'd mourned until tonight. Tonight, she was glad she had it, glad every time she saw the flare in Cade's eyes.

"Yes," she said, "I've found something in Texas that I like." The sweep of her lashes lifted, and she fastened her eyes on Cade's face as if trying to memorize every harsh angle and plane. But could she ever really forget him? Even his cruelties faded now, now that she knew she was leaving him behind. Somehow, all that remained of the past month was the passion between them, and she could see from the curl of his lips that he was thinking of it, too.

The glitter in Cade's lazy eyes flared into a passion that she recognized for an instant, and in spite of her resolve not to let him affect her, her heart beat faster.

"Care to dance?" he asked, and she found herself nodding acceptance, putting her hand in his palm and swinging into the graceful steps of a waltz. She was vaguely aware of the stares of other diners, but dismissed them with reckless abandon.

"We're shocking all the staid matrons," Laurie murmured in his ear, and she felt the laughter rumble in his chest.

"I guess the waltz hasn't reached San Antonio yet," he whispered back. His breath was warm, spiced with brandy, seductive. Laurie shivered. "Cold?" he asked then, and she shook her head.

"No."

River breezes flowed across them, lifting the filmy hem of her gown, ruffling Cade's hair, fanning the fever that was building hotter and higher in her body. Laurie pressed her face into his shoulder. When the musicians switched to the fast tempo of a peasant dance, she gave a regretful sigh and Cade laughed again.

"We don't need the music, you know."

She smiled. "No, I suppose we don't."

And then he was taking her hand and leading her upstairs to her room. For the first time since the night in the arbor, Laurie felt the pleasant thread of anticipation race through her, the quickening of her pulses and the heated thrum of desire.

Almost shyly, she undressed for him in the soft glow of a lamp, letting her gown drift to the floor, feeling his gaze rest on her body as she removed all her clothes. There was a bittersweet quality to the moment, a knowledge of the morrow that colored it with regret as well as passion, but she would not have changed it. What would be, would be. And this was here and now, and though she'd never admit it to him, she would miss Cade Caldwell as much as if he were a part of her.

And perhaps he was, she thought when he began to kiss her, his mouth moving from her lips along the arch of her throat, then down to the shadowed, perfumed valley between her breasts. As he moved downward, tracing a moist path over her skin with his tongue, Laurie tangled her fingers in his thick, dark hair and pulled him up to stare into his eyes.

Still shy, she whispered, "Let me undress you."

Cade wasn't about to argue, and he helped her first clumsy attempts to unbutton his crisp white linen shirt, then his form-fitting pants.

When he lay as bare as she in the glow of lamps and moonlight, he smiled up at her.

"Satisfied, love?"

"Not yet, Cade Caldwell, not yet."

"Let's see what we can do about that, then." He pulled her to him, his hands cupping her breasts, his mouth seeking and finding her lips.

Laurie let all other thoughts slip away as she thought of only Cade, his warm hands and mouth, his hard, lean body so close to hers. The world was ablaze with colors, all the colors of the rainbow, and she was bathed in stardust and moonlight as she let her reserve fade away. This would be her last night with him, and it would be a night they would never forget.

And when the release came in a thundering rush, she sobbed his name aloud, over and over, until he muffled her cries with his mouth.

"I'll never forget you," she whispered, her drowning eyes glistening with unshed tears.

"Maybe you won't have to," Cade said, then smothered her questions with his mouth. She would not remember them until later.

Chapter Twenty

Cade slipped from the hotel and walked down the deserted streets of San Antonio toward a small tavern on the river. It was still dark outside, and the glow from the tavern windows threw a bright square onto the dirt road. He paused for a moment, then pushed open the door and entered the smoky tavern. A voice came to him from the far shadows.

"Come in, Caldwell, come in," General Sam Houston said with an affable smile and an expansive wave of one arm. "I appreciate your promptness."

It was just before first light, and Cade had slipped from bed and Laurie's warm protests regretfully. But he was wide awake now, and tense with expectations.

"You said it was important," he said, accepting the cup of coffee Houston gave him and sliding into the chair he indicated.

"It is, Caldwell." Houston frowned slightly, and his bushy brows lowered over keen eyes as he silently contemplated his knotted hands. "You know what has been happening in the Republic." Cade nodded. "Well, I've received word that my duties are once more desired as its president." A wry smile accompanied this statement as Houston added with a dry chuckle, "Since I am now a *respectable* married man, it seems that I have regained some favor with the public."

Cade grinned. "That can't be all bad, General."

"Oh, it's not. But I must admit Lamar is taking Texas to hell much faster than I—or Santa Anna—could." There was a short pause, then Houston leaned forward over the table to say softly, "I need to find out more about his plans. Lamar was a better Secretary of War than he is a president, I'm afraid. I understand from reliable sources that our president has all but abdicated his office in favor of that idiot vice-president, Burnet." He snorted with disgust. "Burnet favors pounding a Bible and bellowing against me as his form of politics, while Texas currency is now worth twenty cents on the dollar, the public debt has increased by several million, and all the credit is gone. If matters continue, Caldwell, the Republic of Texas for which so many men died will also die." His craggy features creased into a fierce scowl. "I won't allow that!"

Carefully, Cade asked, "How can I help?"

"By going to New Orleans and meeting with a certain gentleman by the name of William Fisher. I understand that Mister Fisher has only recently returned from a stint in the Mexican Army as a colonel. He's most dissatisfied, but he also knows a great deal about Santa Anna's plans. That wily Mexican general has not given up hope on regaining Texas, nor has he ever forgiven us San Jacinto."

"San Jacinto hasn't forgiven him, either."

Houston looked up and met Cade's dark gaze, and a slight smile hooked his lips. "Yes, you were there, Caldwell, and you remember, too."

"I'll never forget it."

Nodding, Houston stared into the faint flicker of light from a guttering candle in the middle of the table. "It can't have been for nothing. And President Lamar, in his desperation, is now entertaining some idiot notion about a territorial grant of gigantic proportions to some French company. Sam Swartwout has been pressuring me to lend my support, but I'll be dead and damned before I will! No, that would ruin Texas for sure, and I won't have it."

"The Franco-Texienne Land Bill?" Cade asked, rubbing the stubble of beard on his jaw. "I heard about it, and wondered if Lamar was able to see the eventual complications that could arise if he pushed it through Congress."

"Well," Houston said grimly, "he won't! I'll see to it, if I have to call out every man in Texas! You see, I intend for Texas to become a part of the United States one day, and I don't want anyone making that impossible."

There was a moment's pause before the general continued, "You know, Caldwell, that this will be happening out in California one day."

Cade shrugged. "I've already seen the beginnings of it. Right now there is a brutal leader who is terrorizing my home. My grandfather had written to me about him when I was in New Orleans. After San Jacinto, I went to Mexico City, where I talked to — or tried to talk to — officials about his removal." Cade gave a half-smile of resignation. "Unfortunately, my recent service in the Texan Army was discovered, and my efforts cost me a while in prison. After that, I left the country, and didn't go back to California until nine months ago." Another shrug lifted his shoulders. "The alcalde is still there, but I intend to go back." His voice hardened when he added, "And he won't be there long after I get back."

"You have a plan, I presume?" Houston said with an enigmatic little smile tugging at the corners of his mouth. "It's always best to have a good plan."

Cade agreed. "I had one before, but an unexpected woman managed to ruin it." His lips twisted

297

into a mocking smile. "Once I get her safely settled in New Orleans, I'm going back to take care of it. I've heard the rumblings of statehood for California, too, and Texas will set a precedent." He grinned. "Once we get all of this other out of the way."

Houston agreed with a booming laugh. "Then you obviously don't mind going to New Orleans to meet Fisher!"

"It's on my way, General."

"Good, good. It all falls in place! Meet Fisher, but don't let him know who you are. He likes to play cards, so it shouldn't be difficult for you to wangle an introduction to him, and besides, he doesn't hold his whiskey well. He's on his way back to New Orleans now."

Cade's brow furrowed, and he said slowly, "Maybe I should tell you, General, that I'm not exactly favored in New Orleans."

"Bah! I heard all about that five years ago. And if the truth were known, I've not always minded my manners with the ladies, either."

"But this particular young lady was the governor's niece—and besides, I haven't seen her since our wedding night."

A booming laugh filled the air. "And you wonder how she might feel when you arrive in New Orleans with the very lovely Miss Allen, heh?"

"Something like that. I had intended to send Laurie on ahead of me."

"Take her yourself. It's the perfect reason for going to New Orleans, and my wife needs a safe escort, too. You can all travel together. Just tell Miss Allen the reason, and I'm sure. . . ."

"General, I'm afraid that Miss Allen won't exactly care about helping with your plan. She doesn't give a damn about Texas, and she certainly doesn't give a damn about me. All she wants is to go home, and if she arrives in my company, her reputation'll be ruined. She's bound to make trouble."

"Most women make trouble, Caldwell, but you'll just have to do what you can with her." His eyes narrowed on Cade. "And I might add, you need to tie up your loose ends while you're in New Orleans. Two wives can only cause more trouble, believe me. I speak from experience."

Knowing something of the rumors of Houston's former marriage to Eliza Allen from Virginia, Cade nodded. No one knew the exact truth, and Houston refused to tell it. That marriage had been years before, and Houston had since divorced Eliza Allen, and only recently been remarried to Margaret Lea from Alabama.

Shifting in his chair, Cade had the cynical thought that Houston had not been married to a willful, spoiled heiress liked CeCe, nor had he become involved with a woman like Laurie Allen, another spoiled, willful female. Two women so much alike in the same city — and connected with the same man? It was bound to bring trouble — *big* trouble, and he wanted no part of it.

Cade left the small tavern just off the San Antonio river as the sun pinkened the eastern horizon. He walked slowly, his mind turning again and again to the warm woman waiting him in a soft bed. Laurie. She'd be furious, of course, if he told her that he was going to escort her back to New Orleans. She counted on him going as far away from her as he could get, and in a way, he admitted grudgingly, he couldn't blame her. He hadn't played fair with her, dragging her from San Diego to Galveston, then across miles of hostile country without telling her why. But it was hard to tell her something he wasn't quite sure of himself.

Why had he brought her with him? Why hadn't he

let her go in Galveston? It would have been a lot easier. And why did she, of all the women he had known, have the ability to make him mad enough to want to strangle her? And, damn it, why was Laurie so easily able to make him want to put himself inside her and stay there forever?

Cursing softly, Cade had the cynical thought that they definitely brought out the worst in each other, even in passion. Laurie Allen was the most complex woman he'd ever known, soft and yielding and loving one moment, vixen the next. And now he had reluctantly agreed to escort her to New Orleans, and once there, it would be difficult to explain her to everyone.

A wry smile curled his mouth as he had the thought that it would be just as difficult for Laurie to explain him to her relatives, and that was some consolation. It should make her a great deal more cooperative. But after last night, when she'd come so willingly to his bed thinking she would never have to see him again, she would not be happy to find out otherwise. Damn women, anyway, he thought with a scowl, for being such contrary, necessary creatures!

As he had expected, Laurie was not delighted with the change of plans. In fact, it was so disagreeable to her that she flatly refused to cooperate.

"No!" she stormed. "You promised that I could go home and everything would be as it was!"

"And I'm keeping that promise," Cade said evenly, trying to keep his temper. "It's just that I'm going to be the one to take you."

"If I show up in New Orleans at your side, the entire town will gather to throw rocks at me! Have you forgotten that you have a *wife* there?" As much as she hated the reminder herself, Laurie's practical side prompted the objection. It was one thing to be with Cade in California, and even Texas, but to show up in New Orleans with its strict social code for unmarried young ladies, and in the company of such a renowned renegade — a *married* renegade — would destroy her reputation. And she had had enough of that in California. No, she didn't want to endure the snide remarks and sly glances again, not in New Orleans, where she still had family and friends. Wasn't that the reason she'd left California? And if there wasn't a future with Cade, she saw no reason to try and invent one. She could never be happy just being his mistress instead of his wife.

"Forget it," she repeated. "I won't go."

"Laurie, you don't have much of a choice," Cade said, and she whirled to glare at him.

"What do you mean by that?"

Shrugging, his cold dark eyes narrowing on her face, he said, "Either you go willingly, or you'll go unwillingly."

"Oh, I see! I'm still your prisoner, then, and all those fine words last night were meaningless." Tawny eyes flashed with hot sparks from beneath her sweep of lashes, and her chin lifted. "You never meant them at all."

His jaw tightened. "Whether I did or didn't doesn't matter much right now. And this conversation isn't doing anything but making us both mad, so I'll leave."

He'd reached the door before she reluctantly said, "If I decide to cooperate, will you pretend you don't know me when we get to New Orleans?"

Cade half-turned, and there was a gleam of devilry in his eyes when he said, "Gladly!"

"Then make the arrangements, but remember — I don't want to be associated with you when we get there. It's going to be hard enough explaining to my

301

aunt why I left California without a proper chaperon anyway."

"Oh, you'll manage that easily enough," Cade said with a sardonic laugh. "You always have."

He shut the door on her furious retort, leaving Laurie alone and fuming and damning Cade Caldwell for a scoundrel.

"The damned, blackhearted wretch! Why, if I showed up in New Orleans at his side, I could never hold my head up again." She sank to the edge of the mattress and stared at the closed door, chewing her bottom lip. Why did the memory of his wife, of Cecelia de Marchand, bother her so badly? Good heavens, it wasn't as if *she* wanted to marry him, for heaven's sake, because God only knew that she wanted to be rid of him as soon as possible. *But still,* a small voice in the back of her mind whispered, *he can't marry you if he's already married to someone else.*

Laurie's mouth tightened. Well, she'd soon be shed of him, and then she wouldn't have to think about him anymore. Cade Caldwell would be just a distant, distasteful memory.

But somehow, that didn't comfort her as much as she would have liked for it to in the following days.

The small cavalcade left San Antonio early, riding through the market plaza just as it was coming to life. Dogs barked, and chickens squawked, and farmers rode in with *carretas* heavily burdened with produce and other goods. Cattle bawled, and horses snorted as they were shown to interested buyers. Children ran about, and there was the enticing fragrance of frying tortillas in the air.

"I'm hungry," Laurie muttered sleepily, and Cade slid her an impatient glance.

"You should have thought of that earlier."

She glared at him. "Well, you were in such a hurry, and you wouldn't let me stop to even grab

302

some fruit!"

"Will a tortilla do?"

"And some chocolate," she added, but he was already spurring his horse toward the line of vendors.

In the end, she settled for a corn tortilla stuffed with shredded meat, and water from Cade's leather pouch. But it was enough, and she didn't want to appear too fussy in front of Margaret Houston, who was riding quietly with a sad face.

It was apparent that Margaret would greatly miss her husband, and Laurie had witnessed their bittersweet parting with something like envy, then wondered why. At least she had no ties, she told herself. Once she got back to New Orleans she would be free to do as she pleased—within the confines of social restrictions and her aunt's wishes, of course.

There would be no more arguments with Cade, no more ridiculous scenes between them.

And no more passion, or the moments when I can pretend he actually feels tenderness for me.

Laurie thrust those thoughts firmly away and concentrated on the movements of her horse, and the dust rising behind the loaded burros carrying baggage and supplies. She wouldn't think about Cade Caldwell anymore—not that way. He was only a guide, a man she'd once known but chose not to know anymore. And in a way, she thought as she glanced at him, it was true.

Cade was once more the remote, dangerous outlaw, wearing his Texas revolver in his belt and a sword at his side, and even a long, wide-bladed knife that he called a Bowie knife in a sheath on his lean hip. He looked harder, somehow, disreputable, and not at all like the kind of man Sam Houston would want to escort his wife back to Galveston for him.

The little cavalcade was heavily guarded, with Cade, Tyler, and Davis as well as several other hired men riding escort. Laurie and Margaret Lea Houston—who was also part French—rode together, and Laurie discovered that though quiet, Margaret had a quick wit and pleasant nature. And she did not look down her nose at Laurie, in spite of the fact that she must know of her relationship with Cade.

The journey back to Galveston seemed much shorter than before, maybe because Laurie knew what to expect. The days were still long and hot, the nights still crisp and clear. A few times a storm whipped across the prairie. Then they would all huddle beneath any shelter they could find while the wind blew dirt and grit and stinging pellets of rain at them, soaking everything. When it was over, the sun would come out, and the ground would dry quickly, leaving it as arid as before.

After a rain, the plants seemed greener, the tiny prairie animals more energetic. Cade and the other men refilled wooden casks with water, and then they pushed on toward the endless horizon.

Fortunately, there were no run-ins with the Comanches or any other Indians on the return to Galveston, and once in Houston City, Laurie and Margaret parted company with the promise to correspond.

Cade had hired a carriage for Mrs. Houston that would take her on to friends in Houston City, while he and Laurie rode south to Galveston.

"I intend to stay in Houston City to be nearer my husband," Margaret said in a soft, firm voice. "But I pray that you will write to me."

"You have been more than gracious, Mrs. Houston, and I will write you at the first opportunity," Laurie promised.

"Aren't you the proper little hypocrite?" Cade said into Laurie's ear as she waved good-bye to Margaret and settled back into the carriage cushions beside him.

"I don't know what you mean, Cade Caldwell!" she said sharply, giving him a furious glance.

Laughing, Cade shook his head. "You don't have the first intention of writing her a letter, and you know it. And I could have sworn I heard you tell her that you were — how did you say it — 'devastated that I have to leave Texas and such good friends behind?' You're a cool liar, Miss Laurie Allen."

"And you are too uncivilized to be polite enough to say what people want to hear, Cade Caldwell!" She tugged angrily at her skirt, the hem of which was caught on the seat beneath his lean thigh. "I don't know why you always have to be so rude, when if you would just try to behave civilly, people would think more highly of you."

"Like they do you?"

She gave an irritated flounce on the seat and stared out the carriage window. Galveston was another forty-five miles away, and she was alone with Cade again.

"What happened in California wasn't my fault," she said after a moment of bristling silence. "I tried to tell you, but you're too pigheaded to listen. And people there were wrong about what they thought, you know they were."

"Do I, Laurie?" His hand reached out to turn her face toward him. The big gold eyes were smoky with some emotion he couldn't place, and her long lashes veiled them quickly from his searching gaze. A faint smile curled his lips. "I know that you let me take all the blame for something you did. Somehow, that seems a lot worse than having people whisper that you're my mistress."

"Why do you always have to make everything sound so much worse than it was?" She jerked her face back to the window, and her voice was tight.

"Besides, you know that's not the entire truth."

Abruptly changing the subject, Cade said, "We'll be in Galveston tomorrow morning. This is the last night we'll have to spend alone together."

"Thank God!" She turned to look at him, and the sunlight streaming through the carriage window backlit her hair and turned it to molten gold. "I can't say I'm sorry, but I do wish you well, Cade," she added after a moment. "And, whatever the reason for your going to New Orleans, I hope it turns out like you want."

His dark eyes crinkled at the corners as he smiled at her, relaxing back against the cushions and slapping the reins over the horse's rump. "Thanks. I do, too."

There was a brief moment of time when each looked into the other's eyes, a moment in which they almost came to terms with one another, but it passed quickly, and was lost.

Seagulls wheeled overhead as the steamer chugged into the New Orleans port and bumped into a quay. Standing at the rail, Laurie was almost breathless with excitement. She held one hand at her throat, and her eyes glittered with unshed tears as familiar buildings came into view. How she had missed it! There had been times when she'd thought she would never get back, and now here she was.

"Happy enough?" a faintly mocking voice asked in her ear, and she didn't even care that Cade was teasing her.

"Delirious with happiness! I can't wait to see my aunt, and I just know she'll be surprised to see me here at last. Do you think she got the message I sent ahead, Cade?"

"Unless there's been a dire calamity, I'd say she

has," he answered, watching the wind blow back the gold curls from Laurie's face. Her eyes shone with excitement, and her cheeks were flushed, her mouth curved in a delighted smile. It'd been a long time since he'd seen her so happy.

Lacing and unlacing her hands in a nervous gesture, she waited impatiently for the steamer to let down the gangplank to the dock, almost dancing with nervousness.

"You'll call a carriage for me, Cade? And you'll be certain my baggage gets to Tante Annette's house?"

A wry smile crooked his mouth. "Yes, Miss Allen, anything you say, Miss Allen, whatever you command, Miss Allen."

"Wretch," she muttered, but smiled up at him with a saucy tilt of her head. "I'm almost sorry to see the last of you."

"Why is it that I think you're just being 'civilized' again?"

"Because you're a confirmed cynic, Cade Caldwell."

"Maybe I've got reason to be."

Her smile faded, and Laurie had the thought that she really would miss him. It surprised her, especially when she recalled how irritating he could be, and even savage at times.

"Yes," she said, "maybe you do."

"That's the first time I can remember us agreeing on something," he said with a laugh, and put out a hand to guide her down the steep walkway to the dock.

People crowded around them, all anxious to disembark, jostling for room and surging forward. Laurie and Cade were swept along with the crowd, and when they reached the dock she felt herself being tugged to one side.

"Let them pass," Cade said. "If we don't, we'll end up in the Gulf."

They stood there to one side, the tall dark man and his blonde companion, a striking contrast that was certain to attract attention. Laurie's lush beauty did attract quite a few male stares, but none had the temerity to approach. Perhaps it was Cade's unsmiling face or the protective arm he put around her waist that branded her as his. He looked rough and dangerous, his weapons worn for everyone to see.

"You look like a renegade," Laurie observed, skimming his frame with a glance.

"And you look like an opera singer," he retorted, making her chin lift again.

"You *would* think of a tawdry comparison like that! Why can't you ever think of nice compliments?"

"And turn your head? You're already too vain as it is." Cade's arm pressed her forward when she would have given him another indignant remark, and he signaled for a hired carriage to stop.

Laurie was swept forward, her eyes down, concentrating on keeping the hem of her skirts from dragging the dock and becoming too dirty, when she stumbled. Cade caught her, his arms circling her body and bringing her up short against him.

"I guess a farewell kiss is too much to expect," he said with a quirk of his lips, and there was a distinct challenge in his dark gaze that made Laurie respond recklessly.

"Yes, but I'm feeling extremely generous."

Lightly, teasingly, she stood on her toes to give him a swift peck on the cheek, but he quickly turned her head so that her lips pressed against his mouth. As always, the touch of his mouth against hers made her breath quicken, and she allowed her body to respond for just an instant before drawing away.

Rather shakily, she said, "Well! Perhaps you won't forget me too easily now."

"Maybe not," he drawled, "but I've never forgotten

308

the time I got shot in the butt, either."

"Wretch," she said with a laugh, turning away from him with whirl of her skirts. Her forward motion carried her into a man standing close by, and he half-turned with a sound of surprise. "Oh, excuse me!" she said, looking up, and the rest of her words froze in her throat.

Pierre DuBois, her older cousin, was looking at her with wary surprise. "Laurette! I did not expect to find you so quickly—or so occupied. *Maman* sent me after you, and I've been waiting . . . but who is this?" he finished, his indignation superceding good manners when he noted Cade's protective arm so familiarly around her waist. "I was not told that you were . . . with someone."

"Oh, Pierre, *s'il vous plaît*—I am not really with him, you see, it is just that . . . just that. . . ." Words failed her in the face of her cousin's condemning stare, and she jerked away from Cade's embrace.

Slightly built, dark, and hot-blooded, Pierre DuBois glared at Cade with narrowed eyes. "I believe we have met before, monsieur," he said stiffly. "If I am not mistaken, it was at the gaming tables."

Cade gave a mocking half-bow. "Correct, sir. But that was over five years ago. I'm honored that you remembered me after all this time."

"One does not forget a man who insults his family, nor a man who creates such a huge scandal before running away."

Bewildered, Laurie looked from Cade to her cousin. "I take it you two have met?" she murmured.

"I am sorry to say that is so, Laurette," Pierre said in his stiffest tone. "How is it I found you in his company in such a—familiar embrace?"

Her cheeks burned, and she knew that there was very little she could say that would explain. So she gave a very Gallic shrug and a sigh. "Mister

Caldwell was kind enough to give me a safe escort from . . ."

"So what I heard is true!" Pierre cut in. "I had hoped it was only jealous gossips with misinformation. News travels even from so faraway a place as California, *ma petite cousine*."

Her heart plummeted to her toes at the censure in his unsmiling eyes. Laurie recognized in her cousin's face what she would see in others.

Straightening her shoulders, she stared her cousin in the eye and said, "So it seems. And Tante Annette—what does she say?"

"*Maman* does not read the papers, and knows nothing of the gossip. I would not have repeated it to her until I was certain." A note of sadness crept into his voice as Pierre said, "How could you be so heedless of your reputation, *petit chou*? You know that you are ruined here now, especially when it is known that you have arrived in the company of a married man, a man who left New Orleans under—shall we say—less than favorable circumstances? What shall I say to people?"

"Say what you like, Pierre," Laurie said shortly. "It is obvious to me that you will think and do so anyway. And tell Tante Annette whatever you like." Her chin lifted in defiance, and her voice was steady. "I will find lodgings elsewhere, so that I will not be an embarrassment to the family. Good day, Pierre."

When she turned away, Pierre put out a hand, then let it fall to his side with a shrug. After a moment's hesitation, he turned and walked quickly away, leaving Laurie standing at Cade's side. She looked up at Cade with eyes filled with hurt, angry tears.

"What will I do now?" she whispered. "I had not thought that word of what happened in California would reach here so quickly."

310

"It's only good news that travels slowly, Laurie." Cade put out a hand to touch her gently on the shoulder. Neither of them paid any attention to the curious stares in their direction, and the bustle of activity on the docks that had been so loud earlier, was now just a faint roar in her ears as Laurie briefly indulged in tears.

It didn't last long, and she swallowed her tears along with her hurt pride and said, "Well, I must make the best of it, I see. Perhaps I can find lodging in one of the smaller hotels, where no one will care about . . . about my past." Her voice almost broke on the last word.

Crossing his arms over his chest, Cade slid an impatient, annoyed glance toward the waiting carriage. "I guess there's only one thing you can do," he said. "You have to let me find you a place until you decide what you want to do next."

She wiped at her eyes with one corner of a wrinkled handkerchief, and her words were muffled. "That would only make things worse. Then the gossips will say they're right about everything."

"They're going to say it anyway. Human nature loves it when another human shows weakness." His tone was hard. "If you want to let them lick their chops over this, fine, but I thought you had more courage than that. I guess I was wrong."

Indignant, she glared up at him. "How can you say that! You know how much I wanted to come home, and now it's all ruined because of you! If you'd just stayed in Texas, or if you had stayed on the boat. . . ."

"Or if Tuesday didn't come after Monday—" He grabbed her, his face angry. "Look, Laurie, life doesn't work that way! You can't blame wrong decisions on bad luck all the time. Sometimes a thing just doesn't work out as it's supposed to do. So we

311

made a mistake or two, so what? The world doesn't have to end."

"Maybe *your* world doesn't," Laurie put in miserably. "But mine does. I've nowhere to go, and my reputation — or what was left of it — is shredded."

"What are you going to do, sit in a corner in sackcloth and ashes and whimper? Damn it, Laurie, what's the matter with you? You certainly don't seem like the same woman who took up a sword for a lost cause, a woman who fought bravely, if a bit foolishly."

Jerking away, she glared up at him, her gold eyes hot and angry.

"What do you suggest I do? An unmarried woman alone in New Orleans is not at the top of everyone's social list."

Cade made a disgusted sound. "Is that what's bothering you so badly — not having a full dance card?"

"You know it's not!" Angry tears spurted anew. "I just don't know where to go now."

She sounded so forlorn and pitiful that Cade' s anger faded. "All right, sweetheart, all right," he said, and his touch was gentle. "We'll figure out something. Until then, you can stay with some friends of mine."

"But I don't know anyone . . ."

"I do." Cade's arm slid around her waist, and he turned her back toward the street edging the docks. "I'll get another carriage and we'll worry about the rest later. For now, the main thing is to get you away from here."

Miserable, dejected, and crushed, Laurie offered no more protests as Cade hired a carriage and put her into it along with her baggage. She paid very little attention when he gave the driver the address, but sat huddled in the corner, lost in the misery of her thoughts.

What would she do now? She'd not thought her aunt might hear of her shame in California, but apparently she'd been too optimistic. And now that she was not welcome here, where would she go?

To compound her misery, it began to rain as the carriage drove through familiar streets, wetting the cobblestones and making them slick. Cade remained quiet, barely looking at her, his face creased in a frown. Was he regretting the fact that he'd offered to help her? Was he remembering how she had said so many times that she'd be glad to be rid of him? Probably, she answered her own silent questions.

It was only when they arrived at 84 Rue Royale and Cade instructed the driver to stop, that Laurie understood her true predicament. The house was in the fashionable district of New Orleans, but she didn't recognize it as one ever visited by her family or friends. In her miserable, confused state, Laurie wondered if she'd forgotten so much about the city. Of course, she'd been gone so long, perhaps things had changed much more than she realized.

A light rain still fell as they alighted from the hired carriage and Cade walked her up to the door. It swung open almost immediately, and a woman threw herself at Cade with a glad cry.

"We only received your message this morning, and it seems like you've taken forever!" she cried, wrapping her arms around him and clinging to him. "Why have you stayed away so long?"

Disentangling himself, and throwing Laurie a wickedly amused glance, Cade said as he wiped lip rouge from his mouth, "I want you to meet someone, Pamela."

Then the woman noticed Laurie standing just behind Cade and glaring at her, and her lips pursed in a slight pout. I thought you were alone."

Ignoring that, Cade reached out and drew Laurie forward with one hand. "This is Laurette Allen, and she will be staying here with me. Laurie, this is Pamela Goff."

"How do you do," Laurie said stiffly, and noticed that the brunette was just as displeased to meet her, too.

An awkward silence fell, and before anything else was said, a big, burly man appeared behind Pamela, his affable face creased in a huge grin.

"It's about time you showed up, Caldwell! Don't keep him and his purty lady-friend standin' out there in the rain, Pamela. Let 'em in!"

Wincing slightly, Laurie allowed herself to be tugged inside the house, and her suspicions were immediately confirmed that she was not in a house of high social standing. An air of ostentation filled the rooms, an overcrowding of furniture and knickknacks that verged on gaudy. There was none of the impeccable taste of her father's home or her aunt's, and when she glanced up at Cade and saw the amusement in his eyes, she grew silently furious.

"Looks like you've done some redecorating since I was here last," Cade observed, and Pamela smiled broadly.

"Yes. But only the best things, Cade. John and I were very careful to keep the house as nice as when we moved in. See that darling little statue over here?" she asked, pulling Cade with her to look at an atrocious figurine of a pair of entwined lovers. Laurie winced, and looked away.

How dared he bring her here! These people were obviously the *nouveau riche* who were coming to New Orleans in droves, rich on land schemes and speculation on the cotton market. As they drank tea in the parlor it was apparent from Pamela Goff's snide comments about the citizens, and her efforts to be

314

haughty to Laurie, that she had met with more than a little censure since arriving with her brother in New Orleans.

The brunette was pretty in a hard kind of way, with small brown eyes and a mop of curly brown hair. She was tall and slender, and had a quiet way of looking through her lashes at Cade that was supposed to be seductive. A hot flash of anger shot through Laurie, but she said nothing. Why give either of them the satisfaction of knowing what she thought? Or thinking that she cared?

She was so quiet that John Goff went out of his way to draw her out, asking her questions about where she was from and how she'd met Cade.

"You could say it was a case of mistaken identity," Cade said, overhearing, and laughed when Laurie flung him a sour glance.

Pamela leaned forward, primly pursing her lips. "I read an article in the *Picayune* about you, Miss Allen. It was very interesting."

A cold lump settled in her stomach as Laurie saw the spite and enjoyment in the woman's brown eyes, but she kept her face impassive.

"Really?" she murmured indifferently as she took a sip of tea. "It's encouraging to know that you can read, Miss Goff."

Pamela stiffened, and her voice was tart. "Not only can I read, but I can read *between* the lines! It was a long article about how you were with some Mexican bandit who robbed the mayor of a town, and when he was caught, you tried to say it was you who had done it. Of course, anyone could see that you were only protecting him. I was embarrassed to know that a woman from New Orleans would stoop so low."

Placing her cup and saucer on the table, Laurie kept a cool smile on her face as she gazed at Pamela. "In the first place, Miss Goff, he was Spanish, not

315

Mexican. And in the second place, you might be very surprised to learn the true facts of the situation which, I might add, are none of your business. I will not dignify either the article or your insinuations with any reply, so do not expect one. If my presence in your home is embarrassing to you, please be assured that it is equally so to me. I am not accustomed to such rudeness from a host, regardless of the circumstances, and I will be more than happy to leave at once."

"Pamela!" John Goff said angrily, rising to glare at his sister. "Apologize!"

"I will not," the woman said sullenly. "It's true. You read it too, John."

Cade, who had remained quietly listening, stood up. He stared down at the woman with a frown, and she flushed. "Knowing your background as well as I do, Pamela," Cade drawled, "I think you shouldn't be throwing rocks at anyone else. Maybe you're just glad they're writing articles about someone besides you."

An ugly red color stained her face and neck, and she looked down at her clenched hands. "All right. I apologize for saying anything."

Laurie sat rigidly, wishing she could fall through the floor. How dare this woman say anything to her! And when it was so obvious she was only a shade above reproach herself! And for Cade to come to her defense . . .

Standing abruptly, Laurie said, "I'm leaving. Please have my baggage brought round, and I will hire a carriage."

Cade stepped quickly to her, his voice low. "Where do you think you'll go at this late hour?"

She flashed him a furious glance, and her voice was taut. "I don't care! Anyplace has to be better than here, where you've allowed me to be insulted and ridiculed!"

Shaking his head impatiently, Cade snapped, "Do you think staying alone in a hotel is less scandalous? Are you going to allow Pamela to run you off? This isn't her house, anyway."

"I suppose that's why she's living in it!"

A tight smile curled his mouth as Cade said softly, "She's living in it because I allow her and John to stay."

There was a short silence while Laurie digested that fact, and instead of making her feel better, she became coldly furious.

"How convenient for you. And of course, now I understand why she's so distressed that you brought me here. It must be terribly awkward for you to have two women under the same roof, Cade. And what would your *wife* say if she was here?"

Cade shook his head. "Look, you had no place to go and I couldn't let you just wander off. I'll find better accommodations for you in the morning."

"With your wife, perhaps?" Laurie turned angrily away, and saw that Pamela Goff was just as angry. Well, she didn't care about her or what she thought. That was her problem. "Just show me to my room and leave me alone, Cade Caldwell!"

"John will show you," Cade said abruptly. "I've got some business to attend to."

"Very well. Mister Goff? Would you be so kind as to show me to the room I am to occupy?"

John Goff stood slowly, looking at Cade before he gave a nod, and said, "Sure, little lady. We didn't know Cade was bringing a friend, so we just fixed up one room, but I'm sure you don't mind . . ."

"On the contrary, I mind very much!"

Somewhat startled by her vehemence, John slanted an inquiring glance toward Cade, who said in a pleasant voice, "One room will be fine, John. I'll probably be out late tonight, anyway."

"I'll fix up the daybed in the study for you," John said quickly, his fleshy face hopeful, and Cade gave an indifferent shrug.

"Thank you, Mister Goff," Laurie said stiffly, and preceded him up a flight of stairs to the room she was to use. There was an outside entrance from the enclosed courtyard, a steep flight of stairs with a wrought-iron railing. The main feature of the room was the bed, a heavily draped piece of furniture that dominated the entire room. Laurie averted her gaze, and John Goff smiled.

"Thar's a small sittin' room through that door," he said to Laurie, and pointed.

Her smile was genuine, but she could hardly wait until he left. When he did, softly shutting the door behind him with the parting comment that she shouldn't mind Pamela too much as she and Cade had once been close, Laurie suppressed the urge to throw something.

By the time Cade came upstairs she had bathed in the room Goff had politely referred to as a "sittin' room," and the black maid who had attended her was brushing her hair with long, smooth strokes, exclaiming over the pale color.

"Such purty hair, you got, Miss," the maid was saying in admiration. "Looks almost lak new-minted gold, it does, an as soft as silk from th' Market."

Tiny wisps curled around her dark fingers as she held the weight of Laurie's hair in her hands, then twisted it into a smooth rope and secured it with a long ribbon on the nape of her neck.

"Thank you," Laurie murmured sleepily. The hot bath and the maid's gentle touch had lulled her into a languor that she had not felt in a long time, not since that night in San Antonio, when she had drunk brandy with Cade and made love most of the night.

318

The memory brought a bright flush to her high cheekbones.

She didn't realize she'd closed her eyes until she felt a hand on her shoulder, and lifted her lashes to stare at Cade's reflection in the dressing table mirror. The maid was gone and they were alone in the room.

"What do you want?" she demanded, but her voice was much softer than earlier.

"Do I have to want something?"

"When have you not?"

Cade's dark eyes crinkled with amusement, and he folded his arms across his chest and leaned against the wall to stare back at her in the mirror.

"I just came to tell you that you won't be bothered by me tonight, love."

Irritated, she rose and walked across the room to gaze out the window at the rain-swept streets. "Am I supposed to be glad?"

"Aren't you?"

She turned and glared at him with contempt. "I suppose you intend to renew your *acquaintance* with the sulky Miss Goff!"

"Ah, so you know about that, do you?"

"Bastard!"

Cade pushed away from the wall, his expression suddenly hard. "Since we're back to that point, my dear, I think I'll leave you to your dreams."

With a half-mocking bow, he was gone, going down the outside stairs to the courtyard without another word. Laurie stared after him, hating him yet wishing he hadn't left her alone in a city that had grown suddenly friendless and vaguely frightening.

Chapter Twenty-one

Laurie woke the next morning to an empty bed and bright sunlight pouring through half-opened draperies over the window. The pungent fragrance of hot, thick coffee and fresh croissants filled her nostrils, and she turned to see the maid—Lucy—smiling down at her over a heavy silver tray.

"Good mawnin', Miss. Hyah's yo' breakfuss."

"Thank you," Laurie said, sitting up and pushing her hair from her eyes as Lucy set the tray over her.

She wanted to ask about Cade, where he was and where he'd spent the night, but didn't. As Lucy chattered about trivial things—Laurie's pretty clothes in the trunks and the welcoming sunshine and balmy weather—Laurie sipped at the hot coffee and stared out the window. It wasn't until Lucy mentioned casually that Cade—Mistah Caldwell—was on his way up to visit her that her interest sharpened.

"Now, Lucy?"

"Yas'm." She giggled. "An' he's feelin' fresh as a new-laid egg this mawnin'!"

"Wonderful," Laurie muttered as she flung the covers off and scrambled from the bed. "Help me find something to wear, Lucy, quick!"

Snatching a rose-colored muslin gown from the armoire where Lucy had recently hung it, she struggled

320

into it, and Lucy was pinning up Laurie's hair when Cade walked into the room unannounced and without knocking.

"You look as fresh as a spring flower," Cade said with a wicked grin that made her want to slap him, and Lucy giggled again.

Suppressing the desire to say something sharp, Laurie managed a cool smile. Her gaze flicked over him with some surprise, noting the change from his usual knee-high boots, gunbelt, and vest and trousers, into an elegantly cut coat, vest, and cravat.

"Too bad I can't say the same thing for you," she said at last, and his grin widened.

"Always the flatterer, aren't you, Laurie?"

"When the occasion warrants. Lucy, leave us, please," she said, and the little maid giggled again as she left.

"Did you sleep well?" Cade asked, flinging his long body into a chair that was ridiculously small to support his large frame.

"Much better than I have since I found you in San Diego," she retorted, her voice sharp in spite of her resolve not to let him prick her into an argument.

"That's what I like best about you, Laurie—you're so even tempered. I always know what to expect."

"What do you think I should do, when now I'm a social outcast in all of New Orleans?" She hugged herself, her mouth turning down in a bitter smile. "I looked forward to coming home so much, and now—now it's ruined. I might as well be back in California."

Arching a dark brow, Cade stared at her thoughtfully. "It is awkward, isn't it?" he said in a surprisingly regretful tone.

She gave him a suspicious stare. "A lot you care! What do you intend to do now? Am I still your captive, or have you decided to allow me to go free?"

"I thought your cousin decided that for you." Cade rose from the chair and stood looking down at her, his eyes growing opaque again. "But I didn't come up here to argue with you, Laurie."

"How novel," she muttered sullenly.

Raking a hand through his thick, dark hair—which he'd gotten neatly trimmed, she belatedly noticed—he gave her a sort of half-smile.

"I went to visit your aunt."

Laurie stared at him with wide golden eyes, unable to speak for a moment. Then, "You *what?*"

"Visited your aunt."

"How could you! Oh God, now I'm totally ruined! I'll never be able to get back into anyone's good graces, and . . . oh, you've ruined everything!"

Cade's eyes narrowed. "Don't be too quick to judge, my love. As a matter of fact, your aunt, whom I found to be quite pleasant and willing to listen, unlike your cousin, will be here shortly."

"Here?" Laurie squeaked, and Cade nodded.

"Repack your bags, love. She means to take you home with her."

"Knowing . . . knowing that you and I . . . that we . . ."

"No, not knowing anything. She's willing to take you on faith. I told her that since we were traveling in the same direction, I had graciously lent my escort in spite of your unwillingness. I told her that I felt responsible for a woman without an escort, especially as you were from a fine New Orleans' family." His mouth twisted mockingly, and she flushed.

"Thank you, Cade."

"Don't mention it—please. I don't want to be reminded that I'm an idiot."

"You just want to get rid of me," Laurie observed with an irritated snap.

"That, yes. But more than that, I want you safely with your family."

She looked at him for a long moment. "Why?"

"So I'm not responsible for you anymore. I found out

that it's not the best job to have."

"And you've done it so graciously, too," Laurie said in a waspish voice.

"Haven't I?" He grinned. "But now I've got more important things to do, and I don't need to be worrying about anyone else."

"I'm gratified to know you worried about me," she said, and meant it. A faint smile curved her lips, and she added in a soft voice, "I do appreciate your doing this, Cade."

Uncoiling his long body from the chair, Cade stared down at her. "Take care of yourself, princess."

After he left, quietly shutting the door behind him, Laurie felt a pang of regret.

To Laurie's complete and welcome surprise, her aunt had no intention of allowing circumstances to stand between her and her favorite niece.

"You are my poor, dead sister's only child, and even if you have been unwise in your choice of companions, I cannot find it in my heart to refuse you my house," Annette DuBois said when she came for her. "I insist that you come home with me. But you understand, of course, that I cannot allow Monsieur Caldwell my home." She cleared her throat and did not look directly at Laurie. "He is not received in certain circles since he was last here. His reputation, you understand, is very bad because of a duel and his, er, shall we say *association* with a certain young lady."

"Are you referring to his wife?" Laurie asked with an acid edge to her voice.

"You knew, then?" Annette sounded shocked, and Laurie had to smile.

"Yes, I knew, but it didn't seem to matter when we were in California, you see."

Staring at her niece's flushed, defiant face, at the wide-spaced amber eyes and the mane of golden hair piled atop her head, Annette suddenly understood that it was much more involved than Pierre had admitted to her when he'd repeated the rumors.

She knew, of course, about the rumors, even before her son had told her. Gossip that scintillating would not be hidden for long, but she had refused to allow anyone to speak ill of her niece. Now she gazed at Laurie's flushed face with intense speculation. Was there a connection between the man in California and Cade Caldwell? She seemed to recall that Caldwell had Spanish ancestry, and suddenly it all fell into place. *Ma pauvre petite,* Annette thought with a pang. No wonder Laurie was so upset, and so on edge!

"You are in love with this Monsieur Caldwell," Annette said, startling a quick reaction in her niece's eyes. "That is unfortunate, for he has compromised you when he is already married. There is no honorable solution to your problem."

"I did not expect one."

"I see."

"I don't think so, Tante Annette. I'm not in love with him, but he and I have endured misfortune together, so I suppose that in a way I feel some ties to him. Do you understand what I mean?"

Putting a soft hand on Laurie's, Annette said, *"Oui, ma petite,* I understand. But put this Cade Caldwell from your mind, for it will be very difficult for others to accept."

"I know."

Annette DuBois's words turned out to be a grim prophecy. The citizens of New Orleans were not at all willing to allow such a juicy tidbit of gossip to go without embellishing it, and though no one had the actual temerity to say anything to Annette or Laurie, she knew from the whispers that stopped when she entered a room that they were talking about her.

But, defiant and composed, Laurie pretended she did not hear them, sweeping through a room as if she was still the same girl who had been the darling of New Orleans. Only her aunt knew the true cost of her bravado, and it was Tante Annette who comforted her at times, and told her it would soon be over and that she was a brave, beautiful girl.

"Why is it that I don't feel so brave when they're all staring at me and whispering behind their fans?" Laurie asked with a rueful sigh. "All I feel is awkward, and foolish, too."

She didn't add the word *used*, though tempted to. Why upset Tante Annette, who was trying so hard to get her niece through such a difficult time?

The news had come from California about Nicólas Alvarez' arrest by the alcalde of Higuera through an article in the New Orleans *Picayune*, written by a man by the name of Warren Hughes. Mr. Hughes had written a scathing report of the arrest, and had not failed to include Laurie's reported claim that it was she, not Alvarez, who had acted as the infamous El Vengador. Hughes had also given the article the slant of illicit romance, an affair between the grandson of a rich Spanish *grandee* and the daughter of an American diplomat from New Orleans. Readers had been voraciously interested in the story, especially as Laurette Allen was well known in New Orleans.

"I feel like a tragic heroine," Laurie had muttered in disgust when she'd read the paper Annette had saved. "Or a stupid one."

"*Non, non!* It is that Monsieur Hughes who was so wicked to misinform the public, that is all," Annette had declared loyally, and Laurie had not had the heart to correct her.

Gilbert Rosière, who had taught Laurie the art of fencing, suspected the truth, and he came to visit her at her aunt's home. Though disapproving, Annette did not speak out against the visit, because, after all, Rosière was from a good French family.

Rosière held Laurie's hand between his own and

looked into her eyes with a smile as they sat stiffly in the parlor. "So, you used your skills to advantage, I hear," he said in a whisper that made her smile.

"Monsieur Rosière," she replied archly, "do you think I would be so bold as to do such a thing?"

"Oui, ma belle mademoiselle, I know you would! I have taught you, you will remember." There was a twinkle in his dark eyes that made Laurie laugh, and she lowered her voice to a whisper, too.

"It is too bad that you did not teach me how to skewer meddling journalists also, Monsieur!"

"It is never too late to learn," he said solemnly.

Gilbert Rosière tilted his head to one side, gazing appreciatively at Laurie. She had matured a great deal from the impetuous, willful girl of sixteen that he had last seen. The years in France had lent her a grace and polish, and there was a new awareness of her femininity that made her infinitely more desirable. She held herself with a poise that was rare in one so young, and she still had the spirit that had made her unique. *Dieu!* but he wished the gulf between them was not so wide. But her family would never allow her to be courted by one such as he, not even in her present disgrace.

Gilbert smiled to himself. That disgrace would soon be forgotten, replaced by another's downfall, and the so-beautiful Laurette would create quite a stir among the bachelors of New Orleans. Already he had heard many a man declare that he did not care about the scandal if he could only kiss Laurette Allen's ripe lips, or gaze into her wide golden eyes. For it was only unproven gossip, after all, and with a woman as lovely as Mademoiselle Allen, a little experience might improve a man's chances.

What a woman, *quelle femme!*

Slowly at first, Laurie found that people began to accept her again, the men more quickly, the women with a guarded reluctance. But there was a tinge of mystery about her that made even her most haughty friends wonder, a hint of forbidden excitement that made them wonder if she had truly been the *petite amie* of a dangerous renegade.

Though furious that Cade was not recognized as Nicólas Alvarez, Laurie did not attempt to clear up the misconception. It would only compound the problem if she were to point out that the infamous Cade Caldwell was also the infamous Nicólas Alvarez—El Vengador. Then she would be doubly damned. So she kept her silence and her secret, bitterly wondering why it was that a man could do the most horrendous things without being socially ostracized, while a woman reaped censure and scorn.

Tidbits of gossip about Cade's return to New Orleans with Laurie on his arm reached her, and though he was whispered about and held to be a generally scandalous man, he was also much sought-after. It didn't seem fair, for he had left New Orleans after marrying and almost literally leaving at the alter his prominent bride, and was now welcomed back into the some of social circles that had once condemned him.

At night, alone in her bedroom, Laurie wondered if he had gone back to his bride. No one seemed to know, but there was a great deal of conjecture about their reunion. Angrily, hopelessly, Laurie fought the tears that would come whenever she thought about Cade—she hadn't heard from him since he'd left her at the Goff house a month before.

Maybe she should be glad, but somehow, when she thought of him, she felt an overwhelming sadness that was often tempered with anger. How could he forget her so easily? And why was she the only one to suffer for something that had been partly his fault? After all, if he'd left her alone in San Diego, she could have come back to New Orleans much sooner, and perhaps defused the rumors that Warren Hughes's article had provoked. Damn that vicious Hughes for a nosy old meddler anyway. And damn Cade for forgetting her so quickly and easily.

But Cade hadn't forgotten Laurie, and he hadn't gone back to his wife.

He had arranged an introduction to William Fisher, the man Houston had sent him to meet, and engaged in several very profitable card games with him. Noting that Fisher was prone to talk more when he was winning, Cade managed to lose tidy sums of money quite graciously. It helped pay the rent in the shabby French boarding house where Fisher was staying, and the former colonel in the Mexican Army looked forward to their games.

"A pair of tens," Cade said as he spread his cards on the table, and hid a smile when Fisher triumphantly spread out two pair.

"Sevens and eights!" Fisher crowed. Sitting back, he lit a fat cigar and took a deep puff after raking in his winnings.

"Brandy, Mister Fisher?" Cade inquired politely, and signaled to the mulatto girl to serve them both.

They were ensconced in deep velvet chairs at a green baize table in the Monroe house, where many of the elite of New Orleans often went to play cards. There was none of the rowdiness associated with some of the other houses, and the main reason Cade preferred frequenting it was the privacy. Each table was tucked into a nook, so that there was an air of seclusion to each game.

"You're an excellent loser, Mister Caldwell," Fisher said, and smiled expansively. "I appreciate that in a man."

"It seems to have become habit since I made your acquaintance," Cade responded, gazing at Fisher over the rim of his brandy snifter. He sipped slowly, watching with narrowed eyes as Fisher took a deep gulp. "I understand that you are recently returned from Mexico," he said when Fisher had made headway into the brandy.

Nodding, the lanky, rather threadbare man opposite him said, "That is true. I spent some time in the Mexican Army as a colonel, but it was rather—unstable employment, I fear. And I became increasingly aware that there was far greater chance for gainful opportunities at home."

Cade swirled his brandy, gazing at the amber liquid in a thoughtful silence. Then he looked up at Fisher. "How did you reach that conclusion?"

Shrugging as he put down his brandy and reached for the pack of pasteboard cards, Fisher said, "I had hoped that war would break out with England, thus providing me with stable employment, but am now come to the conclusion that this age of diplomacy prevents that. So, after studying the situation in Mexico—where Santa Anna has amassed a huge force of over twenty thousand men—I decided that Texas may need the services of an experienced officer not loathe to fight for a portion of the conquered land instead of a hefty commission. And I can bring a force of up to six hundred men if given a little time."

Cade's expression didn't change as he gazed at Fisher with a half-smile curving his lips. "Why is it no one in Texas has heard of this massive force of soldiers Santa Anna has?"

Taking another swallow of brandy, Fisher rolled it over his tongue appreciatively before he answered. "They are in San Luis Potosi. Mexico intends to invade Texas and bring her to her knees. Santa Anna's revenge."

"And your educated guess as to the outcome, Mr. Fisher?"

A sly expression crossed his features as Fisher paused, then said, "I would not be here in New Orleans unless I thought Texas had a chance."

"I see." Cade leaned forward, smiling at Fisher over the rim of his brandy snifter. "And you are willing to raise a force of men to fight for Texas?"

Settling back in his chair, Fisher nodded. "I am."

"Who have you contacted about this?"

"No one as yet, but I am acquainted with General Felix Huston. I intend to advise him of my intentions at the earliest opportunity."

"You will be visiting him, then?"

Looking faintly embarrassed, Fisher shook his head. "No, I am unable to do that. I had thought a written correspondence might be the best."

"I see," Cade said again, realizing that Fisher was pressed for funds. "Another hand of cards before you leave, sir?"

They played for several more hours, with Cade allowing Fisher to win a modest sum from him, and parted congenially just before midnight. Cade walked outside the elegant house and stood on the sidewalk for several minutes, clearing his head of tobacco smoke and brandy fumes.

It was a clear night. Wisps of cloud scudded across the face of the moon, and the wind blew softly through the gray streamers of moss hanging from the trees. Cade signaled for a carriage, and stepped inside and settled back against the cushions, his mind spinning.

So it was true — Santa Anna had already amassed an army to fight against Texas. He would see that Houston got the information quickly. It would be useless to inform the president of the Republic, because Lamar was in a spin and couldn't function. Vice-President Burnet was just as bad, and the citizens of Texas were becoming worried and restless.

And Lamar had only recently presented a new idea, in stirring speeches about extending the Lone Star boundaries to the gray towers of El Palacio Real. The leaders were desperate for new revenues, and the wealth of the Santa Fe trail would bring in enough to boost the new Republic's coffers. Santa Fe and most of New Mexico already lay within the boundaries of the republic as drawn up in 1836, but as yet, the Republic had not attempted to assert dominance. Houston was of the opinion that it would be foolish to the extreme to attempt such a thing now, should resistance be offered.

Cade looked out the windows of the carriage and thought that Lamar must be ten different kinds of a fool to even seriously contemplate such an action. It was too risky and would cost too much, besides splitting Texas once more.

Stretching his long legs out in front of him, Cade cast another idle glance out the carriage window and signaled to the driver to halt. He was already running late because of his game with Fisher, but that didn't really matter.

Carriages were lined up in front of the sprawling, well-lit building, and Cade looked for and recognized an especially plush carriage. He grinned to himself and wondered how CeCe would react when he finally visited her. He'd received her imperious messages and had ignored them all, except this one. What better place for a confrontation than in public? Not even CeCe would risk a potentially embarrassing scene in front of half of New Orleans. Cade waited as the driver opened his door, rearranging the lace folds of his shirt and his neckerchief.

"Wait for me," he said as he leaped down and strode up the brick walk.

Chapter Twenty-two

Warren Hughes had the bittersweet pleasure of meeting, at last, the object of his damning article at the opera. A tall, lanky man with sandy hair and the habit of squinting, he stared at Laurie for a full minute before managing to speak.

"Now I understand why a Mexican bandit wished to carry you off, Miss Allen," he said, lifting her hand to his lips and placing a kiss on her knuckles. "My facts are well proven, I see."

Withdrawing her hand, Laurie gaped at him with a glacial stare. "Do you, sir? How fascinating, since your article was so obscure on most points."

A faint smile curved the lips beneath a thin mustache. "I welcome the opportunity to discuss those points with you at length, Miss Allen."

"I'm afraid you find me quite indifferent, sir. Now, if you will excuse me, I see that my aunt is waiting."

Laurie swept away and entered the DuBois box, aware that Hughes was staring intently after her. Her cheeks flamed, and she could feel other stares in her direction, too. She kept her chin high, and sat down next to her aunt with a rustle of satin skirts.

Annette leaned close, her painted fan fluttering to hide her nervousness as she asked softly, "Did I actually see Bertrand Dupree introduce you to that nasty Monsieur Hughes?"

"You did."

"Le cochon! I shall severely chastise Bertrand later. And what did Monsieur Hughes say to you?"

"He told me that he would welcome the chance to discuss the article he wrote." Laurie met her aunt's startled gaze. "I think that perhaps I will oblige him soon — but not too soon."

She'd seen the interest in Hughes's pale eyes, the twitch of his lips beneath his ridiculous moustache, and knew instinctively that he was interested in more than a discussion.

"He's dangerous, that Monsieur Hughes," Annette said with a frown, and Laurie nodded.

"I know. But I can be, too."

Annette slid her a curious glance, while Pierre, at the back of the box behind them, glowered. He had seen Warren Hughes greet Laurie, had heard Dupree introduce them with a rather puckish glee, and had been as insulted as he thought his *petite cousine* should be. Why didn't she act more embarrassed by the situation? Pierre had always been half in love with Laurie himself, from the time she began to blossom into a lovely young girl with high spirits and a maturing body. The gossipy newspaper article had infuriated him, humiliated him, and chagrined him. Perhaps, he admitted to himself, he was jealous of that Nicolas Alvarez, and then when he had seen her kissed on the dock — in a public place! — by Cade Caldwell, he had known that the virginal girl he had loved and admired had changed more than he liked.

Yet Pierre could not resist being near her, watching her artless flirtations with a resentment he didn't really understand.

Laurie understood it much more than Pierre would have liked for her to, and she felt awkward around him. It was another regret in her life, she thought sadly, that she could not enjoy her cousin's companionship.

Lately she had been talking with her aunt about going back to France. She would not feel so ostracized there, with the gossip always hanging over her head as it was here in New Orleans.

But there, a small voice whispered silently, *you will never see Cade again.*

Irritably, she turned her mind from Cade, wishing he would not constantly pop into her thoughts. Why couldn't she just forget him and all the misery he had caused her?

And in the next instant, as she lifted her eyes toward the stage where a big-bosomed woman was singing in Italian, she saw Cade Caldwell. He was standing in a box on the left side of the stage, and she saw him bend and say something to a woman seated near the front. Her attention was riveted on him, and she could feel the sudden pump of blood through her veins escalate. Cade, here, at the opera, and not even dressed properly, though, of course, he wouldn't care about trivial things like that.

Even with the lights low and the action on the draped stage, Laurie could easily recognize him. Maybe it was the way he walked, with an easy, loose stride that bordered on arrogance. Or it could have been because he was taller than most men, and carried himself with a languid grace. But whatever it was, she knew him, and her heart was in her throat.

It had been a month — would he see her? Would he acknowledge her if he saw her? Or would he politely pretend that he did not see her, and what did it matter anyway?

Laurie's breath came more quickly when she saw him take a chair beside the woman, and she lifted her opera glass with shaking fingers and stared in their direction. Who was she?

The next instant her heart plummeted to her toes as she recognized Cecelia de Marchand . . . Cade's wife. Were they together? Tante Annette had heard rumors, but she said she did not believe them because no one ever saw Cade with her.

"And you know how gossips love to invent new topics," Annette had added with a comforting smile. "I'm certain it is just to spark new rumors."

But Laurie had not been so certain, and said so. And

now she saw Cade talking with Cecelia, who was tossing her head archly and smiling at him, leaning close so that her bosom almost fell out of her low-cut gown, her smile growing wider at something he said.

Burning with anger and heartache, Laurie stumbled blindly to her feet, not caring that she was drawing a few stares and whispers, not caring about anything but escape. She could not watch another moment of Cade with Cecelia. And it didn't occur to her then to wonder why.

"Laurette!" Pierre snapped, and grabbed her by the arm. "Do you want everyone laughing at you? *Oui,* I see him, and so do others. Do not run now, or everyone will say that you are broken-hearted, and that there must have been more between you and Monsieur Caldwell than you are admitting."

Realizing that he was right, Laurie hesitated, and her cousin took pity on the pain etched on her face.

"*Ma petite cousine,* do not show your feelings so openly for everyone to see," he whispered, and took her cold hand between his palms. He smiled at her, and Laurie's chin lifted and she managed to smile back.

"*Merci,* Pierre. You are right. I will stay here, and I will not let anyone think that I care."

It was much easier said than done, Laurie discovered as she flirted first with her attentive cousin, then with the young men who came to her box during the intermission. Drawn by Laurie's beauty and vivacity, they lingered even when the lights once more dimmed and the opera began again. The DuBois box was crowded to overflowing, and from time to time Laurie managed a glance toward the governor's box, where Cade still sat with Cecelia.

He'd seen Laurie, of course. How could he not, when she was so gay and laughing, tossing her blonde head and fluttering a painted fan as expertly as any coquette? She had drawn the attention of more than just those hungry for new tidbits of gossip. His showing up so unexpectedly was like throwing raw meat to the lions, Cade thought wryly. If he'd known Laurie would be there, he would not have done it.

But now he was here, and Cecelia, he was finding out, was furious and vengeful.

"You were gone so long—and without a word of explanation," she was saying, leaning close, her dark eyes glittering with malice. "Everyone in New Orleans laughed, and said that you could not bear to be married to me!"

Cade smiled, fully aware that he and Cecelia were now the main interest instead of the opera.

"I married you because you had me thrown in prison, not because I wanted to," he commented wryly.

"I know. But I have decided to forgive you for that," she said after a moment. "We can begin again."

"You can't force a man into marriage and expect him to like it, CeCe," he drawled lightly.

She glared at him over the edge of her furiously fluttering fan, and her voice was hard and brittle. "I should have you thrown out of here! If my uncle were here, you would not be so cocky!"

"If your uncle were here, I would not have come," he said.

His dark eyes were hooded and unreadable in the dark, and Cecelia, who had always gotten whatever she wanted, felt a mounting frustration. After he had left her on their wedding night, she had gone abruptly to Europe, making a Grand Tour and trying to forget him. Once back in New Orleans, however, no one had let her forget him, and because they expected her to do so, she had not had the marriage annulled in spite of her uncle's urgings. Now she knew the real reason why.

Cade Caldwell, for all that he had humiliated and insulted her, was the only man who had ever intrigued her. Other men were so easily manipulated, but not this one. No, he had not allowed her to make him say this or do that. And instead of making her angry, it was a challenge. Cecelia smiled at him, and her eyes sparkled with an excitement she hadn't felt since she'd last seen him as she leaned forward to murmur, "You will visit me at home tomorrow, and we wills discuss our marriage — and divorce."

To her surprise, Cade did not agree, but merely laughed at her. "CeCe, you never cease to think all you have to do is snap your fingers, do you? No, I won't be there tomorrow, but I will send a note when I can come."

"And if I refuse to see you?" she snapped, stiffening and tossing her dark head.

"You won't. And before you try, let me inform you that I have listened to a few gossips myself, and have learned that you haven't exactly been a faithful wife in my absence."

"Pah! Do you think me foolish enough to believe that you have been a faithful husband — when you would not even stay for our wedding night?"

Laughing Cade shook his head. "You should know that a wandering husband is expected — a wandering wife is not. And remember, CeCe, our marriage was not consummated. I do not need a divorce, just an annulment."

"With everyone in New Orleans knowing that it was you who left me?" she spat before controlling herself. She could feel the eyes in their direction, and had no desire to set herself up for more ridicule. Schooling her features into a calm smile, she added, "My uncle has a great deal of influence, *chèr*. But we will talk more when I see you again. *Au revoir.*"

Rising, Cade pressed a kiss on the hand she lifted to him, and had to admire her cool composure as she inclined her head. Cecelia de Marchand was a very lovely, spirited woman, but much too calculating.

Even more calculating than the blond vixen who sat in the DuBois box surrounded by admirers, he thought as he left the opera house. He knew Laurie had seen him, had seen her look toward the governor's box more than once. By tomorrow morning it would be all over New Orleans that he had visited his wife while his mistress looked on.

Chapter Twenty-three

"Cousine Laurette?" a voice inquired from the doorway, and Laurie struggled from the merciful folds of sleep to sit up in bed. Her youngest cousin Marie was smiling at her from the doorway, and she managed to smile back. Marie's dark eyes gleamed with sympathy as she crossed to the wide bed. Laurie patted the mattress beside her, and Marie stepped up and seated herself primly.

"I have a message for you," the girl said with a self-important tilt of her head.

"Oui, ma petite chou, what is it?"

"Maman wanted me to remind you of the ball tonight, and that you promised to attend."

Frowning, Laurie wished she could refuse. How could she face everyone, knowing that the whispers had begun again? But, she reminded herself sternly, she wasn't a coward, and would not let them all think she was!

"Tell Tante Annette that I will attend," she said, and smiled at Marie's delight.

"Oh! I told Maman that you would, but she was afraid that perhaps you did not feel like it."

"Is that why she did not come herself?" Laurie teased. "Did she send you to coax me into it?"

The girl giggled, bouncing on the bed with suppressed excitement. "No, that is part of the surprise."

"Surprise?"

Marie nodded. She leaned forward to whisper, "But I am not allowed to tell you — that is why it is a surprise."

The surprise, Laurie learned, was a new gown, one that would certainly attract attention.

"But Tante Annette — why?" she asked, gazing at the ballgown with widened eyes. "It's beautiful, but I don't understand."

Annette's mouth puckered into a prim rosette, and her eyes flashed. "Because everyone expects you to be the cast-off woman, that is why! And you cannot let them think that. You must enter that ballroom tonight with your head held high and wearing the most beautiful gown in the room. All eyes should go to you, and there will not be a person there who will not think Monsieur Caldwell a fool."

Laurie smiled. "Vindicate the family name, *n'est-ce pas?*"

"*Oui!*" Annette replied with a vigorous nod of her head. "I will not have people saying that a de Monchy was spurned by such a man."

Wryly, Laurie observed, "If it doesn't bother me, it shouldn't bother you so badly."

"But it does bother you, and don't pretend that it does not. I saw it in your face last night, and so did anyone looking at you."

"Was I that transparent?"

"*Oui, ma chère.* But only to those who know you," she hastened to add, and Laurie hesitated.

"Uncle Jean-Claude?" she began, and Annette said quickly, "Feels the same way I do, *chère.*"

"If it will please you for me to wear a new gown and act as if I am happy, I will, Tante. And Cade Caldwell will never know that I am aware of his existence."

"*Bon!*" Annette approved with a clap of her hands. She held up the silk dress. "And now you will try it on, *oui?*"

"Yes, now I will try it on."

But before she could, a visitor was announced, and Laurie went downstairs to greet Warren Hughes.

"Mister Hughes," she said graciously, indicating that he should sit in a chair drawn close to the fire. "How interesting that you should come to visit me."

His thin lips twitched. "Interesting? That's an unusual word to use, Miss Allen."

"No more unusual than some of those you used in that article," she said with a smile that did not reach her eyes.

Hughes had the grace to look embarrassed, but he did not back down. "Well, was I right in what I printed? Or do you intend to deny the rumors?"

"Ah, so you admit you printed a story based on rumors instead of irrefutable facts, Mister Hughes? Tsk, tsk. How unprofessional!"

"I didn't know you then, Miss Allen," he said, switching tactics. "I had never had the pleasure of meeting you, and seeing that you are a very lovely young lady."

"And now that you have, Mister Hughes?" Laurie held out a glass of port she'd poured for him, and her mouth curved into a smile as his fingers closed convulsively around the stem of the glass.

He took a quick, deep gulp of the port, then said in a breathy voice, "I find it most difficult to believe that you and the irresponsible young lady in California are one and the same."

Laurie replaced the stopper in the crystal decanter of port with a slow, deliberate motion, then looked up at Hughes. "And if I were to tell you that I did not do those things — what would you do?"

"If you could offer proof, Miss Allen, I would gladly print a retraction or correction to my article," he said promptly.

Moving across the floor with a measured tread that

made the satin skirts of her green-striped day dress rustle in a provocative whisper, Laurie smiled down at him. "Well, I cannot offer you proof, Mister Hughes. And you seem to be a man who would take nothing less."

"In fairness to my editor, I cannot see how . . ."

"In fairness to your editor?" Laurie's brows rose, and there was a note of anger in her voice as she said, "What about in fairness to the subject of your articles, Mister Hughes? Do you think it more important to be fair to an editor worried about circulation than to be fair to two people who could be quite innocent? Think about the families involved, and the lives you could ruin!"

Hughes put down his unfinished glass of port and stepped nearer to Laurie, his voice quivering. "Perhaps I was not fair, but it was such a ridiculous story that you—instead of this Nicólas Alvarez—should be dashing around the countryside brandishing a sword and humiliating a troop of soldiers! It was too good to ignore, and perhaps you can appreciate that."

"Being the subject of vicious gossip since your article surfaced here," Laurie said dryly, "I find it very hard to appreciate that."

"Forgive me, Miss Allen!" Hughes said then, daring to reach out and grasp her hands in his. "Since I met you at the opera last night I have been consumed with the desire to see you again, to have you smile at me! I do not want you angry or hurt."

Gently removing her hands, Laurie took several steps away from him. "Mister Hughes, I'm afraid that you and I could never be more than casual—*very* casual—acquaintances at best. Please do not embarrass either of us with more intimate conversation."

Even to her own ears it sounded stilted and blunt, but she could not bear another moment of the man's wide-eyed scrutiny. She almost winced when he recoiled, and his eyes grew narrowed and hard.

"Well. Perhaps I have been impertinent, but now I know how things are."

"I don't think so," she began, but he cut her off with a wave of his arm.

"It doesn't matter. Warren Hughes knows when he's not wanted, and I shall depart. Good day, Miss Allen."

After he'd gone, stalking out of the parlor like a man insulted, Laurie stared after him with a worried frown. For some reason, she had the inescapable feeling that Tante Annette had been right and Warren Hughes was dangerous. But for the man actually to hint that she might have a fondness for him had been too much, and she had to stop him at once. Now he was really angry, and she wondered what he would do.

"But I can't worry about it," she murmured resentfully. "There's too much else to worry about! And I have to go to that ball and watch everyone stare at me without trying to, and—oh, *mon Dieu!* It is just too much!"

"What is too much, my sweet?" her uncle, Jean-Claude, asked as he stepped into the parlor. He stared at her with a peculiarly owlish expression that made her smile, and she ran to him and pressed a kiss to his cheek.

"The sum Tante Annette must have paid for my new gown! It is too beautiful, and I don't deserve it."

He gave her a clumsy, fond pat on the shoulder. "Nonsense, child! You deserve only the best. Only the best. Never accept less."

"I'll remember that this evening when I am wearing the new gown," Laurie promised with a laugh, and ran upstairs. She would not think about Warren Hughes right now. She could think about him later, after the ball was over and she had time.

When Laurie was finally ready that evening, she had to admit Annette had chosen well. The silk ballgown was solid black, making her creamy skin appear even paler, and her hair had been done up in curls atop her head. In the recent weeks she had lost weight, so that her cheekbones stood out, emphasizing the catlike slant to her huge gold eyes. There was no denying that she had grown more alluring than she had ever been and she supposed that it was all because of heartache. Maybe it was a sort of compensation for the pain she had suffered, she thought as she gazed at her reflection without the slightest interest.

"Mon Dieu!" Annette whispered as she looked at her in rapt admiration. "The black of the gown sets off your fair coloring, and you look quite the sophisticate. In a sea of brightly colored gowns, you will stand out tonight."

"I'm dressed the part, is that what you're saying?" Laurie murmured, wondering how she would get through an entire evening of forced gaiety.

"The part, *chère?*"

"The part of the *fallen woman*," Laurie said with a dramatic flourish. "Is that not my role, now? After all, he is married to Cecelia, and it appears that he has chosen to return to matrimonial bliss."

Her voice was tinged with bitterness, and Annette put out a comforting hand. "You must have the strength to accept the things you cannot change, Laurette. That is a lesson your poor maman never learned. Françoise could not deal with the realities of life."

Remembering that long-ago day when Isabeau had told her much the same thing, Laurie nodded. She would go on, would accept what could not be changed, and would be stronger for it.

She tried to remember that when she stepped into the vast, glittering ballroom of the DuMont residence. Everyone in New Orleans had been invited, it seemed, and the halls were crowded with women dripping with jewels and expensive gowns.

Pierre was her escort, and he protectively steered her through the receiving line with an economy of comments.

"You did that well," Laurie whispered when they were in the ballroom among the other guests Her eyes were full of laughter. "I have never heard you say so little to such lovely women!"

A gleam of mischief shone in his eyes, and he had to laugh, too. "There is always later, *petite cousine*. And besides, Madame Remy looked too full of questions to linger very long in her company."

Aware of the gazes in their direction, Laurie looked up at Pierre as if he had just said something very clever, and said, "She is not alone. Everyone here seems to be waiting for something to happen."

"Let them wait." Pierre bowed slightly from the waist and held out his hand. "Shall we dance, mademoiselle?"

"Delighted."

Laurie felt more comfortable in the familiar steps of a quadrille, and less conspicuous. And when the music had ended, she was claimed by another partner for another dance and then another, until she forgot that she was supposed to be in disgrace and the subject of speculation.

Pierre watched her and smiled. In spite of his anger toward her at first, he did not want to see Laurie sad. And perhaps, though she was his first cousin, there was a chance she would turn to him one day. He consoled himself with that thought as the night wore on and he could not get close to her because of the ardent beaux.

One of the most ardent beaux was a young French vicomte who had met Laurie before, in California, he said, and he could not believe his good fortune in finding her again.

"I was dancing with her," he told Pierre, "and then went to fetch her a glass of punch. When I returned, she was gone, poof! I was told later that she had become ill, and as I had to leave a few days later, I was never fortunate enough to see her again. It is the best of luck that I have found her again!"

Rather grudgingly, Pierre agreed with him as the young vicomte hurried back to Laurie's side.

Jacques Poirier was smitten with Laurie. How could he have ever thought she might change? If anything, she was even more beautiful than she had been when last he'd seen her. The daring black gown clung to her like a glove, with a low decolletage that exhibited a creamy swell of bosom and a form-fitting waist that only showed how tiny she was. There were no frills, no adornments on the gown. Her only adornments were the glittering diamonds in her ears and the huge garnet stone surrounded by diamonds around her neck. The jewels could not rival her glowing eyes, Jacques said gallantly, and Laurie smiled with delight.

"*Merci, monsieur!* I had not forgotten how flattering you could be."

When she'd seen him, Laurie had been startled at first, remembering that night in Los Angeles when she had gone with Cade into the arbor. Then she had become deliberately gay and carefree, laughing and greeting the vicomte as if he was an old and valued friend.

Smiling, Jacques had been only slightly surprised at the reaction he'd received, then decided that Laurie must have thought about him, too. He could not believe his good fortune when she teased him, calling him a rogue and a heartbreaker for leaving her in Los Angeles without saying farewell.

"I tried, but was told that you were not receiving visitors," Jacques said, and Laurie laughed again.

"You were too easily discouraged. I am almost tempted not to speak to you again," she said with a pout, then added when he grew alarmed, "But I will not. It is too good to see you here in New Orleans. And this time you will not run away without saying good-bye."

"No, never," Jacques vowed fervently.

They drank champagne punch as if it was water, and Laurie did not notice or care how many times her glass was refilled. She drank much more than she should have, and it still did not seem to be enough. She could still sense the occasional stares in her direction, the whispers behind hands, and several times she could hear her own laughter, sounding much too loud and forced. Jacques Poirier did not notice that she was too gay, too glad to see him.

He knew only that Laurette Allen was beautiful and desirable, and that she flirted shamelessly with him. And if her face was thinner than he remembered it, it only made her look more delicate, made her mouth look riper and more promising, and her huge amber eyes larger. Jacques could hardly tear his eyes from her that night, and he was not alone.

Warren Hughes, a guest of the hosts, stared tightly at Laurie as she gaily flirted with Jacques, and Pierre DuBois's terse explanation that Laurie had known the vicomte before, in California, did not remove the fret from his eyes. Hughes had not known how lovely Miss Allen was, or how heartless she could be. Now he knew, and after their unpleasant interview earlier, he felt a burning resentment. Why should she spurn him so coldly and casually? It wasn't as if she was still one of the demure young girls untouched by scandal. And garbed in the black gown that set her apart from all the others—made her pale beauty stand out like a fallen star—she looked more desirable than ever.

Hughes glared at her as she swung by, laughing with the Frenchman, her lovely face glowing and happy.

He had thought about her all night the night before, and after leaving her home earlier. A chance meeting with an old acquaintance had given him more food for thought. Hughes had, of course, already heard the gossip and rumors about Cade Caldwell and

346

Laurie, had heard that the bold and dangerous Caldwell had escorted Miss Allen from Texas to New Orleans, and that it was whispered that they were lovers. What made it infinitely more interesting was the fact that Caldwell had a wife in New Orleans, the governor's niece whom he had married and left on the same night.

Hughes's natural predilection for juicy stories had made him ask for more details, and there was a certain Miss Goff who had been very obliging. None of this, however, had lessened his desire for Laurie Allen.

Now he stared at her with hot eyes, wondering if she was really as fascinated by the fair French vicomte as she pretended to be.

She wasn't. Laurie's champagne spirits rose dangerously high as she drank more and more. She didn't care. A spirit of recklessness drove her, and even the knowledge that the potentially dangerous Warren Hughes was there and watching her didn't matter.

But if Laurie didn't care about Warren Hughes, she did care that Cade Caldwell was there. Not even her alcohol-induced gaiety could smother the feelings that seeing him invoked, and she asked gaily for another glass of champagne to be brought to her.

"Another?" Jacques Poirier lifted a brow as he eyed her flushed face. "Are you sure that is wise, Mademoiselle?"

She made her voice deliberately cutting. "If you do not wish to fetch it for me, Monsieur, I am certain that I can find someone who will be so kind as to . . ."

"No, no," he said hastily, though he was frowning, "I will be glad to get it for you. I was merely concerned that you might become ill again, as you did the last time you drank champagne punch."

The memory of that night still had the power to make her wince, and Laurie wondered vaguely if she should stop. But she had gone too far now, and besides, she could see Cade lounging indolently against a wall.

"I am quite well," she said to Jacques, "but very thirsty."

She didn't even notice when he left her side to fetch the punch; her eyes returned again and again to Cade.

Elegantly clad in tight-fitting pantaloons, silk vest, starched cravat, and cummerbund, Cade was aware of Laurie, too. He had seen her immediately after arriving, and had watched her without her being aware of it. He knew her too well to think she was truly having a good time, and he was fairly certain of the reason for it.

Cecelia de Marchand noticed him at almost the same time as Laurie did, and she did not hesitate or try to pretend she did not see him. She walked swiftly to his side.

"You did not come today," she said without preamble.

Politely smiling, Cade lifted a dark brow. "I said that I would not."

"But I told you to!"

"And I told you, CeCe, that I don't come when you whistle. Maybe you should get a dog."

He took a sip of brandy as she glared at him, and could feel the stares in their direction. All of New Orleans must be agog with avid curiosity, he thought wryly. What a show they were getting!

"I know about your *petite amie*," she said then, her dark eyes flashing, and conversation around them quieted as people strained to hear.

"Which one?"

"Don't play me for the fool, Cade Caldwell!" Cecelia stiffened angrily, her bosom heaving with agitation. "It is all over New Orleans about the woman you brought with you from Texas! And don't try to deny it, for I know her, and I have asked my uncle to investigate."

"Your information is slow, CeCe," Cade drawled.

"I've been back a month. and you should have heard all about it long before now."

"Perhaps no one wished to upset me."

"Perhaps, but I don't think so." Cade took a sip of his brandy, gazing at the furious brunette over the rim of his glass.

"Is she the reason you came back?"

"If you've heard the gossip, *cherie,* you know that she is not." Cade put one hand on her arm and turned her toward the walled terrace just outside double doors. "Why don't we go outside, where we can talk more privately?" he suggested, and Cecelia went with him quietly, if sullenly.

Watching, Laurie felt her heart drop. First that *puta* Rosa, whom Cade had mistaken her for at his grandfather's fiesta; then Linda Navarro; the alcalde's accommodating niece; then Pamela Goff; and now there was Cecelia de Marchand. Would there never be an end to the women in Cade's life? Must she be thrown into awkward situations every time she saw him? And damn him — why did he still have the power to make her ache for him?

To hide that longing, and to hide the surge of emotion she felt at seeing Cade again, Laurie was gayer than ever when Jacques returned with another glass of champagne for her. Surprisingly, instead of making her drunker, it had the effect of clearing her head. Or maybe it was seeing Cade walk out with Cecelia de Marchand that cleared her head, but whatever it was, Laurie decided after only a few more minutes that she wanted to leave the ball.

"Leave?" Tante Annette echoed with some concern. "But it is not even midnight!"

"I don't care," Laurie said stubbornly. "I'm tired, and I want to go home. I can have Pierre take me, or even the vicomte."

Quick to leap at the opportunity, Jacques said, *"Oui, madame,* I will be more than happy to see Mademoiselle Allen home for you."

"Well," Annette began uncertainly, her troubled gaze going from Laurie to the *vicomte*, "I suppose it would be all right. You do understand, monsieur, that my niece must go straight home. And that you have an obligation as a gentleman to see that she comes to no harm?"

Whatever Jacques would have replied remained unspoken, for Cade Caldwell chose that moment to approach them. Aghast at his temerity, Annette DuBois just stared.

"Madame DuBois, I apologize for disturbing you, but I would like a moment alone with your niece."

"With . . . with my niece? But monsieur, I'm afraid that I do not think . . . I mean . . ."

"It will only be a moment," Cade said, taking Laurie's hand to pull her with him.

"Monsieur," Jacques interrupted coldly, and Cade paused to look at him inquiringly. Jacques shifted, glancing from Laurie to Cade. "I do not believe we have met — or that we have heard what the young lady wishes," he said.

Annette said quickly, "This is Monsieur Jacques Poirier from France, Mister Caldwell, and . . ."

"*Vicomte* Jacques de la Poirier," Laurie put in with a snap, and earned an amused glance from Cade, who still held tightly to her hand.

Jacques flushed, and said in an unhappy tone, "I do not use my title here, monsieur. I have learned that it annoys certain people. I have the honor to be addressing . . . ?" He left the sentence unfinished, and Cade supplied the answer.

"Cade Caldwell. And I only want to speak with Miss Allen for a moment. I trust it will not inconvenience you, sir."

As he did not wait for a reply but pulled Laurie with him, Jacques was left with little to say. If Laurie had called out, or refused to go, he would have interfered, but she had only glared up at Caldwell with huge golden eyes as he escorted her through the crowd.

Annette wheezed, "They have met before, you understand. I think they do not like one another very much." There seemed to be nothing to say after that, and she lapsed into silence as she looked around frantically for Pierre or Jean Claude. Oh, she fumed, they were never near when she needed them! And Laurie, being led away like a lamb to the slaughter, with her arm being held by that disgraceful man!

After the first moment of shock, Laurie recovered enough to say sharply, "What do you think you're doing? Isn't it enough that everyone is already staring at us? And now you leave your *wife* to come and talk to me?"

"I wouldn't cause any more of a scene if I were you," Cade commented dryly. "People are enjoying it too much."

Furious and embarrassed, Laurie allowed him to take her out on the veranda he had just occupied with Cecelia. She stood stiffly, quivering inside but determined that he would not know it.

"What do you have to say that's so important?" she asked when they were alone on the veranda, where an icy moon shone down on them. She shivered slightly, for it was, after all, December, and the night winds could be brisk and cold. She wished her head would clear of lingering champagne fumes, and that she could see Cade more clearly. He was looking at her so oddly. . . . "It won't take long," Cade said, "and then you can go back in to your French count and your aunt."

She stared at him. His expression was unreadable, his dark eyes hooded. What was she supposed to say? He apparently expected her to say something, so she dredged up the first thing that came to mind. "I imagine," she said acidly, "that your wife must be wondering why you have brought me out here!"

Impatiently, Cade said, "Forget CeCe. You need to think about what you're doing, Laurie. Have enough sense not to ruin what's left of your reputation by flirting so openly or getting drunk in public."

"Are you daring to judge my behavior? You, of all people? The man who ruined me in California and almost ruined me here?" Her voice had risen, and Cade took a quick step forward to seize her by the wrist when she would have turned and run back into the ballroom.

"You little fool, you've managed to quiet the rumors until now! Don't be stupid enough to start them up all over again."

She gave a scornful laugh, shivering with reaction and chill, glaring at him in the moonlight. "As if our being out here together won't add fuel to the fires of gossip!"

Shaking his head, Cade said harshly, "I should have known better than to try and tell you anything. You're too stubborn and hardheaded to listen. Go ahead then, and be a little fool."

Furious tears stung her eyes, and her chin lifted as she said, "I will do exactly as I please, Cade Caldwell, and you can go to the devil!"

From behind them, a voice inquired softly, "Do you mind if I quote you on that, Miss Allen?"

Whirling, Laurie saw Warren Hughes in the shadows, and he was smiling oddly at her. Her brain reacted sluggishly, and to gain time, she said the first thing that came to mind.

"Sir!" she began, "You have startled us. Please, be good enough to explain yourself."

Stepping into the light from the open doors, Hughes slid Cade a sly smile as he said, "It's simple, Miss Allen. You said I should have proof, so *voilà!* Here I am to gather my proof! That's all. Your conversation has cleared up quite a few puzzling points, I might add."

"You would not print anything so scandalous!" Laurie said with a snap, but Hughes merely laughed.

"Oh, wouldn't I? I wondered if a woman who looked as sweet and pure as you could actually do all the things some people said. I see that you not only can— you have."

Cade spoke at last, his voice light, but his eyes were narrowed and dangerous.

"I suggest, Mister Hughes, that you think about what you plan on doing. Not only would it cause the lady great harm, but it might endanger you, also."

Tilting his head to one side, Hughes asked, "Endanger me, sir? What do you mean?"

"I mean that if I don't like what you print in the *Picayune* or whatever publication will accept such scurrilous ramblings, I may call you out."

Even Hughes had heard of Cade's reputation with a sword and a pistol, and he paled.

"It . . . it's against the law to duel!"

Cade laughed outright, and Hughes belatedly recalled the reason he'd been arrested five years before. Taking a step closer to Hughes, Cade said softly, "Then I will arrange to have a 'legal' duel, Mister Hughes."

Swallowing hard, Warren Hughes said weakly, "Suppose I think about publishing this story a bit more. Perhaps I can find another article."

"Perhaps you can. And if not . . ." Cade shrugged. "Then I will be happy to meet you at the Oaks."

When Hughes had scurried away, giving Laurie a last, blistering glance, Cade turned to her. "He won't forgive either one of us, you know. And now he's figured out that Nicolas Alvarez and Cade Caldwell are the same person."

She nodded mutely, her face pale. Complete sobriety returned in a rush, and she shuddered. "I know."

They stood there silently for a long moment, then

Cade said in a curiously gentle tone, "Go back to your aunt, *chére*. I'll try to think of a way to smooth this over."

But Laurie knew there wasn't a way. Warren Hughes would not rest until he had told what he'd learned, and it did not have to be in the newspaper. The truth would come out.

She was ruined, utterly ruined, she thought miserably, and what would she say when she rejoined her aunt? She did not have the heart to tell poor Annette yet. Let it come in the morning, after she had had a night to rest.

Chapter Twenty-four

"But what can we do, Cade?" she whispered.

"We? Nothing." His voice was slightly impatient. "I told you, go back to your aunt and I'll do what I can."

"Hughes will tell everyone."

"I know, Laurie. Look—you should have thought about it all a long time ago, before you started that idiotic game. Now it's too late. People don't forget that easily." His eyes grew cold and mocking. "I'll never be able to forget it—why should they? And now is not the time nor the place for regrets. It's a waste of time, and that's something in short supply for me."

Her face paled with shock, and she saw in his eyes that he had not forgiven her—and might never forgive her. Her chin lifted, and her voice was cold. "Excuse me for being bold enough to inconvenience you with my petty problems. Somehow I thought you were just as involved in this as I am."

Cade shrugged indifferently. "My reputation was ruined a long time ago, princess. It's yours that's on the line now. I'll convince Hughes it wouldn't be too healthy to print what he overheard, but you'd better be ready to answer some questions from the fair citizens of New Orleans."

Hot tears stung her eyes, and they glittered with pain. "You don't really care about me, do you?"

"That's not the point. And you don't need to hear

the answer."

"I see. Well, I am quite certain that there are men who care enough about me to want to protect me instead of tell me it's all my fault I'm in this predicament." Her voice grew low and spiteful, and all the pain she was feeling was in the words she threw at him. "I have had plenty of offers you know—Jacques, Gilbert, Paul, Jean—well, as you must be able to see, I certainly don't need *you!*"

"Maybe not. But then again—I'm not sure I'd want a woman who goes from man to man so easily . . . ."

His voice was tight and bitter, and when she would have thrown an angry reply at him, he grabbed her and jerked her close to him, molding her body against his hard frame with a rough embrace. "It's not enough that you have to haunt me when I'm with you, is it?" he rasped against her ear, his breath warm and smelling of brandy. "You haunt me even when you're with someone else, damn you!"

Before she could reply his mouth seared across her half-open lips, and his arms were tight around her. There was no reprieve, and Laurie wasn't sure she wanted one. It felt right to be held by him, right for him to be cursing her in one breath and kissing her in the next. Wasn't that the way she felt about him, too? Didn't she love him and hate him and want him? And God help her—didn't she want to be with him forever?

But then he was pushing her away from him, one hand still on her arm to steady her when she would have swayed back into his arms, and his tone was harsh.

"Get back in there to your aunt, Laurie! Damn your gold cat-eyes to hell, stay away from me before you ruin everything!"

Reeling with shock, she was only barely aware of his voice in her ear as he half-walked, half-pulled her back to her aunt's side, vaguely aware of his terse nod toward Jacques before he was gone again, leaving her standing beside her shocked aunt and the count.

"Oh dear," Tante Annette was saying, vigorously waving her fan back and forth, "oh dear! We need to leave—people are staring so at us . . . ah, *Bon Dieu!*"

Jacques Poirier offered to escort Laurie home, and Annette was so distressed by the buzz of conjecture and curious glances Cade's appearance had sparked that she said she wanted to go, too.

"Shocking, simply shocking," she kept muttering to herself, and Laurie silently agreed.

If Cade cared for her at all, he would never have left her standing there with her aunt and Jacques, walking away without looking back at her. He'd gone straight to Cecelia de Marchand, who'd looked at him with something like triumph in her eyes, and Laurie had hated her at that moment. She'd hated Cade, too, but her hate for him had been mixed with pain and embarrassment. She hoped he'd heard her say, "Well, that finally seems to be the last of that man!" in a cutting voice, hoped it made him think she didn't care if she never saw him again.

Fanning herself rapidly with her painted Chinese fan, Tante Annette asked plaintively, "Just *where* are Pierre and Jean-Claude when I need them?"

Laurie turned abruptly to Pierre and accepted his offer of an escort home, while Tante Annette wavered back and forth before finally deciding that she would go, too.

There didn't seem to be much to say about the incident on the carriage ride home, and fortunately, Jacques seemed more concerned with getting her alone than he did anything else.

"Don't you care what people were saying?" Laurie asked irritably as they sat in the DuBois parlor. She sat stiffly beside him on the parlor settee as he drank the brandy Annette had insisted he have. Poor Annette had gone up to her room immediately, pleading a headache, but had insisted that Jacques come in for a brandy, for after all, he had been kind enough to escort them home in his own carriage after neither Pierre nor Jean-Claude could be quickly found.

Jacques looked at Laurie curiously. "Am I supposed to care about it?"

"Yes! No—oh, I don't know. All I know is, every time I have the misfortune to see that man, there's trouble!"

She could feel Jacques looking at her, his blue gaze steady and faintly inquisitive, and flushing, Laurie looked up and sighed when he asked, "Is there something between you and Monsieur Caldwell that I should know?"

Rising with a quick, impatient motion, Laurie paced the floor, finally pausing in front of the cheery fire in the parlor grate and turning back to look at him with a soft rustle of her silk skirts.

"Yes," she said with brutal honesty. "Gossip has it that he and I . . . that we traveled unchaperoned together from Texas. And he is wed to Cecelia de Marchand, the governor's niece."

"And is it true?"

"Yes," she said again. Her chin lifted, and the glow from the fire flickered over her face as she gazed at Jacques with a faint challenge in her eyes.

He smiled. "I see. Then perhaps I am—in the way."

"No, it's not like that. But you must know the truth, or at least, what is being said."

"Why?"

"Excuse me?"

"Why must I know the truth?" Jacques set his glass on a table and rose to walk to her. "Is it important that I know 'this person said this' and 'that person said that'? I think not. I think what is important is what you have said to me. And if you want me to go away—I will go. But if you want me to stay—I will stay."

"Don't you care about the gossip? About the truth?"

He shrugged. "About the truth, yes. But what is

more important to me is how you feel. If you are in love with this man. . . ."

"No!" Laurie burst out, her eyes darkening. "I am not in love with him."

Jacques gazed at her shrewdly. "I think you are not being honest with me or yourself," he said slowly.

"I can't help what you think!" Laurie snapped, then regretted her hasty words. "Oh, do forgive me, Jacques, but I am so upset! This evening has been dreadful, and I have a headache. . . ."

He took her hands in his and gently kissed her forehead as if she was a small child. "You are tired, and any woman would be upset after such a night. May I call on you tomorrow?"

She nodded, suddenly unutterably weary and longing for her bed and oblivion. "Yes," she murmured, "tomorrow will be much better."

Jacques turned her hands over and pressed a kiss on the heel of her palm. *"Bonne nuit,"* he said, releasing her hands with a regretful sigh.

After he'd gone and she was upstairs allowing a maid to brush out her hair and help her into bed, Laurie had the wrenching thought that Cade was probably with his wife. Why wouldn't he be? She'd seen the possessive looks Cecelia had given him, the way she had walked boldly up to him. It did not matter to Cecelia if New Orleans gossiped, but she had always been that way. She'd never cared what the good sisters said at the convent school, nor what the other girls thought of her. Cecelia had always considered herself above the others, above censure. And maybe she was, Laurie thought wearily. She certainly seemed to have emerged unscathed from her groom's abandonment five years before.

Laurie sighed heavily, then gave a soft cry as the maid gave a sharp tug on her hair with the brush. It had caught on a tangle, bringing tears to her eyes. The maid dropped the brush, jerking her head up to look at Laurie's reflection in the dresser mirror.

"Oh, I'm sorry, mamselle!"

"That's all right, Dorothée," she told the maid with a forced smile. "I'm tired, too, and want to retire now."

"*Oui*, mamselle," the maid said, and quietly left.

It was late. The small ornate clock on the fireplace mantel of her room struck the hour, chiming twelve times. Laurie counted them, forcing her body to relax, wishing she had not seen Cade again. How could she ever forget him if she kept seeing him? And did she really want to?

He had looked at her with a wary watchfulness this evening; she had seen it in his narrowed gaze, the way he'd stared at her through half-lowered lashes. What had he seen in her eyes? Had she betrayed herself?

All the memories of the past months flooded back and she buried her face in her cupped palms; she didn't know, didn't know if she loved him or hated him or just wanted to feel him inside her. Her lips twisted at the last thought. It was ridiculous that she — Laurette Allen — should be weak enough to ache for a man like Cade Caldwell, but God help her, she did.

But how cruel and harsh he'd been earlier! He had bluntly admitted that he would never forgive her for what he considered her betrayal of him — *her* betrayal, as if he had no part in what had happened in Higuera! Dear God, what could she do now? She had hurt so much over everything, had hoped for so much, and now it all seemed to be crashing down around her ears. Perhaps she should have told him that she loved him, but her pride — her stiff-necked foolish pride — would not allow her to tell a married man that she was in love with him.

She meant nothing to him, nothing but a warm, willing body, and he'd proven that to her tonight by his rejection of her in front of half of New Orleans. Her cheeks still flamed with the insult and humiliation.

At least, she consoled herself, he had never made false promises, never pretended to love her. And at least she had never told him she loved him, she told herself in the next moment. Yes. Perhaps her pride had saved her from that last humiliation, after all.

And it had been Cade who had dragged her with him, Cade who had held her prisoner, refusing to let her leave him. And it had been Cade who had jerked her into his arms that night and kissed her, angrily, passionately.

Pacing from the bed to the window, Laurie looked out on the street. Moonlight silvered the world, and wrought-iron railings cast patterned shadows across the slanted threads of light. Leaning against the wooden windowsill, she remembered another night when the moon had been full and bright, spilling over flat, arid land. Cade had been angry with her, and she had been angry, too, but the passion between them had flared hot and high. Was that all there was between them — passion? Was there any love at all?

Miserable, Laurie sank to the edge of a chair, staring bleakly out the window. Cade was probably still with Cecelia. It had certainly looked as if he meant to linger with her, and really — wasn't that where he belonged?

They were two of a kind in a way, both hard people who didn't mind stepping on others to get what they wanted. She had thought for a time that maybe Cade was different, that he cared about people, but she must have been wrong. She had thought that he cared about her. . . .

Abruptly rising from the small boudoir chair, she paced the carpeted floor in front of her window. Even if Warren Hughes had not begun the gossip again, it would never have died out completely. Everytime she and Cade accidentally met at a social function, it would begin all over again. It seemed that there was only one solution to the situation, but for some reason she hesitated.

Putting so many miles between them — was it really what she wanted? She hated and loved him with an intensity that was frightening, yet being so far away from him would give her time to think, time to discover what she really wanted from life. Would she be content being Cade's mistress instead of his wife? She didn't think so, and anyway, he already had a wife. So what was she to do?

Sadly, Laurie reached the inevitable conclusion.

She would leave New Orleans, leave the United States. She would go back to France, but first she would go back to California, back to where it had all begun. She had to exorcise her memories, make peace with her father and Carlota, and then she would leave forever. There was nothing here for her anymore, nothing but heartache and the emptiness of her soul.

It was that decision which helped her in her confrontation with Cecelia de Marchand the next day.

"Mamselle," Dorothée came hesitantly into her room and said, "there is a woman downstairs who — she will not tell me her name — insists upon seeing you at once."

"At once?" Faintly surprised by the maid's obvious distress, Laurie went downstairs. When she entered the parlor, she was shocked, then angry to find Cecelia de Marchand waiting imperiously by the fireplace.

Pausing in the doorway, Laurie wished briefly that she had seen to her *toilette* before coming downstairs, because Cecelia looked as if she had just stepped out of the pages of *Godey's Ladies' Book of Fashions*. Her ermine-trimmed cape swung gracefully from her shoulders, and the rich crimson color of her gown perfectly set off Cecelia's dark coloring and flashing dark eyes. Laurie couldn't help the twinge of dismay at seeing how beautiful Cecelia had grown through the years.

Uncertain how to address her — did she call her Madame Caldwell or Mademoiselle de Marchand? —

Laurie did neither.

"How may I help you?" she asked, skirting the haughty Cecelia by a wide margin as she stepped to the settee in front of the fireplace. Her chin was unconsciously lifted in a gesture of challenge, and her amber eyes flashed gold sparks that made Cecelia look at her warily.

"Not as you may be thinking," Cecelia said shortly. "I have come to offer you a way to look less foolish." Her dark eyes darted toward the servant hovering near the door with a tray of refreshments. "Dismiss your servant at once. I have no desire for this to be all over the servant's quarters within the next quarter hour."

In spite of Cecelia's haughty tone, Laurie felt the same way. "Gaspard," she told the older servant gently, "I will ring if I need you."

"Oui, mademoiselle," he muttered. "I shall be only a short walk away." His old eyes darted to the imperious figure glaring at him, and he gave a shrug as he backed from the room. It was obvious he had no liking for Cecelia, and Laurie smiled faintly. Cecelia must be formidable indeed, if even Tante Annette's faithful servants felt the need to protect her!

When the door had closed behind him and they were quite alone, Laurie turned to look back at Cecelia. She saw her appraising glance, but refused to give in to the urge to smooth her hair or skirts. She walked to the window, then turned to look back at Cecelia.

"Well?" she began in the same haughty tone Cecelia had used a few moments before, "Why have you come to visit me? And what causes you to think I appear foolish?"

"Pah!" Cecelia said with a shrug. "Everyone in New Orleans must think so, especially after last night. It is well known that you arrived in New Orleans on the arm of my husband, and just as well known that he enjoyed your favors in California." Her tone whipped across Laurie cruelly. "I have spoken with a Monsieur

Hughes, who confided to me that you were lovers. Though Monsieur Hughes is too much of a gentleman to print such news in his publication, I think it will be all over New Orleans by this evening." Her eyes glittered with malice. *"N'est-ce pas?"*

"I understand that you are as vicious as you are dull-witted," Laurie replied with a careless shrug that masked her anger and pain. "What I do not understand is why you are here."

"Fool! I have come to offer you a graceful way out of this!" Cecelia sauntered to the settee and sat down in a rustle of satin skirts, her smile wide and predatory. "I am quite determined that my husband will remain here with me, and am concerned that he might feel some compunction to protect your name, as he did last night. He feels burdened with the responsibility for what happened, you see."

"And well he should, though I don't think you really see the truth at all!" Laurie shot back. A tiny smile curled her lips as she saw Cecelia's eyes narrow. "You keep referring to Cade Caldwell as your husband, but in truth, I seem to recall that he left you on your wedding night, and that he has not been back to New Orleans in five years. It would seem to me that *you* are the one trying to save face."

Jerking upright, Cecelia spat, "You were always stupid! I should never have come here . . ."

"You're quite right about that," Laurie said coolly. "I intend to do what I want to do, without any encouragement from you. As you obviously came here to suggest that I leave New Orleans . . ."

"For the sake of your reputation!"

". . . so that you won't have to wonder where your *husband* is spending his nights—" Laurie saw that her shot had struck home, and was suddenly, fiercely, glad to discover that at least Cade was not spending his nights with Cecelia de Marchand—"I will ease your mind. I am leaving very soon and do not intend to return. But that does not mean that I am doing it because of you. I simply have no desire to be associated by gossip with Cade Caldwell, as will surely happen if I remain. You are welcome to him."

But for Cecelia, that statement did not have the desired affect. She gazed at Laurie with doubt in her eyes, and it was obvious she now wondered if Cade had been spending his nights with Laurie, and if not — with whom?

Laurie held to that small comfort as Cecelia swept from the DuBois home and into her waiting carriage, but it was a small enough comfort.

Cecelia de Marchand was just as upset as Laurie, and just as uncertain of her future. Had Cade truly spent any of his nights with her old schoolmate? Cecelia's hands curled into fists in her lap, and she snarled an order at her coachman to take her home at once or she would lay the whip across his back.

As the carriage lurched forward, Cecelia sat back against the plush velvet cushions and thought of her last, frustrating conversation with Cade. He'd been so cold and distant with her, especially when she had raged at him for being lovers with Laurette Allen. Damn him! And damn her, too!

How dare that blond vixen stare back at her so coolly, and she had looked beautiful even with her hair uncombed, and in a plain gown. It had been most disconcerting, and any advantage she had hoped to gain by arriving unannounced and unexpected had been shattered by Laurie's appearance. She had remembered Laurette Allen as a gawky, spirited child, but had been confronted with a cool, poised woman.

Furious, Cecelia clenched her teeth together, then gave a sharp order to the coachman to take her to 84 Rue Royale.

"And quickly!"

Cade was faintly amused by CeCe's furious tirade against him and against Laurie.

"But you knew all that, CeCe," he drawled, gazing at her with an impudent grin. "Why did you ever think going to see her would gain you anything?"

Storming around the room, CeCe stopped to glare at him. "I thought she was smarter, that she would see the sense in leaving New Orleans!"

The amusement in his face quickly disappeared, and Cade uncoiled from his chair and stood up, stepping to CeCe and grabbing her by the shoulders.

"Now, see here," he growled dangerously, "she doesn't need to go anywhere! New Orleans is as much her home as it is yours, and if anyone needs to disappear for a while, it's you."

"How can you say . . ."

"I can say the truth, and you need to hear it." His face was grim, his mouth taut with anger. "I don't want any more of your tricks, CeCe. You leave Laurie Allen alone, and you better do what you can to stop the gossip, because whether you realize it or not, it makes you look just as bad."

Cecelia glared at him. "*I* am not the one who traveled with you unchaperoned! *I* am not the one who caused a great scandal out in California, and . . ."

"And you don't know the truth of the matter, so you don't need to feel too smug." Cade released her shoulders, and his eyes were bleak. "For your information, CeCe, all that happened was my fault, not hers, and she had no choice in the matter. I goaded her into doing what she did, and I should have known it then, but I didn't. And as for traveling unchaperoned with me—I kidnapped her. Does that make you feel better?"

"No. Still, she was compromised, and the facts are the same as before." Cecelia gave a light shrug. "Whether it was her choice or not, she was unchaperoned and in the company of a married man. She will not live it down. It is not like it was a romantic elopement, and after all, you are *my* husband, not hers!"

"Odd you should mention that, CeCe. I've been doing a lot of thinking on that score. We need to talk about our annulment."

Cecelia's eyes widened. "I would never agree to a divorce or an annulment!"

Cade's mouth twisted, and he reached out to lift one of her dark curls in his palm. "You will not have much of a choice when I mention Monsieur Remy, or Counte de Saligny, or any of the other men you have entertained. Does your uncle know of your romantic activities? I don't think so. Shall I tell him, or . . ."

"All right!" she spat at him, her eyes blazing. "We will talk more of this later." She started to move past him and he grabbed her, his fingers coiling around her arm and swinging her back to face him.

"No, we'll talk more of this now. And we'll also talk about your emphatic denials that Laurie Allen was anything more than an innocent woman under my protection." His voice softened. "In fact, CeCe, you'll swear to everyone who'll listen that your old school chum fought off my improper advances quite vigorously. Do you understand?"

"No! I do not understand why you are doing this!"

"Neither do I, except that I have to leave New Orleans and I don't need anything coming back to haunt me." His voice grew rough again. "Now listen to what I'm saying. . . ."

"But I don't understand why you must go back to that barbaric place, *chère*," Annette DuBois said unhappily. They were standing on the crowded docks, and the steamer *Dearing* was taking on passengers.

"I know," Laurie said softly, "but I must. And Papa's letter said that no blame has been placed on me for Cade's escape, so I don't feel that I can't go. And it's not as if I'll never see you again."

Staring at her niece through tear-drenched eyes, Tante Annette slowly shook her head. "I don't know why, but I feel as if you will stay there."

"In California?" Laurie smiled. "No, only for a little while. Then I am going back to France. I have already written to *Cousine* Mignon, and told her I will join her in Calais."

"Paris is better," Annette muttered, then hugged Laurie tightly. "Ah, what does it matter, if you will only be content? And since that dreadful Monsieur Hughes has said all those terrible things about you, and everyone now knows that Cade Caldwell and Nicolas Alvarez is the same man, is the bandit from California — New Orleans is not the place for you."

"At least I have the satisfaction of knowing that the cowardly Mister Hughes fled rather than fight a duel with Cade," Laurie said grimly, and Annette laughed.

"Qui! And Pierre called him out, too! And Jacques Poirier, and even some *bourgeois* by the name of John Goff tried to get him to fight because of the comments about his sister. But no, the not-so-brave monsieur ran away, and no one knows where!"

Annette sounded fiercely glad, and Laurie hugged her back. "They're blowing the whistle again, and I have to go now," she said, fighting the tears that welled in her eyes.

"Will you write to me?" Annette asked around the lace handkerchief she pressed to her nose. She lifted a hand in farewell as Laurie strode up the gangplank to the waiting steamer, and remained there on the dock until the vessel had faded from sight in the gray-blue waters of the Gulf.

Her heart was heavy, and she hoped that her niece would find the peace she deserved. Of course, Laurette could not remain in New Orleans with all the gossip. It was impossible even with Cecelia de Marchand vowing that her old school friend was innocent. What a turn-around that was! But it was said, of course, that where there was smoke there was fire, and there had been enough smoke to obscure all of Louisiana lately. Annette's lips thinned into a grim line as she stepped up into her waiting carriage and gave the order to go home. How dare that brazen Cecelia try to make amends for all the things she'd said earlier. It had only made it worse, much worse.

And Cade Caldwell, for all his pretensions to civility, was just as bad. Why, if it were not for him, Laurie would not be so sad, and would not be on her way back to her papa in that godforsaken foreign country called California. For all she had seen of Californios, they were a savage, uncivilized lot, and poor Laurette would be better off not going back there but going on to France.

"And I shall tell Pierre again that he should have stopped her," Annette said aloud, and gave an impatient shake of her head when the coachman leaned back to ask if she had said something. "Not to you. Drive on!"

"I think, Maman," Pierre said when confronted by his mother, "that I could have done nothing to stop her. Laurie would not have been happy."

"You could have made her happy! You could have introduced her to someone, or encouraged her to allow Jacques Poirier to pay more attention to her, or . . ."

"No," Pierre said gently. "She did not want any of that. Her heart belongs to another. There is no substitute when that is true."

Distressed, Annette stared at her son. "Still? I had thought she would have realized that he is only a renegade! I thought . . ."

"You thought wrongly, Maman. Laurie did not admit it, but I know that she cares for him. And it would have been useless to coax her to love another."

"She is foolish," Annette said with a long sigh, and Pierre smiled sadly.

369

"She is in love."

If Laurie had heard their conversation, she would have agreed. But she would have added that it did not matter. It was a matter of conscience now, not love, that sent her back to California and her father.

Leaving New Orleans again had been hard, much harder than she'd thought it would be. She felt as if she was leaving a part of her behind, and in a way, she was. She had grown up in New Orleans, and it was like abandoning her childhood to leave again. But she was no longer a willful child, but a woman, and there were things a woman had to do that children never faced.

A slight smile curved her lips as Laurie thought of how she had been so insistent about returning to New Orleans when Cade had been dragging her over half of Texas. She had regarded it as a healing place where all wrongs could be made right, and all hurts soothed away, as if she was a child again. Until Cade, annoyed and impatient, had told her that she could never recapture the past, she had believed that she could. He'd been right. But she'd had to find it out for herself.

And, sadly, in the process, she had discovered how painful it was to hurt someone she cared about.

Jacques Poirier had been terribly upset with her when he'd found out she was leaving. He had come to the house the morning of her departure and insisted upon seeing her, his face dark and angry.

Laurie had felt ashamed of herself for allowing him to court her when she loved someone else, but sorry for herself, too, when he told her she was foolish and selfish.

"I cannot believe that you truly mean to leave because of that man!" he'd burst out, raking a hand through his fair hair in agitation so that it stood up on end and gave him a distraught appearance.

"I'm sorry, Jacques, but . . ."

"I thought perhaps you were beginning to care for

370

me! I hoped that after you realized who truly loves you, you would . . . would come to your senses." He had gazed at her in frustration, and accused hotly, "You're still seeing him, and can think of no other!"

Laurie had winced at the pain she saw in his eyes, but replied honestly, "No, Jacques. I have not seen or heard from Cade since the night of the ball." She had not added that she'd prayed she might even when Jacques sarcastically voiced his opinion of Cade Caldwell.

When she'd burst into tears he had grabbed her hands and kissed them fervently, begging her not to do anything foolish until he was able to join her in California, and to end the unpleasant confrontation, Laurie had finally agreed to wait.

Once Jacques had left her, she had felt emotionally torn, drained of the desire for anything in her life but peace. Yet she knew she had to go back.

She held to that purpose during the rough steamer ride across the Gulf, when winter winds buffeted the craft and the water was gray and stormy. And she held to it when she crossed the Isthmus of Panama, that mosquito-infested, disease-riddled land of humidity that needed to be traversed before she could board another vessel. Finally, she was aboard a steamer bound for Higuera, facing two more weeks of sea travel.

And when the steamer cruised up the California coast and she saw the familiar red-tiled roofs and swaying palms, she took a deep breath to steady her resolve. She was back where it had all begun nine months before, and she drew her lace mantilla close around her face as she prepared to disembark.

Chapter Twenty-five

Southern California was, as last, warm and balmy. Laurie lay on the patio in the bright sunshine, not caring if it beat down on her uncovered face in spite of Carlota's worrying that it would make her skin brown and dry. Why should she care? It had been so long since she had felt its warmth. Her voyage had been cold and rainy, and rainshowers had swept up and down the coast for the past week since her arrival. The sun felt good, and anyway, she had to re-gather her courage and strength.

Her days were no longer governed by a whirlwind of social events. She had uninterrupted hours of leisure. Carlota always seemed to be there when she needed feminine companionship, and her father—well, Philip Allen was still smarting from Laurie's angry departure months before, but he was trying to understand.

For the first time in a long time, Laurie had the leisure to read some of the books in her father's vast library. The year before, she had been too unhappy, too unsettled to read; but now she found it stimulating.

It wasn't until she found the pressed flower in a book left on her night table that Laurie gave in to the tears that were long overdue. It was the flower that Cade had given her that night, the first night they had made love, and she had pressed it between the pages of a book and forgotten about it. Now it lay stiff, a fragile reminder of all that had been between them, a reminder of her broken dreams and hopes as dry as the blossom itself.

When her eyes were dry and she could face her family, she went down into the *sala* to visit with Carlota. Often they had endless discussions of world events, or played lively games of chess that ended in a stalemate.

The only subjects that were never discussed were Cade Caldwell and El Vengador.

"What do you think of California becoming a part of the United States?" Carlota asked her one evening over their glasses of port. She peered at Laurie in the candlelight, her face serene. "I understand that there is talk of it, much as there is talk of the Lone Star Republic becoming a state."

Laurie almost winced. Texas. It reminded her of Cade, and how he loved that vast, arid land full of nothing but dust and death. She recalled the Comanches, and how scared she had been, and how she had fought back, surprising Cade and herself with her ferocity. Until then, she had not known she had the capacity for it.

"A state?" she said when the silence stretched too long and Carlota stared at her curiously. "Well, I think it will eventually happen, of course."

"Why?"

Shrugging, Laurie observed, "Because more and more Americans are coming to California, and it cannot continue to remain loyal to Mexico for long. I have heard that the Russians who owned large amounts of land near Monterey, have sold it to a Swiss-born man by the name of Sutter. This Sutter runs his lands as if they were a European nation. And when I was in New Orleans, I heard rumors that people intend to travel by wagon to California, many people who intend to settle here." She shook her head slowly. "It is only a matter of time before California and Mexico go to war."

Worried, Carlota put down her glass of port and stared anxiously at Laurie. "Do you really think so? Phillip says the same thing."

"Papa should know. Doesn't he correspond with Señor Mariano Vallejo near Sacramento?"

Carlota nodded, her brow still furrowed. "Si, and Vallejo is uncle to the governor, Juan Bautista Alvarado, who is also a distant cousin of mine, but I understand that Señor Vallejo wishes for Mexico City to send more troops into California, that he is worried about the lack of troops to protect us from the Indians who raid our fields and cattle."

"There has been a lot of talk about war, Carlota. But there is always talk of war if you listen to men." She gave her stepmother an encouraging smile. "Try not to worry. I am sure that everything will be fine."

Laurie understood Carlota's concern. The Alvarado family had been in California for generations, as had the Alvarez family. Their ties with Mexico were long and firm. A war could cost them dearly, if they chose the wrong side.

A month passed, and Laurie listened to Serita at night telling her about the latest atrocity by the alcalde. Don Luis had not learned anything from his humiliation by El Vengador, it seemed, Laurie thought wryly. If anything, he was bolder than ever, perhaps because he considered the threat to his esteem far removed. Word had filtered back from Mexico about Cade's escape, of course, but as that had been months before and there had been no sign of the masked night raider who had terrorized the alcalde's *soldados*, Don Luis had dismissed any threat.

"There has been no improvement, Serita?" Laurie asked the maid, and she shook her head.

"No, Doña Laurie. And Juan—he is my *novio*, you remember—labors under the taxes he must pay." She looked sad. "We will never be able to marry, I fear."

"If the taxes were not so high, or if the alcalde were more patient, perhaps then you could wed?" Laurie asked, and the girl nodded.

"But that will never happen."

"Perhaps one day it will, Serita.

After replacing the empty teacup Laurie had used on a tray, Serita slid her a wan smile. "I don't think so, but it is nice to dream about it. No one seems to think the alcalde will ever be out of office."

"And if he was? Would life be that much better?"

Serita stared at her, the tray trembling in her hands. "It would be as it was before Don Luis was the alcalde, I believe. There would be laughter again, and small children would not fear to run about the streets, and there would be enough food, and the occasional bottle of wine at the end of a workday. Oh, it was not an easy life before he came, but at least there was enough to eat, enough to buy sandals and treats for the children—but I should not say all of this."

"Why not?" Laurie impulsively reached out to put a hand on her shoulder. "One day, Serita, life will be as it was before. One day Mexico City will discover how evil and greedy Don Luis is, and then things will get better."

"Perhaps." Serita did not sound convinced, but she tried to smile back at Laurie. "I only hope that there are some of us left to see that day, Doña Laurie."

After she'd gone, softly shutting the door behind her, Laurie closed the shutters over her windows and drew the drapes over the patio doors. In just a few moments she was clad in snug-fitting pants and a loose blouse. She looked in the mirror with a smile of satisfaction. What would Phillip Allen say if he saw her in the garb of El Vengador? He would probably rage at her, threaten to lock her in her room again, and destroy the tenuous peace that had been made between them.

But it was something she had to do. She only felt alive when she took her epée out of hiding, when she feinted, lunged, and parried with imaginary enemies in the privacy of her room at night. It had become a ritual every evening to practice with her epée — and Phillip would definitely stop her if he knew about it.

Springing from the floor to the seat of a broad chair, Laurie pretended that a fat candle in its holder was the alcalde. The blade swished viciously and swiftly, and the tip of the candle toppled from the wall sconce to the floor. Swirling, she leaped lightly down from the chair, landing on her bare feet with all the agility of a cat.

Her bed became the top of a wall around the *presidio,* the chair her saddled horse, and all the candles were the *soldados* who guarded the alcalde. If Serita ever wondered why there were never any candles in her mistress's room in the morning, she never mentioned it. Nor did she mention the congealed wax she found scattered on rugs and even the walls. It was a well-kept secret, and Laurie pursued her "enemies" with a vengeance at nights, until she was panting from the efforts and damp with perspiration.

Since coming back to Higuera, she had toyed with an idea that was as dangerous as it was foolish, but it would not be lightly dismissed. If she was to show the alcalde that it was truly she who had been El Vengador instead of Cade, then her conscience would be satisfied. All charges against Cade would he dismissed, and he could come back to Higuera when and if he ever wished to do so.

It sounded so simple in theory, until she realized the realities of it. The consequences to herself would be dire and dreadful, she knew, for the alcalde would not take it lightly that his nose had been tweaked by a woman. He would take it as a direct insult, but she would have accomplished her purpose.

Dared she do it? And why did she even consider it? Was it for love or vengeance that she contemplated such a foolhardy act? Cade had called it an idiot game.

The slender blade of the epée cut through the empty air with a hiss, and the lit candle in its tall holder did not move until she reached out with the tip of her sword to give it a gentle nudge. Then the severed tip fell to the floor, scattering hot wax in its wake. She could still do it, if she chose; she still had the skill to outduel any of the alcalde's clumsy *soldados!*

Even the boastful José Garcia.

She thought longingly of that when she saw him the next day. She was leaving the hacienda when she chanced upon Garcia. The captain was riding on the main road with a group of soldiers, and when he saw the Allen diligencia he rode closer. She tried not to look at him, but the captain put out a hand to stop the driver.

"So! It is you, señorita," he said, peering into the vehicle to confront Laurie. He smiled when she looked up at him. "I had heard rumors that you were back in Higuera, but did not dare to hope they might be true."

"And now that you know they are?" Laurie asked coldly. "Do you intend to arrest me?"

"Arrest you, señorita? For what?" Garcia put a hand over his heart, and his lips twitched under his mustache. "I am grieved that you would think so badly of me."

"Not as grieved as you were when I last saw you," she retorted, her face grim as she stared at the captain's lean face. A brisk breeze blew in from the bay so that she pulled her rebozo closer around her shoulders. "If you are through speaking with me, Capitán,

I will go home now."

"For the moment. But I intend to call on you later," he said, his gaze raking her. "We have unfinished business to discuss."

"I don't. And I am certain your business will not interest me in the least."

"Ah, but I am certain it will!" He bowed from the waist and signaled to the driver to move on, laughing as Laurie looked away angrily.

His laughter echoed in her ears almost all the way to the village, and she silently cursed his effrontery. She knew what he meant. Because she had been Cade's mistress, he thought he could take his place. Fuming, she knotted her hands together and wished she had an epée in them. Then Garcia would not be so bold! She itched to see his sardonic face blanch with fear, and to have him at her mercy.

If anything, Garcia was even more brutal than the alcalde, more harsh than the commandant. At least Trujillo possessed some objectivity with his duty; not so Garcia. The captain was harder on the peons than anyone, and they scurried out of his way when he rode through the mercado, or through the streets.

In spite of the warm sun, Laurie shivered. She had heard from Serita that Garcia could be ingenious when it came to extracting information from possible informants. Knowing that, she wondered how Cade had withstood Garcia's attempts to force a confession from him. He'd never told her the details, only — sarcastically — that it wasn't pleasant.

And she had seen the marks of the whip on his back, and felt a twinge of guilt every time. Could she make it up to him? Laurie wondered with a twinge of apprehension if Cade would ever know or care if she made such a sacrifice for him. And if he ever intended to return to California. . . .

Cade Caldwell, at that moment, was wondering the

same thing. He'd completed his business for Sam Houston, and had delivered the information himself while Houston was attending the Congress being held at Austin. He wasn't in the best of moods, but Cade's temper improved slightly when he met with Houston in the crude log building that passed for the Republic's Hall of Congress.

Houston met him with a grin and a twinkle in his eye. "Caldwell! I see you made it back in one piece — your two women didn't take advantage of the wisdom of Solomon to cut you in half!"

Respect for his former commander made Cade force a weary grin, and his voice was dry.

"Don't be too certain. If I turn my head too fast, it may fall in my lap."

Houston's loud laughter boomed across the yard muddy from a recent rain. His beefy arm fell companionably over Cade's shoulders as they walked.

"It went well with Colonel Fisher?"

"Very well." Cade briefly described the facts he'd learned, including the number of troops Santa Anna was said to have. Houston nodded thoughtfully.

"Texas needs money and good men now more than ever. I hope you will stay with us," he said, and Cade shrugged.

"I'm needed at home, as I told you a few months ago, but when I have matters settled there I'll be back." There was a brief pause, then he asked, "Is there any possibility of getting funds from France?"

Rather ruefully, Houston said, "Not since the pig incident."

Cade laughed. "So the French have still not forgiven us for that?"

Houston began to laugh, too, his big shoulders shaking. "Innkeeper Bullock was a mite put out when Monsoor de Saligny's servant killed his pig just for eatin' a little French corn! I do think that Frenchman

379

was more upset about being put out of a comfortable hotel than he was about the innkeeper thrashing his servant for killing the pig."

"The fate of Texas rests on the head of a dead pig," Cade said, grinning as he shook of his head.

"Just her finances, son, just her finances." Houston was quiet for a moment as they strode down Congress Street. "And your immediate plans? Are you headed for California?"

"As soon as I leave Austin. There are rumblings of war out there too, General. My grandfather will need me."

Clapping a hand on Cade's back, Houston nodded. "I understand, Caldwell. And I don't blame you a bit." He grinned. "That purty blonde filly waitin' out there for you, too?"

Cade shook his head. "No. I left her in New Orleans. The last I heard she was with a French count."

"Not de Saligny, I'll bet."

"No, not de Saligny." Cade's voice was bitter, and Houston looked at him closely.

"You sure that's where you wanted to leave her, Caldwell?"

"That's where she belongs."

Houston didn't say anything for a moment, just gave a noncommittal grunt. Then he commented in a deceptively casual voice, "I thought she fancied you, myself."

"I don't think she knows who she fancies." Cade tugged at the brim of his hat, shading his eyes, then changed the subject. Houston didn't push it, and they embarked on a discussion of who would be the best man to lead troops should Texas engage in another war with Mexico. That conversation evolved into speculation about California and Mexico.

"So you think it certain that California will rebel?" Houston asked, and Cade nodded.

"Definitely. It's only a matter of time." Cade added grimly, "And I intend to be there to help with it."

"I wish you luck, Caldwell. Revolutions are a risky business."

Cade thought about Houston's prophecy in the following days, but he thought about a lot of things. Most of all, he thought about Laurie, and damned her and himself for it. Why should he feel guilty for having left her like he had? And why did she keep intruding into his thoughts even when he should be thinking about business?

It was especially bad at night, when he rolled up in a blanket and lay on the hard ground, looking up at the stars overhead. Then he would recall how they'd ridden across Texas together, and the feel of her next to him, her own special fragrance, and the way her sweet body curved into his when she was asleep. When she was awake she was like an angry cat, claws and hisses, but asleep she fit into his angles as if made to go there.

He couldn't forget her face the last time he'd seen her, the shocked, disbelieving expression when he had left her standing beside her aunt, and the almost childlike look of abandonment in her wide golden eyes. It had taken all his strength of will to keep walking, but he'd had to. And because he'd left without telling her the real reason, he couldn't get her out of his mind.

Cade wondered where she was and if she was happy, then had the cynical thought that like a cat, she would land on her feet. She always did. Lovely Laurie, with the clouds of golden hair and exotically tilted amber eyes—she was probably in the arms of her French viscount, the frowning Jacques de la Poirier. They could even be married by now, and really, he didn't blame her. Why should she have waited for a man already married? He'd never promised her anything, never even told her he loved her.

And now he was going back to California and would never see her again. Which was probably best. There were too many memories between them, too many unsolved problems. He could forget how she had betrayed him, and he'd even begun to believe her story of being drugged, but there were other nagging questions that hadn't been answered.

No, Cade decided as his ship sailed up the coastline of California toward Higuera, there was nothing else to do but forget her. If he could.

Laurie had the same problem, and she finally sought diversion in the company of Carlota's family. The Alvarado family was vast, and scattered all over California. Those that lived near Higuera visited frequently, and Carlota did her best to entertain them with picnics, long rides in the hills, and shopping excursions to the ships that put into port.

Instead of waiting for the ships to secure a berth in the bay, many of the Alvarado women would have servants row them out to the anchored vessels, and climb aboard to view the array of goods before others could go through them. It was a good way to get the best, and the Alvarado women were notorious for being shrewd bargainers.

Laughing, Laurie held up a bolt of shot-silk material that Carlota's sister Carmencita had brought her. It was a deep rose, flattering her coloring, and Carmencita had not been able to resist purchasing it for her.

"I'd never realized the advantages to a large family until now," Laurie observed, Carlota laughed with her.

"There are times the disadvantages seem as numerous as the advantages, but those are few. Most of the time my sisters and cousins are a comfort to me. I never knew that I would miss them until I was away from them for a while."

"That was when you went to New Orleans," Laurie said, and Carlota nodded.

"I was very happy when your papa took the position as ambassador, and for him to be sent here, to Higuera, was like a dream come true."

Laurie smiled at Carlota. Her stepmother's narrow, sallow face glowed with contentment, and she actually looked pretty. She'd put on some weight, so that her gowns fit better, and her dark eyes usually sparkled with a calm self assurance.

"Papa makes you very happy, doesn't he?" Laurie asked softly, and Carlota nodded.

"Very happy."

For the first time since Laurie's return, Carlota considered asking the question that had been in the back of her mind, and often, on the tip of her tongue. But when she looked at her stepdaughter, she held back, seeing the still haunted look that always shaded her eyes. It was the first time she'd ever seen that look in a person's eyes, and she thought that it was one she would never want to see again.

"I'm glad," Laurie was saying with a smile. "You two deserve some happiness together. I know it was very hard for Papa all those years after my mother died. He must have felt, somehow, that it was partly his fault, since she did not want to live."

Puzzled, Carlota asked, "Who told you that?"

"Isabeau. It was a long time ago—when I first found out that you and my father were to marry, I think. She told me how my mother lost her will to live after her oldest child died, and how devastated Papa was that she would not try harder even for him."

Carlota looked stricken. "Oh! *Madré de Dios!* I never knew that!"

"I'm certain it would not be something Papa would want to recall, and anyway, it was sixteen years before you."

Laurie reached out to touch her shoulder, and Carlota immediately covered her hand with her own. "And so you too have been left with feelings of guilt all these years."

Startled that Carlota should read her so well, Laurie could not speak for a moment, then said, "I suppose I have. But mostly I've felt a great determination not to allow life or disappointments make me give up."

"Sí, you are very determined, very stubborn, but it is also your strength. What would break another person only makes you stronger."

"And speaking of stronger," Laurie said with forced gaiety when the silence grew too long, "Shall we go down to see who is the stronger in the bull tossing?"

Carlota laughed. "My foolish nephew must always try his strength against that of the bulls! His máma swears he will be killed before he is twenty!"

Laurie tried not to think about the last time she had attended a festival, the time when she and Carlota had been accompanied by Cade, and they had watched the young men try their skills against one another in horsemanship. Today it was the tossing of bulls, tomorrow perhaps a contest between a bull and a bear.

An odd feeling of restlessness swept over her, and she urged Carlota to attend the bull tossing. They called for their horses to be saddled, and changed into more comfortable riding clothes, then rode down through the winding streets of the village to the beach.

After only a short time of watching the *vaqueros* ride past the bull on their horses and attempt to throw it by the horns, Laurie begged Carlota to excuse her.

"I think I'll ride back to the hacienda and lie down for a while," she added when it looked as if Carlota might go with her. "I have the beginning of a headache."

"I will go with you, if you wish," Carlota began, and

Laurie shook her head.

"No, but thank you. You stay with your sister, and tell me later how your nephew has ridden."

Wheeling her horse around, Laurie urged him up through the sandy dunes to the sea road just above. The sound of the breakers constantly rolling to shore almost drowned out the excited cries and hoarse shouting of the participants and spectators, and she could almost feel the mist of spray in her hair. It was a windy day, and though the sky was clear, she wondered if a storm was brewing.

It was March, and frequent storms buffeted the coast and village, sometimes sending entire hills plunging into the ocean with loud roars and the high shrieks of trees being ripped from the ground. The first time she had seen it she had been frightened by the storm's intensity, then had thought it majestically overwhelming.

Laurie nudged her mount into a canter, wishing she could ride as she had once ridden across the hills, straddling the animal instead of sidesaddle. It was much more sensible, and she thought crossly that it must have been a man who had decided women were to ride this way. No man would do it!

Instead of riding back to the hacienda, where she would be met with questions from servants and possibly her father Laurie decided to ride into the hills. Her earlier restless energy had returned, and she felt like riding until she could go no farther, ride without thinking, without feeling anything, just riding to keep her thoughts from making her so miserable.

The wind blew, lifting her skirts and tugging at the ends of the *rebozo* over her head, making it whip in the air with loud pops. She laughed exultantly, wondering why she suddenly felt so free. There was something in the wind that drove her, made her reckless.

She let the *rebozo* slide from her head, not caring if it

blew away, not caring about anything but feeling the wind in her hair. The daily restrictions she endured faded away in a heady rush of freedom, and she felt nothing but the pounding rhythm of the horse beneath her, the wind in her hair, and the threat of rain in the air.

Laurie paid no attention to where she was going, but simply rode her horse across the folds of hills. It was the same freedom she'd felt as El Vengador, the sort of reckless danger that made her adrenalin pump and her heart race. With no one to see, she straddled the horse, her legs on each side and her skirts pushed knee-high. She didn't care. She didn't care about anything right now but the sweeping rush of freedom and excitement, and some of her excitement must have infected the horse, for he pounded faster and faster over the hills, leaping obstacles as if they weren't there, his nostrils distended and blowing, and his long mane whipping in the air.

Laurie bent low over his neck, letting the wind tangle her long hair that had come free of its combs and was flying wildly around her face. She felt the first large drops of rain splatter on her face, and didn't care. She didn't want to think about how worried Carlota would be when she returned home wet and weary. She didn't want to think about the inevitable scolding Phillip would give her for racing about and not observing the proprieties. She didn't want to think about anything. This was a time for feeling, for feeling alive instead of dead as she usually did.

As she rode over a low rise she heard the heavy beat of wings and saw a flock of swallows fly into the air just ahead of her. Just below was the ocean, pounding against the sandy beach that stretched for miles without interruption. Reining her mount to a heaving halt on the crest overlooking the ocean, Laurie sat there for a long time, breathing in the salt tang and watching the endless washing ashore of frothy waves. It was stimulating and soothing all at once, the timelessness of it appealing to her. Long after she was gone the ocean would still be here, still be rushing shoreward, then rushing back out. Somehow it seemed to put all her problems into perspective.

It began to rain harder, slashing down in stinging pellets that pelted her upturned face. The horse began to snort and dance nervously, and she turned him back down the hill toward a grove of trees she had seen. There was an abandoned hut there, with half its roof fallen in, but still some sort of shelter. She would wait out the storm there, then ride back home to a scolding from her father.

Shivering as the cold wind and rain penetrated her clothes to soak her skin, Laurie ducked into the hut and found an old wooden crate to sit on in the crumbling structure. Her horse was tied to a spreading tree outside the hut, half-hidden by thick branches budding with new growth, but she could hear the jangle of his bridle as he shook his head. Clumsily she tried to pull back her long, wet hair into some kind of knot on her neck, to keep the wet, clinging strands from her face.

Unbidden, the memory of the fierce storm she had seen came back to her, terrifying in its intensity, and she shivered as she recalled how an entire hillside had skidded into the ocean. Watching it from afar was quite different from being out in it, she discovered, and she shuddered when a loud thunderclap sounded, making the old hut rattle.

Huddled on the crate, Laurie wished she had turned around and gone back home as the storm raged around her.

Laurie wasn't the only one caught out in the storm. A rider appeared on the crest above the hut and nudged his horse toward the shelter, cursing as sheets of rain dripped from the brim of his hat. Damn it, why hadn't he had sense enough to turn back? He knew well enough how quickly these storms could come up, but he'd not wanted to return home. A chance encounter with an old acquaintance had made him more wary, and he had ridden out across the hills to vent his frustration in solitude.

Now here he was, caught in a storm. But it looked like he wasn't the only one, he thought as he saw the horse tethered beneath a tree. Another fool's company might help pass the time until it blew over.

Dismounting, he ducked into the low-roofed hut, pausing in the doorway to let his eyes adjust to the dim light.

Laurie, still seated on the crate with her arms wrapped around her shivering body for warmth, jerked her head up as the apparition appeared in the doorway, a large, dark form silhouetted against the light from outside. The apparition was accompanied by a particularly loud rumble of thunder and flash of lightning, making her scream.

Another scream erupted as the lightning bolt crashed to earth, and she leaped up from the crate. Pure terror filled her as she saw the large form step quickly toward her, and she gave another scream.

"Don't come near me!" she screamed, wildly looking around her for a possible weapon. "Stay away!"

"Still as sweet as ever, I see," a familiar voice mocked her, and Laurie froze, dropping back to the crate.

"Cade?"

"Who did you think? Your friend Garcia? Damnit, Laurie, what are you doing here?" Cade demanded angrily. "I thought you were safe in New Orleans!"

She was staring at him in stunned surprise as he stepped inside the hut, his dark hair plastered close to his skull and his dark eyes glittering in the odd half-light of gloom.

"What's the matter with you?" he asked in the same mocking tone. "You look as if you've seen a ghost. Surprised to see me, too, Laurie?"

Reason fled, and she was glad, angry, and frightened all at the same time as she sprang to her feet to glare at him.

"I can't believe it's you! What are you doing here? I thought you'd be in New Orleans with your wife!"

"Did you, now? That's interesting." Cade smiled at her, with his eyes still leaping with angry lights. "I thought you'd be in New Orleans with your count."

He stood there looking at her with an enigmatic expression on his face, his booted feet slightly apart and his thumbs tucked into the red sash around his lean waist. Now why did he terrify her so? she wondered with a fleeting surge of panic. He was still the same Cade, the same man who had taken her virginity and made love to her, then dragged her with him for three months, alternately hateful and loving by turns. Why did he affect her so?

Maybe it was the storm outside, she reasoned as another bolt of lightning cracked, making her leap and shudder with fear. And maybe it was the storm inside. . . .

Laurie could almost sense it now, Cade's awareness of her, the way her riding habit clung wetly to her body, outlining her curves, the thin material almost transparent over her breasts. She knew she must look like a frightened rabbit with wide eyes and half-parted lips as she gazed at him with irrational fear.

As they stood looking warily at one another, she became aware that his clothes were drenched, clinging to his hard, lean frame and leaving nothing to her imagination—or memory. And as she looked at him without thinking, she saw that he had begun to desire her, and her eyes jerked back up to his face with a shocked ex-

389

pression.

Cade was grinning wickedly. "Maybe I haven't forgotten you, Laurie. There were times when we didn't disagree, if you'll remember."

Taking an instinctive step backward, her voice came out as a hoarse whisper.

"Don't come near me, Cade Caldwell! I'll . . . I'll scream if you do!"

But even as she said it, she knew that she wouldn't, and that her heart had begun to race in a familiar pattern. In spite of her reluctance to begin it all over again, to surrender the resistance she'd built up, she could feel the slow yielding of her doubts to the rationalization that she had not seen him in so long, had not thought she'd ever see him again.

"Scream?" he mocked her. "Do you think anyone would hear you? We're three miles from the nearest hacienda, and the storm is loud. . . ."

A sudden clap of thunder seemed to rattle the small hut and Laurie jumped, gasping with fear, as frightened by his mocking words as by the storm. Then, as if sensing how afraid she was, Cade shrugged lightly.

"But don't worry, *love* — " He emphasized the word, and she remembered how she used to hate him for saying it so carelessly — "I have no intention of hurting you, though I don't know why I shouldn't."

Her chin lifted, and she said in a steady voice, "I don't know why you think you should. I've done nothing to you."

When he just looked at her, she amended lamely, "Nothing lately."

"I'm glad you thought of that last." His tone was dry as he began to shrug out of his wet shirt, and Laurie took another step backward, her heart pounding. Cade slid her a wicked smile. "I ran into Doña Carlota a little while ago, and she was surprised to see me, too."

390

"C-C-Carlota?" she stammered, hating herself for showing her fear but unable to stop.

"Your teeth are chattering, Laurie," he said in a brisk tone. "You need to get out of those wet things. I'll build a fire so we can dry out, while you take off your gown."

Her chin lifted defiantly. "I have no intention of taking off my gown, Cade Caldwell!"

He shrugged. "Suit yourself. Stay wet then, but I should warn you that these storms often last a while. You may end up with pneumonia if you don't get warm and dry."

And because he was right, and she felt slightly foolish and ingenuous at refusing, Laurie reluctantly began to unbutton her gown where it fastened at the side. Her fingers were chilled and clumsy, and in the end it was Cade who helped her unbutton her gown, his fingers swift and efficient as he peeled it from her wet, quaking body.

Pushing at the ends of her wet blond hair, Laurie took the blanket he held out to her, grateful that he'd thought to bring one on his saddle. She wrapped it around her body and spread her palms out to the fire he'd built in the center of the dirt floor of the hut. The wood was wet, and it gave off almost as much smoke as heat, pricking her eyes and stinging her nose as she knelt beside the fire.

"What are you doing back in California, and what did you say to Carlota?" she asked as she finally began to get warm again. Rain rattled down, occasional drops spattering into the fire through the chinks in the roof, making it hiss. Laurie looked up at Cade when he didn't immediately answer, then quickly looked away again.

He seemed harder somehow, his lean face sun-browned and harsh, his well-muscled, slim-hipped frame more dangerous than ever before. And more attractive. She couldn't help but remember the long nights she'd spent with him, the hours on the steamer, then the star-frosted nights out on the open Texas prairie. Did he ever think of them? Did he ever miss her? And why did she have to remember so well? Laurie tried to concentrate on what he was saying, his reply to her question.

"I came back to California to help my grandfather," he was saying, crouching down by the licking flames to feed in another stick of damp wood. "As for Carlota—I had the good sense not to say much at all. It seemed best."

"You're still a renegade," Laurie said, her amber eyes widening. "Why haven't you been arrested yet?"

"Because they haven't seen me yet. It was just by chance that I ran into Carlota." His voice was still mocking, still angry.

"Aren't you taking a big chance just being here?"

Cade nodded. "Not that it makes much difference. I had to come back."

Laurie was silent for a moment before looking up at him with sudden understanding. "That's why you wanted me to stay in New Orleans. You didn't want to see me again, and you knew you were coming back to Higuera."

Cade gave an impatient shake of his head, and droplets of rain flew into the fire. "No, you're wrong. I didn't want you back here because you don't belong here. You belong where there are operas and theaters and people like you. California is still too primitive for a woman like you. And besides, I'm not certain California is ready for you."

"What do you mean by that?"

Cade laughed at the indignation in her voice. "I mean that you turned poor, lazy Higuera upside down with your El Vengador, and if you stayed long, there's no telling what else you might do."

Stiffening, she glared at him in the dim light. "And it is much easier to forget me if you don't have to see me—is that it?"

He looked at her, and all the amusement vanished from his taut features. "Yes."

Sudden tears pricked her eyelids, and Laurie realized that she didn't want him to forget her, didn't want to forget him, to spend the rest of her life without him. But how could she tell him, and if she did—would he care?

Arming herself against inevitable hurt, Laurie quavered, "Get out, then!"

"Ride out into the storm? That's not very charitable," he chided with a narrowing of his dark eyes.

"I don't feel very charitable!"

Cade's glance raked her, and he stood slowly, his lean frame uncoiling from a crouch to tower over her. Laurie shrank away from him without meaning to, her eyes growing wide with apprehension.

"How do you feel, Laurie?" he asked in a soft, husky voice. He reached out to lift a fat, wet coil of her hair in one hand, and she shivered at his touch. "Are you afraid of me? You shouldn't be. Have I ever hurt you?"

She almost gasped, and managed to say shortly, "All you have ever done is hurt me!"

He crouched down in front of her, only inches away, and she could feel the heat of his body close to her.

"Laurie, Laurie—you know I'd never really hurt you."

She looked into his dark, simmering gaze, almost felt the odd, inquisitive look in his eyes, and looked away.

"I don't know anything like that," she murmured in a tone that was sulky, penitent, and hopeful at the same time.

Cade smiled, and let the curl he was holding drop

to her shoulder. He gently pushed it to her back, and let his hand linger on the curve of her blanket-draped shoulder.

"We always manage to argue, don't we." It was more of a statement than a question, but she felt the need to agree and nodded. Cade shrugged. "That was one of the reasons I left you in New Orleans, you know. The other was because it's probably too dangerous for you in Higuera now. Especially now that I'm back." His smile widened slightly, and the pressure of his fingers tightened.

Laurie was more aware of his proximity than she had ever been aware of anything in her life, and her blood ran from hot to cold and then back again. She shivered, and her teeth chattered, but her face was flushed and hot as Cade let his hand drop along the length of her arm.

Shaking away the feeling of lethargy that invaded her body at his touch, Laurie said more weakly than she wanted, "It's always your fault that we argue."

Frowning at her, he felt a muscle twitch in his lean jaw, and he rose, letting his hand drop away from her arm. He took two steps away, then half-turned, his brows drawn angrily over his dark eyes as he glared at her.

"You'd like to think that, wouldn't you? It'd make it easier if it was always my fault, but . . ."

A sudden loud crash of thunder and a bolt of lightning interrupted him, and the tiny hut shook with the force of it. Laurie screamed with reaction as she heard a heavy thud and the sound of screaming wood, and realized that a tree had been struck nearby. Over the sound, she heard the shrill neighing of the horses, and saw Cade reach the door in one long stride. He disappeared into the driving rain and she ran to the door, trying to see through the dense pouring. Another loud crack rent the air, and she was blinded for a moment

394

by a bolt of lightning searing through the sky.

"Cade!" she screamed when she didn't see him or the horses. "Cade!"

He was back in a moment, drenched again, rain running in rivulets over his face and shoulders.

"They're both gone," he said, and when she stared at him blankly, weak with relief that he was back and all right, he clarified in an irritable tone, "The horses. That last bolt of lightning made them break their reins. They'll probably run home. Which means we have to walk back," he ended when she still stared at him.

White-faced and trembling, Laurie didn't think as she threw herself into his arms, lifting her face for his kiss as if she did it every day. And Cade didn't push her away, but coiled his arms around her quivering body and held her closely, his mouth searing across her half-open lips with a hunger he hadn't realized he felt until now.

"Laurie," he muttered in a half-groan. "Laurie."

She was laughing and crying at the same time, kissing him on his face, his neck, his chest. "Cade, oh Cade, I've missed you so! Please don't leave me again, don't be angry, I can't stand it if you are. . . ."

He didn't let her say anymore, but scooped her into his arms and carried her to the dry spot near the fire, laying her down with gentle urgency. Laurie didn't remember later how it had happened, only that it had. She vaguely recalled tearing at his wet shirt with eager fingers while he opened the folds of the blanket and removed her damp undergarments.

A searing fire drove her, made her bolder than she had ever been, seeking out his secrets with her hands, making him want her as much as she wanted him. The rain pounded against the roof as Cade took her, his body driving into hers with an aching satisfaction that made her arch toward him again and again, crying out his name, holding him as if she would never let him go.

"*Bruja*," he muttered against her lips. "You're a witch, a sorceress who's put a spell on me. I must be crazy to be doing this. . . ."

"Hush," she said softly, putting one finger over his lips and smiling up at him with a haze of love in her eyes. "I love you." She held her breath at her daring, wondering how he would react to the word.

Cade stared at her, his dark eyes wary. For a long moment filled with only the beat of rain, he gazed at her without speaking. Then he silently folded her into his arms again and held her close to his heart, so that she could feel its steady beating against her breast.

"I love you, too," he said softly just when the silence stretched so long she thought he wouldn't, and Laurie felt a hot gush of tears sting her eyes.

"I couldn't bear it if you didn't," she whispered brokenly.

His lips captured hers again, smothering anything else she might have said with his kiss, and Laurie forgot everything but the man holding her. The storm outside was nothing compared to the storm inside the small, crumbling hut, and the pent-up emotions stored inside their souls were released at last.

Laurie couldn't get enough of Cade, couldn't feel his hard-muscled body beneath her exploring fingertips enough to sate her longing for him, and he felt the same way as he teased and caressed her slender curves.

And afterward, when they lay exhausted and drowsy in each other's arms with Cade's blanket around them, Laurie wondered if he was as contented as she was.

Tilting back her head, she gazed up at Cade through half-slitted eyes, a soft smile curving her lips. "Had enough yet?" she teased, and his arms tightened briefly around her.

"Of you? Not yet. Soon, though—" He paused as her eyes opened wider, then drawled, "—say, in a hundred years or so."

Laurie relaxed against him with relief, running the pads of her fingertips across his broad chest. She didn't dare ask the questions that pricked her; not yet. She wasn't certain she wanted to hear the answers, and wasn't certain if there were any answers. Right now, all she wanted was for Cade to hold her. She felt warm and secure wrapped in his blanket and love, with a crackling fire for light and the world far away. She wanted no intrusions.

Turning into him, she lifted her face to his and he bent his dark head and kissed her, softly at first, then more fiercely, until she was moving beneath him, opening her body for his love.

The passion that had always been there between them overrode any lingering reservations that Cade had, and he knew that this slender girl was the only one in the world who could truly defeat him. He needed her; he wanted her. And he didn't care if she knew it, not anymore.

He'd dreamed about her, lusted after her, and even hated her for a while, but none of that mattered now. Now she was here, her soft, ripe body opening for him, only for him, and he knew he would never give her up again. If anything, she was even more desirable, more sensual than she had ever been before, and he wondered with a fatalistic twinge why he had ever thought he could live without her.

There was much more than passion between them, and he should have realized it long before this. . . .

Chapter Twenty-six

"But can't we stay here forever?" Laurie asked dully as Cade finished dressing, and he laughed.

"Forever's a long time, love, and we may get hungry before then."

"I won't." She looked up at him. Tears spangled her long lashes like dew, and her lower lip quivered ever so slightly. "Once we go back, it will be just the same. There will be things that come between us, make us quarrel again, and it will be like today never happened."

Cade knelt beside her, lifting her chin in his palm, and his dark eyes were soft.

"Laurie, we can't run away. I can't. Why do you think I came back to California knowing that there's a price on my head? Because I don't want to spend the rest of my life looking over my shoulder."

"Are you sure it isn't because of Doña Linda?" Laurie heard herself ask sharply, then flushed. "Cade—I'm sorry," she said. "I didn't mean that."

He grinned. "Don't worry about her. She left for Spain a few days ago. I have it on excellent authority." When she would have pulled away his fingers tightened gently, and his voice softened to a low, husky murmur. "I won't lose you again, love, I promise."

Her eyes searched his, gold orbs drowning with tears, and he pulled her into his embrace, holding her until she pulled away from him. A faint smile curved her lips.

"All right. I'll have faith in us, Cade. It will be hard, but I'll have faith." She paused, then asked quickly, "Will you go back to your grandfather's? That would be the first place they would look if they thought you were back."

He shook his head regretfully. "No, I can't go back there, but he will know where I am. If you should need me, just go to Don Benito. I'll tell him to forward any message from you."

"Oh Cade, I'm so frightened! How do you plan on proving your innocence? What if you can't? What if they catch you?" Her words tumbled over one another in her haste, and he put a finger over her lips.

"Try not to worry, querida. First I have to talk to my grandfather. Then I will decide what I must do." He smiled at her, his dark eyes glittering as his voice became teasing. "Tell me — does Garcia still have a fondness for you?"

She looked at him warily. "Why?"

"Because he could be very useful. Think about it. Isn't that how you used him before?"

Squirming slightly, Laurie admitted, "Yes, but that was different."

"How? This time I need for you to find out what is going on inside the *presidio*. I need to know what Don Luis is planning, and when."

"Cade, you're not planning to . . ."

"Become El Vengador? But of course! Why not, since I've already been tried and convicted for the crime?"

Gasping with dismay, Laurie recalled her brief decision to do the same, and gave a vigorous shake of her head. "No! It's too dangerous, Cade, I've already considered it."

He rocked back on his heels. "Why did you consider it?"

"Because I thought . . . I thought that if I was captured and proven to be El Vengador, then they would not think that you . . . oh, you just can't, Cade!"

Her last words came out in a wail, and he grinned. "I take it you consider yourself a better swordsman?"

She nodded. "Something like that."

"And do you recall who won our last duel?"

Softly, earnestly, she pleaded, "Don't try it! Think of some other way."

Unfolding his long body, Cade stood up, pulling her with him. "Have a little more faith in me, chica. It's almost dark. I'll walk part of the way back with you. If we see anyone, you go out to meet them, and don't mention me."

"What if your horse has been found?"

Shrugging, he said, "Anyone could have caught and saddled him, remember. Only my grandfather would know that he allows no one but me to catch him, and he won't mention that."

The rain had made the roads slippery and sticky, so they walked through long grasses as the sun sank behind the horizon. The storm had freshened the air, and there was a crystal-clear quality to it that made Laurie wish she could stay in California forever.

"Cade?" she murmured after a few minutes, and he slanted her a glance. "I know this isn't the time to ask, but—do you intend to stay in California if Don Luis is still the alcalde?"

Another shrug lifted his broad shoulders, and he

looked out to where the sky met the sea. "Probably. For a while, anyway. Events are changing everyday, and I think an entire new world is about to open for California. I feel now like I did about Texas. Change is coming, and I want to be here."

Laurie shivered. Change . . . why did it sound so ominous now that she'd found Cade again? She was afraid of losing him, afraid he'd be taken away.

When they finally stood on the edge of the Alvarado *estancia,* Cade turned to Laurie and kissed her gently and quickly.

"Remember what I told you to say," he reminded her. "And don't let anyone make you say anything different. And don't believe everything you hear, either. Promise?"

She nodded, wiping at the tears that crept maddeningly from her eyes. "Yes, I promise."

"You'll be all right, Laurie. Any woman who can run off an entire band of Comanches has nothing to worry about from Don Luis's *soldados.*"

"I'm glad you think so," she muttered unhappily. "But I refuse to be too nice to José Garcia, even for you."

"We need to find out what the alcalde plans, but I'm not willing for you to be *too* nice, either," he said grimly. "But now you need to go. I see lights on, and I'm sure your father has men out looking for you."

"Oh, Cade—you'll be careful?"

He laughed softly. "As always, love!" then he was gone, disappearing into the dark shadows of the trees. Laurie remembered that he had grown up in this area, and claimed to know every hiding place within a hundred square miles. She hoped he was right.

"I can't imagine what has gotten into you, Laurie," Phillip Allen fumed, staring at his daughter in the light of a silver candelabra. She did not look at him, but kept her head bent low, seeming engrossed in her needlework. He ground his teeth together and burst out, "Look at me! Since when did you become interested in stitchery?"

"Is that what you're so upset about, Papa?" Laurie laid her needlework on the small table at her side. "I won't do any more stitchery if it distresses you."

"You know that's not what I'm upset about! I want to know why you are allowing that Captain Garcia to visit! Have you forgotten his earlier behavior? Have you forgotten how rude he was, and how he . . ."

"Papa, I thought we agreed a long time ago that I am well past the age of being protected. If my reputation was intact, perhaps it wouldn't matter, but we all know that is no longer the truth."

Her voice was even, but Phillip flushed and Laurie winced at the calm truth in her words. No young men called on her since her return from New Orleans, and though she was treated politely, she was not invited to the normal affairs that unmarried girls would attend. She was caught in a netherworld, lost between respectable spinsterhood and marriage, and no one knew quite what to do with her. And she knew it, and she knew her father knew it.

Laurie met his perturbed stare with a calm gaze that made him shake his head.

"I don't know what's right anymore," he muttered so plaintively that she felt sorry for him. Rising from her chair, Laurie crossed to where Phillip had sank down on a low bench, and knelt in front of him.

"Neither do I, Papa. I only know what feels right." She cupped her hands over his. "Things have hap-

402

pened that have been beyond our control, and now I feel I have to take control of my life. For the past six years, others have been telling me what to do, where to go, who to go with—I am almost twenty-two years old now, and I think I'm ready to make those decisions on my own."

After a moment, Phillip put his hand atop her blond head, and a weary smile curved his mouth. "Perhaps you're right, Laurie. And perhaps I'm just getting tired of this diplomatic post. Trying to keep peace between the alcalde and the American merchants has taken a great deal out of me lately. The merchant ships don't want to stop here anymore because he levies such heavy taxes on them, and so they go farther up the coast, and the people of Higuera have to pay more for their goods, and then the coffers are dwindling and Don Luis levies more taxes on the peons to pay for his necessary luxuries—*Ay di mi!*"

Laurie smiled at the Spanish phrase, sounding so foreign on her father's lips.

"Woe is all of us," she said, still smiling. "But maybe the alcalde will be out of office soon, and things will be better."

"I don't know when," Phillip muttered dejectedly. "Don Benito has petitioned Mexico City many times, and still they take their time. It has been years, and Don Luis has stolen more from the people of Higuera than can ever be returned to them!"

"But he hasn't stolen their pride and dignity," Carlota said quietly, and both Laurie and Phillip turned to stare at her. Carlota walked quietly into the room, and her big dark eyes were filled with tears, as she added in a quavery voice, "It hurts me to see how much my home has changed, and how my servants quake at the very mention of Don Luis!

403

And I cannot protect them! We, who took pride in treating them as good and obedient children, cannot even offer them shelter from the alcalde!"

"But they aren't your children, *mi corazon*," Phillip pointed out softly, rising to go to his wife. "Don't fret over what you cannot change."

"You don't understand! The Indians are little more than gentle, childlike creatures who have depended upon the Alvarado family for generations, and the others, the ones who came to us from Mexico, they have their pride, too, and it is being trampled in the dust. How much longer can Higuera exist under the shadow of that vulture?"

Laurie felt a tightening in her chest, and Carlota's next words fell like stones into the silence.

"They took Serita today, for not paying enough. . . ."

Rising swiftly to her feet, Laurie felt a cold anger grip her, and she stepped to Carlota's side.

"Where did they take her? When?"

Carlota looked up at her, her eyes awash with tears, and shook her head. "I don't know where they took her. They came today, the *soldados*, and took her to be questioned."

"I have to go out," Laurie said then, and Phillip gave her a sharp glance.

"Where? It's almost dark."

"Just for a walk, Papa. Please, don't try to stop me. I won't do anything foolish."

"Laurie—I know that you were telling the truth last year when you said you were El Vengador. If you should try to do that again. . . ."

"Papa. I said I was going for a walk, and I am. If you like, you may send someone to walk with me."

Phillip hesitated, then gave a curt nod of his head. "Very well. Take Julio with you. He is young and strong and very reliable."

Laurie took Julio, but made him drive the diligencia to a spot not far from Don Benito's hacienda, where she got down and told him to wait for her. She walked swiftly up the tiled pathway and took a deep breath before knocking on the door. She had not come to see Don Benito since her return, and did not know how he would receive her.

The servant allowed her in, and went to call for his master. Don Benito arrived several moments later, leaning heavily on his goldheaded cane.

"Ah, Señorita Allen," he said with a lift of his brow. "What brings you to my house at this hour?"

"I apologize for intruding, Don Benito, but I've been told that I may leave a message with you," Laurie said in a soft voice, and the old man narrowed his eyes at her.

"That is so. But I must warn you—the walls have ears since I was bold enough to petition Mexico City for the removal of the alcalde." He tapped a finger on his closed mouth, then indicated with a jerk of his head that she should step outside with him. Not quite certain, Laurie walked with him toward the open patio doors, and Don Benito paused beside his writing desk for a moment, then gestured to her to go with him out onto the vine-covered patio. "How may I help you, Señorita?" he asked loudly, and handed her a small square of paper and pen.

Speaking loudly as she scribbled on the sheet of paper, Laurie said, "My stepmother wishes to borrow some of your peons for the tending of her vineyards. Several of her people have gone, and she is in need."

Don Benito nodded approval, his eyes crinkling at the corners as Laurie handed him the paper. He scanned it quickly, saying aloud as he read, "Of course! I have often lent some of my most trusted people to Doña Carlota, and I will be glad to do so again."

After scrawling a reply on the paper, Don Benito gave it to her, and Laurie read it quickly, then held the paper out to the flame of a candle. It caught fire, and she held it until there was only a tiny corner left unburned, then let it flutter to the stone tiles and burn itself out. Don Benito smiled at her, and she smiled back.

On the way home Laurie plotted on ways to rescue Serita, and hoped Cade would get her message in time. Poor Serita! How frightened she must be, and in despair, thinking there was no hope for her. But there had to be a way to get her away from the alcalde, there had to be!

The next day, riding with Captain Garcia, who still preened his mustaches and puffed out his chest like a vain bird, Laurie did her best to be charming and gay.

"And to think that I actually missed California while I was away!" she said, smiling at him with a tilt of her blonde head.

Garcia looked at her with an odd smile. "Is that so, Señorita? Perhaps that is why you were so charming to me when you first came back."

Laurie pretended to pout. "Oh, that! Well, I couldn't let you grow too cocky, you know. I mean, there you were, acting like I should have fallen at your feet, when you know you were much too bold."

Smoothing his mustaches with one finger, Garcia said, "Somehow, I thought you preferred bold men. If I recalls correctly, you were quite taken with Nicólas Alvarez."

"A girlish fancy, of course. I'm certain you have a great deal of experience with women, and understand that at times, girls become infatuated with a man who only appears to be bold and dangerous. Alas, when it is discovered that he is not, the image

406

vanishes, *poof!*, and all dreams are shattered." Laurie edged her horse closer to Garcia, still smiling. "Real heroes are the men who stay true to their role, who do their duty, and risk their lives for others. Don't you agree?"

Still wary, Garcia nodded, and his eyes were watchful. "Si. I just did not know that you agreed with that theory, Doña Laurie."

Encouraged by his use of a familiar term, Laurie cajoled and flattered and teased all during their ride, and when the captain rode her home, she even let him kiss her, though she wanted to scrub her lips before he was through.

Garcia was breathing heavily when he lifted his head from hers, and Laurie wished someone would interrupt, Carlota or her father or a servant—anyone! When his hand fell to her knee, she resisted the impulse to slap him but kept her smile intact. He grew bolder with every time she rode with him, and soon he would expect her to bed him. He had told her bluntly that since she was no longer a virgin, she should not expect to be treated as one.

"But I am very generous to my women," he added in such a smug, confident voice that Laurie longed to throw his words back into his face.

Swallowing her hasty comment, she murmured a noncommittal reply and kept her eyes lowered, hoping he would think her shy.

Garcia chuckled, and as a servant appeared in the door of the *sala*, he rose from beside Laurie.

"You can still be a shy dove," he said to her. "I like that in a woman. As well as—other things."

Burning with indignation, Laurie wished she could tell him her true opinion of him, but remembering Serita, she didn't dare. Instead, she changed the subject so he wouldn't grow suspicious, speaking lightly about the paucity of social events in Higuera.

José took both her hands in his. "There is a fiesta in a few days. You will go with me. The alcalde will not mind, I am certain."

"The alcalde?" Laurie gently withdrew her hands and rose from the bench where she sat, sliding a glance toward the hovering servant. Another spy? She didn't know who to trust anymore, for someone here at the Alvarado hacienda had betrayed poor Serita. Keeping her tone light, she said, "I did not know the alcalde had to supervise your social activities, Capitán."

Grinning, José said, "Just when it will be at his hacienda, my sweet."

Laurie jerked to look at him, her eyes wide. "A fiesta at his hacienda? You are inviting me there?"

"Why not?"

"I suppose—I mean, doesn't the alcalde hold a grudge against me? After all, I was involved with El Vengador."

José's face tightened. "We will not remember that. And Don Luis is more than generous. He will not mind."

"I see. Of course, I will be glad to go with you," she said with a smile. Her heart raced, and she saw the endless possibilities in the situation. Why not go with him? She could do some spying of her own, perhaps discover more about Serita. . . .

"Don't be stupid!" Cade growled when Laurie told him what she intended to do. They were in an arroyo on the Alvarado rancho, and it was dark, with only a sickle moon overhead to provide any light. She had come to meet him after receiving a message from Don Benito, and now he was glaring at her angrily. "It would be dangerous, and I won't let you do it."

Laurie tossed back her head, and her eyes were fixed on his shadowed face with determination.

"Cade, I won't do anything foolish. We need to know where she is, and if there is any way to release her, don't we?"

Grabbing her by the shoulders, Cade ground out, "Don't be in such a hurry that you end up in prison yourself! If Don Luis imprisoned Serita, he wouldn't hesitate to imprison you. It's too dangerous, Laurie. For once in your stubborn, headstrong life, listen to me!"

A faint smile curved her lips, and she leaned into his arms, laying her head against his chest without speaking. A sigh stirred her hair as Cade surrendered and held her, and some of the tension eased from his taut muscles.

"You intend to do it anyway, don't you?" he muttered, and she nodded. There was a long moment of silence in which she could hear nothing but the wind and the metallic jangle of their horses' bridles as they grazed not far away. After a moment he pushed her slightly away and gazed narrowly into her moonlit face. "Maybe it's not such a bad idea, if you don't begin thinking of yourself as El Vengador again."

Her chin lifted indignantly. "What do you mean by that?"

"Simply that if you try to rescue Serita yourself, it will end very badly for all of us. Leave that to me. Just find out what we need to know, and we . . ."

"*We* who?"

Cade grinned and shook his head. "Oh no! I'm not going to tell you anything yet."

"Why not? Do you think I'd tell anyone?"

"It's not that, Laurie, and you know it." His voice had become serious again, and he put a hand beneath her chin to hold her face up to his. "There's too much that could go wrong, and it has taken a long time to come this far. If you knew everything, you would be in more danger than you can guess."

409

A shudder rippled through her body, and she flung herself into his arms again. "Oh, Cade! If anything happens to you, I'll die!"

He laughed softly. "Always the melodramatic for you, Laurie. Don't borrow trouble."

"That's easy for you to say," she sniffed, "when you know what's going on. I hate to be left out."

"You're not being left out. You're being protected."

"It's the same thing—I don't know what's going on!"

Cade shook his head. "You will when the time comes."

She had to be content with that, with that and the memory of his strong arms around her and the little arbor of leaves where they had lain together until just before dawn. Her lips were still swollen with his kisses when she slipped quietly into her bedroom, grateful for the few hours of rest she would get before having to rise.

If anyone noticed her sleepy eyes or quiet manner, it was not mentioned. Carlota was subdued, too, worrying over Serita. Phillip was more concerned than he wanted to admit to his family, but it was easily readable in his eyes as he quickly finished his breakfast and left the hacienda.

"Would you like to play a game of chess?" Carlota asked Laurie with a forced smile. "It is a long time until noon."

"No. I don't think I'm in the mood for chess," Laurie replied, and Carlota nodded.

"Neither am I." She rose to pace around the *sala*, her straight dark brows drawn into a worried frown. "Oh Laurie, I don't know what to do about Serita! And Phillip, for all his goodness, cannot think of a solution either. The poor girl is doomed to remain in prison."

"Perhaps a miracle will happen," Laurie said, and

410

wished she had a better reply.

Carlota smiled wanly. "Yes, a miracle. I think I shall go to the church and light some candles and pray. That is the best I can do at the moment."

"Say one for all of us," Laurie said, and Carlota looked at her strangely.

"The alcalde is giving a grand fiesta," Carlota said after a moment, "and has sent us an invitation."

Surprised, Laurie looked at her stepmother with a slightly open mouth. "Are you going to attend?"

Carlota shrugged. "I do not want to, and neither does your father."

"How do you refuse the alcalde?"

Sighing, Carlota murmured, "Not easily."

"I have received an invitation, too," Laurie said as Carlota picked up her needlework. When she looked at her inquiringly, Laurie added, "Captain Garcia invited me to attend with him."

Carlota put down her needlework. "And you are going with him?"

"Yes, I think I am." Laurie recognized the bewilderment in Carlota's eyes, but before she could explain, her stepmother gave a firm shake of her head, her lips pressed tightly together.

"I saw Nicolas Alvarez," she said abruptly, noting the way Laurie's face flushed. "You have seen him, too."

It was a statement, not a question, and Laurie hesitated with a glance around the *sala* before asking, "Why would you think that?"

"Why would I not?" Carlota took two quick steps toward Laurie and grasped her by the hands, her voice low and soft as she said, "You know that the alcalde will have him shot if he sees him! Don't endanger yourself too!"

Laurie searched Carlota's face for a moment before saying in a gentle tone, "I will do my best to

411

stay safe, of course."

It wasn't an admission or a denial, and Carlota gave a heavy sigh. *"Ay di mi!* Don't be foolish, I beg of you."

"Someone, sometime, has to risk something, or Higuera will soon be empty of courage as well as happiness." Laurie smiled encouragingly. "Just pray for everyone."

"I will do that, and I will pray that your father does not find out about your foolishness until this is over with." Carlota shook her head. "I can see that you will not rest until all is done."

"No, I won't."

"And El Vengador? Does he ride again?"

Because she wasn't certain, Laurie shook her head and said slowly, "I don't know. Perhaps he should."

Crossing herself, Carlota murmured a prayer, then gave Laurie a faint smile. *"Dios mediante,"* she said.

God willing. Laurie hoped that He was.

Chapter Twenty-seven

Don Luis played the part of a perfect host. Laurie held her breath when Capitán Garcia introduced her to him, wondering if he would remember her or harbor a grudge, but the alcalde was effusively pleasant, eyeing her with a speculative smile.

"Ah, so we meet under much better circumstances, Señorita Allen. And your padré—he was able to attend with you?"

"I'm afraid he must send his regrets, Your Excellency," Laurie replied politely. "He and my stepmother were most disappointed at not being able to attend because of illness. He begs your forgiveness and hopes that the gift sent in their place was acceptable to you."

"I have not seen it yet, but I am certain it will be," Don Luis said with a smile. "Doña Carlota has long been known for her exquisite gifts. But my hacienda is graced with your lovely presence, and for that I am grateful." He waved an expansive arm, and recited the customary Spanish phrase, *"Mi casa es su casa."*

Captain Garcia smiled widely as Laurie swept the don a graceful curtsy, quite pleased with her reception and his. He had long coveted a high position, and it seemed as if even a lady with a questionable reputation was much more acceptable than one of the women from the *cantinas*, or his home village.

"See?" Garcia said in Laurie's ear as they stepped aside and allowed the alcalde to greet more guests. "I told you that he could be quite charming."

As a snake, Laurie thought to herself, but managed a calm smile and casual comment.

"He has his hacienda quite well decorated," she said, and José nodded as happily as if responsible for it.

Lanterns were strung under huge tents, and the archways to the patios were to be lit as well. Long tables groaned beneath the weight of huge platters, and the tantalizing aroma of beef filled the air. It was spring, and the cattle round up to brand the new calves had produced a surplus of meat.

There were wines and fruit from the mission, olives from San Diego, pastries and wheat bread from a distant mission, and the huge slabs of beef that roasted over open pits filled with live-oak coals. Music filled the air, lively tunes played by Indian musicians, the *jota, son, contradanza,* and peasant dance, the *jarabe,* as well as the waltz.

Guests had come from miles away, and the fiesta had begun early in the day with a *merienda,* or picnic out in the green hills. Indian servants carried a multitude of huge woven baskets out into the hills for the guests, who sat on grassy hillocks and ate and watched a succession of entertainments planned for their amusement. There were cockfights, bull tossing, and a *rodeo* where dusty *vaqueros* proved their skills on horseback to the accompaniment of cheers and waves from the *señoritas* watching.

After a noontime *siesta,* the festivities had continued in the cooler halls of the alcalde's hacienda adjoining the *presidio.* A bullfight was to be held in the mercado, and the peasant merchants had been cleared away by the *soldados* so that it could be done without interference.

Dressed in a new gown made of a shimmering gold satin, Laurie read admiration as well as lust in Garcia's eyes as he stared down at her, and she moved

414

slightly away. Though admittedly handsome in his red and blue uniform, José did not appeal to her at all, and she hoped she would not have to remain in his company for too long.

"Do you wish to see me ride?" José asked Laurie, and she smiled.

"In the bullfight?"

"If you wish, though I was thinking of exhibiting some of my superior skills at horsemanship."

"I thought fencing was your greatest skill," Laurie said. "Are you excellent at everything, Capitán?"

Leaning close to her, suggestively close, José let his hand move to the small of her back, pulling her into him. "I have yet to show you my best skills, *amante,*" he said softly, and she stiffened at the innuendo.

Tapping him lightly with her folded fan, she said, "You grow far too bold, Capitán!"

"*Todavia no.* I am just confident of pleasing you," he said huskily, and Laurie stifled the desire to jerk away from him.

"Not yet? You sound *much* too confident now!" She moved away slowly, and José smiled smugly, smoothing his mustache with one finger in the gesture she had grown to despise.

"It has grown warm in here, no?" José took her by the elbow and led her outside under the shade of a live oak. He gazed down at Laurie's flushed face, wondering if she was angry or just flushed by the reminder of his masculinity. His hot gaze roamed over her slender body, admiring the beautiful gown she wore. It was different from those that the village girls wore, more daring, with no scarf covering the ripe suggestion of her breasts. They thrust out, almost begging for his touch, the rich golden material of her dress molding snugly to her curves, and José thought that he could not wait for her much longer. He wasn't certain of her yet, not yet. She still remained remote and distant at

415

moments when she should be soft and yielding. It was as intriguing as it was maddening, and he grew impatient with the waiting. Tonight . . . he would have her tonight, would not take no for an answer again.

Laurie stirred uneasily, sensing what José intended, and she wondered how she would be able to put him off any longer. He was growing bolder and bolder, with his hands as well as his words. But she took a step away from him, and kept her voice determinedly light as she said, "It is much cooler out here under the trees, Capitán. perhaps you should stand in the breeze for a time."

He laughed softly. "For now. Until later. . . ." He let his voice trail into a silence ripe with meaning, and she managed a smile.

"You promised to show me the *presidio*, remember? I have not seen it."

"You do not remember seeing it," he corrected with a sly grin. "You were here before."

Shuddering, she said weakly, "Please! Don't remind me of it!"

José put his arm familiarly around her waist. "That was a bad time for everyone. But now things are quiet in Higuera, and I believe it is because of my leadership." He laughed. "Trujillo is weak, and too soft! I carry out Don Luis's orders just as he wishes, and often, he does not even have to tell me what to do!"

"But — you are the captain of the guards, isn't that right?" Laurie asked in confusion. "Trujillo is the commandant."

"*Was* the commandant," Garcia corrected proudly. "Or at least, it will be announced this evening. He will be most surprised, I think."

"Trujillo doesn't know?"

Glancing around and lowering his voice, José said, "No, my dove. Not yet. You will be with the new commandant of the *presidio!* Doesn't that make you

416

proud?"

Looking up at him, Laurie felt a twinge of dismay. With Trujillo as commandant, there had been a chance for Serita to be treated fairly. But with Garcia in charge . . .

She drove the thought from her mind. They had to act tonight, could not wait any longer. How could she get word to Cade?

"So? What do you say to that?" José was asking, jerking Laurie from her thoughts, and she smiled quickly.

"I am very proud! And excited . . ." She stood on tiptoe to press a kiss to his cheek, and Garcia quickly turned his face so that her lips grazed his. His arms closed around her and pulled her hard against his frame. When he finally released her, his voice was hoarse, and his black eyes glittered.

"Come! Come with me into the *sala,* where we can be alone."

"No. Not yet." Laurie looked around nervously, and was glad to see a fat matron approaching. "There are too many people — later, when the sun has gone down and there are dark shadows to hide us so that we can steal away to be alone . . ."

She let her voice drift into meaningful silence, and when it looked as if José might insist, she added with an arch of her brow, "Waiting only makes the moment sweeter . . ."

Giving a frustrated groan, José muttered, *"Dios!* But I know you are right, my dove."

"And now you will take me for a walk? To the *presidio,* perhaps?"

"If that is what you wish," José said with an effort.

The early April sun smiled warmly down, and Laurie pretended an indifference she didn't feel as they strolled from Don Luis's hacienda through the gates to the *presidio.* An aura of quiet prevailed, a silence as pervasive as the thick walls surrounding the grim building. Wide steps led up to the heavy wooden doors, and as a *soldado* recognized the captain of the guards, he snapped to attention.

"El Capitán!" he said loudly, and other soldiers suddenly appeared at their posts.

"Lazy dogs," Garcia snapped. "If I were not in the presence of a lady, I would deal harshly with you. You may thank your good fortune that she is here."

"Sí, mi capitán!" the unhappy soldier said, keeping his eyes straight ahead of him. He stood stiff and still as they entered the main building, not relaxing his posture until the doors had shut behind them. Then he slouched back into his former position and waited. Why not? It was warm, and the sun felt pleasant on his face, and he had eaten too many enchiladas at noon, and was sleepy. What could happen?

It was much cooler inside the *presidio* walls, and Laurie shivered, pulling her light rebozo closer around her shoulders as José escorted her down the empty, echoing halls. Their footsteps sounded overloud in the silence, and she felt an odd premonition.

"It . . . it's very quiet," she said softly, and Garcia grinned at her.

"Not always. When the criminals are here—lining the hall sometimes—it is very noisy with their silly whimpers and excuses." He sounded so contemptuous that Laurie looked up at him curiously.

"You hate them, don't you? The peasants who come here."

He nodded. "Sí. I hate all of them. They are a dirty rabble of illiterate beggars, and should be little more than slaves."

His voice was casual, almost indifferent, and Laurie felt her throat tighten at his callous attitude.

"You will make a formidable commandant," she murmured, and he slid her a narrow glance.

418

"You sound disapproving, Doña Laurie."

She managed a smile. "No, just observant."

He laughed at that, his good humor restored. Reaching around her, he flung open a door, and they stepped inside a large room with an ornately carved table and chair at one end, and several rows of benches.

"This is where the *corregidor* hands down his decisions on civil matters," Garcia said, and Laurie looked around the room, wondering if this was where she had condemned Cade. It was vaguely familiar, with the high, lace-grill-encased windows. Long shadows fell across the floor, and the sun filtering through the grillwork seemed shallow and pale. The air was thick and oppressive, musty with the reminders of human misery.

A shudder racked her body, and Garcia laughed softly. "Does it make you nervous to be here?"

"It's not very pleasant," Laurie murmured, then tried to look more interested. "But is this where the prisoners are kept? Here, in the *presidio?*"

Giving her a long look, Garcia shrugged and said, "No, they are kept below, in the *mazmorra*. Is there a particular criminal who interests you?"

Feigning surprise, Laurie said with a little laugh, "Should there be? I merely wondered if there were many. Higuera seems such a quiet place, with so little for the *soldados* to do except collect taxes or have parades, that I wondered what you would do as the commandant."

Having successfully pricked his professional pride with her air of condescension, Laurie smiled as Garcia said shortly, "I will show you what there is to do! There are many who break the law, who show insolence to the alcalde and to the rules of the government!"

"That's so difficult to believe—oh, not that I think

419

you are not telling the truth, Capitán, but one hears so little of crime here, except for the Indians who are ignorant and know no better—that I find myself amazed to think there may actually be some vicious criminals nearby!" She feigned another shudder, and José put a protective arm around her shoulders.

"Come with me, my dove, and I will show you evidence of criminals in Higuera! Of course, I will protect you, so you have nothing to worry about," he added, placing a hand on the hilt of the sword at his side.

Laurie allowed his touch without moving away, and said in a small voice, "I know I have nothing to worry about in your company, mi capitán."

Garcia took her to a door, and unlocked it with a huge ring of keys that hung from a peg beside a soldier's station. Laurie glanced shyly at the soldier, who stared at her with a knowing smirk.

Ignoring him, and pretending she did not see the glance between the guard and Garcia, Laurie stepped through the opened door and down a steep flight of steps. She fought against the urge to flee back up into the light and fresh air as they went deeper and deeper into the dungeon, and a huge lump settled in the region of her chest as she thought of poor Serita and how terrified and miserable she must be.

She tried to remember every twist and turn so that she could describe them to Cade, then wondered if he had been kept here, too.

Long rows of *calabozos*, or individual cells, ran the length of a dark hallway lit only by a few sputtering torches. It looked to Laurie as she imagined hell would look, and she could hear muffled groans and moans from the cells.

"These men—what have they done?" she asked in a hoarse whisper when José paused before a dank, foulsmelling cubicle that housed several prisoners.

Shrugging, he said, "They have been foolish enough to disagree with the alcalde, or to refuse to pay their taxes. One of them was caught stealing bread from the mercado. Another stole shoes for his children."

Horrified, Laurie said, "For that they have been imprisoned?"

"They are fortunate. A less merciful alcalde would have put them to death."

She felt a surge of revulsion but swallowed it, trying to avoid looking directly at the poor, wretched human beings crowded into the cell. She wondered what they must think of her, coming down here to view them as if they were exhibits at a marketplace, then thrust that thought from her mind. She had a purpose for coming, a firm purpose, and she must stick to her resolve.

"And all of them are here for such things? No murderers or heretics? No women who have committed crimes?" She made her laugh light and airy. "I see that only men are capable of evil!"

"You think so?" José took her by the arm and pulled her with him, deeper into the passageway that smelled more and more strongly of human misery. The keys to the cells clinked invitingly in his hand, and when he paused in front of another large cell inhabited by women in tattered gowns, some of them with children in their arms, Laurie had to restrain herself from trying to snatch them away from him and opening the cell. "Here! Is this evidence enough that men are not the only criminals in this village you thought so quiet and peaceful?"

Laurie struggled to keep her composure as she looked into the cell, and could not speak for the horror clogging her throat. She scanned the pitiful women holding their children, some of the infants crying, some of them ominously silent, and finally recognized Serita. She leaned against the far wall, her face turned up toward a tiny square of light near the top of the

421

high wall.

Serita did not glance at them, but kept her face turned away until Laurie summoned the strength to speak, her voice loud enough to reach her former servant as she said, "Oh, my goodness, Capitán! You were so right about the prisoners! I vow that I won't be able to sleep at night thinking of what heinous things they must have done!"

Turning her head at last, Serita looked directly at Laurie, but did not visibly react. She remained still and quiet, but there was a quick flash in her dull eyes that let Laurie know she was still able to recognize her.

"I'm so glad I don't know any of these people!" Laurie said quickly so that Serita would not be tempted to speak to her. "Please, Capitán—take me out of here. I cannot bear it another moment!"

As she turned to follow Garcia back down the hall, Laurie cast a quick, reassuring smile to Serita that she hoped would let her know she was trying to help.

The memory of Serita's thin, haunted face stayed with her for a long time.

Once back out in the fresh air of the *presidio* courtyard Laurie sucked in a deep, cleansing breath, not even minding the smell of the hide warehouses down by the bay. The wind had shifted direction, blowing in from the bay, lifting her hair and whisking it across her face as she stood quietly beside Garcia while he berated a sleeping guard.

"Imbecile! You shall feel the whip for this laxness in my command!" José shouted at the cowering soldier. "Report to your sergeant, and I will deal with you later."

"Si, mi capitán, si," the guard stammered out, and cast a surly glance toward Laurie. It was his opinion that Garcia was only trying to impress a woman, for he usually did not care about such things.

Laurie lifted a brow, watching the guard leave his

422

post by the entrance, and when Garcia turned to speak to another soldier, she said quickly, "José—I mean, Capitán—isn't it time we returned to the fiesta? It grows dark early in the spring, and the lanterns will be lit soon, making it difficult to see."

Her inference was not lost on Garcia, who grinned at her shy impudence. "You little minx! So you wait on the shadows, too, do you? And you pretend to be so cool!"

In spite of his native caution, Garcia let his conceit convince him that Laurie longed to lie with him, to feel him inside her. She was shy, yes, but she had been born a lady, not one of the Indian peasants such as those he'd been born into. And because he believed that there was an inherent difference in the classes, that those born into wealth and position were better, he allowed himself to think that she wanted him but was too shy to openly show it.

The thought of the night ahead kept Garcia sharp and oblivious to anything else around him as he escorted Laurie back to the fiesta. The bullfighting had ended, and there were to be contests of skilled horsemanship. Laurie urged him to compete, hinting that a *caballero* who carried her scarf into competition would be greatly rewarded. At first hesitant, Garcia capitulated quickly enough at that last, and fervently kissed her hand as she gave him the modesty-bit from her bodice. It was still warm from nestling in the swell of her breasts, and carried her light fragrance with it.

Inhaling deeply, Garcia leered at her over the flimsy bit of silk, whispering, "After I have captured the prize, my dove, I shall show you an even greater skill!"

Forcing herself to look down so that she wouldn't glare at him with undisguised contempt, Laurie murmured, "I count the hours."

"Minutes, fleeting moments of time," Garcia said as he grabbed her hands and pressed wet kisses on her palms.

Restraining the urge to jerk them away, Laurie watched as he turned and strode toward his saddled mount. Trembling with anxiety, and wondering if Cade would meet her as the message from Don Benito had indicated, she stood where José had left her until he was mounted and wheeling his horse around to ride toward the stretch of ground where the contests were to take place.

"Señorita?" a voice at her elbow said just as Laurie started to turn away, "I am Sergeant Ramirez. Capitán Garcia asked me to be your escort until the contests are finished."

Hoping her dismay didn't show on her face, Laurie smiled and said, "How nice! Thank you, Sergeant— Ramirez, did you say?"

Flushing—he was quite young and looked like a beardless youth—Ramirez said, "Si. Sergeant Raul Ramirez."

"It is very nice to have you as my escort, Sergeant. Shall we go and stand by the side in the shade?"

Maneuvering their way through the crowd of people lining the street to watch as riders thundered past, Laurie silently cursed Garcia. How would she rid herself of the very polite and very dedicated Ramirez?

Shifting from foot to foot as she stood at the sergeant's side, Laurie watched as riders spurred their horses into hard runs down the middle of the dusty street. To demonstrate their skills, the riders were to scoop up small objects placed in the street, gold coins so small that it was hard for anyone to see them. Only the best could successfully complete the test of skill.

Laurie noted that Ramirez was intensely interested in the contest, and asked, "Do you know anyone competing, Sergeant?"

He nodded eagerly. "Si! My brother Juan, he is one of the best."

"Competing against Captain Garcia? Does he have a chance?"

Rather scornfully, Ramirez boasted, "Juan cannot be beat by anyone, not even the capitán."

"Ah," Laurie said, and the sergeant looked at her quickly as if realizing that he might have spoken unwisely.

"But of course, señorita, the capitán is the best there is, and my poor brother, he will not win today."

Laurie smiled reassuringly. "I am certain that your brother is very good, Sergeant, and that the captain will have to work very hard to best him."

A doubtful smile curved the young man's face, and he gave a tentative nod, not quite sure what he was supposed to do or say.

After several riders had competed unsuccessfully, Ramirez pointed out with pride that his brother was to ride. Laurie leaned toward the sergeant and pretended to be very embarrassed, her words slow and doubtful, her eyes downcast as if she could not bear to look at him.

"Sergeant Ramirez, I do not want to take you away from the contests, but I must attend to my needs. Would you be so good as to—wait here until I return?"

Ramirez's face flushed crimson, and he gave a quick nod of assent. "I will be most happy to wait right here, Señorita. Are you certain you do not need me to—"

"*Por favor!* I am certain," Laurie burst out with her eyes still downcast. "I won't be long."

Worming her way back through the crowd of exuberant spectators, Laurie almost broke into a run once she was away. It was growing late, and she hoped Cade was there, or that he would wait.

Several acquaintances from when she had lived in Higuera before saw her, nodding coldly as she passed, and Laurie wondered with a sigh if she would ever be able to live down her infamous reputation. Perhaps not. But if she had Cade, nothing else mattered.

Turning a corner and stepping into the shadowed arch of a high column, Laurie felt her heart quicken as she spotted a flicker of movement only a few yards away. Cade? Or someone else?

Her steps slowed, and she tucked her shaking hands into the folds of her skirt as she continued walking, aware that she was in an almost deserted area. No one else seemed to be near, and the distant clamor from the contest grew even fainter as she kept walking. Her steps echoed faintly on the stone walkway, and when she paused she heard another, different echo. Not daring to call his name, Laurie paused in an agony of indecision, hoping it was Cade.

A darker shadow fell across the walkway as a man stepped out from behind the thick column, an old man, it seemed, garbed in the simple loose clothing of an Indian peasant. A shabby sombrero covered the man's head, and a filthy serapé was draped over his upper body as he shuffled along in the hesitant gait so common to old men. Laurie felt a surge of relief, and gathering her courage again, began walking toward the far end of the path.

She had almost passed the old man when his hand shot out to grasp her by the wrist, yanking her with him into the deeper shadows. Before she could scream, she heard Cade hiss "Shh! It's just me, querida."

Relieved, frightened, and irritated at the same time, she snapped, "Then why didn't you say something instead of scaring me half to death?"

He leaned against her, and she could feel the cold stone column against her back as his body pressed into hers. "Because I like scaring you," he said, sweeping the sombrero from his head and kissing her in the same, lithe motion. It was several moments before Laurie could speak again, and when she did, all the irritation was gone from her voice.

"At least you taste the same," she said calmly, and edged slightly away to look at him.

His usual dark complexion was even darker now, more the color of an Indian's, and his thick dark hair was uncombed and unkempt, and looked as if it hadn't been washed in a month. Her nose wrinkled.

"You don't smell the same, though . . ."

"I'm not supposed to. Well? Would you know it was me?"

Her heart skipped a beat as she met his gaze, and she gave a slow nod. "Yes, but I have an advantage over most people."

He grinned. "Maybe you do, love, maybe you do."

Laurie said quickly, casting a furtive glance around her, "Garcia took me into the *presidio*, Cade. Serita is in the dungeon with the others, only at the far end, in a cell with other women."

"Any windows?"

She shook her head. "Only one, a small one at the top."

"Describe the interior for me," Cade said, and she gave an impatient shake of her head.

"Don't you remember it from when you were there?"

Shrugging, Cade drawled, "I was in a special area, my love, an area where only the most — stubborn — prisoners are kept. I don't think Serita warrants such special attention."

Shuddering at the images his words invoked, Laurie shut her eyes and tried to recall, step-by-step, her descent into the dungeon. Cade occasionally interrupted her to ask how many steps or how many feet she had walked before turning, but other than that, he just listened intently.

"And Cade," she added when she was through, "there is no guard at the entrance to the *presidio* tonight!"

"Why?"

She explained how the man had fallen asleep and Garcia had reproved him, sending him to his superior officer but forgetting to replace him. "And I tried to distract him so he wouldn't think of it." She looked around, nervous at every sound. "Garcia claims that he will be made the commandant tonight in Trujillo's place, and that Trujillo does not know it yet."

Cade's eyes narrowed, and he muttered, "That's very interesting. And Trujillo has no idea?"

She shook her head. "Not according to Garcia."

Grinning, Cade said, "I have a feeling the good Trujillo would be quite surprised and gratified if someone were to warn him."

She stared at him. "Who?"

"I have someone in mind. Is there anything else I should know before I go?"

Shivering, she shook her head again. "Nothing I can think of. Hurry, Cade! It will be dark soon, and—how many men do you have with you?"

"You worry too much," he said, and pulled her into his arms again to smother her protest with a kiss. When he let her go, he pulled the sombrero back over his head to hide his face. "Rejoin Garcia. When the commotion breaks out, I want you to try to slip out in the confusion and go home. *Go* home," he repeated when she opened her mouth to argue. "I can't be effective if I have to worry about you. Do you understand?"

Sullenly, she nodded, biting her lower lip between her teeth as she looked up at him. "Cade—*vaya con Dios*," she said softly, and he grabbed her and kissed her again, fiercely, his lips bruising her mouth. Then he was gone, shuffling back down the long walkway and fading into the shadows.

Chapter Twenty-eight

Fortunately, she didn't have to explain to anyone where she had been or why it had taken her so long. The young sergeant barely acknowledged her return, and José was still competing in the contests. Laurie watched with grudging admiration as Garcia rode at a dead run down the center of the street, scooping a shiny gold coin from the dust without breaking his horse's stride. She had to admit he was an excellent horseman, and hoped he was not equally adept with a sword.

Dreading yet anticipating the confrontation to come, Laurie wished Cade had not ordered her to go home. She, who had out-dueled every *soldado* when she was El Vengador, was to be sent home like a naughty child. A surge of rebellion made her long for a sword in her hand and her trousers and shirt, but to disappear without explanation might alert Garcia to trouble, and she couldn't afford that.

So Laurie remained quiet and reserved, wondering how Cade planned to free Serita.

She wasn't quite prepared for the method he had chosen.

The lanterns had been lit, casting swaying patterns of light across the tiled floors of the huge patio, and the musicians had begun to play again, the guitar and violin blending together to the melody of a *fandango*. She and José paused, caught by the excitement of the dancers and the sultry throb of the music.

One of the dancers was a slender young woman of exceptional beauty, with long ebony hair caught up on one side with an ivory comb, and swirling yellow skirts that flashed around her long legs as she danced. Laurie felt a twinge of envy as she watched the girl dance in the center of a circle of clapping, enthusiastic spectators. She held a pair of clicking castanets over her head as she moved with sinuous grace to the music, reminding Laurie of the dancers she had seen in Spain. This was sensual, passionate and moving, and had caught the attention of many of the guests.

Even José seemed affected, and bent to whisper suggestively in Laurie's ear that they accept the silent invitation of the dance.

"It is dark now, and there are shadows," he said softly in her ear, his breath stirring coils of her hair that had escaped the combs holding it atop her head.

Pretending not to understand, Laurie murmured softly, "These dances always affect me, too. Look how gracefully she moves, her body telling a story."

With the setting of the sun the night winds had grown cool, yet the dancer's body was slick with a sheen of perspiration as she danced, her eyes half-closed, her lips slightly parted as she moved to the rhythm of the throbbing guitars and sobbing violins. José's gaze shifted from Laurie to the dancer, and lingered.

"I know that girl," he said softly, and Laurie did not reply. "Her name is Lolita, and she comes from my village."

"She is Spanish?"

José shook his head, his gaze still lingering on the

girl. "No. She is Mexican, an Indian from the province of Chihuahua."

"Is that her husband dancing with her?" Laurie asked as a lithe young man leaped into the circle and began to dance. She felt José shrug.

"I do not know. But it doesn't matter. They dance well together."

Laurie watched as the young man seemed to stalk the black-haired girl, his heels clicking against the stone tiles and the gold ornamentation edging his sleeves and pants glittering in the light of the lanterns. The girl—Lolita—tossed her long mane of hair, appearing seductive, then rejecting, leaning forward in the movement of the dance to tease, then whirling away from him when he grew too close. Her lips were pursed in a sultry pout, her eyes inviting, her body tempting, and every man there wanted to be her partner.

Tearing her gaze from the dancers, Laurie looked across the circle of spectators and felt a jolt of surprise. Just across from her, wearing the garb of a servant, was her father. His blond hair had been darkened with hair oil, and his skin looked much darker, too, but she knew him. Her lips parted slightly, and her eyes widened as Phillip Allen scuttled from table to table with heavy baskets of food to replenish the platters. What was he doing?

When she would have gone to ask him, she felt José's hand on her arm, and paused. It occurred to her then that he must have a reason, a reason that he did not want her to know. As she stood there uncertainly, heedful of José at her side, Laurie's gaze encountered another familiar face in the guise of Don Luis's servant. Julio, one of Carlota's coachmen, offered a tray of drinks to guests. And over there, near the door to the main *sala,* stood old Tómas, the man who had met her on the docks her first day in

Higuera.

Suddenly it all fell into place, and Laurie knew what Cade must have done. She wasn't surprised to see Alvarez servants there as well, quietly serving the guests, mingling with the others as unobtrusively as if they worked for Don Luis.

A thrill shot through her, and she knew the time was almost at hand. Would it work? Would Don Luis be overthrown and sent back to Mexico? Or would the rebellion be put down by his soldiers, the ones such as José Garcia who had their reasons for working for the alcalde?

Turning, Laurie said in a halting voice, "José, I am unwell. Will you please see me home?"

He tore his gaze from Lolita, looking down at Laurie with a frown. "You are ill? Perhaps you just have not had enough to eat, or you may need a drink . . ."

"No, I need for you to see me home. Please. And if you could stay a little while?"

Her innuendo made José brighten, and his mouth curled in a knowing smile. "Ah! Of course, my little dove. It is dark now, and you wish to be taken home." He smoothed his mustache with a finger, and cupped her elbow in his other hand. "We'll leave at once."

Laurie's heart was pounding fiercely, and her mouth was dry and her hands shaking. She could feel the blood pulsing through her veins in anticipation, and felt the same way she had felt all those times she had ridden out as El Vengador. She would lure José to her house, then pretend to be very ill. And she would retrieve her sword and costume and join Cade, risking his anger, but it was better than waiting and wondering.

José was escorting her through the courtyard, his head bent as he whispered in her ear, when a loud shout rang out and he stiffened, jerking up his head.

"What was that?"

Quickly, Laurie said, "I don't know—perhaps someone has had too much wine."

José laughed, relaxing. "You are probably right. It is probably that pompous fool Mendoza. He always drinks too much and ends up under the tables."

They were almost to the wrought-iron gates when another shout erupted, followed by immediate chaos. Women screamed, a shot rang out, then several more, and men roared with rage and the heat of battle. José paused for only a moment before he thrust Laurie into a small room with the command to stay there, then he was running back across the crowded courtyard, drawing his sword as he ran.

Left to her own devices, Laurie only briefly considered going home as Cade had told her. She had no intention of missing the action, and she might be able to help in some way.

But the sight that met her eyes when she made her way through the throng of fleeing women, fighting against the current of bodies pressing toward the gates, was one of pandemonium.

Indian servants with pitchforks had rallied against the alcalde, and she could see the soldiers fighting them with drawn sabers. The untrained peasants would be no match for even the undisciplined men of the *presidio*, and Laurie felt a sick twinge of dismay. She had thought—had hoped—when she saw her father and the Alvarez servants that there would be trained men among the rebellion, but she must have been wrong. If the rebellion was put down—

Swirling, Laurie ran back toward the gates of the *presidio*, fighting her way through the crowd. If all was lost, she must rescue Serita before it was too late.

The front doors to the *presidio* were still unguarded, and there was no sign of activity beyond a few distant shouts. She could hear the uproar from the alcalde's hacienda, and decided that all the soldiers must have run to Don Luis's aid.

Her hair had fallen from the combs and was dangling in front of her eyes, and Laurie pushed at it impatiently as she pulled open the heavy wooden door to the *presidio*. It was as quiet as a tomb inside, and her footsteps seemed to echo too loudly on the tiled floors. She walked swiftly, a sense of urgency prodding her, and when she reached the door to the *mazmorra*, she saw with relief that the ring of keys was still hanging on the hook over the deserted guard's station. She had wondered what she would say to him if he was there, and spared a brief prayer of gratitude that he was not. It saved her the necessity of inventing an implausible tale, and her supply of ingenuity was almost gone.

The keys clinked loudly as she took them down, and her hands shook like leaves in a high wind as she fit the key into the lock and turned it with a loud grating sound. When she was inside the deep, dark hallway, Laurie was assailed with doubts. Could she find Serita again?

Her gold satin skirts dragged across the dank stones as she hurried down the hallway, turning and twisting, coming to a dead end and retracing her steps. Men stood silently at the barred doors of their cells, watching her, and when she asked frantically where the women were kept, they only stared at her blankly.

"Please! *Por favor!* Don't any of you know where the women are held?"

One man finally lifted a shaking hand and pointed, and Laurie blessed him as she hurried in that direction. The light from the torches was fitful at best, but she found the large cell at last, and fumbled with the ring of keys.

"Serita! Serita!" she called softly, not quite daring to be too loud. "It's me—Doña Laurie!"

There was a stir of movement in the cell, and several women came to the barred door to stare curiously at Laurie.

"You are here to help us, sí?" one of them asked, and she nodded her head.

"Sí, but quickly now! You must be very quiet so that no one will hear us."

Finally she found the right key and heard the tumblers of the lock click with a surge of relief. She swung open the door, still searching for Serita, and when she saw her, she felt hot tears burn her eyes.

"Serita!"

"Doña Laurie—but I don't understand . . ."

"There's no time to explain," Laurie said quickly, "and we must hurry! Does anyone know another way out?"

A woman holding a small child nodded. "Sí. I do."

"Quickly, then! Lead everyone out!"

"But where are you going?" Serita asked as Laurie turned back down the hall.

"I'm going to see how many of those prisoners want to risk their lives fighting the alcalde," she said grimly. "It seems a better way to die than this."

"I'll go with you."

"No, you go with the others. . . ."

"No, you have risked much to free me, and I will stay with you," Serita insisted, and Laurie flashed her a grateful smile.

"Good. Here, take some of these keys, and let's see what fits. . . ."

In their haste and the rustle of men surging to freedom, Laurie failed to hear the slamming of a door. It wasn't until she led the way back up the long, narrow passageway that she saw their path was barred by a tall figure silhouetted against the light from the torches.

"It's a trap!" one of the men cried, and Laurie felt her heart drop to her toes as she recognized José Garcia. He stood with his legs apart, his sword drawn, and behind him she could see the uniforms of several more *soldados*.

"So, this is why you were so anxious to see the dungeon. I wondered at your curiosity, but then you have always been an enigma." He sauntered closer, his face shadowed and grim in the pale light. "You have played me for a fool, *puta!*"

Laurie could feel the press of bodies behind her, and heard Serita's quickly indrawn breath. Their fear had the effect of strengthening her courage, and her chin lifted in a gesture of defiance.

"But you fit the part of a fool so well, Capitán, that it was very hard not to do so."

Garcia recoiled as if struck, and his black eyes narrowed with rage. "You will regret those words," he ground out angrily, and she shook her head.

"No. I may regret the consequences, but I will never regret the truth!"

Angrily tapping his drawn sword against the palm of his left hand, Garcia walked quickly toward Laurie, and when he drew back his weapon she did not flinch, but remained stiff and glaring at him with unconcealed contempt.

"Yes, kill me! Your men will certainly respect you if you cut down an unarmed woman, Capitán!"

"You tempt me too much!" Garcia spat, but he hesitated. He was aware of the men behind him, and the promised status as their new commandant. If they did not respect him, he would never be able to command them effectively. "Perhaps making a public example of you will be just as satisfying," Garcia said then, and drew back his open hand to slash it across

Laurie's cheek.

She reeled, and Serita caught her, her dark eyes flashing hatred and fear at the captain. Garcia laughed.

"Be glad I did not use my sword to mark your face," he sneered, then gestured for one of his men to come and take her. "Bring her upstairs, while I put the rest of this worthless rabble back into their cages like the dogs they are."

As the soldier stepped forward to take her, there was a loud crash behind them, and Laurie jerked her head up to see a uniformed soldier sail from the top step over their heads. No one moved for a moment, surprise rendering them motionless, and it was only when Garcia moved with a professional soldier's reaction that he avoided being struck by the soldier's body. He knelt quickly beside the fallen man, and looked up at his stunned men with a narrow glare.

"He's dead! Quickly, behind you, now!"

"Too late, Garcia," came a familiar, mocking voice that made Laurie want to weep with relief. Her relief turned to shock as she saw Cade appear above them, clad in the black cape and garments of El Vengador, a mask over his head and his sword drawn.

"El Vengador!" one of Garcia's soldiers cried fearfully, and shrank away, ignoring his captain's furious shout.

"Fool! He's not invincible! Get him!"

But Cade quickly stepped forward, his sword flashing in the dim light provided by the torches, and the half-hearted resistance of the nearest soldier was met with a ringing clang of blade against blade. The soldier's sword went flying through the air, and it had the paralyzing effect of sending the others into flight.

Ignoring Garcia's furious shouts, they dropped their weapons and ran, pushing through the prisoners behind Laurie and Serita as if they weren't there, fleeing toward the back exit like men possessed.

Garcia, however, wasn't frightened. He was only blindly angry, and he turned to meet Cade's onslaught with expert thrusts of his blade.

"I always thought we might test one another's skill one day, Garcia," Cade said with a laugh. "The day has finally come."

Parrying Cade's deliberate thrust with his blade, Garcia fought viciously and well. They met, closed, sprang apart again, and the metallic clash of swords filled the close air of the dungeon.

Laurie watched with her heart in her throat, frantic as Cade slipped on the damp stone floor, then regained his balance just in time to parry Garcia's forward thrust. He met it with the edge of his blade and gave Garcia a harsh shove, leaping to his feet again and turning with his blade slashing.

Over the harsh breathing of the combatant's and the clang of their blades, Laurie could hear a muted roar outside in the *presidio* courtyard, and wondered what was happening. Had the rebellion worked? Was Don Luis alive or dead? But then there was no more time to worry about what was outside, because Garcia managed to get in an agile thrust with his blade, slicing through Cade's shirt sleeve.

Laurie heard Cade's quick, indrawn breath, saw his lips thin with pain, and held her breath. His dark eyes were glittering with cold fury now, and somehow the mask he wore only intensified the effect.

"First blood," Garcia taunted, then had no time to say more before Cade pressed a vicious attack.

"Madre de Dios!" Laurie heard Serita moan behind her, and she wanted to add a prayer but couldn't think clearly. What if Garcia won?

"Quick!" Laurie snapped to Serita. "Hand me that

sword at your feet!"

"*Que?*" Serita mumbled in confusion. "What sword do you mean?"

"The dead man's," Laurie said, stooping to get it herself. "He won't need it anymore, and we might."

"*Ay di mi!*" Serita gasped as Laurie hefted the blade in her hand, briefly testing the balance. "It is true, then!"

"If you are referring to my being able to use a sword, yes," Laurie said, reaching down to jerk up the hem of her long skirt and tuck it into the waistband. She had to have some freedom of movement.

The hallway was almost clear now. Most of the prisoners had fled out the back exit, panic-stricken and escaping while they could. They would be of no help whatsoever, she decided with grim acceptance. It would be up to Cade to do what he could, and if he was defeated, she would fight until all was lost.

"Flee, Doña Laurie!" Serita begged, clutching at her arm and trying to tug her down the hallway, but Laurie shook free.

"No. I can't, Serita. You go, and be careful."

Terrified, but unwilling to leave her, Serita clung by her side, her body quaking with fear. Serita watched with her brown eyes wide, cringing at every clash of blade, praying that God would strengthen Don Nicólas's arm and keep him safe from harm. She hid her face in the crook of her arm, shuddering at every curse and blow.

"Damn you, Alvarez!" Garcia shouted when Cade's sword slipped beneath his guard to pink his arm and bring blood. Desperately, he thrust forward, trying to ignore the wicked slash of Cade's blade, but it was too late.

Throwing all his weight into a fierce lunge, Cade fought savagely, beating Garcia back farther and farther while the tiring captain tried to parry the blows.

439

He was growing weak, and Cade could see it. A mocking smile of satisfaction curled his lips and infuriated Garcia into recklessness, leaving just the opening he'd been waiting for.

Stepping forward in a smooth motion, Cade slid his blade beneath Garcia's, plunging the point into his chest. A bright spurt of crimson appeared on the red uniform, and Garcia looked down in surprise.

Wordlessly, he slipped slowly to the damp, dank floor of the hallway, and Cade jerked his sword free of the body.

Looking up at Laurie and Serita, he said in short, panting gasps, "Quickly! Go out the back way!"

Laurie cast a last glance toward Garcia, then did as he said, pushing Serita ahead of her. Cade followed. She could hear his bootsteps echoing eerily behind her.

The roar from the courtyard grew louder as they got closer to the exit, and she saw that the heavy wooden door was ajar. Serita was trembling, but managed to flash a brave smile as they reached the exit, and Laurie wedged herself out the door just ahead of her.

She was met by a soldier, his face dirty and bloody, his sword lifted high to meet this new threat. Behind him, chaos raged across the courtyard, men battling and shouting and the clang of weapons loud in the air.

Without stopping to think about it, Laurie met the threat of the soldier with the sword she still held, bringing it swiftly up to parry his blade. She fought the surprised soldier fiercely, her movements instinctive. She was hampered by her long skirts, but the soldier was still reeling from the shock of a beautiful woman wielding a sword so viciously, and it took him a moment too long to recover.

Laurie slid her blade up and under his guard, and

felt it slide into his body with a shock that vibrated down the length of her arm. She couldn't stop to think about it; she was only dimly aware of Serita's scream behind her, and then Cade was at her side, lifting a foot to shove the man from her blade. He took her sword and flung it away, then grabbed her arm.

"Come on, Serita," he said over his shoulder as he dragged Laurie with him. Using his sword, he hacked a path through the throng of fighting men, then up and around the stone path to a small balcony overlooking the courtyard. It was deserted except for a few broken pots of flowers, and he pushed them up against the wall outside a door.

"Stay here," he told the two women, "and you will witness the end of the battle."

Still shivering with reaction from her brief battle, Laurie nodded numbly. The courtyard was a blur of torchlight and death, and she huddled against the wall of the *presidio* with Serita as Cade disappeared inside.

It had been like fighting the Comanche all over again, and she was still shocked by her ability to kill. It was a horrifying discovery, and she wondered if there was something innately wrong with a woman who could do it. But then Serita was weeping, holding her arm and telling her she was so brave, so magnificent, and that she had saved their lives.

"But . . . I killed a man," Laurie whispered, shaking from head to toe.

"Sí, but only because you had to. He would have killed us, and you did what you must, Doña Laurie."

Wondering if she was right, Laurie thrust the thought away, staring down into the courtyard and wondering about Cade and her father. Were they still alive?

Then she saw Cade below, his dark cape swirling

and his blade flashing, and she heard the cries of "El Vengador! El Vengador!"

The name seemed to strike terror into the hearts of the *soldados,* and the fighting slowed. Indians with long, curved pitchforks and scythes used in culling the grapevines rushed forward, capturing those who faltered, and slowly the chaos ceased. Laurie could see them being rounded up into groups, the torchlight and lanterns flickering across the milling men.

Leaning weakly against the wall, she heard Serita break into relieved tears, and felt like doing so herself. Then Cade leaped the low stone wall just below the balcony, and disappeared into the *presidio.* Moments later he appeared in the doorway beside her, Don Luis shoved roughly ahead of him.

The alcalde was bruised and bloodied, his face grim and fierce with rage as Cade pushed him out onto the balcony, and Laurie could see that his hands were tied behind him.

"Attention, *caballeros!*" Cade shouted, "Attention!"

Below them men grew quiet, even the soldiers subsiding into silence as they recognized the alcalde in the light of the torches.

"Our alcalde has something he wishes to say to you," Cade said, and it was then that Laurie saw the point of the knife pressing hard against Don Luis. She felt a grim satisfaction, and when the alcalde swore softly and Cade pressed harder, Don Luis capitulated.

"Good people of Higuera," Don Luis began, and at Cade's nudging, cleared his throat and said loud enough for all to hear, "As your alcalde, I am empowered to make appointments to government seats. I step down from my position, and relinquish it to . . ." He paused, half-turning as much as possible to snarl at Cade, "Just who am I supposed to appoint, El Vengador? You?"

442

Cade gave a careless shrug and a soft laugh. "No, I have other plans, Don Luis. Why not appoint Don Benito Alvarez as alcalde. He is a good and honest man, and will not rape the people as you have done."

Swearing, Don Luis turned back to the crowd, his voice sullen as he shouted, "Don Benito Alvarez! He is to be your new alcalde! And he is welcome to the position," he added softly as he looked up at Cade with hatred flaring in his eyes. "And now you will kill me, I suppose?"

Laurie held her breath. She could see the fires of vengeance in Cade's eyes, and saw his hands tighten on the Bowie knife pressed against Don Luis's spine. But slowly his grip loosened again, and he managed to say in a light voice, "Death is too good for you, Don Luis. I think you should be sent back to Mexico City with the evidence of your years of theft from the government in your pocket. Don't you?"

Don Luis paled, and Laurie saw the white lines on each side of his mouth deepen. "I will be executed!"

"That is up to the government, such as it is. But don't be too frightened, Your Excellency—they've taken years to study the evidence I've gathered, and it will probably be years before they get around to executing you."

After Cade delivered Don Luis into the safe company of guards headed by a grinning Phillip Allen— who flashed his daughter a wink—he turned to his grandfather.

Don Benito stepped out onto the balcony slowly, his face flushed with pleased pride. "My first official act will be full pardon for my grandson! It was an excellent plan, Nicólas. But why appoint me as alcalde? The people would probably prefer the man who was El Vengador. And to think that I once thought it was—ah, but it was you! And I called you a coward because you would not do more for your

443

people!" Tears glistened in his eyes, and he clasped his arms around Cade. "You should have confided in an old man, my son. I would never have betrayed El Vengador."

Grinning, Cade reached out and pulled Laurie close to him. "But it was not my secret to tell, Grandfather. I am not the real El Vengador."

Don Benito stared at him, and Laurie jerked up her head to look at Cade.

"What?" the old man was saying in shock. "You are not? But you . . ."

"Borrowed the disguise because I needed to roust the peasants into fighting. They would not fight for me, an ordinary man, but they would fight for the brave El Vengador." His lips twisted into a faintly mocking grin. "I have to admit my pride suffered a bit, but there was too much at stake to worry about it."

Laurie began to laugh, and Serita—who had been staring at Cade as if mesmerized—looked from one to the other with a puzzled frown.

"But who is the real El Vengador?" Serita asked, and Laurie put her fingers over Cade's lips when he would have answered. She smiled, and her voice was light.

"Perhaps that should remain a mystery, Serita. For one never knows when he will be needed again."

As Cade pulled Laurie closer into his embrace, his head bending to kiss her, Serita shook her head slowly, and she was smiling when she said, "I don't think El Vengador will be needed for a long, long time."

Epilogue

"Do you know I was almost too late to rescue you, you hard headed female?" Cade demanded, and Laurie smiled in spite of the harsh edge to his voice. "By the time I got free and heard from your father that you were foolish enough to be seen going into the *presidio*, Garcia had enough time to drag you anywhere."

"But he didn't," she reminded softly, "and you were in time to save me."

They were lying in a large bed in the local *posada*, with seabreezes wafting in through an open window and over their entwined bodies. She could still envision the shock on Carlota's face when Cade had told her shortly and firmly that he was taking Laurie straight to the local priest, and that he was no longer married to Cecelia de Marchand. He had glanced at Phillip Allen, his face hard as if he expected an argument, but Phillip had merely shrugged and wished him well.

"You'll need my good wishes if you are to marry my daughter, I'm afraid," Phillip had added with a smile. "She is not known for obedience or listening to good advice."

And now they were married, she and this handsome, dangerous *caballero* who had successfully planned and led the rebellion to expose and depose Don Luis. Even now, Don Luis was on a ship going to

Mexico, and his heavy guard was led by Trujillo and Juan Gonzalez, Serita's *novio*. It seemed fitting that Juan be one of the men instrumental in the alcalde's eviction from office, and when he returned, he would be wed to Serita. Smiling, Laurie murmured, "You're not still angry because I felt it necessary to rescue Serita, are you?"

Cade stretched lazily, and rolled to his side to stare down at her face with dark, narrowed eyes. "I should beat you for it," he said in a flat tone that didn't frighten her in the least. "I should beat you like a stubborn burro."

"But you won't. . . ."

Grinning, his eyes flaring with the lights she had come to recognize so well, Cade said softly, "No, not now. Maybe later, after I make love to you again."

Lifting her arms and putting them around his neck, she had the thought that nothing would ever come between them again, nothing. Not time, nor distance, nor war, even the war that threatened between California and Mexico. Cade would go, of course, that was one of the reasons he had returned to California. But then he would come home, home to her and to a new life together.

Cade's mouth drifted from the hollow of her throat to the lush valley between her breasts, and Laurie shivered with reaction. She stopped thinking, stopped everything but responding to his hot, searing kisses and caresses, and when he whispered love words to her, words she had wanted to hear for so long, Laurie knew she would never be alone again.

"Laurie, *vida mia, mi corazon, amante* . . ."

"Oh Cade, I love you, too."

Let Sonya T. Pelton
Capture Your Fantasies!

Captive Chains
(2304-9, $3.95/$4.95)

Shaina Hill had always yearned to be a teacher. Heading out for the remote area of Thunder Valley in the Washington Territory, she never dreamed her employer would be the rugged rancher Travis Cordell.

Inexperienced in the ways of the heart, Shaina was a willing and eager student when Travis took her in his tanned, powerful arms. When the virile, handsome rancher branded her with his kiss, Shaina knew she would be bound with Travis in love's *Captive Chains*.

Dakota Flame
(2700-1, $3.95/$4.95)

Angered by the death of his father at the white man's hands, Chief Wild Hawk wanted to lead his people to peace and obey the call of his dream vision: to capture the beautiful young girl who possessed the sacred talisman of the Dakota people. But Audrina Harris proved to be more of a captive than Wild Hawk had bargained for. Brave and fiery, she soon tempted him with her auburn hair and lovely fair skin. Each searing kiss and passionate embrace brought their worlds closer together. Their raging passion soon ignited into a fierce *Dakota Flame*.

Love, Hear My Heart
(2913-6, $4.50/$5.50)

Her mother wanted her to marry a wealthy socialite; her father wanted her to marry his business partner, the handsome river pilot, Sylvestre Diamond. But radiant Cassandra St. James needed to know what *she* wanted to do, so she slipped on board the *River Minx* for a trip down the Missouri River.

One moonlit night, she shared a passionate kiss with the one man she had sought to escape. The satiny kiss and powerful embrace of golden-eyed Sylvestre captured her desire, yet he knew it would be more difficult to claim the rebellious heart of his blue-eyed love.